Needle on the Haystack

by

Richard Bergeron

ISBN: 0989354318
ISBN-13: 978-0-9893543-1-8

DEDICATION

This book is dedicated to my wife, Barbara, who encouraged me to write and edited the story many times to make it immeasurably better.

CONTENTS

ACKNOWLEDGMENTS

Many thanks to the following people:

My wife Barbara for her encouragement and her great ability as an editor/continuity editor.

Barry Kleider, photographer, who did some great work one afternoon to provide me with the professional personal photographs.

Bart Palamaro of indieauthorsupport.com who designed and created the cover.

The Office of Naval Intelligence (ONI) agent on the USS Meredith (DD-890) who gave me some idea how Navy undercover agents worked. I never knew who he really was until the duty driver told me (six months later) what he overheard while driving this man to the airport. The fictional OCI of this novel is based on this early ONI, which gave birth to the Naval Investigative Service (NIS) and then the now famous NCIS.

National Novel Writing Month, which got me to write down the basic novel.

People of every race and ethnic group who showed remarkable patience with an outsider willing to learn from them, especially the American Indian people of Minnesota. I must also thank African Americans, Latinos/Chicanos/Spanish-speaking people, and Asian people of many backgrounds. And I can't leave out European Americans who helped me understand many of their traditions.

Everyone who supported me and taught me how to write better: in writing clubs, creative writing classes at the University of Minnesota and The Loft of Minneapolis. Special thanks go to the fine editors I had at work, especially Coventry at Control Data Corporation and Ray at MECC/The Learning Company.

PROLOG

A sailor named Terry Adams stood alongside a Corvette. He glanced down at the driver and said: "The stuff you been selling me is weak. I still hurt after I shoot up."

"Izzat so?"

"Yeah." Adams swallowed hard and glanced through the night at the abandoned warehouses around them. "I need more of it every time to do the job."

"Hmmm."

"Come on. I need stuff like I used to get."

The man shook his head and looked up at the sailor. "Ya get what ya get. That's what the boss says to sell for a nickel or a dime. Name your size and pay your dough."

Adams clenched his fists, raised his eyes, looked at the sky in exasperation. "You gotta let me have something better, man. I shoot up an' I still hurt. Bad. But I'm paying the same price. What you're selling me isn't strong enough."

The man's eyes turned to ice. "That's what you said before. It's already an old story."

Adams examined the car. It was bright red and looked brand new. He knew his money helped buy this shiny bauble. "Come on. I'm a good customer. That's got to count for something."

The driver stared at his steering wheel. "You got a point, kid. You're one of my regulars." He reached into the glove compartment and pulled out two small folded squares of white paper. He held them out between two fingers. "Here. Coupla dime packets for you. Like you were getting a year ago. Gimme twenty bucks."

Adams slipped the drugs into his inside jumper pocket as he sauntered away, smiling in anticipation of his trip later that night.

The driver smirked as he slammed his Corvette into gear and sped off.

"Enjoy yer trip to eternity, kid."

* * *

Seaman Charley Simms had been playing after-hours poker in his barracks on "Mainside," Naval Operations Base, Norfolk. He had also been drinking a lot of soda pop. As he relieved himself at the trough that served as a urinal, he heard someone come in behind him. He glanced over his shoulder.

"Hey, Adams, what's up?" he greeted.

"Nothin'. Everything is copasetic."

Simms turned back to finish as Adams slammed the door to the commode stall and latched it. Simms returned to his poker game and his soda pop.

* * *

The last showing of the movie was over and half the theater lights were off. A middle-aged man sauntered into the lobby of the theater in Virginia Beach. Tonight he had watched a newly released romance comedy called "Come September" starring Rock Hudson and Gina Lollobrigida, which was not the type of film he ever went to see. He would rather have watched his favorite flick again, "The Guns of Navarone," but it had been out for some months and he'd already seen it three times. Besides, it was playing at a different theater, one where he often went. And he wanted to be sure that certain people didn't know where he was.

He acted nervous. He looked around, checking out the people in the crowd. He passed a public telephone, walked by it, then turned and looked around. He returned, entered the phone booth and closed the door. He picked up the receiver. He rested his shaking hand against the case of the phone in order to get his dime in the coin slot. His finger shook as he dialed the number he had taken pains to memorize. When he finished dialing, he turned his back to the phone so he could keep an eye on the lobby.

A voice on the other end of the line answered: "Office of Criminal Investigation, Conway YN2 speaking."

"Yeah," the man began. He swallowed, cleared his throat, tried to swallow again. "Uh..., I... uh... want to report a bunch of drug pushers. They're selling stuff to sailors here."

"Where are you, please?"

"In the Norfolk-Virginia Beach area."

"Please identify yourself."

"Uh-uh. I just don't want to see these young swabbies getting hooked

4

on this stuff. But I'm scared of these guys so I won't identify myself. Just in case. But you guys should send some folks down here to investigate this mess. This gang is really big. And mean."

"But we may want to contact you. Please tell us who you are."

"Sorry. That's all I can say." The man hung up the phone and quickly walked out of the theater.

Conway logged the call: "Saturday, 2 Sept 1961. 0115. Unidentified man called to report drug-pushing activity in Norfolk-Virginia Beach area. Gave no other information."

Then he called Commander Blount in the middle of the night.

* * *

The loudspeaker was done squawking "REVEILLE, REVEILLE." Charley Simms rubbed the sleep from his eyes and went to the head. He noticed that the door to the stall Adams entered the night before was still shut. He wondered about that, a little, but shrugged it off. After breakfast and morning quarters, he returned to start his daily cleaning. Rough day ahead. Two commodes were left unflushed. Someone barfed on the floor. And it smelled like more than one drunk missed the urinal completely. He chuckled. "Hope they pissed on their shoes."

The door of the same commode stall was still shut. "Hey!" he called out. "Hurry up in there! I gotta clean the damn thing."

There was no reply.

"Hey! Get out of there! Who the hell's in the shitter, anyway?" No response. "What the hell's goin' on?" he grumbled. He put down his buckets, brushes and rags, and strode over to the stall. He banged on the door with his open palm. "Hey! Wake up in there!"

He pounded on the door and shouted a couple more times. Another sailor came in to check what was happening. "What the fuck's all the noise about? You're gonna wake up the dead!"

"I saw Adams go in there last night. He fell asleep on the shitter before. And I gotta clean the damn thing. I don't know who's in there, but he's gotta come out."

"So climb under the door and see what the problem is!" the newcomer laughed.

"Hmmm, I got a better idea," Simms said. He entered an adjacent stall and stood on the commode so he could see over the partition. "Aw, shit. It is Adams," he reported. "And he don't look too good...."

He pulled himself over the partition. He unlatched the door as he landed in front of the other man, and then backed out quickly. "Fuck! Get the Master at Arms! Somebody get the MAA! Fast!"

1. TROUBLE IN NORFOLK

I stepped out of a miserable drizzling rain my first day in town and entered a building that was identified only by a number on a sign in front of it. I knew the office number I was supposed to go to. When I found it, I paused. The door stood there staring at me. The glass in it, emblazoned with bold black letters, announced the agency on the other side of it:

OFFICE OF CRIMINAL INVESTIGATION
NORFOLK, VIRGINIA

I glanced at the paper in my hand, the summons the Navy called "orders." I had no idea what lay ahead but I had to go through with this now. I tried to build up my courage. I took a deep breath and reached out to open the door. It opened before I could touch the doorknob.

My heart pounded. A yeoman second class stood there. He looked at my collar rank insignia.

"Good afternoon, Lieutenant. Can I help you?"

I swallowed hard. "Uh, yes. I'm Lieutenant Eric Matthews. I have orders to report here."

He acted like he recognized my name. "I'm Conway, YN2." He motioned to an empty desk in the office. "Won't you have a seat, sir? I'll be right back to process you."

I nodded and stepped into my future.

Conway returned from the head. He checked me in and made a phone call. Within an hour some other folks had me measured for uniforms.

The following day, Sunday, Conway called me back to the office early and gave me my seabag, the uniforms all tailored to fit. Now I had to stencil each piece like enlisted men did in boot camp. Even the skivvies. Even the silly shit, like the flat hat, which nobody's used for years, maybe even since

World War II. At least they weren't issuing dress whites any longer, an older style white jumper with a pale blue collar.

The OCI office was almost deserted. It was the weekend, after all. I sat at an unused desk, stenciling my new clothing with my last name and initials. The stencil paint didn't dry very fast, so I had stuff spread all over that end of the office. I was getting tired of seeing my own name, MATTHEWS E M. The initials stand for Eric Michael.

I'm a full lieutenant in the U. S. Navy, the same rank as a captain in the Marines or Army. Soon I'd be pretending to be a raw recruit right out of boot camp going to my first duty station. I'm twenty-nine but look twenty-two, which is the age shown in the service jacket I'd take with me. I'd be impersonating an older recruit—most guys joined the Navy at seventeen or eighteen.

By education, I'm an electrical engineer. I specialize in complex electronic equipment. My analytical ability gives me a knack for solving problems. That's how I got into OCI in the first place. Now they needed another undercover guy and I needed this assignment for advancement to lieutenant commander. So they flew me here from Great Lakes, Illinois.

Conway, the duty yeoman, was shuffling papers and answering phones while I painted my new clothing. I didn't pay much attention to the calls that came in. After one of them, the yeoman phoned Commander Robert Blount, the commanding officer of this OCI branch, to keep him up to date. Blount would be in Monday morning, unless something really big happened. By that time, I'd be out at the Destroyer and Submarine Piers waiting for a ship.

When Conway hung up, he turned to me and said: "That call was connected to why you're here, Lieutenant. Seems some addict died in one of the barracks."

"I'm going onto a ship," I reminded him. "How does that relate to me?"

"We're getting a lot more of these cases. And if you ask me, they're all related. I think you're gonna be part of a big operation, sir."

I nodded. That was possible. The captain of the destroyer USS *Hestek* had called OCI about possible drug use on his ship. That's where I was going. But if drugs were on the small ships, you could bet they were also on the big ships and on the largest navy base in the world, Naval Station Norfolk. That's its official name. Thousands of sailors still call it N.O.B., from its older name, Naval Operating Base.

* * *

Commander Blount showed up at the OCI office at eleven hundred hours. "Okay, Conway, I came over right after church. Bring me up to date."

"Yes, sir. First, Friday night's phone call." The yeoman pointed to his log. He repeated the conversation almost verbatim.

"You try to get more information from him? Where he was or where he thought this gang is?"

"He refused to say anything else. 'Just in case,' he said. Like he didn't want anyone to know who he was. He sounded pretty scared, sir. Then he said that was all he could say and he hung up. I heard people in the background, like he was around some public place."

"OK, what else do you have?"

Conway held out a letter for Blount to examine. "Just this morning, the Admiral sent a special courier with this from Norfolk Naval Station headquarters requesting action. It looks big, Commander. Three men died last month from heroin cut with quinine. The people are dying from the cutting agent, not the drugs. That's not counting Seaman Terry Adams, the man who died Friday night."

"That's the man you called me about last night?

"Yes, sir. But the medical examiner said this guy didn't die from the cutting agent. For some reason he was given a deliberate overdose of one hundred percent pure."

"Murder," he observed, frowning. "So, we hear about a gang pushing this stuff. We have a number of deaths from the cutting agent, a call for help from three ship's captains now, and an outright murder." He tapped his lower lip. "This is too much for our present staff. We'll need help. I'll check the registry and see who else we can bring in. Get Knox in here."

He entered his office and closed the door. Soon another man came in and shut the door with a minimum of noise. Even so, Conway heard him, looked up and went back to work without saying anything. The new arrival sat down and waited. After a half hour Commander Blount stuck his head out and called: "Knox?"

"Here, Commander." The new arrival stood up and entered Blount's office. I later learned that Charles Knox was a civilian contract OCI special agent. Now he stood in front of Blount. "Charlie," the Commander said, "I'm putting you in charge of a new investigation team. I talked with Admiral Schoonover in Washington. He approved these transfers. Get Captain Rena Skye, USMC, in here from San Diego. Have her pick two or three of the best operatives out there and bring them with her. Cut the orders for Skye to get here tomorrow and start setting up immediately. Her people can come in ASAP."

"One day from California, sir?"

"Affirmative."

Knox took a deep breath. "All right, Commander. Any special arrangements?"

"Get her an overnight flight to Norfolk Naval Air Station. Wait for her

8

at NAS. Get her oriented. Have her find off-base living quarters and a civilian job. I'll be getting more agents for you. They'll all be going undercover."

"Yes, sir. Commander. I'll get right on it."

As I sat there painting my uniforms and listening to my future hitting me in the face. My heart beat heavily in my ears. I'd been hoping to chase down some slush funders or something like that. Get my undercover experience the easy way. Then I got assigned to look for drug users on a destroyer, a fairly small ship, and try to trace his source of drugs.

I rubbed the scars on my cheek. I was very unsure of how I would perform under those circumstances, but one of my goals in life was to get rid of as many drug pushers as possible. They deserved no leniency whatsoever. Death was too good for the snakes that pushed that poison onto others.

I was already nervous about going undercover. But with a bunch of killers on the other end of the line? I'd do what I had to, of course, but I sure wasn't thrilled about it.

* * *

Captain Rena Skye paused outside the door to adjust her uniform jacket and skirt. Nineteen hundred hours on a Sunday evening was a hell of a time to get called in to see her boss, the Commanding Officer of OCI San Diego. She entered the office as fast as she could while still presenting the proper image of a United States Women's Marine Corps officer.

"I believe the Commander is expecting me," she said to the Wave yeoman behind the duty desk.

"Yes he is, Captain Skye," the Wave replied. "I'll let him know you're here." She entered the door behind her. In a few moments she motioned for the officer to enter as she returned to her desk. "He's ready to see you now."

"Thanks." Skye entered the office, hat under her arm, and stood at attention. "Captain Skye reporting as ordered, Commander."

"Stand easy, Rena." The senior officer sat looking out the window. He motioned to a small refrigerator in the corner. "Have a drink. There's soda, water, other stuff.... Grab what you want, then have a seat."

The woman's eyes turned cautious. The section chief was never this familiar. She sat down right away. Her left hand started to reach up to twist her hair around her forefinger as she often did while trying to figure something out. But she thought better of it here. She put her hand back into her lap, frowned and asked: "What's up, Commander?"

He didn't meet her eyes for long seconds. He opened a desk drawer. From behind his hanging files he extracted two glasses and a bottle of eighteen-year-old Glenlivet.

The look in Skye's eyes changed from caution to alarm as her boss opened the bottle of single-malt scotch. She sat straight and tall, waiting.

"I'm afraid I have some good news and some bad news," the Commander said while he poured two stiff drinks. He slid one toward Skye. "Take it. You're going to need it."

She tried to stop her hand from shaking while she reached out for the glass. "Give me the bad news first."

"That's going to be difficult to do, there's so much of it." Raising his drink in a toast, he finally looked her in the eye. "Here's to your advancement. Regrettably, not rank, but certainly a higher position in the organization." He took a good swallow. "Drink. That's an order."

Skye took a sip. "Please quit dancing all around this. What's happening?"

The Commander sat with lips pursed. He finally replied: "Most of the bad news is mine. I'm losing you. Best damn operative I ever had."

"Where are they sending me?"

He took a deep breath and let it out slowly. "Nor-foke, Vah-jin-ya. Heart of the east coast fleet."

"When do I leave?"

He looked at his watch. "In three or four hours."

"What!"

He nodded. "As soon as you can pack your bags—a few uniforms and all your civvies. They want you there tomorrow. A plane is waiting to take off when you're ready."

"But, I have other things I have to do before...."

"We'll sell your car. Send you the money. Pack up the rest of your stuff. Send it to OCI Norfolk. And I know what this does to your personal situation. We'll try to get that settled for you." He swallowed another healthy jolt of his scotch. "When you get to Norfolk, they'll have a car ready for you. Then you will go out into Adventure Land, get an apartment and a job, and play like a civilian."

"What's my assignment?"

"Field coordinator. Twenty-some operatives. Some in the fleet. Some ashore. Military. Civilian." He emptied his glass and poured another drink. "It seems that you're supposed to close down one of the biggest drug rings outside of the Mafia that they've ever discovered."

Skye stared at her boss. Ex-boss. She took a healthy drink from her own glass. After she caught her breath, she asked, "I get an instant transfer, have to cross the country overnight, don't get to take all of my stuff with me, and take on this huge drug ring. I appreciate the advancement to field coordinator. I suppose we could call that good news. I've been undercover before but never, not ever in charge of a team, let alone such a big one. Is there any actual good news, I hope?"

"Yes. You get to choose any three of our operatives here to take with you. Like I said, a lot of the bad news is mine. I don't lose just you, but my four top people because I know you will take some of the best. In fact, I will demand that you do so. Who do you want?"

Skye answered after mere seconds. "Jennifer Powers. Daniel Han. Tony Alvarez."

"Any others you want me to try to get for you?"

"You have anyone special in mind?"

"Morgan Delano impressed me when he was out here."

"Sure. I'll take him if OCI New York will cut him loose again. And try to get me Glenn Oliver from Charleston."

"Will do. And I'll notify the others of their transfers. They've been given more time to get to Norfolk because they'll be attached to military units as determined by the Norfolk office. You have to set yourself up as a civilian and get ready to coordinate your team. OCI Norfolk will let you know who your other people are as they determine them." He stood up and held out an envelope. "Here are your official orders, Captain Skye. Good luck. Go catch your flight."

* * *

Skye woke up with her heart pounding. She lay in bed, quietly, listening. Yes, there it was, the sound that woke her up. Soft footsteps. She pulled back the covers as quietly as she could and made her way, barefooted, across the bedroom. She stood at the door and listened. All was quiet. She held a Tae-Kwon Do karate brown belt, so she mentally prepared herself, clenched her hands into fists, slid into the hallway and walked toward the front room. A rough hand clamped over her mouth. It had to be a man. It was a big hand. Strong. She tried to shake loose but he held her too tightly. She kicked back with her foot, hoping to smash his shin.

"Don' even think about it, lady," the man growled. "I know all those karate tricks, too. So just quit yer squirmin'."

She tried to scream but it came out as a muffled squeak.

'Shut up! Don' try nothin'. So ya wanna take down our drug ring, huh? Well, honey, you just run outa luck."

Rena felt the icy cold of a knife blade at her throat. She tried desperately to think what she could do. Her heart pumped wildly.

"Good. Yer real scared. I can feel yer pulse in yer neck. You'll bleed real fast."

He pulled the knife across her throat. She felt the blood spurt out....

11

2. REPORTING ABOARD

I reported to the OCI Norfolk office very early Monday morning. Even so, Conway was there and brought me up to date concerning Skye. She would contact me in her own way and the yeoman couldn't tell me what to expect. He did provide the recognition sequence of code words we would use when that time came.

I didn't know Rena Skye then. But she had to be good to get a call like this. Better than good—she was a woman in an all male outfit. I'd never heard of this kind of thing before. And Blount had to be pretty special for giving a field coordinator position to her, no matter how good she was. A woman just didn't get this kind of a job around this man's Navy.

We double-checked that I had everything in order and looked exactly like a seaman apprentice right out of boot camp. Like a young, scared dip-shit. I didn't have to invent the scared part. Then Conway arranged for a driver to get me to the Norfolk Greyhound bus station moments before a bus arrived from Chicago. I took a cab from there. Everything had to appear exactly like I was a boot arriving for my first duty station.

* * *

"Ma'am? Capt'n Skye? Time to wake up! We're almost at Norfoke, ma'am."

Rena woke up. She jumped as far back as she could on top of the pile of cargo where she'd fallen asleep. She raised a hand to her throat. Everything was intact. She leaned back and groaned. The startled plane's radio operator looked at her.

"Are you all right, ma'am? You're white as a ghost!"

"Just let me catch my breath. I was having a nightmare, that's all...."

"All right. If you're sure you're okay...."

"I'm fine. Thank you. Carry on."

"All right, ma'am. I have to get back to my station now."

She nodded. She recognized the roar of the aircraft engines that filled the cargo compartment. When she was sure that he was out of earshot, she took a few deep breaths. "Just what the hell did I get myself into?"

* * *

The taxi crept onto one of the Destroyer and Submarine Piers of the Norfolk naval base. It came to a standstill near the end of one of the four large piers. The driver stopped the meter and turned to me. "Here y'are, bub! That'll be four thirty-five."

"There's no ship here!" I protested.

"This is where the gate guard said it would be."

"But it's not here!"

"Yet, sonny. Not here yet," the cabbie insisted. He pointed to the only empty berth on the pier. "That's where the guard said it'd be. That's where it's gonna pull in."

"When?"

"Sometime soon. Betcha within an hour or so."

"What am I supposed to do 'til then?" I asked.

"Well, I can charge y'another four thirty-five an' you can go back into No-foke. Run around fer a while. Then hire another cab to get back out here."

"I'm supposed to drag a full seabag around with me?"

The driver shrugged. "Yer choice!"

I stepped out into the concrete pier. It was a hot September day in Norfolk. It felt like I was standing on a charcoal grill. I pulled the heavy seabag out after me, handed the driver a five-dollar bill. "Keep the change."

I stood upright and looked around as the taxi wound its way back to its land domain. The pier was about a thousand feet long and fifty feet wide with train tracks running down the middle. Machinery and spare parts lay scattered all over.

Cables as thick as my wrist provided power to the ships. Thicker hoses supplied water and fuel. The stench of oil and garbage was everywhere. The noises of blowers and machinery came from every ship, creating a constant dull roar in the background.

A large ship, a destroyer tender, was tied up on the south side of the pier, near where it connected to land. A number of destroyers were moored outboard of it. They were much smaller than the tender, their bridges reaching not much higher than the tender's main deck. Two other nests of destroyers were tied up on the north side of the pier.

I noted that each nest of ships had a series of huge dempster dumpsters positioned slightly off the train tracks. Each dumpster was clearly labeled for the type of garbage it held. One was labeled "EDIBLE GARBAGE" and another "EGGSHELLS." I smiled to myself. The Navy sold its garbage to farmers who fed it to their pigs. Pigs evidently didn't like eggshells.

I wondered how much of the garbage in the dumpsters was leftovers. I heard the chow wasn't great in the fleet.

"Hey! Where ya supposed to go?"

I turned toward the voice, that of a petty officer standing watch on a ship moored directly across from the empty berth. "Got orders to the USS *Hestek*, D-D-eight-fifty-six."

"Yeah, she'll be here soon. She's supposed to tie up right over there." He pointed to the place where the cab driver dropped me off. "I'd guess she'll be coming in pretty soon. Not long to wait!"

"Thanks!"

I picked up my seabag, leaning almost forty-five degrees away from it for balance. Carried it a short distance and dropped it on the pier next to a dumpster that didn't smell too bad. I sat on the seabag so I wouldn't mess up my whites. I'd positioned myself on the side of the pier where the *Hestek* was supposed to berth, but out of the way of those who'd be helping her tie up. I leaned forward, elbows on my knees, lit a Marlboro and watched the sea gulls scold each other over scraps.

I reached up and scratched an itch on my right cheek. Above that was a series of ragged scars I had since I was sixteen. I shuddered, feeling each blow anew from a nightmarish scenario.

Bored, I reached into the top of my seabag and took out a paperback book of crossword puzzles. I took out my pen and began to fill in the little squares.

Some time later, a small group of women and kids began to gather in an open spot near the empty berthing space. Wives and children of the *Hestek's* crewmen.

In less than half an hour a working party came over from the tender. They reached the empty berth and lit up their smokes, waiting. That was the Navy enlisted man's motto, "Hurry up and wait."

"Mommy," a little girl asked. "When will the Old Haystack finally get here?"

"Be patient! Daddy's ship will be here soon."

Old Haystack? I had to think about that for a second, then realized it was the nickname of the *Hestek*. Every ship has a nickname, often a play on its proper name.

"There it is, Mommy! Look!" The little girl danced around while she pointed. "Mommy! Here comes Daddy!"

I looked out over the water. A destroyer slowly turned toward us. The large hull number, 856, was clearly painted on the bow. The USS *Hestek*. I closed my crossword book and watched as the ship pulled in.

My heart boomed like a base drum. Could I pull off this assignment? What if they found out who I was? I was sweating like a stuck pig and it wasn't because of Norfolk's summer sun. This was my first undercover job. I sucked on my cigarette and exhaled slowly. Well, I'd chosen this work and needed field experience for advancement. I knew that failure here would effectively end my Navy career.

Other things motivated me to make this assignment a success. First, I welcomed the chance to grow. And this assignment would let me get a certain measure of revenge.

My job was to track a suspected drug user back to the parasites that supplied him. I rubbed at the scars on my right cheek and thought. Drug dealers were all vermin. I wouldn't mind shooting every one of them. Not the users, though. They were trapped in a hell they never wanted. But the pushers earned a long slow death, like what they sold. I'd love to provide it for them and their bosses. And I'd love to start with the street dealers.

I wiped my forehead and ran my fingers through my hair. Put my white hat back on and squared it according to regulations. Pushed my horn-rimmed glasses into place and looked around again.

The *Hestek* was a *Sumner*-class destroyer. It hadn't gone through the Navy's Fleet Rehabilitation and Modernization, or FRAM, program so it had a lot more guns than many other "tin cans." Destroyers, small multi-purpose ships, were the workhorses of the fleet. With their guns they could shoot at ships, planes, and shore targets. They had different weapons to fight against submarines. And they performed a number of other kinds of duties for fleet formations.

The *Hestek* maneuvered almost all the way to its berth without any help from the tug that stood by. A man at each of the six main-deck stations of the special sea detail threw his heaving line to the pier. The landside crew pulled over this light line, then the heavy nylon mooring lines. The pier detail placed the large eye splices of these over the bollards embedded into the concrete.

The 1MC announcing system on the ship called out in its semi-mechanical voice: SHIFT COLORS. The American flag on the main mast instantly came down and another was raised on the fantail. I nodded. This ship was manned smartly. It should be a good one to serve on.

The ship's crew manipulated the mooring lines from the main deck, pulling them in when the *Hestek* closed on the pier, holding them fast when the vessel tried to drift away. They gradually pulled the destroyer to its berth. Once they had all six mooring lines taut and holding the ship snugly against the protective bumpers between the hull and the pier, they doubled up the lines.

I ground out a finished cigarette under my shoe. As I observed the operation, I was careful to show only the awe and wonder of a young sailor anticipating his first fleet assignment.

Six seaman, one at each of the six main deck stations, stepped outside the lifelines, turned their backs to the pier, and straddled the tripled mooring lines. They bounced down the lines, tenuously holding themselves upright as they slid toward the pier. On the way, they lashed the doubled up mooring lines with lengths of "small stuff" using half hitches. They also pulled conical rat guards with them, until they reached a point halfway between the destroyer and the pier. There they tied the rat guards to the mooring lines so that the large flared ends faced the shore.

Now any invading rodents couldn't take those routes to the vessel. They'd have to go up the brow just like any other life form. But then they could be detected and batted or kicked into the water.

The cockroaches were probably already on board.

"NOW, SET THE IN-PORT WATCH, SECTION ONE," the 1MC broadcast.

The quarterdeck watchstanders, an officer, a petty officer and a seaman messenger, were already at their stations. The enlisted men wore what was now called dress whites: clean, pressed regular white uniforms with a black neckerchief.

The sailors riding the mooring lines continued to tie the lashing around the big lines until they finally reached the pier. By this time the brow had been placed from the quarterdeck to the ship and they could get back aboard easily. As they returned to the *Hestek*, they rapidly and nonchalantly flipped salutes to the flag on the fantail, then to the Quarterdeck Watch Officer.

NOW, ALL HANDS SECURE FROM SEA DETAIL.

I stood up, looking up at the towering superstructure like I was anticipating duty on my very first ship. Okay, I thought. The lights are dimming. The curtain is rising. The play is about to begin. I had a few college experiences on stage—I knew I could keep the butterflies under control and stay in character. That wasn't my problem. One tiny unconscious slip-up would give away my real identity. That's what I was nervous about.

I slung my seabag onto my left shoulder, stumbling like a boot not used to balancing every one of his worldly possessions stuffed into one canvas bag.

All three men on the quarterdeck were watching me.

I approached the brow, the narrow metal bridge between pier and vessel. I reminded myself to make the mistake of calling it a gangway a few times. I crossed to my new home, stopped, faced aft and crisply saluted the flag on the fantail. I turned back to the Quarterdeck Watch Officer with another snappy salute. "Matthews, Eric M., Seaman Apprentice, 546-99-46, reporting for duty, sir!"

"Come aboard," the officer replied. His return salute was as lax as mine was smart. He looked at the two stripes on my arm and spoke to the petty officer on watch. "Shepherd, take care of this man. He's probably one of yours, anyway."

Shepherd was a Negro with light brown skin and sparkling eyes. The crossed anchors under the crow on his left arm and above the single chevron showed that he was a third class boatswain's mate. I already knew I was going onto the *Hestek's* deck force. I'd be working with this man.

"Aye, aye, sir," the petty officer replied. He turned to me and smiled. "Hi! Call me Shep. Where the hell you been? We've been waiting for you for a month now!"

I shrugged. "I got out of boot camp at Great Lakes and took my two weeks' leave. I came here just like my orders said. Why were you guys waiting for me?"

"We're a man short and we need your muscle power," he grinned.

"How come you're short? Someone get out?"

"Nah! We lost a guy in an accident. They sent him away to get fixed up. Or he died. We don't know which." He pointed to a location a few yards away. "Give me your papers and put your gear off the quarterdeck over there."

I dropped my seabag and gave Shepherd the manila envelope with my service jacket and orders. Shep wrote my information in the ship's log. Name, service number, time of arrival, all that good stuff. I couldn't help but notice his .45 caliber semi-automatic pistol. It was in a holster hanging on his right hip from a khaki web belt. The piece didn't have a clip in it. I could see the empty slot in the handle where it could be inserted when necessary. There was a clip of ammunition in a special holder on the left side of his pistol belt.

I glanced at the Quarterdeck Watch Officer and almost laughed out loud. Ensigns are the boots of the wardroom. This one stood with a telescope in the crook of his arm, trying to look every inch the naval officer.

The messenger of the watch, well, he was the messenger. He stayed off to one side of the quarterdeck, ready to do whatever he was told.

Eyes wide, I gazed around the ship. This was my first chance to evaluate my new home. I knew the name of one suspected drug user, but had no idea if there were more. Or who supplied him. It could be a crewmember or a civilian. Or a sailor from the base.

Shepherd looked up from his log, keeping tabs on what was going on. I must have been playing my role pretty well, because he laughed and said, "Bet I know what you're thinking."

"What?"

"You look like I must have looked when I first came aboard."

"What do you mean?"

"I looked around and thought to myself, so this is a small ship? It sure looked big to me. And noisy too!"

"You got that right."

"You'll get used to it," the petty officer said. "One night you'll wake up at oh-three-hundred, worried, maybe even a little scared, 'cause you don't hear the blowers, the fans, and the shafts driving the ship's screws."

"I can't imagine that."

"It happens to everyone," he said. He completed his logbook entry. "Okay, I'll get someone to help you settle in."

"Who's your duty PO today?" the officer asked.

"Cisco, sir," Shepherd replied. He went to the quarterdeck 1MC panel, pressed a switch and announced over the loudspeaker system: NOW, CISCO, BM2, LAY TO THE QUARTERDECK IMMEDIATELY. CISCO, BM2.

A second class petty officer soon arrived. He was tall and had crew cut blond hair. He seemed to take everything in at a glance. He held a large book in one hand. A spring-loaded metal clip hung from a belt loop on his right side, carrying a full key ring that clanked against his similarly held coffee cup. Shepherd turned to him. "We got a new guy, Al. Would you take him below and get him settled?" Cisco nodded. Shepherd turned back to me. "He'll take care of you, Matthews. See you later."

Cisco walked aft, through a watertight door and down a hatch into the bowels of the ship. I had to run with my seabag on my shoulder to keep up.

The berthing compartment was a deck below the main deck. Every cubic inch of space was used. The bunks, in tiers of three, were made of metal tubing bent into six-by-two-and-a-half foot rectangles, with large canvas pieces lashed to them. Each had a thin mattress covered in a huge pillowcase-like mattress cover, generally called a "fart sack." Pillows were set on alternating ends of the bunks with folded wool blankets at the feet.

Three lockers were welded to the deck below each tier of bunks. Each locker was about two and a half feet square and a foot and a half high.

Around and over all of this was a wild array of cables, pipes, valves and blowers. Hisses, rumbles, creaks and groans accompanied the smells of fuel oil, paint and sweat.

The compartment was full of guys in various stages of undress.

"Who's this?"

"New guy?"

"'Nother deck ape?"

Cisco simply nodded.

Suddenly the 1MC speakers drowned out the ship noises: NOW, LIBERTY CALL! LIBERTY CALL! LIBERTY IS GRANTED TO ALL AUTHORIZED PERSONNEL IN DUTY SECTIONS TWO AND

THREE, TO EXPIRE AT ZERO-SEVEN-THIRTY TOMORROW MORNING. LIBERTY CALL!

More than half the guys stampeded for the exit.

"Hey, Preacher!" a seaman shouted.

A big man stopped on the companionway ladder going up to the main deck. He turned and glared at the seaman.

The seaman grinned. "Goin' over for a piece of ass?"

Preacher scowled. "Smith, you're all a bunch of reprobates, drunkards, and whoremongers! I wouldn't want to be in your shoes on Judgment Day."

Smith laughed as the big man scooted up the ladder. "Sure! Get a little for me, Preacher!"

Cisco ignored the two seamen. He walked to an empty bunk, unfolded its mattress and tossed the pillow to one end. "You can use this rack and this locker, here." These were his first words. He spoke with quiet authority. He pointed to a sailor painting in a corner. "Jovan, there, is our compartment cleaner." He turned to the other man. "Pete, get Matthews a pillowcase, blanket and fart sack."

"Coming right up."

NOW, SWEEPERS, SWEEPERS, MAN YOUR BROOMS, the 1MC blared. SWEEP DOWN ALL DECKS, FORE AND AFT. SWEEP DOWN ALL PASSAGEWAYS, LADDERS, AND COMPARTMENTS. DUMP ALL TRASH ON THE PIER. SWEEPERS.

Cisco turned back to me. "You can start stowing your gear. It'll be time for supper soon. Use your seabag lock on your locker."

I began to place everything in neat piles inside the locker. No one bothered me and I was done by the time the 1MC came to life again.

NOW, KNOCK OFF SHIP'S WORK. EARLY SUPPER IS BEING SERVED FOR FIRST CLASS PETTY OFFICERS AND OTHER AUTHORIZED PERSONNEL.

The rest of the guys drifted topside, some giving a wave or nodding as they passed me.

Jovan re-appeared and put the bedding on my bunk.

"Finish after supper," Cisco said. "We should get in the chow line now, if we don't want to be last."

The food wasn't great, but it was better than I expected. But then, hungry people don't often gripe when being fed. After supper, I made up my bunk, putting on the pillowcase and the fart sack and folding my blanket according to regulations. When I was done, Shepherd tapped me on the arm. "Let me introduce you to the guys. This is Phil Le Blanc." He pointed to a man already asleep in his rack. "We call him 'Cajun' 'cause he's from Louisiana."

He walked to the center of the compartment. "That's Billy Bob Coe over there." That man looked daggers at Shepherd, but his handshake with me was friendly enough. "How y'all doin'? Where you from?"

"Illinois."

"Awww, 'nother dam' Yankee. Why don't we get more good ol' boys on the deck force?"

"Then we'd never quit hearing that lazy drawl you talk," another man chided. This was the guy who'd hassled "Preacher." His eyes were glazed but there was no scent of alcohol. We shook hands. "Name's Ron Smith."

"Over here," Shepherd continued, "we have Joe Monnyng. He's the third class in charge of the paint locker. And these guys are Brian Grengs, Chet Lyell, Pete Jovan, who you met earlier. That's Clement Jackson who we call 'Jax,' Sam Deram and Rob Roy Davern." Each guy made some kind acknowledgement. "Then we have Stef Roma, another BM3. Most of the other guys are on liberty or on duty. The Preacher's probably already on a street corner in downtown Norfolk."

"You really have a preacher in the division?"

Another man in a rack chuckled. "Not quite, even though he might wish to be. The Preacher is Luke Raynes and he's a slightly overzealous brother in Christ." The man held out his hand. "My name's Stephen Zoss and I won't preach to you."

"Thanks, Steve. I appreciate that. I'm Eric Matthews."

"Stephen, please. That's the name my parents gave me, and the one I prefer. Glad to meet you, Eric."

I sat down on some locker tops and lit a cigarette. "Glad to meet all of you, but I won't be able to remember your names for a while."

Just then the 1MC announced: NOW THE MOVIE FOR TONIGHT IS "THE BRAVADOS" STARRING GREGORY PECK AND JOAN COLLINS. IT WILL BE SHOWN AT TWENTY HUNDRED ON THE FANTAIL. JIM DOUGLAS PURSUES FOUR OUTLAWS WHO KILLED HIS WIFE. HE FINDS THEM IN A TOWN'S JAIL WAITING TO BE HANGED. HE STAYS TO WATCH THEIR EXECUTION, BUT THEY BREAK OUT OF JAIL. THE PEOPLE OF THE TOWN GET DOUGLAS TO HELP THEM RECAPTURE THE OUTLAWS. "THE BRAVADOS" WITH GREGORY PECK AND JOAN COLLINS ON THE FANTAIL AT TWENTY HUNDRED.

One of the guys plopped onto the lockers next to me. "Don't worry about remembering all of us right away. Then it'll happen faster. Welcome aboard. Always glad to have new help. Lightens the workload," he grinned. "My name's Hank Reston."

"Eric Matthews," I said. "Glad to meet you." We shook hands. "What do you do around here to pass the time?"

"Movies. That's mostly all we have for entertainment. We even like the old TV shows they put on film for us. Different flick each night. They start at twenty hundred. On the mess decks or the fantail in nice weather. We've also got a small ship's library. Some decent stuff there. And someone's always buying books ashore and bringing them back, but they're mostly fuck-books, and...."

"Fuck-books?" I had to play dumb on this one.

"Stories of people screwing any way you can imagine and a few you hadn't thought of yet. Most don't have any plot at all."

"I've never seen one."

"You will. I find them more frustrating than doing without. Know what I mean?" I nodded. Reston looked at his watch. "It's almost twenty hundred now. Want to go watch the flick?"

"Sure." I snuffed out my cigarette in a nearby butt kit. "Let's go. It'll take my mind off all my confusion."

We went topside and picked a spot to sit on the deck in front of the crowd of chairs people had brought from their workspaces. A movie projector sat on a table behind everyone. Somebody lowered the five inch gun barrels of Mount 53. Another guy tied a large white sheet between the two barrels. Then he shouted to raise the guns to the right elevation. A slight breeze moved the bottom of the sheet ever so slightly, so the man tied the bottom corners to a couple chairs to anchor the screen. We sat outside in the pleasant night air and enjoyed the movie.

When the movie was over, we went below and read for a while.

NOW TAPS! TAPS! LIGHTS OUT. ALL HAND TURN IN. MAINTAIN SILENCE ABOUT THE DECKS. TAPS!

I lay in my rack and tried to analyze the situation. OCI had given me the name of the man the Captain of the *Hestek* suspected of using drugs. I already met him. But I also had to find any other drug users on the *Hestek*. Ron Smith exhibited some of the signs. And I had to prove my suspect was a user. Even tougher, I had to learn who supplied him. Were there other suppliers? Tears welled up in my eyes as I lay there in the dark. I grieved for the trap the users had fallen into. Then the anger rose up, anger at the pushers of this poison. I clenched my fists. I wanted to strangle all of them, slowly, to provide the kind of slow death they were selling to the now-helpless addicts they'd made. I fell asleep wondering how the hell I was going to find the other users, the sellers and how I could strangle the latter.

3. CHECK-IN AND GRAND TOUR

In the morning, Shepherd and Reston escorted me to breakfast on board the *Hestek*. Then came morning quarters for muster and inspection. Chief Boatswain Gascomb went through roll call. I tried to memorize the names and faces.

"Ackerman?"

"Here?" the man answered.

The Chief shook his head. "Everything's a question for you guys from Minnesota."

"You betcha, Chief. That's the way we talk."

"So I hear. Every day. Okay, Burch?"

"Here!" he practically shouted.

"Cisco?"

"Here," he said quietly but clearly.

"Coe?"

"Heah!" I remembered his southern accent from last night. I noticed that he stood as far away from Shepherd as possible.

"Davern?"

"Yup."

"What kind of response is that, Davern?"

"Here, Chief!"

"That's better. Dean?"

And it continued with every man in the division, alphabetically. I met many of them last night.

"Matthews?"

"Here," I replied.

"Shepherd and Reston will get you started with your check-in after quarters. Shepherd, get him to the Exec and return to your duties. Reston, wait for Matthews and help him find everyone." He turned to me.

"Matthews, we'll cover your duty assignments later. You'll be working for Shepherd. His group takes care of the fantail."

"Yes, sir," I replied

"I'm a chief petty officer. You don't 'sir' a chief."

"Yes, Chief."

"Okay, let's finish this. Raynes?"

"Here, by the grace of God." This was "The Preacher." He was big. Tall and well built, like a weight lifter. He looked like he could be quite a presence when he preached.

"Reston, I know you're here. Roma?"

"Here."

"Shepherd, you're here."

Coe mumbled a few words that didn't sound nice. Something like "fuckin' nigra." Or worse. Neither the Chief nor Shep seemed to hear him.

"Smith?"

"Yo!" The Chief merely shook his head at the improper response. Maybe he knew something about Smith the rest of us didn't.

"Zoss?"

"Here, Chief."

FIRST CALL TO COLORS, the 1MC announced. The color guard was now armed and making its way to raise the flag on the fantail and the jack on the bow.

Ensign Reynolds, the First Division Officer, arrived from Officer's Call. He made his announcements then said: "We have a new man. Matthews, isn't it?"

"Yes, sir."

"Welcome aboard. We'll have a formal meeting later. Anything else, Chief?"

"A couple more assignments, sir." Gascomb told some petty officers to have their men do various repair jobs or to get things checked out by others.

After colors, Shepherd, Reston and I got my check-in sheet from the Ship's Office then went to the Executive Officer's cabin. Shepherd knocked on the steel bulkhead. The Lieutenant Commander looked up. "Good morning, Shepherd! How can I help you?"

"Our newest man's checking in, Mister Monroe. Sir, this is Seaman Apprentice Matthews."

The officer nodded to Shepherd, who departed. We could hear him talking to Reston.

"Come in, Matthews." The Exec invited. He closed the door. "Sit down. Make yourself comfortable. Who's waiting for you?"

"Reston, sir."

He nodded. "I'm the Executive Officer, often called the Exec or XO.

I'm second in command of the *Hestek*. The Navy assigned you to a very good ship. The crew is conscientious. Everyone works together as a team. You know why?"

"Efficiency, I suppose, sir. Make the ship run well."

"Right. And we must do that. We're here together. When we get out to sea, just look around and realize you can't go very far from the rest of us."

We talked for about half an hour. I didn't tell him who I really was.

When we were done, Reston took me around the ship to complete my check-in. After a few stops, I asked, "Will I ever quit seeing new places."

"You'll feel right at home in a month."

Chief Gascomb told us I'd be standing underway watches as a phone talker on the bridge. So we went up there where I "learned" how to use these communication devices that generated their own electrical signals. Needing no power, they could be used as long as the circuit cables were intact. Reston also covered how to keep the two status boards up to date for skunks or unidentified surface craft, and bogies, unidentified aircraft.

After completing my check-in, I reported to Shepherd. The check-in acquainted me with many places, especially the locations where I'd stand watch and sea detail. But there was a lot more to a ship. Shep gave me a detailed tour of spaces where the deck force worked. We began at the front of the ship. "Just remember, this forward part of the *Hestek* is the bow. This deck portion is the fo'c'sle." He grinned. "It's the pointy end of the ship. And the rear of the ship is the stern." He pointed aft. "The deck back there is the fantail. You can remember that because it's at the tail end."

About mid-afternoon, we rested on the platform of Mount 33, one of the 3"/50 caliber anti-aircraft guns on the 01 level, one deck above the main deck. I shook my head and said, "I'm glad I didn't get put on a larger ship. How do you ever learn your way around a carrier?"

"I hear you never learn it all. Only what you need for your work and your watches. You just don't bother with the rest. Me, I'd just as soon stay on a tin can."

"Even this is something else," I remarked. "Right now, I'm not sure I could tell you the difference between the location of Chief's Quarters and the Ship's Office."

Shep handed me pencil and paper. Under his direction, I drew the ship's outline, the three five-inch twin gun mounts, the two three-inch single mounts near the bridge, and the two three-inch twin mounts aft of the stacks where we were.

"Remember, the crew is organized into divisions that are part of departments. We have four departments on this ship. Ours is the Deck Department but there are a lot more people than us in it - the gunner's mates, torpedomen, sonarmen, fire controlmen. Another department, Engineering, handles the boilers and all the stuff that makes us move when we're out at sea, including electricity. They also do all the repairs. Operations runs the radars and communications stuff, which includes signal flags and signal searchlights. They also have the quartermasters, yeomen, personnelmen, hospital corpsmen, all those ratings. Supply handles all the stores, pay disbursement, mess decks, cooking, all that stuff. Now, mark down on your drawing where all their living compartments are. You'll probably need to know all of them to wake people up when you stand watches as messenger."

Under Shep's direction, I added all the berthing compartments. Then he named the different divisions and the job ratings of the men in each of them.

When he was done, I shook my head. "God, I am so mixed up. But at least I have a map now."

"Yeah. And use it. In time, you'll learn it all by heart. For your in-port messenger watches you'll need to know where your watch reliefs sleep and how to get messages to anyone in the crew. On a ship this small, you do have to know everybody and every living compartment."

I lit up a cigarette and crumpled up the empty pack. I was looking for a place to throw it when one of the bos'n's mate seamen came up to us, carrying a trashcan that was about one-fourth full.

"Shep, I'm gonna get a standby fer later," he said. "Townsend said he'd take my duty. Just ta let ya know."

"Thanks, Derella. I appreciate the heads up. Got something special going on?"

"Just going out lookin' fer a little." He wiggled his hips to emphasize his words.

"By the way," Shepherd said. "This is Matthews, our new guy."

"I noticed ya at quarters. Glad ta meet ya. Well, gotta run." I assumed he was going to dump his trash can, so I tossed my empty cigarette pack in it. Derella whirled to face me and shouted with blazing eyes, "Hey, ya don't use my shitcan without askin' my permission first! Ya understand?"

"All right," I shrugged, reaching for the trash can. "I'll take it back."

"Don't get so fuckin' smug with me, boot! Or I'll knock yer face in!"

"Cut him some slack, Derella," Shepherd said. "He's new."

"Well, he better learn pretty fuckin' fast!" He turned and strode away.

When Derella got out of earshot, I asked: "Did I do something wrong?"

"He's just a mean sonofabitch, one of the few you have to watch out for. He's always nasty and a fighter, too. He's bounced up and down between seaman apprentice and third class so many times, some guys nicknamed him 'Yo-Yo'." Shepherd grinned. "But don't let him hear you call him that. Leave him alone and you'll be all right."

When our tour around the ship was over, I went below to the living compartment to wait for chow. Billy Bob Coe came over and asked, "So, how's it goin' for y'all?"

"All right, I guess. Everything's new and confusing."

"Yeah, and I bet that there nigra didn't help things, either, did he?"

"What? Who're you talking about?"

"Shepherd, of course. Realize, I don't mind nigras, as long as they're respectful and stay in their place."

I couldn't believe this. "Shepherd seems like a pretty nice guy."

Coe looked around the compartment. "Nice is one thing. And the Navy in all its wisdom saw fit to make 'im a petty officer. I don't envy ya, though, gettin' put in his work group. I wouldn't work for 'im. I just wouldn't. Y'all understan', don'tcha? I mean they oughta know not to put one of them as boss over his betters."

"And how do you handle even being in the same division with him?" I tried to be as sarcastic as possible.

Coe took me all wrong. "Patience. The sign of a superior man. I'll get out of this here canoe club soon and go home down South where the natural order of things still reigns supreme."

"Oh, you mean, like in Little Rock? And where the white man reigns supreme at the lunch counters all over the South?" I laughed. "I never gave it much thought before, Billy Bob, but by the time you get back home, your natural order of things just might be changed. Those civil rights protestors will tear your old system apart, bring it down." I turned my back on the bigot to leave the compartment.

"That'll nevah happen, Matthews! Nevah!"

Right before taps, Reston asked how my tour had gone. I propped my head up with my arm and expressed my confusion. "Mount 53, Mark 63 gun director, flying bridge, after steering, engine room, ship's office, foul weather gear locker, torpedo tubes, ship's store, shipfitter's shop, plotting room, gun director barbette, paint locker, hedgehogs, five-inch loading machine. I'm overloaded. I'll be dreaming about places on the ship all night long."

"You'll do fine," he assured me. "Get a good night's sleep. It'll already be easier when you wake up tomorrow."

"I hope so," I mumbled. "Hey, Hank, what the hell's with Coe. This afternoon he gave me a tirade about Shepherd in particular and Negroes in general."

"He's a bigot. He hates anyone different than him. And he makes no bones about it. Ignore him." He walked over to his own bunk and climbed in, ending our conversation.

The next day, I started working on the Old Haystack.

4. THE TENANT

Skye stepped from her 1957 Chevy Bel Air into Virginia Beach's hot morning sun. She looked around the semi-residential area, turned her back on the houses and leaned against the car.

"OCI brought me clear across the country overnight," she muttered. "No time to pack. I'm supposed to close down a drug ring big enough to make the Mafia gag. Bastards aren't just selling heroin, they're cutting it with poison and killing someone weekly. I have to find them and stop them."

She lit a cigarette, inhaled deeply then hurled the smoke from her lungs. "Why'd they pick me for this damn job? Got no sleep in two days. Got personal problems to take care of back on the other coast. Don't have a place to set my ass. This operation's been FUBAR since I started. I appreciate the advancement, but I've never been a team leader before, let alone for something this big.

"My operatives are coming from all over the country. I know five of them. Maybe six. Got to get an apartment. Get a job. Start managing my people. Have to contact them first. Rots o' ruck." She shook her head. "Well, I chose this career. And Dad always said 'be the best at whatever you do. If you're going to be a street sweeper, be the best damn street sweeper in the world.' So, here goes."

She snubbed out her smoke and turned to the house where she'd parked. "Apartment for rent. That sign agrees with what Central told me. Maybe they're right this time."

She walked up the short driveway to the front porch. The rental sign was on the left door, so she knocked there. No answer. She knocked harder. A balding man on the older side of middle age appeared.

"Hi!" she greeted. "Are you the landlord?"

"Yes I am," he smiled. "Would you like to see the place?"

27

"Please."

"Fine." He said in a slight southern drawl. He opened the door on the right and started up the stairs. "Follow me, Miss."

At the top of the stairs he opened a door to the left and held it for her. "I'm Mr. Scott. What's your name?"

"Rena," she replied, looking around the kitchen. "Rena Skye. S-K-Y-E. How much is the rent?"

He shrugged. "Probably not what it's worth. Fifteen a week includes all utilities. There's lots of room in the kitchen here, even with a table and chairs. The living room is in here." He said as he walked toward the front of the house. "That couch is as comfortable as it looks. So are the two easy chairs. The bedroom's in front, large closet here on the left, over the stairway. Nice wide bed."

Skye sat on the bed. It felt comfortable, but any bed would have felt that way right then. The front window had thin curtains and a window shade. "Fifteen a week?"

"Yes. I have no use for the space any more. I'd rather let someone live in it than have it collect dust."

"Who used to live up here?"

"Mother-in-law. After she died, my wife wouldn't let anyone up here where Mama used to live. Then she passed a few months ago. Now I'm alone with a small pension. I cleaned the place and got some furniture. The rent will help me a lot."

They returned to the living room. Skye looked around again. "I'll have to get a television."

"I have an older set you can use, if you want. No extra charge. You can put it on that table there. And I have some extra rabbit ears. Pretty good ones, too."

"You're very kind, Mr. Scott. How long a lease do you want me to sign?"

"Don't know anything about leases," he drawled. "I'm a simple man, Miss Skye. If you want to rent it, all I ask is a couple weeks notice before you leave."

"Mr. Scott," she smiled. "You have a tenant."

Rena paid two weeks' rent, then returned upstairs with a suitcase. The small kitchen window let some sunshine in. A normal sash window lit up the eastern side of the living room. The larger bedroom window at the front of the house was a double sash dormer. She leaned against the wall, watching the traffic on the boulevard. "I like this view," she nodded. She turned to the closet. "I really like this. Room for clothes on one side and a chair and small table for the police-band radio on the other."

She brought up a few small boxes full of Melmac dishes, towels, sheets and a couple of blankets. She sat down on a kitchen chair and looked around. "Home sweet home. I'll wait 'til dark to bring up the radio set. Now I need to get some groceries and start looking for a job."

* * *

My *Hestek* shipmates taught me how to chip and paint metal. They also showed me how to do coxcombing, the wrapping of railings with half hitches. These simple knots are decorative when painted, and the ridges made by the knots provide an excellent grip, even when wet.

After work, I went below to the living quarters to change uniforms and get ready for dinner. Clement Jackson, one of the seamen, was sitting on the locker tops, sharpening a knife. I greeted him: "Hi Clement. How's...?"

He jumped up and waved his knife right in front of my face. "See this?" he shouted. "It's sharp as hell. Cut up anything. Even a person...."

5. NEW JOBS

Rena Skye divided her time between the newspaper ads and the TV news. Her attention was caught by praise for a local businessman. "Frank Murphy did it again. His church was raising funds to build an orphanage. This afternoon, the owner of the celebrated Bogie's Club announced that he would give two hundred fifty thousand dollars of his personal money to complete the fund drive. Mr. Murphy once again lives up to his nickname of 'The Saint.'"

Skye looked over the ads for waitress openings. Bogie's wasn't one of them. "Too bad," she mused. "I bet he pays pretty well. Anyway, there are a few open waitress positions. I'll start checking them out tomorrow."

* * *

I backed up as I looked at the knife being waved in front of me.

Jackson continued ranting: "Don't you ever call me Clement again or I'll use this on you. Call me Jax. I hate Clement! My name is Jax!"

"All right, Jax. I'm sorry, I forgot."

He lowered the knife. "Just don't do it again." He leaned down to pick up his whetstone. When he stood up again, he was smiling. "You're new, so maybe the mistake was honest."

"Why do you keep your knife so sharp?" I asked.

"That's somethin' they don't teach you in boot camp." He looked down at my beltline. "Here's some advice to a new shipmate. You're on the deck force. Get a knife of your own. Wear it like this." He returned his knife to the sheath hanging from his belt and tucked into his back right pocket. "We always need something to cut lines. And you may have to cut yourself clear to save your life. Position it like this. It stays out of the way and you can get it fast. Get a knife—and keep it sharp."

30

The next day I was given a section of *Hestek's* railing to work on. Shepherd loaned me his knife until the ship's store opened, when I bought my own.

I cut off the old, damaged material on the railing. Next, I scraped and re-primered the metal with red lead. I looked up from my work a few times and saw Cisco watching from the oh-one level, holding his ever-present cup of coffee. He never said anything. Just watched.

Before I began the new coxcombing, Shepherd inspected my work. "That's pretty good. Okay, you know what a fathom is?"

"Six feet," I replied.

"Right. Easy to measure." He held both arms straight out sideways. "Fingertip to fingertip. So, go and get six fathoms of shore line to wrap this with."

"Shore line?" I asked. I'd heard about this. Now I was caught up in it.

"Yeah. It's a special kind of sturdy line that looks terrific when you're standing on the pier looking at the decorative work."

"Okay. Where do I get it?"

Shepherd took off his work baseball cap, ran his hand through his short-cropped black hair. "Ask Monnyng in the paint locker. He might have some."

When I finally found the paint locker, the third class boatswain was inventorying his supplies. "Monnyng?"

"Yeah, Matthews, what do you need?" He was thin, but not emaciated. His movements flowed and he gave the impression that he was a spring ready to pop under the right circumstances.

"Shep sent me to find six fathoms of shore line."

Monnyng stood up, wiping his hands on a rag. He took one look at me then pointed to the side of the ship. "No smokin' here. Douse the fag. Don't want any fires, with all this paint." He spoke softly but with a veiled strength. After I flipped my smoke over the side, he lifted some rags, mumbling just loud enough to hear. "Lemme see. I'm sure I put that stuff here. Nope, not there. Maybe back here. No...."

"Maybe it's in that metal box in the corner." I suggested, stepping into the small compartment.

He dismissed my suggestion with a wave of his hand. "Nah. That's personal stuff in there."

Monnyng pointed out the door. "Why don't you stay out there? I'll get your stuff for you."

"Okay." I backed out of the paint locker. I didn't want to trespass on anyone's territory. "Why're you so touchy about me being in the compartment?"

"Not just you. Stuff gets spilled or rearranged. Can't find what I'm looking for." He took a deep breath. "I have a system all worked out. Don't want anyone to mess it up."

I looked around. A raised lip on every shelf held paint cans in during rough weather. Removable metal bars across the front held the cans in. The paint was arranged by color: deck gray and haze gray on the bottom, lime green and white for living compartment walls on the shelf above that, various colors of enamel on top. Another shelf held red lead primer for steel and yellow zinc chromate primer for aluminum. Another area held painting supplies, brushes, turpentine, stuff like that. There was even one area for empty paint cans. Impressive organization.

Monnyng didn't have any shore line left. He sent me to the gunners mates in Mount 52, a deck up and all the way forward on the 01 level. As I left, he reached down, seeming to double-check that his metal box was locked.

The gunner's mates sent me to the Mark 56 secondary gun fire control system. The FT there, the gun fire control technician, said some shore line might be on the floor of the gun director. When we got up there, I found out that it was a tiny box-like thing that could barely hold two men. I found myself hanging upside down looking for the line. It wasn't there. The FT had to help me get out of the director. He checked that an FT on the *Peter I. Johnsten*, tied up outboard of us, had returned what he'd borrowed, then sent me to the torpedomen. They sent me to a machine shop. They sent me to the quartermasters on the bridge. They sent me to the signalmen.

I went out onto the open bridge and aft to the signal bridge. One man was replacing worn out signal flags in a flag bag. Another was cleaning the lens of a signal searchlight, used for flashing light Morse code communications. I approached two guys standing and talking. "Shepherd sent me for six fathoms of shore line. I've been all over trying to find it. The quartermasters said you guys were using some this morning. Can I please get enough to do my job?"

One of the signalmen, a first class, grinned. "Hi! My name's Dasso. When did you get aboard the Old Haystack?"

"Four days ago."

"Where have you looked for your shore line?" he asked with a twinkle in his eye.

"Oh, God. Lets see." I explained all my adventures to him, ending with, "What the hell does a guy have to do to get some of that stuff?"

"Follow me," Dasso said. We crossed the signal bridge to the other side of the ship. He laughed as he motioned across the open water of Hampton Roads. "Your shore line is over there. See it? I'm sure there's more than six fathoms of shoreline along that beach over there!"

Showdown time.

"What?" I stood with my mouth hanging open.

"It's a game, man. All the boots go through some wild goose chase like this." Dasso chuckled at the look on my face. "If they're gullible enough! Be glad you're not a snipe, an engineer. Their initiations are a lot greasier!"

"What a waste of time! I could've...."

"Hold on! It's tradition to razz new guys. But think about it. I bet you learned something about where places are and who works there. In fact, I'd guarantee it!"

I grinned. "Guess I did. And I met some people I might not have met for a while."

When I turned to leave I almost bumped into Cisco. He was standing by the doorway to the bridge, sipping coffee.

"Hi, Cisco. How you doing?"

"All right," he said with a knowing look. "How about you?"

"Learning a lot," I grinned as I moved past him. "Real fast."

At supper, I was asked at least six times if I ever found my shore line.

*   *   *

Skye spent a couple days learning the layout of the area: Norfolk, Virginia Beach, Portsmouth, other nearby towns. Now she was looking for a job where she could watch sailors for drug activity. She parked in front of a nightclub in Virginia Beach.

"Damn!" she mumbled. "This is the third place I've tried. 'Sorry, miss, we just hired someone.' What're the odds that two bars in a row just hired someone? Maybe they don't like my accent."

She slid out of her '57 Bel Air. She glanced at the unlit sign above the front door: Blinker's Bar and Grill. A sign in the window said "WAITRESS WANTED."

"At least that's still up," she said. "Here we go again, Dad. I'll be the best damn waitress in the world."

The front door was locked. She knocked. No answer. She knocked harder and looked into a window. Nobody was there.

She looked around the corner, down the right side of the building. There was another door two-thirds of the way down this longer side. The large parking lot to her right was empty. She glanced through the windows on her left as she walked. The dim interior was one big room. This door was unlocked. She entered.

"Hello!" she called. "Anybody here?"

"We're closed!" a distant voice replied from behind the bar.

Skye crossed the room, stood on the heavy brass foot rail and looked over the bar. A trap door was hooked open. Stairs descended to a basement. A muffled curse issued from below.

"I'm here to see about your ad in the paper." She heard footsteps before she saw the mop of gray hair. A large man came up the stairs carrying two full cases of bottled beer. "Is the waitress job still available?"

"Yeah," the man grunted as he put the boxes on top of the coolers. His face reminded Skye of an ingrained roadmap with two pools of clear blue where the eyes should be. This man had spent a lot of time outdoors. Or boozing. Or both. "I'm Nick Davenport, the owner. What's your name?"

"Rena Skye."

"Where you from, Rena? Sure isn't Virginia."

"Originally northern Illinois, near Rockford. Then we moved to California during the War. I just spent a number of years in San Diego."

Davenport nodded. He lifted a hinged countertop section and came out from behind the bar. He sat on a stool. "Been around myself. Retired from the Navy ten years ago. You must be familiar with swab jockeys, being in Dago for a while."

Rena nodded. "Yeah, I met a few sailors."

"You like 'em?" He looked her up and down, taking in her nice figure, deep tan, shoulder-length auburn hair, and dark brown eyes in one long glance.

She forced a smile. "Some of the younger ones are all right."

Nick looked puzzled for a moment before he understood. "No! I mean as customers. Let me rephrase that. Do you get along well with swabbies?"

"Absolutely!"

"Good. This is a sailors' bar. I serve good, inexpensive food. Drinks aren't watered down. Live music for dancing. We do a good business almost every night, but we're closed on Sundays and Mondays. You waited tables or been a barmaid?"

"Both. Few different places. If you want, I can give you references."

"I want. Got 'em written down?"

Rena pulled a paper out from her purse and handed it to him.

While Davenport examined it, she looked around. Complete sets of signal flags hung from the ceiling. Authentic signal searchlights stood at the ends of the bar. The neatness of the liquor bottle shelves reminded her of the way a flag bag might be laid out: in alphabetical order—bourbon, brandy, cognac, gin, rum, scotch, tequila, vodka—with the quality stuff on the higher shelves. She mused, "Bet you were a signalman."

The bar owner gazed around and nodded. "You'd win. In fact, I was so fast on the signal lamp, there, that they called me Blink or Blinker. Thus the name of the bar." He re-folded her paper and handed it back. "I know three of those places. How long you work at them?"

"Eight to ten months each. I was at the last one for just over a year."

"Navalese doesn't bother you?"

She laughed. "Nope. And I can give as good as I get."

Nick nodded, smiling. "I do try to keep the real foul language down. Lady customers, you know. And the swabbies are actually pretty well behaved. Why'd you leave those jobs in Dago?"

"Better pay, usually."

The owner raised his eyebrows. "How much do you want here?"

Rena shrugged her shoulders. "What're you paying?"

"Forty cents an hour plus all your tips. You don't have to tip out anyone. I cook. You bus your own tables. You clean up each night, wipe down everything, sweep up. High school kids come in to scrub the floors on the evenings we're closed. So, no need to share tips with anyone. Sound okay?"

"Yep."

"Any questions?"

"Two. What are your hours and how many other waitresses do you have?"

"Tuesday through Saturday from eleven a.m., to pick up the lunch crowd. We close at two a.m. With you and the other new waitress, I'll have a total of six full timers. A part-time woman stands by for when someone takes off, which I don't mind as long as Janet's available. The shifts are ten-thirty to seven and six to two-thirty. The extra time on first shift is for set up, on second shift for clean up. You get two ten-minute breaks. You can eat and work at the same time if the service isn't hurt. Okay?"

"Sounds good!"

"When can you start?"

"Whenever you need me."

"How about tomorrow, six p.m.?"

"I'll be here."

"Where you living?"

Rena pointed to the east. "I found an upstairs apartment a couple blocks away."

"Good. There are a number of nice places around here like that. Hope you found a good one."

She nodded. "I like it. So I'm hired?"

Davenport walked to the front window and took down the "WAITRESS WANTED" sign. "Yep. Far as I'm concerned, you're now an employee of Blinker's Bar and Grill!"

* * *

I watched my primary suspect leave the *Hestek* as soon as liberty call went down. He returned less than an hour later, carrying a small paper bag. He went through all the trouble to shit, shower and shave, get into dress uniform to go ashore for a very short time. I thought I knew why, but I had to make sure.

6. CO-WORKERS

Skye heard the car door. She glanced out the front window of her Virginia Beach apartment. A tall, slim Negro woman stepped from a green 1955 Dodge. She had skin the color of milk chocolate and short, straight hair. Rena smiled. She waited for the knock on the door. After a short delay, she opened it. The visitor's hand was raised to knock again. "I'll be damned!" Rena said. "Look what the cat dragged clear across the country!"

"Uh-huh. Look here, honey, I know you. You knew I was here soon as I got out of the car. Then you made me stand here and knock. Now, are you going to invite me in or keep me out here like an unwanted aunt?"

"I should make you wait for not letting me know you were arriving from California today."

"Lady, you sent word to get here A-SAP. That means no delays. Not even for a phone call. Jennifer Powers, at your service ... ma'am!"

"Oh, shut up and get in here!" Rena pulled the other woman into the apartment. "I'm glad to see you, Jennie. Sit down. You eaten yet? Want a drink?"

"My, what a change from making me stand there knocking!" Powers said. She took off her light coat. "You have a hook for hanging stuff up or should I toss it in the corner like at your last place?"

"Give it to me and quit your bitching." Rena closed the door and hung the coat on an empty hook alongside hers.

"Yes, sir, ma'am, honey. You have any good bourbon?" Jennie asked while walking around and inspecting the apartment. Her eye caught the chess set on the board like it was the middle of a game. "You still play against yourself?"

"Sorry, no bourbon. How about a beer?"

"Guess that'll have to do."

"Yes, I still play against myself. That setup there, I'm going through some Bobby Fischer moves." Rena pointed back to the kitchen table. "I'm having lunch. Join me?"

"Sure. We can eat and talk! How'd your… uh… special problem turn out?"

"I'm really pissed," Skye answered. "The C. O. in Dago said they'd take care of it out there. But if this turns angry, the lawyers will screw me royally. I hope we won't have to pick up where we left off when I go back to Dago. You probably noticed that I'm using my maiden name again."

The two friends brought each other up to date. Finally, Rena asked over dirty dishes, "So, are you up to speed on what we're doing here?" Powers shook her head. "So, you don't know yet?"

"No details," Jennie said. "OCI San Diego set me up with enlisted uniforms with second class storekeeper crows."

Rena nodded. "You're assigned to the Naval Operating Base. I'm glad they're making use of your business degree somehow. But that psychology minor won't help much."

"Yeah, nice of them to make me a storekeeper. If I can't work in my field, I can always pretend to be something similar."

"Well, you volunteered for this duty. God, I've never seen anyone gripe like you!" Skye teased.

"Honey, a bitchin' sailor's a happy sailor, right? So I'm happy." She finished her third beer. "How about you?"

"I must not be too happy 'cause I don't gripe so much. Another beer?"

"First, tell me what we're into."

"I have a job as a waitress at Blinker's Bar and Grill, a couple blocks from here. And I get to play mother to the bunch of you guys. I can only suspect how nasty this case will be."

"I don't like that word, 'nasty.' You work tonight?"

Skye nodded. "I start at six."

"Then I won't drink any more. I don't want the cops to stop me on the way to the base. Not in the South!"

"You can always stay here."

"Can't. I checked in already and they gave me duty tomorrow. Wasn't that nice of them?"

"Okay. But the invitation's there whenever you want a place to flop."

"Yeah, sure. I'll be too busy watching half of Norfolk Naval Station to get here very often."

"Maybe not. You're the mother to two other Waves. But, if you need a break, come on over." Rena went into her bedroom and opened the combination lock on a metal box. She extracted a business size envelope and some photographs, which she gave to her friend. "Here are your official orders and some other details. Top secret."

"Yeah, I know. 'Burn Before Reading.' I'll read it here and you can set fire to it yourself." Powers tore open the envelope and quickly read the single sheet inside. "Okay, I knew we were out to get drug dealers, but what's this about quinine?"

"Dealers cut their drugs. If they cut it to fifty percent, they double their profit. Heroin today is usually about four percent pure."

"Big profits!"

"Exactly. Many use powdered milk or powdered sugar to cut the stuff. But that makes the bitter heroin too sweet. That's why users taste what they buy. If it's not bitter enough, they know it's not very pure."

"So what's the quinine do?" Powers asked.

"It's also bitter. The dealer dilutes the drug and a user has a hard time tasting the difference. Tastes very pure. But you can overdose on quinine, too. Right now, roughly half the heroin deaths are actually from quinine."

"Got it. So, I'll watch out for my helpers. Who are they?"

"I haven't met them yet." Skye reached into another envelope and extracted two photos. "This is Lieutenant j-g Laura Jaf, who'll play the role of a seaman apprentice. And this is Ruth Gardner a hospital corpsman second class. Both are your operatives."

"What am I supposed to do with them? Maybe I can use my psychology."

"You'll be working in supply. Gardner's at the base sick bay. And Jaf'll be compartment cleaning, mess cooking or whatever they tell her to do. All of you are to be socially active. Keep your eyes open. Try to detect drug users, at work and at play."

Powers chewed on her lower lip for a moment. "You're pulling people in from all over the country?"

"OCI Norfolk is. A hand-picked team from Newport, Great Lakes, Dago, Jax, all over."

"How many of us are there?"

"Twenty one so far, military and civilian."

Powers whistled. "That's a big crew!"

"It grew on them. They got some drug use calls. They assigned ten of us to take care of that. Then came a very nervous anonymous call. He might be an insider who wants out. That's always helpful. If we can find him. About the same time the commanding officer of Norfolk Naval Station sent a request for help. They're finding dead bodies on the base. Quinine overdoses. So Central doubled the size of the team. Okay now, here are Gardner's and Jaf's files. Read and memorize."

Powers read the files quickly. She looked again at the photos. "They're so young!"

Skye nodded. "So were we, when we first started. This is their first field assignment. They were very sharp on their previous duties. They may require some mothering, but Central feels they'll do fine."

"I suppose we have to listen to Central, don't we?" Jennie sighed. "Who else do we have from California?"

"Daniel Han is on one of the ships here. Tony Alvarez is working as a waiter at the Windjammer."

"That one of the clubs?"

Skye nodded. "Acey-Deucey Club. And Morgan Delano. He's from New York, but I worked with him out west, too."

"Del? I remember him. Anyone else interesting?"

The team leader shrugged. "Don't know. Negro guy from Charleston named Glenn Oliver. I worked once with him, too, and he impressed me. A Sioux Indian guy from the Midwest. A real savvy guy named Terry Irwin on the *Valcour Bay*. And a guy named Eric Matthews, an electrical engineer, analytical type. Like your partners, he's done some good work at Lakes, but he's never been undercover before. Commander Blount at Norfolk Central assigned him to the USS *Hestek*, DD-856, before we were even brought out here."

"What set that off?"

Skye shrugged. "The ship's captain called about suspicious activities."

"Interesting...."

"I'll be directly coordinating a number of operatives. And we have a few other people assigned to base security, mess decks, fix-up and clean-up crews."

"Enough, already. I won't remember it all anyway." Powers stood up. "We have any leads on suppliers?"

"Nothing. Matthews knows of a suspected user. A couple other guys are in the fleet following leads called in by the ships' COs. That's it. Most of our team's been involved with heroin users in their private lives or on other cases. We have to find users and backtrack. We're supposed to break the whole drug ring. Pass that on to your people. A drug ring causes a ripple effect radiating out from them."

"Yeah. And taking them down will cause a different kind of ripple effect when the drugs are gone," Jennie observed.

"That'll be someone else's problem," Skye said. She wrote something on a piece of paper. "Here's my phone number. Give it to your two and tell them to use it—if necessary. And then with caution. Okay, let's get this show on the road. I want to finish this up and get back out west so I can get unmarried."

Powers looked at her watch and stood up. "I better let you get ready for work."

"You keep in touch."

"Yes, sir, ma'am, aye, aye, roger wilco, and all that stuff." She put her coat on. Then she gave Rena a hug. "You take care of yourself, girl. You hear? This doesn't feel like the jobs in Dago. This time could be dangerous."

Rena shivered at the memory of her nightmare on the flight from San Diego. "You watch out, too, Jennie. You're right. We're not chasing down loan sharks or petty thieves. When the shit hits the fan here, we don't know where it's going to splatter."

"What's the matter, girl? You just turned white as a sheet. What's wrong?"

"Nothing. I just had a flashback to a dream I had."

Jennie looked at her friend. "Must have been one hell of a nightmare, honey...."

"Like I said, when the shit hits the fan here, we don't know what'll happen." She hugged her friend good-bye. "Go on, now, and get yourself set up."

7. LEADERSHIP AND NEW PEOPLE

I stood my first in-port messenger watch on the quarterdeck of the *Hestek*. Tanglewood, third class gunner's mate, was Petty Officer of the Watch and Lieutenant (junior grade) Dapp, Fox Division Officer, was Quarterdeck Watch Officer. It was a slow morning.

A Navy car pulled up to the foot of the brow.

"Here comes the Captain!" Dapp observed. Tanglewood turned on the 1MC announcing system, then waited for the Old Man to come up the brow.

Captain Lorman stepped out of the vehicle. He patted the back of the drivers seat. "Thanks, Ross. I have to meet some people at the Officer's Club for dinner at 1230. So pick me up at 1200 hours. I don't believe any of the other officers are going anywhere this morning."

This told the driver he could do whatever he wanted until then. "Aye, aye, Capt'n. See you at noon."

Lorman came up the brow, smartly saluted the ensign, and stepped on board. Tanglewood rang the ship's bell and announced:

[DING-DING. DING-DING.] HESTEK ARRIVING.

The Captain waited for the honors to be completed. The scrambled eggs on the bill of his hat and the gold stripes on his sleeves sparkled in the sunlight. All of us saluted. "Good morning, Captain."

Lorman returned the salutes. "Good morning, Mr. Dapp. All's well?"

"Aye, Captain. All's well."

Lorman nodded and headed forward toward his stateroom. Even though he wore the three stripes of a full commander, he was the destroyer's Captain. The commanding officer of any ship was always referred to as "Captain" in the same way that a four-striper, a Captain, who was in charge of a destroyer division was always referred to as Commodore, a rank that didn't exist during peacetime.

All the men Lorman met stepped aside and saluted. The Captain stopped and spoke to one of them. "Fowler, how's Terry doing? I heard he went to the emergency room."

"He's fine, Capt'n. Thanks!" the man replied. "He just banged his head pretty bad and needed a couple of stitches. He was released right away."

Lorman smiled. "Glad to hear it."

The Captain continued on to his stateroom. Fowler came onto the quarterdeck, shaking his head. "How does he know that stuff? We went to the emergency room at ten-thirty last night when my two-year-old son fell down the stairs. How does the Old Man get his information so fast?"

"The Wardroom doesn't know either," commented Dapp. "He seems to know everybody and they all feed him information. He has quite a network."

Tanglewood turned to me. "The Captain knows the names of all the crewmember's wives and most of their kids," the petty officer explained. "He learns about everyone's family and how they're doing at almost every moment. This crew would follow that man into hell."

After I finished my watch, I ate lunch, then went up to the 01 level and sat inside a 3-inch gun tub to compare my watch experiences with the diagram Shep and I drew earlier. Corrected some of it. When the 1MC announced, "COMMENCE SHIP'S WORK," I took the long way to go below, forward and down to the main deck, looking around to continue learning the layout of the ship.

As I headed for the living compartment, I passed the paint locker's open door. Monnyng sat in front of his metal box, now unlocked. Soon as he saw me, he slammed it shut and sat on it. He looked up at me warily. "Need something, Matthews?"

"No, just heading back to the compartment."

There weren't many guys in the compartment when I got there. Ron Smith knelt in front of his locker. He straightened up quickly with a wary look. He locked his locker and quickly left. He was short and squat but muscular. Looked tough as nails, the type you'd prefer not to get into a scrap with.

But what was with all this slamming shut of metal boxes and lockers? What did they have to hide?

As far as Smith went, I was already developing a profile of him. A couple days ago, I came down the companionway pretty fast. Must have taken him by surprise. He threw something into his locker, slammed it shut and jumped around to sit on it. Swallowed hard, tears in his eyes. Swallowed again. A couple times.

"God, you gave me a start!" he gasped.

"Why? Aren't you used to someone coming down that fast? What's wrong?"

"Nothing! Leave me alone."

I bet he had to quick-swallow a mouthful of straight booze. I knew he was a big drinker but didn't know how far gone he was. He would rush off on liberty as soon as it went down and come back late. He'd either make too much noise and "shush!" himself, or he'd take baby steps, holding on to bunk frames for balance. Then he'd pour himself into his rack. He had a hangover every morning, which disappeared by morning quarters.

After changing into my work dungarees, Shep had me help chip the deck. Others primered it. We'd paint it tomorrow. Chipping is an arduous task: hit the deck with a special hammer to take the old paint off. Over and over and over. My arm ached after ten minutes, so I alternated hands to hold the hammer. The constant jarring of hitting steel helped the muscles turn to mush. And the noise of four or five hammers going at once was just about deafening. I was glad to hear the announcement to knock off ship's work.

When I got to the living compartment, most of the other guys were already there, changing into the appropriate uniform for supper or liberty. Phil Le Blanc was already climbing into his rack. "No supper, Cajun?"

He looked around with his nervous deep brown eyes. "Nah. I had a couple candy bars. I'm not hungry."

Smith returned from showering and put his shaving kit away. He lit up a cigarette, placed it carefully on top of the butt kit and started changing into a dress uniform.

Luke Raynes came down the companionway. He began to rant the instant he smelled the cigarette. "Heaven help us all and keep us from that poison. That smells terrible. You smokers ought to show some respect for those of us who try to keep our bodies pure."

"Go to hell!" Smith said.

"Not me. I'm saved." He glared at Smith. "I suppose you're going ashore to wallow in sin." Raynes turned to me. "Fornicators are everywhere. And blasphemers. Every other word is foul and unrepeatable. And they're so lazy. Sloth is one of the seven deadly sins, you know."

I turned away, trying to ignore him.

Raynes changed out of his dungarees. He was a big man, six feet two and shaped like a boxer. But he didn't seem like he cared much for his physique; he had other priorities. Like converting the world.

Smith, ready for liberty, slammed his locker shut. "Well, I'm off for another hot time on the old town."

Le Blanc half rolled over. "I thought you didn't have any money, Smith."

"I don't," Smith said. "But I'll get some."

"Where?"

He looked around to be sure no senior petty officers were around. He shrugged as he continued. "I'll roll a couple o' queers. They always have money."

Raynes looked up, eyes blazing. "That's robbery! And even though they are reprobates, thou shalt not steal!"

Smith grinned. "Then they can stay away from me. If they're where I can find them, they're fair game."

"You'll go to hell for that!" Raynes warned.

"I don't like homos, either," said Le Blanc, rolling over again. "But that's going too far, Smith."

"Tough shit. They can bring charges against me, if they catch me. If they can get witnesses. Queers don't like the limelight. Well, I'm off. Wish me good hunting. Maybe I'll only have to roll one of 'em if he has a enough dough." He ran up the companionway.

Raynes was leaning against his rack, praying out loud. He stopped after a minute. "Matthews, are you saved?"

"From what?" I asked.

"Have you accepted Jesus Christ as your Lord and Savior?"

"In my own way."

"There's only one way to be saved. You confess your faith before everyone. Come to services with me. We can go to the altar together. I'm in church almost every night. You can come with me any time."

"That's all right. I'll do it my way," I replied.

"Well, brother, whenever you're ready, let me know."

Zoss was changing his uniform over in the corner where his bunk and locker were. He came to my rescue. "Raynes, leave the man alone. The only way being saved is meaningful is when people do it on their own."

"That's what you say. And I know what kind of so-called Christian you are."

Zoss shook his head. "Strong-arm missionaries," he muttered to himself. He looked Raynes right in the eye and demanded, "Leave... the man... alone."

That night I fell asleep reviewing the people in the division. The petty officers seemed stable and above suspicion, but I'll watch them anyway. Most behaved like the seamen, except for Al Cisco, the quiet, ever-present, ever-watchful second class who read tomes instead of books.

The seamen were fairly squared away, with some exceptions. Rebellious Toby Burch had just been busted to seaman apprentice. Billy Bob Coe was a bigot. Brian Grengs was just plain lazy and had to be told to do everything at least twice. And for him gross was hilarious—he'd light his farts with a Zippo and get pissed when it burned his ass. "Jax" Jackson hated his given name of Clement and raged at anyone who dared use it. Phil "Cajun" Le Blanc slept every free moment. Luke Raynes was a religious zealot and missionary. Ron Smith was a drunken hater of homosexuals. Quiet,

44

unassuming Stephen Zoss showed his religion but never preached it. Hank Reston was a nice, easygoing kid. Charlie Wu was quiet, easy to work with and willing to help. But both Reston and Wu kept to themselves and had no shipboard friends that I could detect.

The rest seemed to be guys trying to get their required military time done. Hard working, but not too much so, obedient enough not to get into trouble. The most suspicious person was Joe Monnyng, with his guarded steel box hidden in the paint locker. Nobody else, other than my known suspect user, seemed to be a good candidate for user or pusher.

I was probably derelict in my duty for quite a while. My job was to get to know the crew but I steered clear of Raynes, "The Preacher." I have my own beliefs and I don't appreciate pressure from others. So I kept away from him as much as possible. Luckily, he worked on the fo'c'sle, the full length of the ship away from where I worked.

* * *

Rena Skye tried to meet all her operatives face to face. She arranged to meet Laura Jaf at the public library, but got involved in talking with someone else. Laura was late and overheard Skye talking, so she waited outside for the team leader to leave. Even then, she didn't catch Skye in time. She followed her to a grocery store where she engineered an "accidental" meeting.

One night, civilian agents Leonard Ford and George Stolichek showed up at Blinker's. They irritated Skye—they messed up their cover stories. Being insurance salesmen was okay, but when she asked which company they worked for, they answered with two different names.

That didn't make a good impression. Skye commented that just because Ford was a frog out of water, he shouldn't behave like he didn't belong where he was.

"I'm a good part French. Is that a slam on my background?" he asked.

"No," she frowned. "I was referring to you as a frogman. I know the superb training you've had. But I don't need those skills right now. You're stuck on land for a while, Len, and you have to be just as careful here as if you're on an underwater demolition job."

He nodded and gave her an "OK" sign as he apologized for both his bad cover story and his ethnic sensitivity.

* * *

Finally, the weekend arrived. In our living compartment on the *Hestek*, some of the deck force prepared to go ashore. Local slush funder Derella was "manning the compartment" to make last minute loans. Smith was obviously going out to get drunk. Le Blanc wasn't in his rack. He had the 16-to-2000 messenger watch. Monnyng was silently getting dressed.

"Going out to rob someone again, Smith?" Raynes asked.

"Maybe I'll roll a couple queers just for you, Preacher. I can always use the extra dough. Want me to donate some to your church?"

"Reprobate," Raynes mumbled, leaving the compartment.

"Where you going then, Smith? Lovey's?" Jovan asked, referring to a popular bar on the "strip" just outside the Main Gate of the base.

"Not me. I got a hard-drinkin' gal in Virginia Beach."

"She actually talks to ya?" Derella piped up. "Or do the two of ya just sit around suckin' on a bottle?"

Everyone laughed, Monnyng the loudest. Smith slammed his locker shut, gave Monnyng a very dirty look and stomped off to the quarterdeck. I wondered what was going on between those two. That look wasn't just irritation.

*   *   *

That same night Ruth Gardner checked in with Skye at Blinker's in Virginia Beach. Gardner was a pretty woman with bright red hair. She acted very unsure of herself. Skye gave her the address of Cranston's, a nearby café, with orders to meet her there the next day.

When they met, Skye found that Gardner was, indeed, shy and uncertain. She was on her first undercover assignment and she was scared she wouldn't do well. Skye reassured her and gave her some pointers: do her job as a Hospital Corpsman, act like a normal Wave, go out to various social functions. But a major part of her job was to go with friends to bars and nightclubs where there was music and dancing so she could keep an eye out for suspicious behavior.

But Gardner also had another problem that might affect her work. She'd come here from Great Lakes, Illinois, where she had a boyfriend who seemed to be running around. Everything was fine when they were together, but this long distance stuff was a whole different thing.

*   *   *

One day the following week, about 1400, I first heard the shrill whistle of a bos'n's pipe prior to an announcement.

NOW SET THE SPECIAL SEA! SET THE SPECIAL SEA! ALL HANDS TO QUARTERS FOR LEAVING PORT. THE SHIP WILL GET UNDERWAY IN THIRTY MINUTES. SET THE SPECIAL SEA!

"What's happening?"

"Scuttlebutt says all ships are going out," Hank Reston said. "Get into

46

your grubbiest whites."

"Why?"

"This ain't a clean work detail."

There was a bit of grumbling among the crew. "What's this for?"

"Why?"

"Cut the bitching!" ordered Dean, the first class boatswain. "Get changed and get topside!"

After changing again, I was last in the compartment. I started to go topside, but saw a small, neatly folded square of paper on the deck. I opened it. It held some fine white powder. I smelled it. Tasted it. Quite bitter. It was heroin.

8. ESTHER

I was surprised to find heroin this openly. I re-folded the paper and crumpled it in my hand. I wondered whose it was and whether a supplier worked out of the crew's quarters. On the way to my sea detail station, I tossed the packet over the side. I knew more now than I did fifteen minutes ago but that packet could incriminate me.

Gascomb arrived from Chief's Quarters. "Listen up! Hurricane Esther is heading straight for us. We're going out to the hurricane anchorage in Chesapeake Bay."

Each vessel cast off its mooring lines and backed away from the piers. Behind us, more ships slipped out. In front of us, I could see a long line of ships. It was a sight to see, the whole fleet pulling out at the same time.

The water gliding by the ship fascinated me. The vibration of the screw shafts and the whump-whump-whump of the screws pounded under my feet. I smelled something new—salt water without the stale bouquet of harbor. I'd been here before, but I couldn't let these guys know. "Man, this is exciting! We're really going to sea!"

When they secured sea detail, I raced up to the 01 level, near Mount 52. I faced the wind and greeted the elements as the salt spray rose from a sea that was growing rougher by the hour.

Reston came up alongside me. "I was lookin' for you." He gazed intently at my face. "You're really enjoying this, aren't you?"

"Yeah! This is why I joined the Navy!"

The choppy seas soon turned to whitecaps. The ship's rolling grew more pronounced and its pitching increased to the point where spray flew through the air toward the bridge. We stepped back so most of it missed us. Even so, I had to periodically clean off the salt water from my glasses.

I pulled out my cigarettes and lighter.

"I see you got a Zippo," Reston observed. "That's the only lighter made that can do the job in this weather."

"That's what the guy at the ship's store told me."

"Hey, gimme one of them."

I shook the pack so that a cigarette stood partway up, then held it out.

"By the way," Reston said, "you shouldn't smoke at sea."

"Why not?"

"Makes you seasick. Sometimes smokin' makes you sick faster'n anything I know. Some guys never smoke at sea. If I were you, I wouldn't take the chance."

"So why're you smoking?" I grinned. "Go to hell, Reston. I won't get seasick."

"You know what to do if you do feel sick? Come topside for fresh air and watch the horizon."

"Why?" I asked.

"Look out there. The horizon is the only stable thing around. It's always horizontal, no matter what the ship's doing. And when you watch it, there's kind of an automatic connection between the horizon, your eyes, your brain and your stomach. It works."

I smiled. I knew he was right. "Thanks, I'll remember that. Any other old salt's advice to the boot seaman?"

"You start feeling sick? Eat something. Nothin' greasy or anything like that. Get some crackers from the mess decks. Saltines are perfect to settle a stomach."

The bos'n's pipe screamed again. NOW, SET THE ANCHOR DETAIL. SET THE ANCHOR DETAIL.

We watched the anchor crew get soaked. They dropped one anchor and let out some extra anchor chain. Then the ship moved over a short distance. The anchor detail dropped the other anchor with extra chain. The wind pushed us back from the anchors so the chains formed a wide "V." Our bow pointed into the oncoming waves and wind, reducing the effect of both. We were ready to ride out the hurricane.

The *Hestek* continued rolling side to side. Reston unconsciously balanced himself, shifting from foot to foot as the ship moved. He didn't notice I was doing the same thing.

Later, we went down to the living compartment to dry off. Le Blanc sat on the deck sleeping, propped between the floor lockers and one of the triple upright lockers reserved for senior petty officers. It seemed this guy could zonk out anytime, anywhere. I couldn't figure out why he'd need to.

The following day, Esther veered away. She missed us by two hundred miles. Most of the ships returned to port. The *Hestek* went out to sea to replace another destroyer that developed fresh water evaporator problems and had to come into port for repairs.

9. LIFE AT SEA

The *Hestek* steamed out of Chesapeake Bay and headed for the Virginia Capes Operations Area in the open Atlantic. From my position near the status board at the back of the bridge, I could see the great empty ocean through the windows.

This was my first watch as a bridge phone talker on the primary battle circuit. I knew there'd be some initiation pranks with yours truly as the butt of them, but I dared not let anyone know I wasn't a boot.

The Captain sat in his chair on the starboard side of the bridge. The Officer of the Deck and the Junior Officer of the Deck were at their positions on either side of the helmsman and the lee helm. The Quartermaster kept the underway log at his desk on the port side of the bridge. The Boatswain's Mate and Messenger of the Watch waited out of the way to do their chores. The other phone talker on the primary maneuvering circuit was to my right.

"All phone talkers check in," the Officer of the Deck commanded.

Shepherd was the Boatswain's Mate of the Watch. He quit fingering his boatswain's pipe, hanging from a lanyard around his neck, and tucked it into his jumper pocket. He walked over to advise me, leading me step by step through the phone check procedures, until we'd heard from everyone on the circuit and I could report, "Mr. Tower, all JA talkers are on line."

I stumbled a bit when handling the report for skunk alpha, which turned out to be a small merchantman. Shepherd checked on me periodically. I grew more confident as the hours wore on.

Shortly before the watch was over, there was another contact. "Bridge, Starboard Lookout. Bogey at one-one-zero about five thousand."

"Bridge, aye. Sir! Starboard lookout reports a bogey at one-one-zero, five thousand." I reported loud and clear.

"Very well." The OOD strained to see it. "Where is it? I don't see it."

"Starboard Lookout, Bridge. Can you identify the bogey?"

"Bridge, Starboard Lookout. Bogey now at one-one-five, range four-five-zero-zero. It looks like a bee-one-arr-dee. That's bravo-one-romeo-delta."

I dutifully reported, "Sir! Bogey now at one-one-five, range four-five-zero-zero, identified as a bee-one-arr-dee."

Mr. Tower stared straight ahead. "Very well. Tell him to keep me updated."

I looked at the status board where I'd written the type of bogey and groaned. The designation showed me what a B-1-RD really was. Before I could let anyone know I'd caught on, the lookout reported a change with a touch of urgency, "Bridge, Starboard Lookout. It's not a bee-one-arr-dee! It's a gee-you-eleven. They do look alike, you know!"

I had to laugh. I could hardly make the report, but tried to follow protocol, "Bridge, aye. Sir! Starboard Lookout reports that the bogey is not a bee-one-arr-dee, but a gee-you-eleven."

The OOD laughed. "Keep me posted. If you really want to track that seagull."

"No, sir! I don't think we need to."

The OOD turned to me, chortling. "Go ahead and ask the lookout where that gull is now."

I wiped the board clean then asked Shep. "That was some kind of initiation, wasn't it?"

The Captain turned with a twinkle in his eye. "Yes, son, it certainly was. Welcome to the fleet. As obvious as it seems now, I suspect most of us have been caught by that or something similar."

"Okay," Tower said. "Back to serious business."

The Captain returned to gazing out over the sea. That afternoon, the *Hestek* made contact with the task force's type commander. The destroyers typically sailed in an octagonal formation around a carrier to protect it, with more destroyers positioned out "on point." The smaller ships periodically pulled alongside the carrier or an oiler to refuel and to get mail and new movies. They tried to keep our tanks ninety percent full, in case of an emergency.

Captain Lorman silently watched and listened to the officers and men on the bridge. He lifted his binoculars to observe the carrier, the other ships, and our own position in the formation. He kept tabs on everything. But if all was going well, he didn't interfere.

The *Hestek* remained on station with Task Force Alpha, patrolling off Cape Hatteras or Vacapes, short for Virginia Capes. Small ships like ours went through an enormous amount of rolling and pitching. The seas were always high here. One day at dinner I asked why.

Reston and Roma, a third class boatswain mate, explained the way the currents swirled around the landmasses. They told me about the sport the helmsmen played by swinging the rudder at just the right time to amplify the ship's rolls during mealtimes.

This led to school call on how to control one's food tray—hold it at the top center and tilt or twist it to keep it level as the ship rolled and pitched. I made a conscious effort to level my tray for a couple days' meals. Soon I could do it automatically.

Each night when I returned to the compartment after supper, I noticed Le Blanc sound asleep in his rack. He never seemed to eat supper.

In these rough seas, I also "learned" how to sleep. All bunks on the ship were aligned fore and aft. Thus, a man in his rack would be rocked to sleep like in a cradle. It was also much more comfortable than taking large rolls with one's head tilting severely downward, then the same angle upward. I climbed up into my rack and was quickly rocked to sleep.

Suddenly there was a searing pain in my tailbone. I woke up howling.

10. LETTER FROM MOM

As the newest man in the division, I'd been given an undesirable top-most bunk. It was tough to get in and out of, but it didn't seem unsafe until the *Hestek* took a very large roll. I fell out. My tailbone hit the deck. That was why I woke up howling.

Everyone else woke up, too. Someone turned on the lights. Shepherd rushed over to help.

"Shit, he just fell out of his fuckin' rack," Derella complained. "Teach 'im how to sleep and shut the fuckin' lights off!"

Shep helped me up from the floor. "You all right?"

I nodded. "If it still hurts in the morning, I'll go to sick call."

"Okay. Look. Your rack's held up by two stanchions on the inside and two bunk chains on the outside. Right?" I nodded. He continued, "In rough seas, sleep on your stomach. Tuck your feet below the stanchion and the chain nearest to them, so they hook around them. Lay with your hands under your head or your pillow, with your elbows sticking way out. Hook your elbows above that stanchion and that chain. Now you're locked into place. You can take almost any roll. In time, you'll hold yourself in, even when you're asleep. All right?"

I nodded, climbed back into my rack and positioned myself as told. Shep made a couple adjustments, patted my rack and began to leave, when Derella shouted, "Turn the fuckin' lights off and lemme get back to sleep!"

"Derella," Shepherd warned, "if you ever want to get recommended for third class again, shut your trap." He turned off the lights and climbed back into his own bunk.

*   *   *

The sky was clear and the moon was bright. We hardly needed lights as we refueled at sea. This was a first for me. Our fuel tanks weren't topped off when we left Norfolk for Hurricane Esther. Now they were pretty low. The destroyers took turns alongside the aircraft carrier *Valcour Bay*, from which they pumped their lifeblood.

The ship ahead of us finished and pulled away. Oily smoke poured from both stacks, blanking out the stars. The ship's rooster tail was luminescent in the darkness. It flared higher than the fantail, showing the force of the screws carrying the destroyer back into formation.

The *Hestek* maneuvered into position off the starboard beam of the carrier. The bows of the two vessels compressed the sea between them. The water tried to push them away from each other, which amplified the roll of our ship.

The ship providing the fuel kept a straight course. The refueling ship had to match the other's speed and maintain a distance of thirty to fifty yards. Only the best helmsmen were assigned to this detail.

Amidships, the *Hestek* hooked up a strong cable for a trolley to carry bags of mail and movies. The highline detail, wearing helmets and bulky kapok lifejackets, waited. Hurry up and wait.

The carrier provided spanlines for the heavy fuel hoses to ride on, but we had to pull them across. Special details, also in helmets and lifejackets, waited at the forward and after refueling stations to do that.

First Division provided the line handlers for the after hose. We waited. Big swells flowed over the deck. We jumped onto the tops of closed hatches or the rungs of ladders welded onto the side of Mount 53. Everyone was soon drenched. It was a fun way to pass the time, but it was a dangerous game, more so at night when we might not see the rising water in time. Once in a while a guy got swept off his feet and the rest of us scrambled to grab him before he went over the side.

Reston and I stood protected by the superstructure, watching our approach to the carrier. "God! Look at the size of that thing!"

"Yeah, and that's a small bird farm. Hope like hell I never get assigned to one of those goddamn things."

"Bird farm?"

"Yeah. Planes are birds. Carriers are bird farms! Nothing but floating cities," Reston grinned. "If you got one of those bird farmers on the Haystack, I bet he'd be calling for Ralph before we ever left the pier."

"Yeah, worshiping at the porcelain throne," I laughed.

"Better believe it," Reston nodded.

"All right!" Chief Gascomb shouted. "Heads up! Here comes the shot line! Reston! Get on station!"

Reston scrambled up to the 01 level with Shepherd. We heard a shotgun sound. We could see the lights of the carrier, but not the weighted bulb on the steel rod that arched through the air, pulling a light nylon line after it.

When it slammed into the superstructure, Roma grabbed it. Tanglewood leapt to help. Aided only by flashlights, they hauled the shot line over and untied it from the heavier messenger line, which they passed up to Shepherd on the 01 level. Shep ran it through a block and returned it to Roma, who passed it through a series of blocks attached to the main deck.

"Okay, men! Run that line around!"

Each man in turn grabbed the line and ran aft as far as he could. He let go and ran back to where the line came through the final block on the deck, then ran with it again. We pulled the messenger across and then a bigger line that we'd use to bring the heavy span wire across over to our ship.

Everyone could hear Shepherd's clear voice calling out instructions until his crew connected the span wire's end fitting to the pelican hook and secured it. Next, they routed the lines connected to the hose through the blocks.

"Okay, run it!"

Once again, we did our stuff. This time we pulled a heavy hose across. When the ships rolled towards each other, the waves reached up and grabbed the drooping bights of the hose. We stopped dead in our tracks until the waves let go. Then we had to run even harder.

Waves continued to rush over the fantail but if we jumped out of the way now we'd lose control of the lines. So we got wetter. We might fall and land on a padeye, a metal tie-down point sticking up from the deck, and get badly hurt. But that occurred less often than expected because the line in our hands was also a lifeline. Even though the churning ocean often wrenched our feet out from under us, the rushing water usually raised us up off the deck and protected us from more painful falls.

We pulled the heavy hose across with great effort. It rolled foot by foot on wheels that rode the span wire. When the hose was finally across and connected, the carrier began to pump fuel. We were supposed to stand by in case the hose broke loose and we needed to bring it over again, but I snuck up to the 01 level, where I could watch the whole operation.

Near Mount 33, Belisle, an Interior Communications Technician, operated a tape recorder, complete with amplifier and loudspeakers. The *Hestek* was playing music for the carrier! I grinned. "This is really something!"

"Keep an eye on that!" Belisle pointed towards the signal bridge. We could just make out the dim silhouette of a rolled up flag on a signal halyard.

When we received all our mail and new movies, the crew disconnected the highline. The forward fuel team finished. Shep's after fuel station wasn't far behind. When all the lines were disengaged, the *Hestek*, whose radio call was "Roman Legion," was free to leave.

Belisle cranked up the volume on the tape deck. Roman style drums and trumpets blared ancient-sounding marches, like in the movies. One of the signalmen yanked on the halyard with the rolled up flag and another shined a signal searchlight to illuminate the black banner with a golden Roman helmet, shield and spear, now flying proudly to the strains of the music.

"Roman Legion departing!" we shouted as we pulled away, belching clouds of oily black smoke from both stacks.

* * *

NOW, MAIL CALL! MAIL CALL! ALL DIVISION MAIL PETTY OFFICERS PICK UP YOUR MAIL FROM THE POST OFFICE. MAIL CALL.

"That's one time I don't mind the bitch box blaring at me!" someone observed.

I never got mail but this time I received a letter from my "mother." No kidding, it actually had my parents' return address. I knew it had to be from OCI because my family didn't know where I was. After some general news about "the family," it continued:

> "Do you remember my friend Helen Skye? Well, her daughter's on the East Coast. Helen told me Rena went to a place called Virginia Beach. It's supposed to be near Norfolk, where you are. She's has a job as a waitress at a place called Blinker's Bar and Grill. Maybe you can look her up. Love, Mom."

11. SEA STORIES

Sunday at sea. That meant Holiday Routine. The only work was the duty section, which stood watches and cleaned. Because we were at sea, nobody could go home. So we slept, read, played cards, and told sea stories.

The ocean was calm for the Vacapes. Relatively. So some of us sat on the 01 level smoking, "shootin' the shit" and "grab-assing." I listened and looked around regularly from my crossword puzzle book. Le Blanc was asleep against the gun tub. From what I saw, he got enough sleep for three guys. But there he was. Smith was sitting on the deck of the open three-inch gun mount, glassy eyed and silent.

The old salts tried to prove they'd experienced Navy life to its fullest with their stories.

Even Derella, the gruff bos'n seaman, shared a story. "Montego Bay, Jamaica," he said around a cigarette. "What a place! The purty ladies in this one club took our five bucks 'n' led us up to the fuckin' roof. Each one of 'em had 'er own place, like a private room, where she could sell 'er wares, shall we say? Man, I saw four diff'rent little rooms that day! Screwed four colored beauties in one afternoon. An' man did I put away the beer!"

At this point Raynes left, mumbling, "drunkenness and lechery and fornication. That's all you guys talk about. There's no hope for any of you."

Derella gave him the finger as a parting salute. "Anyway, on the way back ta the ship, I lost my balance 'n' fell over a fuckin' four-foot embankment. Lucky me, it had a forty-five degree grade to it. I didn't get hurt but I couldn't stop myself from rollin' down an' smashin' through this picket fence 'n' into this garden. Right in front of a woman an' her two little girls. Man, I dunno what they thought. But I was feelin' no fuckin' pain! I got up, laughin' like crazy, 'n' those two little girls musta thought that I'd a rizzen from the dead, 'cause they ran away screamin' like hell!"

"Then what?"

"I was laughin' so fuckin' much I could hardly stan' up. But I climbed back up that embankment an' made it home ta the Old Haystack. Sure hope that woman got her fence fixed." Derella flipped his cigarette butt over the side into the water.

"That's a great story, Derella. You remember in the Med, when you and Cisco and Smith got tanked up, and...."

"When we got a ride in the fuckin' Admiral's barge? Yeah, that was a good time."

"Well, you gonna tell the story or should I tell it?"

"You can fuckin' try! I'll tell ya the good parts. You can get Cisco up there to tell the perfessor's part."

The men looked where Derella pointed. Cisco was sitting on the 02 level in front of the Mark 56 gun director, crossed knees cradling a tome.

"Okay, this ain't no shit. We were in Naples, where all the ships are Med moored, fantails tied to a seawall 'n' bows pointed into the harbor. That makes enough fuckin' space fer all the ships. We were in a nest with a tender that provided fifty-foot launches ta take us ashore and bring us back.

"The land there forms a big fuckin' circle 'round a wide bay. The seawall makes the harbor pretty big 'n' protected really good from the elements. From the ships you can see the city to port an' Vesuvius to starb'd. Pompeii is way off ta the right.

"We started that day on a tour. We spent the mornin' an' some of the afternoon visitin' the ruins. The best part of Pompeii was this one fuckin' house the tour guide showed us." He laughed at the memory. "Yeah, it sure was a fuckin' house. One panel by the front door had a pitchur of a guy getting' his cock 'n' balls weighed on a balance scale by the taxman. The bigger ya were, the more taxes ya paid. But I guess I'd pay the tax if I was that fuckin' well endowed.

"Inside, they showed us a vomitorium, where the fuckin' Romans went to throw up so they c'd go back to eat 'n' drink some more."

"Sounds like somethin' you'd do, Derella!" Reston laughed.

The storyteller looked at the seaman. "Fuck you, Reston. You 'n' the horse you rode in on." Derella lit another smoke. "They got some encouragement ta return ta their festivities after heavin' their guts out, 'cause all along the wall goin' to that vomitorium were paintin's of people screwin' in different positions. Man, I never knew there were that many fuckin' ways ta do it! I mean front, back, sideways 'n' upside down, either one on top, legs at all fuckin' angles. I'd a loved ta get copies of all them positions so I could try 'em out.

"The rest of the tour of Pompeii was pretty fuckin' tame."

"What're you talking about, man?" Reston protested. "There was some great stuff there. All the plants and the plaster casts of the people and the dogs...."

"The plaster cast of that dyin' dog was pretty cool. But I don't get my cookies off from a buncha fuckin' plaster plants. Now, you want me ta continue this or not?"

Everyone pleaded for him to go on.

"All right. No more interruptions or I'll swab the deck with your fuckin' heads. So, we went to Vesuvius. They drove us halfway up the mountain an' we climbed the rest of the way. I mean we actually went inside that volcano. It was a strange goddamn feelin' standin' there and seein' the steam hissin' out. It's still fuckin' active! An' they told us it could go off any minute! Don' know why they didn't tell us before we went up there.

"If I ever needed a drink, that was it! So I pulled out this flask I had 'n' took a good fuckin' swig. Then Smith grabbed it, took a jolt 'n' passed it on ta Cisco. I was about ready to club 'em upside the head, but they promised ta pay for more later."

"Where's that story about the Admiral's barge?" one of the other seaman apprentices interrupted.

Exasperated, Derella shouted, "Look, shithead, ya want ta hear it my way or ya want ta go deef from me bustin' ya upside yer fuckin' head?"

"Tell it your way."

"All right. So shut the fuck up." He flicked his cigarette butt over the side. "When we got done tourin' some dumb fuckin' cameo factory, my flask was empty. So we left the tour 'n' started walkin' back ta the fleet landing. We musta stopped at every fuckin' bar along the road. We made it all the way 'roun' the bay 'n' back ta the fleet landing, all ready ta pick up a boat ta get back ta the ship. But it was real late by then—the last fuckin' liberty boat already left.

"We didn't know what ta do then. We were all gonna be AWOL 'n' get busted. Believe me, I didn't wanta get busted again. Been there too many fuckin' times already. But it was our lucky night. The cox'n of this Admiral's launch was waitin' fer his boss, but he knew The Man wasn't gonna be around fer a couple hours. Piece o' tail ashore, ya know. He offered ta give us a ride fer six thousan' lira each. That's five bucks apiece in Eye-talian money. Seems he had his own shack-up, but didn't have no fuckin' money fer the morrow. Anyways, we snapped up his offer. So we hopped inta the Admiral's barge fer our ride out ta the nest.

"As the launch pulled alongside the tender, the quarterdeck went crazy. They thought the Admiral hisself was returnin'. They ran aroun' wild, preparin' ta welcome him aboard. I mean they got the Bos'n of the Watch and all the sideboys there ta give 'im all the proper honors. An' out steps us three fuckin' drunk swab jockeys, respectfully requestin' permission to cross the tender 'n' go home. Man, they were fit ta be tied! But we got back ta the Old Haystack early enough not ta be AWOL 'n' put on report.

"An' that ain't no shit! Ya got that Matthews?"

"Got what?" I felt like I was falling into another trap for unwary boots, but couldn't figure out what it was.

"What's the diff'rence b'tween a fairy tale 'n' a sea story?" Derella laughed. I shrugged my shoulders. "Yeah, I thought so. Fairy tale starts out 'Once upon a time....' An' a sea story starts out 'This ain't no shit!'" He laughed uncontrollably at his own joke.

"So you're telling us your stories are all made up?" Reston asked.

Derella stopped laughing long enough to answer. "Well, ya can verify the facts with the people who were there with me. An' that ain't no shit!"

"Derella, you left out the best part!"

Everyone looked up, surprised. Cisco stood with a fresh cup of coffee in one hand and his book in the other.

"What part's that?" Derella asked.

"You were so shitfaced that night, I don't think you even remember it."

"So tell us, Cisco!" Reston urged.

"Derella was so anxious to get home that he jumped out of the launch too early. He caught the edge of the platform at the bottom of the accommodation ladder with the tips of his toes. He teetered there for a few seconds and slowly... oh so slowly... slower than slow motion... arms flapping, he fell backwards into the water. I grabbed him by his jumper collar and pulled him out. Remember that, Derella?"

"Fuck you, Cisco! You're just tryin' ta make me look bad."

"Sure!" the petty officer chuckled. "None of us looked very good that night!"

In a way, Raynes was right. The "sea stories" continued, tales of sightseeing around the world, boozing it up, and carnal knowledge of just about any woman you could imagine.

After an hour and a half of this, I laughed. "Great stories!" I stuck my crossword book into a rear pocket of my dungarees. "But, can any of that help me make seaman?"

"Fuck off. I ain't got no time ta help some boot with what he's gotta learn at work." Derella walked away.

"I'll help you, Eric," Reston volunteered. "When do you want to start?"

"How about now?" I pulled out my Seaman book from under the belt at my back.

Officers have rank. Enlisted men have rates: three for seamen, three for petty officers and three for chiefs. Advancement is called making rate. Each rate has a pay grade designation of E-something or other. A seaman apprentice is an E-2, and a seaman is E-3. I was trying to make rate to Seaman, E-3. The pay was better and being a seaman proved I wasn't right out of boot camp.

We spent two hours going over the book and doing practical things. Reston reminded me about stuff I'd already done in my daily work and how that related to the material in the Seaman book.

For days, I practiced what I had to know. We covered watch standing procedures, rules of the road, compartment numbering, marlinspike seamanship, and a bunch more.

"You know?" I said one day. "I don't feel nearly as overpowered with all this as I did when Shep showed me around. And that feels pretty damned good!"

Reston grinned. "I told you you'd feel at home real soon."

* * *

Rena Skye had met enough of her operatives by now to plan and organize them. None of us knew yet what we were really up against, and certainly not who the bad guys were.

Skye's initial plan was to place people where sailors hid their drug habits among drunk friends—at the enlisted clubs on the various bases of the area and at some of the major civilian clubs. She would watch for users among the clientele of Blinker's Bar and Grill.

She made sure we all knew our jobs. Watch for drug use in work areas. But the hard part was to be socially active after hours, that is, go out and drink and dance and have fun but not get drunk. We still had to identify suspected users and track them to their suppliers. In time, our information would permit her to piece together the whole network.

After we got to know each other better, she told me that when she wasn't at work she sat and worked out her chess moves. But she often lost her train of thought because she'd constantly play her OCI chess game in her head. I could imagine her sitting, thinking, staring out her window, probably twisting her hair, and wondering: Who'd be best for this or that location? Where would someone fit best? He's good at this, I think, but not that. And she knew she could fine-tune each operative's placement later.

And after getting to know her, I could imagine she often reminded herself: *As Dad would say, be the best damn team leader in the world. I hope it's that simple. Then I can get back to Dago and take care of my personal business.*

12. FISHING FOR INFORMATION

The seas in the Vacapes Ops area were calm enough to work on deck. I started my morning waiting at the paint locker. I looked beyond the guys ahead of me, admiring Monnyng's organization.

"Okay, Matthews. You're next," Monnyng said.

"Gallon of deck gray and a big enough brush to paint the fantail."

"You primer? Yeah, I remember you got red lead yesterday. I'll mix your gray."

"I've been admiring your shelf system there. Any of the paint cans ever fall off?"

"Nope. The bars hold them in. Even when we get rolls over forty-six, forty-seven degrees."

I noticed some light blue stationery with flowers along the top and one side, on the metal box in the corner. "You keep your writing stuff in here?"

"What?"

"That stationery, there."

"Oh, no. Just that." He grinned sheepishly. "I should keep it hidden. My mother sent it to me, but when the other guys saw it, I really got razzed."

"Seems like you have a special place for everything. What do you keep in that metal box?"

He whirled around and shook a big paintbrush in my face. "None o' your business. It's personal stuff. I told you that before." Glaring, he handed me the brush and an open can of paint. "Here. Go to work."

I shrugged and took my paint back to the fantail. Monnyng could be strange. He was a quiet guy, until you asked a personal question. Then he turned hard real fast.

I made good progress for an hour. Then the snipes, the engineers, blew the stacks without letting the bridge know and getting the ship to change course. As a result, the wind was fore to aft instead of across the ship. Stack gas asphyxiated us on the fantail. Thousands of small, oily carbon particles settled onto my new wet paint. Hours of work were shot to hell. I'd have to scrape it all down again and repaint.

* * *

The weather turned rough overnight. Reston and I stood on the 03 level alongside to the Mark 37 Gun Director, above the bridge. About as high as you could go without climbing a mast. It was a great spot to watch the ship cut through the heavy seas. We were somewhat sheltered, but we were close enough for the hand of the briny deep to reach out and slap us every so often.

Hammering rain and wind-driven spray hid the horizon. The sea was endless liquid valleys and hills. Towering peaks rolled into deep depressions, undulating, high to low and back again. Gust after gust, surge after surge, everything melted into one hypnotic roller-coaster ride.

The ship was in her rhythm. She plowed directly into the wind and waves. The bow rose high on a groundswell and hung in mid-air. When the swell reached amidships, the bow slammed down, splashing an immense volume of water outward and upward. My stomach got that roller-coaster sinking feeling like when it goes over a high point and begins its run downward.

At this point, the sea rushed back over the bow, plunging it under the next swell. The *Hestek* shuddered under tons of water. It was amazing how rapidly that much steel could shimmy from side to side. She broke loose moments before the next wave pushed the bow high in the air, and the whole process started over.

We watched in awe. We'd taken off our blue work baseball caps so they wouldn't blow over the side. Our hair flew in every direction. Smoking wasn't impossible, just difficult. The wind caused the Zippos to sputter but it couldn't blow them out. We protected our lit cigarettes inside cupped hands. Sometimes we turned our backs to the water rising all the way from the main deck. Our heavy foul weather jackets almost kept us dry.

"I love this!" I laughed. "Told you I wouldn't get seasick!"

"Yeah, I guess you were right."

"Exhilarating! It really gives me a rush," I shouted. "A real rush. Almost as good as.... It's just great!"

Reston looked at me, a combination of fear and wonder in his gray eyes. "What did you say?"

13. COLLISIONS, CONNECTIONS AND SMALL CRAFT

Reston stood there silently looking at me.

I smiled. "I love the feel of the pitching ship, the sting of spray on my face...."

"Yeah." Reston stared at me. I gazed straight ahead. He watched me until a whip of salt spray hit him in the face and poured down his jacket.

"Ahhhhh!" he screamed. "God damn! That's COLD!"

I took my glasses off to wipe them dry with a clean handkerchief. "So pay attention!"

"Don't laugh, man! That was so cold it HURT!"

"Sorry, Hank. Want to go below and dry off?"

"Nah, being wet's nothing new. But, damn, that water was cold!"

We lasted another half hour. "I'm going below. I don't want to get drenched like you did."

We dried off then went to the mess decks to get some hot coffee from the eternally full pots. We sat down, sipping the steaming liquid.

"Eric, how old are you?"

"Twenty-three."

"How long you been in the Navy?"

"About six months."

"Why'd you join so late?"

"No job. No training. No union apprenticeship unless I completed national service. Nobody would hire me. I could get drafted any time. Then I got a letter with a return address of 'Selective Services System.' I knew I'd probably wind up in the Army. My Dad was Army and told enough stories that I didn't want to eat dirt and sleep in mud. I never opened that envelope. I immediately joined Uncle Sam's Canoe Club. How about you?"

"Tried going to college...."

"And?"

"My Dad died and we couldn't afford it any more. And I flunked half my courses the first semester. I wasn't ready. So I joined the Navy. Partly for the 'dirt' reason you mentioned. But I thought I'd get some kind of school."

"Didn't you?"

"Yeah. But I don't do very good on tests. I didn't make it."

We sat in silence for a while. "Where you from, Eric?"

"Rockford, Illinois. Second biggest city in the state."

"I'm from Iowa. I've heard about your part of the country. Ever go to the Wisconsin Dells?"

"Once, but it was too touristy. People tried to sell anything they could to everyone around," I explained. "So, we went to Lake Geneva instead. It's about halfway to Madison and lots nicer than the Dells."

"Sounds like fun."

"Yeah. But I'll tell you something...."

"What's that?" Reston asked.

"None of those places had rides to compare with the one we were on topside. None."

* * *

We patrolled back and forth through the Virginia Capes operations area. One day the *Valcour Bay* collided with a merchantman. The *Peter I. Johnsten* escorted her into port for repairs and immediately headed back out. On the return trip, she detected a probable submarine at the mouth of Chesapeake Bay. She tried to communicate with it but it didn't respond. The brass figured it was a Russky sub watching ship movements, so they had the *Johnsten* stay on top of it and make it worry for seven or eight hours. They never did find out for sure if it was a submarine or not.

We continued patrolling. The crew's available options were standing watch, sleeping, reading and watching movies.

Same old stuff.

* * *

Back in Norfolk, the OCI office coordinated efforts with local authorities. They had Skye meet with Dave Walden, a Norfolk undercover cop. He offered to provide all the help he could as long as it didn't blow his cover.

* * *

South of the Virginia Capes, the weather was bright and sunny. The sea was unusually calm. I was on watch, enjoying the feel of the ship cutting through the sea and its slight movement in gentle waters.

Because of the recent collision, the lookouts were especially vigilant. All of us were. I was on watch when I got a report from a lookout. "Sir, Port Lookout reports a skunk at three-two-five, range three-thousand."

Lieutenant Tower's binoculars were at his eyes before he reached the open bridge. "I can't.... There. It's just a spot in the water." He shouted up to the lookout. "What is it? It's very close. Why didn't you report it earlier?"

The lookout, on the flying bridge, replied without lowering his binoculars. "Just saw it, sir. Too small to make out."

Tower went back into the Pilot House. "Mr. Reynolds, please keep visual track of that skunk."

"Aye, aye."

"Captain, request permission to change course and speed to investigate."

"Granted, Mr. Tower. Let the Commodore know by flashing light."

"Aye, aye, Captain. Messenger, tell Flags what we're up to. Have him notify the Type Commander." The OOD went to the appropriate pelorus to convert the relative bearing of the skunk to a true bearing so he could order, "Lee helm, turns for five knots. Helmsman, five degrees left rudder. Come to a heading of zero-two-seven and hold steady."

Both men responded simultaneously, "Aye, aye, sir!"

The *Hestek* slowed down. The helmsman steered toward the object, now visible without binoculars.

"Port Lookout reports the skunk looks like an overturned small craft," I reported.

"Boats!" Tower called out.

"Aye, aye, sir!" the Bos'n Mate of the Watch replied.

"Get a deck crew on the fantail. Prepare to bring that boat aboard."

"Aye, aye, sir!"

"Stop all engines," Tower ordered. The *Hestek* gradually slid up to the small craft. The deck crew grabbed it with a grappling hook. They soon had it on board.

"Bridge, After Lookout. Chief Gascomb reports three expensive rods and reels are tucked under the seats of the boat. And he says it has an expensive outboard motor. There's also a soaked paper bag with sandwiches. There definitely were people on it."

"Captain, shall we search for survivors?" Tower asked.

Lorman thought for a moment as he looked out over the ocean. "No. Knowing the currents here, that boat probably drifted for quite a while. Secure it. We'll turn it over to the Coast Guard."

"Aye, aye, Captain."

Lorman picked up his radiotelephone to let the Commodore know what we found. The *Hestek* returned to its assigned station. Just before the watch ended, the Commodore called us back.

"Roman Legion, this is Jackalope. We just got the skinny on that boat." The Commodore said with resignation in his voice. "It came from New Jersey. It had four fishermen in it. They were reported lost at sea. The Coast Guard searched for three days, but gave up after finding no trace of the boat or the people. The fishermen were never found. The Coast Guard will be waiting for the whole package when you get back in. Over."

"Jackalope, this is Roman Legion. Thanks, Ed. We'll take good care of it. Out."

* * *

Many of the crew inspected the boat lashed to the fantail. I sat back there "reading" and watching people. At one point, Reston stood alongside the boat. He stayed a long time, hands at his side and head bowed. He reached up once and wiped his eyes. Finally, he heaved a sigh, flung his hands out in a gesture of helplessness, turned and walked away.

As he went through the door leading down to the living compartment, I caught a movement on the 01 level. Cisco was standing at the lifelines, book in one hand, coffee cup in the other. He'd seen Reston and now stood there frowning.

That evening I strolled along the main deck, watching the water go by. The sunset had been striking. The seas were calm and the sun splashed reds, oranges and yellows off the ocean.

The ship now cut through the inky darkness. Excited plankton flashed and sparkled in the wake. The stars shone like diamonds on black velvet. I observed the infinite cosmos for quite a while, then continued along the deck, watching the glittering plankton. It seemed like the water reflected the stars in the sky.

I paused again to watch the sea go by. Noticed a shadow out of the corner of my eye. Reston leaned against one of the exhaust vents that pulled hot air out of the after boiler room.

"Hank, you okay?"

"Pretty much," he said in a dreamy voice.

"What's wrong?"

"Ohhh, just a bit chilly, Eric. So... I'm standing in the heat... coming out of the vent here."

I frowned. The air temperature was a little cool, but not as cold as Reston seemed to think. I looked into his eyes. He could hardly focus. He looked like he was high. "Can I help you, Hank? Want to go back to your bunk?"

"Nobody can help me."

"What're you talking about? Why do you say that?"

Reston mumbled something garbled. I thought I heard the word "killer."

"Who's a killer? Who got killed?"

Reston didn't answer me.

14. SEA BAT

I looked at Reston and asked again: "Who's a killer? Who got killed?"

"Nobody! Leave me alone!"

"You sure?"

"Yeah. Jus' leave me alone!"

I walked away slowly, rubbing the scars on my right cheek. I wondered if there was some connection between his earlier behavior at the fishing boat and his present condition. I thought to myself, *Damn! Another nice kid caught in hell. I wonder if I can save him.*

* * *

The *Hestek* headed south, to an area around Charleston. The sea was calm, sometimes even glassy. On Sunday the Captain got permission to leave the task force and catch up later. When we were on our own, he stopped all engines and had the Bos'n of the Watch announce that the crew could fish over the side.

I stood and watched guys try to catch something. I was thinking about this assignment. I'd been aboard for a month now—this was the first of October—and wasn't very close to getting any real answers. I knew my suspect but so far hadn't been able to follow him off the ship on one of his drug-buying runs. And I still had no answers about any other users or any suppliers on board.

Raynes interrupted my train of thought. He came over to convert me. "Matthews, I can tell you're a good man. Deep down, you are. Why not accept Jesus as your Lord?"

"I have my own beliefs, Luke. Thanks for caring, but I don't want your religion."

"Well, at least read this, won't you?" He gave me a pamphlet. I went down to the living compartment to get away from him. Shepherd and I shot the shit for a while.

After a while, Raynes came down below. "There you are! Let me point out a few things in that pamphlet I gave...."

Luckily, at that moment the 1MC announced: NOW A SEA BAT HAS JUST BEEN CAUGHT. ANYONE INTERESTED IN SEEING THE SEA BAT, LAY BACK TO THE FANTAIL.

I knew about this sea bat thing. It was an old Navy tradition. The Captain had to give his permission when we had some free time for it. Even though I knew what it was all about, I couldn't get out of it because Shep stood right there with me. He escorted me to see this marvel of maritime fauna. "You shouldn't miss it. But be careful, they can bite."

I followed him up the companionway and onto the fantail. The sun reflected off the gently rolling sea. When the breeze was up, the water glittered like dancing diamonds; when it was calm, it reflected sheets of blinding sunlight.

A couple guys were sweeping down the deck and three others hovered over a cardboard box that jumped around a lot. A small group watched the box and offered advice to keep the bat alive but not let it free.

I never did get to see that animal. When I leaned over to look, somebody whacked me on the ass with the flat of his broom. "What the hell you doing?" I hollered. "I'm trying to look at the sea bat. Cut it out!" I turned back to the box. "Okay. Let me see."

I leaned way over to get a better view. The second sweeper took his turn, hitting my perfect target as hard as he could. "Come on, you sonsab...."

The two sweepers burst out laughing. "Well, Matthews," one said, "did you see the bat that time?"

I laughed so hard I had to sit down. "That's good. But what's all the noise inside the box?"

"Look down here between Tom and the box...."

Another man was reaching around Tom's leg so he could scratch the cardboard without being seen. All three guys did their part to make the box hop around.

The bitch box soon passed the word to secure all fishing lines. In fifteen minutes the Haystack was steaming full speed to catch up with the formation.

Later the bridge announced: NOW, THE MOVIE FOR TONIGHT IS "THE TIME MACHINE" STARRING ROD TAYLOR AND YVETTE MIMIEUX AT TWENTY HUNDRED ON THE FANTAIL.

The weather remained calm so they showed the flick outside. The screen was a sheet tied between the Mount 53's gun barrels. After the movie I read for a while on the mess decks. I read past taps. *Of Human Bondage* was too good to put down. I finally hit the rack around midnight.

Life could be good at sea.

* * *

The day we returned to Norfolk, I had the messenger of the watch when liberty call went down. Reston was off with all the married guys rushing to get home to their families. He returned before my watch was over, not carrying anything. Unless it was in his sock. Being under cover I had no authority to search him or even to recommend to the Quarterdeck Watch Officer to do so.

"Hank, that was fast! How come you're back already?"

"Just stopped to see a friend, that's all. But he had something else planned, so it was a quick visit."

I wasn't convinced. I knew I had to follow him somehow when he left the ship.

15. BLINKER'S

It was a warm October evening in Norfolk. I was studying for my Seaman's exam on the fantail. Reston fidgeted next to me.

The 1MC announced the food vendor that had pulled up on the pier. NOW THE ROACH COACH IS ON THE PIER. THE ROACH COACH IS ON THE PIER.

"Want any gedunks? I'll fly if you buy," Reston offered.

"Yeah. Get me a Popsicle. Orange, if they have it."

"And if they don't?"

"Any other ice cream thing." I held out a five-dollar bill. "Here. Use a buck for yourself."

I shut my Seaman's book when Reston returned. "I've been studying for days. I need a change of pace, not just some ice cream. I'm going on liberty."

"I got duty. Where you gonna go?"

"Well," I said, adjusting my glasses. "My mom wrote me that the daughter of an old friend is working nearby. I think I'll look her up and see what happens."

"Well, you have fun. But be careful," he grinned. "And if you can't be careful, name it after me!"

"Yeah. Can you imagine a kid named Reston Matthews?" I shook my head. "No way! See you later." I went below, shed my dungarees and pulled on my blues' bell-bottoms. I chuckled as I fastened the buttons all around the front flap. It took so long to both fasten and undo them that sailors said the buttons were a girl's thirteen chances to say "No."

I slipped into my jumper. Tied my neckerchief in a perfect square knot, arranged so the front of the knot presented a neat flat surface that hid the rest of it. When done right, it looks like a small tube holding the neckerchief coming in from above and the ends drooping out below. I checked that the knot was located right at the "V" of my jumper.

When I was satisfied with my uniform, I got my liberty card from Cisco. I left the ship and headed for the gate. Many guys walked over to one of the locker clubs on the "strip" where they changed into their stored civvies. I didn't mind wearing the uniform, so I hailed a cab just outside the gate. Opening the rear door, I leaned in and asked, "You know where Blinker's Bar and Grill is, in Virginia Beach?"

"Sure, pal. Hop in."

"How much to take me there?"

He named a price. I nodded, jumped in and shut the door. It didn't take us very long to get to there.

Inside the front door, I observed the large open space. Bar in the middle of the long left wall. Restaurant starting in the corner to my left, going across the front and down the right side, past a side door. Good-sized dance floor. Raised bandstand in the far left corner beyond the bar. It was early. The place wasn't crowded. I sat down at the bar and ordered a beer.

"Identification." The graying, hefty bartender held out his hand for my ID card. I gave it to him. Handing it back, his weather-beaten face broke into a warm smile. "Twenty-three—that's about what you look like, but I had to be sure. Okay. One beer coming up."

I lit a cigarette. Gazed left and right. Stared into the long mirror behind the bar. I examined the place carefully. In spite of all the modern decorations and beyond all the signalman's paraphernalia, Blinker's felt like an old building.

I nursed my beer and watched the waitresses a while before asking the bartender, "Does a Rena Skye work here?"

"Why?"

I shrugged. "She's from my home town. Mom wrote me that she worked here. Thought I'd stop by and see her."

"Yeah she works here, but she's not in yet," the bartender said. He glanced at the clock. It was five-thirty. "Another half hour. But remember, she works here, with the emphasis on 'work.' Don't turn it into old home week. Understand?"

"Yep. "

"I'll be watching. Just to be sure."

"Fair enough." I sipped my beer. "Can I ask you another question?"

"About what?"

"The building?"

"Shoot."

"I get the feeling it's pretty old. I'm no architect, but I'd say it used to be a church. How old is it?"

"You got a good eye. It was a church. Long time ago. A Quaker meetinghouse. Hundred 'n' fifty years back. That's why we can keep it this open without it falling down on us. The attic has some beautiful arches, but they're covered by the ceiling to meet the Quakers' call for simplicity."

The next shift came in. One woman was about my age. Shorter than me, shoulder-length auburn hair and brown eyes. Her tan skin suggested she was either from some Latin or Mediterranean country, or recently from a sunnier part of the U.S. It's an understatement to say that she was pleasing to look at. She put her purse in a cabinet under the liquor shelves behind the bar. She grabbed a clean apron from another cabinet, tied it around her slim waist and came back out into the customer area.

The bartender stood in front of me. "Rena, come here!"

"Yeah, Blink, what is it?"

"Blink?" I asked.

"I'm a retired signalman. Some guys said I was the fastest signal lamp operator in the fleet." He shrugged. "They started calling me 'Blink' or 'Blinker' instead of the usual 'Flags' and it stuck." By this time, Rena was at my side. The bartender turned to her, "This guy said his mother told him about you, where you were working, that he should look you up."

"Haven't heard that pick-up line before," she grinned, creating dimples in both cheeks.

"Rena Skye?" I asked.

"Yep!"

"My mom knows Helen, your Mom."

"Small world, isn't it? What's your mom's name?"

"Sorry for not introducing myself. My name's Eric Matthews, and my mom is Martha."

"I don't remember her, but Ma talked about Martha a lot. I think they were into gardening together, especially green vegetables, beans, peas, broccoli, stuff like that."

"I thought it was their common love of dogs," I mused. "We always had at least one dog around the house." So there it was, the recognition sequence, "Mom," "green," "dog." This woman was my contact ashore, my boss.

"Could be," she agreed. "I guess they had a number of shared interests. But that was a long time ago, and I don't remember much." She looked me over, twirling her hair around a finger the whole time. I could guess her thoughts: taller than me, stocky build, sandy hair, hazel eyes, scars on the right cheek, horn-rimmed glasses—definitely not the standard Navy translucent pink plastic things—so there's a streak of independence. She smiled. "Welcome to beautiful Virginia Beach!"

"Rena," Blink nodded to the booths, "the customers."

I didn't dare irritate Blink and get kicked out. I sat near Skye's workstation. We talked when she came over to place an order. We asked questions or continued our conversation while she waited for drinks. It was a tough way to have a conversation.

"So, you're originally from Rockford?" I asked.

"The northern suburbs, Machesney Park."

"Ah, the Harlem Huskies! We played them in football."

"You from the city proper?"

"Yep. Went to East High." I motioned for another beer. I liked the looks of this woman and wanted to make a good impression. I figured I'd be here for a while, so I timed my drinking. "Why'd you move?"

"Dad found a better job in southern California."

"And now you're here? How come?" I asked, trying to look like any other guy hitting on a girl.

"Change of pace, I guess. I had to get away from my parents. They still wanted me to report everything I did."

"I know the routine. That was one reason I joined the Navy. Wanted to be my own boss." I chuckled into my beer glass. "Yeah, right. So I joined the Navy."

It was getting late and I hadn't eaten. "What's good on the menu?"

"I'm the cook," Blink interrupted. "It's all good."

"That's true!" Rena responded. "Try the T-bone and baked potato. Best steak in town. The burgers and fries are good, too. That's what I'm going to have."

So I had the T-bone. It was great. I had another beer before the band started and the prices tripled. Then I drank soft drinks. We talked as best we could around the band's versions of Ray Charles, Ella Fitzgerald, Brenda Lee, The Shirelles, and the Kingston Trio, from "Itsy Bitsy Teenie Weenie Yellow Polka Dot Bikini" and "Where the Boys Are" to "Blue Moon," "Runaway" and "Only the Lonely."

At 0130, a half hour before closing, the musicians packed up and the waitresses sang out their final pitch, "Last call! Order it now or go home sober! Last call for alcohol!"

"Want to go somewhere after work?" I asked.

"What's on your mind?" she grinned, eyes flashing.

"I noticed a café a couple blocks away. If it's open, we could get a cup of coffee, maybe some dessert. Whatever. I'm having a nice time and don't want to quit."

She nodded. "That café is open all night. But if you come to my place, I make some decent coffee. And I just baked an apple pie."

"It's a date." I helped her clean up to leave quicker.

As we walked out of the bar, Rena asked, "Can I bum a cigarette from you?"

"Sure. I get them cheap enough. Ten cents a pack. And I always carry extra." I lit one and handed it to her.

We slowly walked the short distance to her upstairs apartment. I enjoyed her pie and coffee. We talked about everything.

"By the way," I said during a lull in the conversation. "Who was that tall dark-haired man that ordered wine with his steak? You looked like you knew him, but you didn't talk to him like you did."

Skye looked at me, dimples appearing with her smile. "You're good! Glad you're on my team. He's one of us. I recognized him from his file photo. We'll meet later where we can talk more openly. I like to meet all of my operatives face to face. It can be a challenge because I can't talk business at the bar. You have good powers of observation."

"Guess I picked that up by analyzing the electronics circuits I didn't design well enough to work right away."

"With such an analytical mind, do you play chess?"

I nodded. "I can play, but I'm not great. I'm more into crossword puzzles. Sometimes I even do the New York Times puzzle with pen and ink."

She went into the living room, returning quickly with her chess set. We set it up on the kitchen table. Luckily we weren't using a timer. I play even worse under pressure. She gave me the advantage of playing white, so I opened the best way I knew: king's pawn up two spaces, then queen's pawn up one. This would let me get my bishops and knights out to the center of the board and also let me use my powerful queen early on. It's an opening that beginners learn early.

Rena countered my early moves with unconventional defenses. Between moves, she asked: "So, after getting an electronics engineering degree, what persuaded you to join the Navy?"

"I was getting older and due for the draft. I was out of college. My Dad was Army and I didn't want to live in foxholes or eat K-rations. The Navy impressed me as a place to experience man-against-nature combined with man-living-with-nature. Sense of adventure, I guess. So now I get to play the 'Swab your way around the world' game."

She pointed to my right cheek. "How did you get those scars?"

I forced a laugh. "We were playing baseball. We didn't have a catcher and I let the other kids talk me into being one. Didn't even have a mask. The very first pitch hit me here." I pointed to my right cheek. "The stitching on the ball caught me just right and it ripped me open in a few places. I never played catcher again!"

She was twirling her hair around her finger again. "I've seen scars from baseball cuts. That doesn't look like one."

I shrugged. "Sorry, that's how I got these."

She changed the subject.

We talked about many things as we played our chess game: books, world affairs, and pastimes. We both spoke other languages, but different ones. I read the classics and didn't care for spy or mystery novels, which I

76

considered unrealistic. Sherlock Holmes was the single exception. I studied those stories and tried to learn from them. Skye loved to play chess and tried to analyze all the exotic moves, both offense and defense.

She pulled a couple more surprise moves and I was checkmated.

We continued talking, even about some work related stuff. She told me of her final interview with her OCI boss in San Diego, minus some important personal matters, which I heard about later. She also talked about the people she'd had transferred to Norfolk, including her best friend, Jennie. We seemed to click right away, that we could talk about anything and trust each other. Through the coming months, she would tell me about the activities of the whole team, their screw-ups as well as their victories. I got to know my fellow team members through Rena.

At one point I looked out the window and yelped, "God, it's getting light already! We talked all night!"

"I haven't done that for ages!" she grinned.

"I have to be back at the ship before seven-thirty. Can I use your phone to call a cab?"

"I'll drive you."

"No! Don't go through the trouble."

"If it were trouble," she smiled, "I wouldn't offer."

Back at the D & S Piers gate, I got out and walked around to the now rolled-down driver's window. "Rena, I really had a good time."

"Me, too, Eric." Her eyes sparkled.

I had the urge to lean down and kiss her, but didn't. She was my boss and I knew I'd better cool it. Even so I asked: "Can I call you later?"

From what she told me after we got to know each other better, alarms went off in her head at that. She sensed that I was asking to take our friendship beyond the working relationship, which I was. But I needed her number anyway, to report in regularly. So she gave it to me.

Not having any paper, I wrote it on my hand with my ballpoint pen. I turned and headed for the *Hestek* in a very good mood. This meeting went better than I'd dreamed it would.

Back in her apartment, Rena sat a long time, thinking over the events of the night. The last time she'd talked all night with anyone had been with her friend, Jennie. She pulled out my file, reviewed its contents, sat and stared at it for a long time.

I didn't realize yet how well she could read people. She had not believed my explanation for my scars. Evidently she spent some time trying to find out how I actually got them. In time, I also learned that her habit of twirling her hair around a finger was an indication that she was trying to figure something out.

16. LUNCH

Skye walked along the beach, deep in thought. She didn't even notice the crashing breakers. She zipped her jacket all the way up and wrapped her arms around herself to keep out the chill. This definitely wasn't San Diego.

Her OCI job was getting more demanding. She wondered if she was up to it. After more than a month she still hadn't met all her people, though she did know their names and locations. Today she would meet the operative I'd noticed ordering wine at Blinker's.

She heard her father's voice inside her head: "Just be the best damn team leader you can be."

As she walked, sometimes she upset the seagulls around her, and they fluttered into the air. Then a barking dog interrupted the screeching gulls and crashing waves. The birds took wing. She was jolted, lost her balance, and fell.

"Hey!" a distant voice called out. "Tango! Come here!"

Skye sat where she'd fallen in the sand and looked around. A Saint Bernard turned in response to its owner. It made a couple detours to chase more gulls then ran to him. He snapped a leash onto the animal's choke chain. "You must be careful, Tango! You're too big to slam into people like that."

Skye waited for the man. He walked with lengthy strides. He was tall, well over six feet, had a medium build, wavy dark brown hair and sparkling blue eyes.

Now under control, the dog came up and licked her face.

"I'm sorry, Rena. I shouldn't have let him loose."

Skye laughed as she reached out and rubbed Tango behind his ears. "It's a public beach, Brandon. And an animal this size definitely needs to run. Besides, he was having a blast! I just didn't realize we'd meet in the company of a dog half the size of a horse."

Brandon Lunch waved around the area. "It seemed deserted. So I thought I'd give him a treat." He held out his hand. "May I help you up from the cold sand?"

"Sure." She let him lift her to her feet. "Thanks for calling to set up this meeting." She brushed the sand off herself. "Why'd you name the dog Tango?"

The man laughed. "When he was a pup he would dance on his hind legs whenever I opened a beer."

"He likes beer?"

"Loves the stuff. In fact," Lunch laughed, "I often have to drink wine or whisky just to keep his nose out of my glass."

"What if you simply drank from the bottle?"

"Oh, he'd tip it over and spill it so he could lap it up."

Skye laughed. "Does he still dance for beer?"

"He doesn't have to. He can usually reach it simply by standing up."

"I can believe that! And now for the owner. Lunch is an unusual name, too."

"It's an honorable old New England name." He nodded seriously. Then he laughed. "Well, more like stodgy."

Skye turned to face him. Each person could now see the whole beach in one direction. "So, what's your cover here?"

"Freelance writer for travel magazines. I go south for the winter, visiting various places as I travel. I take insane amounts of notes. Then I sit on a beach in Florida and write."

"Where in Florida?"

"A little town on an island west of Saint Petersburg quaintly named Treasure Island."

"Do you have to watch out for pirates?" she laughed.

"No. Too many tourists. All those islands are crawling with them now. Treasure Island is somewhat out of the way, but a short distance to the north they've built a gigantic amusement park. Sunset Beach, on the southern end of my island, is quiet enough for me to get a lot of work done."

"Sounds like you know that place well."

"I actually do go there when I'm able. Some friends live nearby and they keep me up to date."

Skye smiled. "After seeing your pony-sized dog here, I'd have to ask if it's a good place for him to run?"

"Not as out of the way as this. But it is warmer."

"Well, it sounds like you have a good cover. And I'm curious, do you actually write the travel stuff?"

"Certainly! Should anyone check up on me, it proves I'm a real writer."

He took a business card from his wallet. He wrote on the back. "Here's my local number. And where I'm living."

"Thanks. I didn't have that information."

"I stayed in a motel the first night. Found an apartment next day. It's kind of cheery, not too flashy. The Norfolk area looks nice. Is there a lot to do here?"

"I don't think many Navy people would agree with your assessment. I hear that some folks still have yard signs saying 'Dogs and Sailors Keep Off the Grass'!"

Lunch reached down and patted his dog's head. "Hear that Tango? We may not be welcome here." He looked back to Rena. "Is that left over from World War Two?"

"Some of it is the old southern attitude toward northerners, which a lot of sailors are. And then there's the behaviors they exhibit."

"What do you mean?" He shifted as Tango bumped into his leg while lying down.

"Downtown Norfolk used to have an area called East Main Street. It was a cross between Hell and the Black Hole of Calcutta."

"That pleasant?"

"Yeah," she grinned. "It had anything you'd want. Bars, broads, tattoo parlors, sex shows live and on film. It was a rough area. Fights every night. A missing person or murder per week. Even the cops didn't like going there. And the local people are very afraid for their daughters when they think of sailors in that environment."

"So what happened?" he asked.

"Evidently, after many mayors refused to admit the place even existed, last year officials found the money to clean it up. The area was razed and they're now building respectable businesses."

"How's that working out," Lunch mused.

"Fine for downtown. But the strip just outside the Navy base's Gate Two, the main gate at Hampton and Admiral Taussig Boulevards, picked up much of the old business. The locals don't seem to mind that, though. Keeps the animals close to home."

"Interesting." He took a deep breath. "Would you like to go to dinner with me this evening?"

Skye paused. That would let her get to know him better, but.... "Right now things are hectic getting everything set up for this assignment. My team's coming in from everywhere and I have to get to know them well enough to place them. Plus I still have to hold down a job."

"At that club, Blinker's?"

"It's a good cover. And just a couple blocks from home."

"Hmmm, it was all right. Not quite my style. Maybe you'll consider dinner another time. Since I already have your phone number, I can call you later."

She nodded. "All right. We'll see...."

"No fraternizing?" he smiled.

Skye nodded. "That is frowned upon. But I'm also married and going through a divorce that's hung in mid-air. He's back in California."

"Sorry to hear that," he sighed. "I hope it works out for you. And you're a transfer from there?"

"Yes. San Diego."

"So how did you learn about this area so quickly?"

"I do my homework!"

"I guess that's why you're the boss," Lunch chuckled, rubbing the back of his neck. "Puts me in my place...."

"Central provided me with a very thorough rundown," she explained.

"Okay, what shall I do and where?" A sudden gust of wind sent chills through both people. "It is cool out here, isn't it? Too bad. The dog loves to play in the waves."

"Tango goes swimming!" She looked down at the animal. The dog sat up and barked, as if in agreement. She turned back to Lunch. "Let's see.... I'd like you to watch the big naval establishments south of here. Dam Neck is a large Navy training facility. Oceana is a Naval Air Station. Little Creek is an amphibious base. Try to watch those three as closely as you can. I'll send you photos and descriptions of others assigned to those places within a day or two."

"Sounds good. Thanks."

"You have all your identification and cover stories set up now?"

"Yes. Civilian reporter. Navy Times newspaper. Doing stories of interest to the military people in the area."

"Great. I guess you're all set."

"I think so. And I am sorry Tango knocked you down." He looked at his dog. "Well, boy, shall we go home?"

The animal stood up, vigorously wagging his tail.

"I hope I see you again soon, Brandon," Rena said.

"I hope so, too!"

* * *

A sleepy yeoman jumped when the phone rang. Few people called at 0300 on a Monday. He answered on the second ring. "Office of Criminal Investigation...."

An older man's voice interrupted him. He spoke so softly the yeoman strained to hear him. "Yeah, uh... I called you guys a couple months ago about a group selling drugs to sailors. I don't see anything happening, and I wondered...."

"Please identify yourself."

"As I told the sailor then, I can't. I'd be in danger and I'm afraid of these guys."

"Where are you located?"

The man's voice trembled. "I... I'm at a public phone. In the Norfolk area."

"One moment, please." There was silence on the phone for a long minute. "Hello?"

"Yes? Can you tell me anything?"

"We cross-referenced your previous call. We are investigating your allegation. I'm sorry, but that's all I can say."

"That's good enough for me. Thanks." The man hung up.

* * *

After work a day later, Skye sat looking out her apartment window in Virginia Beach. Most of the team was in place: three men on ships with suspected drug problems, three sailors and three waves in barracks on Mainside, one at the Norfolk Naval Air Station, a second man at the Dam Neck amphibious base, one person working at the Tradewinds Enlisted Men's Club, another working at the Windjammer Acey-Deucey Club for first and second class petty officers, ten civilians under contract. Some of the latter were working with base security.

The next moves were up to her people in the field. But she had no idea what would happen. Or when.

17. DATE

My records showed that I'd spent some time at Great Lakes after boot camp and that I'd been a seaman apprentice for six months. I passed the exam for seaman the first time I took it. I'd get advanced on the fifteenth of October, in three days. This put three stripes on my left arm instead of two, proving I wasn't just out of boot camp. I went onto the pier and called Skye.

"Hi, Rena! I've got some good news."

"What's up, Eric?"

"I made the lofty rate of Seaman," I laughed. "I'm no longer a lowly apprentice."

"Well, congratulations!" she chuckled.

"Hey! It's a thirty-dollar-a-month raise. It's already burning a hole in my pocket. Are you working tonight?"

"Yes...." She sounded hesitant. I could hear her take a deep breath. "But, I can get a stand-in. Want me to pick you up at the gate?"

"Sure, if you don't mind the drive over. Maybe we can get some supper and catch a movie."

"That sounds good, Eric. See you about five?"

"Yeah, I can get off the Haystack by then. See you."

She waited outside the gate, standing near her car. She stood on tiptoes and kissed me on the cheek. "Congratulations! So, what are you planning for this big celebration?"

"Like I said, dinner and a movie. My treat. I'm a rich guy, now, you know."

She laughed. "For that, you should take me to a real swanky place. You can dig into your savings account...."

"Except that's pretty empty, too."

"Okay. Where shall we eat?"

"Well, I know of two places...."

"Where?"

"Tradewinds, the Enlisted Men's Club over at Mainside. And Blinker's," I replied self-consciously.

"Tradewinds, then. I shouldn't go where I just said I couldn't work. Want to drive?"

I nodded. She tossed me her keys.

At Mainside's main gate, the Marine guard held his white-gloved hand straight out, palm towards the car. I stopped and showed my Navy ID and liberty cards.

"You don't have a pass to drive on the base. Where are you going?" the Marine inquired.

"Tradewinds."

"Hold on." The guard handed me a pass. "Keep this on the dashboard. Driver's side. Return it when you leave."

"Thanks."

The guard stepped back and crisply swept his right hand across his chest to motion us through.

We ate supper at the EM club. It was good but not up to Blinker's. As we sipped our drinks, I reached over and took her hand. I figured we should at least look like we were really on a date. She hesitated a moment before pulling back, then smiled and asked, "So, how's life on your Old Haystack?"

I gazed into my glass. "I haven't been on a ship since my midshipman tour and some other training a year after that. There's a lot to learn. And I'm learning. But it's Navy. Same ol' same ol'. Day in, day out. Nothing ever new."

"Like they say, 'Hurry up and wait'?"

"Rule number one."

"Have you noted any strange behaviors among the crew?"

"I'm watching a few guys, some out of curiosity, some out of suspicion. Luke Raynes is irritating, always trying to convert everyone. He never lets up. Luckily, he preaches on the street most nights."

"Any suspicious behaviors?" she asked.

"No, not with him. But then there's Ron Smith. Really down on homosexuals. Announces regularly he's going out to roll queers for drinking money. I suspect he also has booze aboard ship. There were times I thought he was taking a swig from a hidden flask. Nothing provable, yet. And another guy, Phil Le Blanc, is always tired, circles under his eyes, even though he seems to sleep twelve hours a day...."

"Drugs?"

"I don't know. When he's awake there's no glassy eyes or anything. But he could be using small amounts."

"He doesn't go on liberty or get up in the middle of the night?"

I shook my head. "Haven't seen him do either. But the one really suspicious guy is Joe Monnyng. He's extremely defensive about a locked metal box in the paint locker where he works. Says it's private property."

"Keep an eye on him. Anything on the guy we got the phone call about?"

"He's a really nice kid. But I've seen him behave strangely a couple times. The first time, he overreacted when I commented that riding the ship in heavy seas gave me a real rush, better than... and I let that hang in mid-air. He didn't quite know how to take it. Another time he seemed to be out of it, talking incoherently, saying nobody could help him. He mentioned something about a killer, but he wouldn't say any more."

"Did he look drugged up at the time?"

"Definitely."

"Okay. Job one, find out where he gets his dope. He is our prime suspect. The others are gravy, if we can prove they're also using."

The band came in and set up. We ordered another drink. For the first dance they played a slow tune, The Kingston Trio's "Scotch and Soda."

"Dance?" I asked. I held her close. She laid her head against my shoulder for a moment then stood up straight. So I leaned into her sweet smelling auburn hair. She didn't respond or pull back. When the music stopped, I held her a moment longer, singing a slightly changed version of the song's final words about feeling high.

"Eric," she murmured. "Don't...."

"I know." I loosened my embrace.

"Another time, another place, maybe."

We stayed for a few more dances, but left before we got into something neither of us could control.

When we got back out to the car, I asked: "Okay, what movie should we go see?"

Rena put her hand on my arm. "We really shouldn't take this any further."

"What do you mean?" I asked to be sure we were talking about the same thing.

"I'm the person in charge of this project. Technically we're fraternizing." She took a deep breath. "But it was a very nice dinner, Eric. Thank you."

"I had a great time, too. Let's do it again, even if there's nothing to celebrate."

"We shouldn't."

"I know," I replied. I had to keep trying. "But let's, anyway. It can be part of our cover. Two people meeting and going out."

"We'll see." She glanced at her watch.

There was an uncomfortable pause.

"Oh, well. Can you drop me off at the ship? I should get back and get some rest. I have duty tomorrow. Have to go on watch first thing in the morning."

She looked down at her hands. "So, the fates help keep us in our places."

"I'm afraid so."

She reached up and put her hand on my right cheek, then traced along my scars with her fingertips. "Baseball wound? Really?"

"I was a lot more stupid when I was young."

"Sure." She rubbed her hand on my cheek. "Good night, Eric. Congratulations again on your advancement."

I chuckled. "Thanks. I do have to keep trying to advance, just so I seem like a normal enlisted man."

She drove me back to the ship. I watched her car turn the corner onto Hampton Boulevard, and thought, *She's really cute, and I like her a lot, but she's my boss. So I guess it's hands off.*

18. ASSIGNMENT

Skye spent her day off reading a murder mystery. She tried to determine who the killers were before the story ended. It was way too easy for her. Then she was studying some chess moves when the phone rang. "Here."

"Skye?"

"Yes." She recognized the crisp tone used by everyone at Central. "What's up?"

"This is Charles Knox, special agent in charge of your project. We got a call today about a sailor at the Naval Air Station. He's on drugs of some sort. We have Wave operatives on Mainside, right?"

"Yes. What do you want us to do?"

"This gal called us, talked for a little while, and hung up. We got her name. It's legit. We checked. She's a Wave on Mainside. She's worried about her boyfriend at NAS. He's been acting strange so she called for help. I guess she got cold feet and hung up. We don't know how you want to do it, but track her down and make a friendly connection. Just remember, we're after the boyfriend's supplier."

"Okay. What's her name?"

"Shirley Card, YN3."

"A Yeoman third. All right. Where's she from?"

"Henniker, New Hampshire. Only place with that name in the world. About twenty miles west of Concord. Right on a river. Has a small college."

"That helps. I'll find it. One of us could pretend she's a local or went to school there. But it may be tough to get more information. If I find nothing else, I'll play her a different way."

"People from that part of the country are pretty private, Skye. But anybody who lives within fifty miles knows about the area. They take turns hosting social affairs and concerts and flea markets, and everyone goes everywhere to do stuff. Handle her carefully."

"Thanks. I will."

* * *

Skye immediately took a change of clothes, hopped into her car, and drove to Washington, D.C. She got a hotel room for the night and was waiting at the door when the Library of Congress opened in the morning.

Henniker was where Highway 114 crossed the Contoocook River. About a thousand people. Twenty miles west of Concord. Seven miles northeast of towns named Hillsboro-something, home of President Franklin Pierce. Henniker once had a number of mills. These days, New England College provided patrons for businesses catering to students' eating, drinking, clothing, reading and music habits.

Census data and newspaper articles informed Skye of the Card family. Shirley's father was a good carpenter. He provided a comfortable house and raised a large family.

Before leaving, Skye researched the local high school, the names of its teachers and the subjects they taught.

She created a believable story. Her agent could be from Antrim, south of Hillsboro, and could display enough knowledge of the area to be believed. She wrote everything down and put it in a manila folder. Now, she had to determine how to contact Shirley Card, make friends, and find her boyfriend.

19. COBBE

The *Hestek* came into port to pick up observers for an exercise. We tied up about noon and got to stay overnight. The crew got early liberty at 1500.

I was miserable. I wanted to see Rena, but I had work to finish. Reston had the duty but got a standby for a couple hours. This instantly changed my plans. I got ready for liberty along with everyone else so I could follow him.

The liberty party rushed ashore. I followed Reston, barely keeping him in sight.

He walked fast out the D & S Piers gate. He took a right on Hampton Boulevard. This surprised me. All the bars and locker clubs were to the left, by the main gate. That's where all the other guys went if they weren't waiting for a bus to downtown Norfolk.

Reston's direction led to an area filled with abandoned warehouses, civilian piers, and railroad yards. Places that no sailor in his right mind would want to visit. So I thought.

I stayed well back in case Reston turned to look behind him. He didn't. Then he disappeared. I stopped dead in my tracks, frowning. The last I'd seen of him, he was about even with one of the run-down warehouses.

I heard the Norfolk bus coming. I flagged it down and went into town for a beer while I thought. Reston and his supplier must meet in that urban jungle somewhere. Or he used the area as a shortcut to the rail yard. I didn't think they'd meet around the piers. Too many people.

I roamed around Norfolk for a while. Checked out some bookstores and bought a few items. Then I caught a taxi back to the ship to drop off my stuff.

After supper, I took a cab to Blinker's. I went in the side door. I sat in an empty booth just inside, facing the front of the bar. I had a good view of the tables and booths. By twisting a bit I could also see most of the dance floor to my right. The band finished "Theme from A Summer Place" for the slow dancers and started into the wildly popular "Twist."

I didn't see Rena, so I watched the crowd. A few people were already pretty inebriated. One gal was hanging all over a sailor. A guy in another booth was hanging all over a woman, feeling her up as if they were already home. A sailor was draped over his table, sound asleep next to a half-finished beer. Another was still sober, sort of, staring into the depths of his brew. When the band took a break, I could hear a number of conversations. One guy was bragging to his friends about his ability to attract girls. A woman was describing her two-timing ex-boyfriend. Four guys were telling sea stories, trying to outdo each other.

"Can I get you something, Eric?"

I jumped at the sound of the waitress's voice at my shoulder. "Oh, hi, Nancy! Where's Rena?"

"In the front section," she replied. "Want me to get her for you?"

"No, thanks. I'll wait until I can catch her eye."

"Okay. See you."

After looking around a while, I finally noticed Rena. She seemed quite friendly with a customer. I mean she acted very friendly. The guy was handsome, muscular with brown crew-cut hair and finely chiseled features. She joked around with him. Flirted. Acted seductive. I wondered if she was working a good tipper or if something else was going on. I got more curious as I watched. She'd never said anything about a boyfriend. I watched for ten minutes or so before she saw me and came over. "Eric! What're you doing here?"

"We're in port for a day to pick up observers."

"Want a beer? This isn't my section, but Nancy won't mind if I get you something."

"Sure."

When she returned with my beer our hands touched. I took the bottle and pulled back quickly before I realized what I was doing. She stood at the edge of the table, head tilted. "Eric, is something wrong?"

"Nope." I took a sip of beer. I stared at the top of the bottle for a moment then nodded toward the front of the bar. "Who was that guy over there by the door?"

She looked where I was gazing. "Him?"

"Mmmm-hmmm." I tried to sound indifferent.

Rena shrugged. "Some business I had to take care of," she explained, shifting her weight from one foot to the other. She smiled. "Eric Matthews, are you jealous?"

"I have no reason to be jealous," I said too quickly.

"You're right. No reason. He was business, and sometimes I have to play to peoples' personalities."

I had no claim on this woman. I knew that. But it seems my feelings didn't. The thought raced through my head that Rena might flirt with everybody.

20. ENTERPRISE

Rena said that other guy was business and I had no reason to be jealous. I couldn't see it. But I nodded. "Okay."

The silence between us was so thick you could cut it with a knife. "Eric?"

"What?"

She placed one hand on each cheek and forced me to look directly at her. "You have nothing to be jealous of."

"Okay," I whispered, swallowing hard.

She sat down across from me and spoke in a low voice. "Listen to me, Mr. Matthews. His name is Everett Cobbe. He's like you. An E-3. Just like you, only he's a Marine stationed at the Dam Neck Training Center. He's here for a meal and a couple drinks. And he's homesick." She grinned. "He kept talking about his mother and their dog." She stood up and returned to work.

He was another one of us.

The *Hestek* went back out to sea in the morning.

* * *

Sunday at sea. Holiday routine. I studied some, read some, and worked a crossword puzzle. I skipped the flick and hit the rack because I had the midwatch.

The messenger normally woke watchstanders about fifteen minutes early. But he woke the midwatch a half hour early so they could get their late night snack. As I dressed in the dark, I saw a movement out of the corner of my eye, like someone was taking a swig. Smith stood by his bunk. I couldn't tell if he was holding a flask, but I sure got the impression he was drinking on board ship.

I straggled down to the mess decks for midrats, the standard midnight rations of chicken noodle broth, crackers, coffee and whatever else the duty cook came up with. Sometimes the "extras" were nice. They were usually non-existent.

We ate, filled our coffee cups and dragged our tired selves to wherever we'd spend most of the night. I relieved the watch and stood there sipping my coffee, trying to wake up. We permitted no white lights on the bridge— they'd blind our night vision. Our red lights let us see and even write in the logbooks.

The bridge was silent except for the occasional command or report. I liked the mid, the darkness, serenity, general warmth and companionship, even in heavy seas. I sipped my coffee.

"Matthews," the Officer of the Deck snapped.

"Yes, sir!"

"Get rid of the coffee! No drinks on the bridge."

"Aye, aye, sir!"

The messenger instantly stood beside me. I gulped down the last of the coffee.

"More?" the messenger asked.

"Yeah, sure."

The messenger chuckled. He took my cup so he could return it to the mess decks. Then he rubbed it in. "Least I can grab a quick cup whenever I'm out and about on watch business."

I grunted an acknowledgement. I stood enjoying the quiet of the night. Jensen, the Quartermaster of the Watch, turned to the Junior Officer of the Deck. "Mister Reynolds, we going to do some kind of special operation this time out?"

"Didn't you read the Plan of the Day?" the ensign asked.

"No, sir. I hit the rack early 'cause I had the mid. The P. O. D. hadn't come out yet."

"The Navy's newest and biggest will be here in the morning, the nuclear aircraft carrier *Enterprise*."

"That thing's supposed to be huge."

"It is," the JOOD replied. "If you stood her upright, she'd be taller than the Empire State Building. She's going through her sea trials and a number of Norfolk ships will operate with her."

Dawn broke on a cloudy day. The enormous carrier had joined the task force in the very early morning. Her square superstructure made her unique. It looked like someone put a huge toy block above the flight deck, smoothed it down and painted it Navy gray.

I was back on watch at noon. The twenty-ninth of October 1969. A day to remember.

The Captain sat in his bridge chair, studying the carrier through his binoculars. The other phone talker announced, "Mister Tower, sir! Boiler rooms report all boilers lit off. The engine rooms report they're ready."

"Very well." The OOD turned to Lorman. "Captain, we're standing by for the run."

"Let the *Enterprise* know."

"Aye, aye, Captain." Tower picked up the radiotelephone handset. "Climax, this is Roman Legion. We are standing by for your first run. Over."

The response came back quickly, "Roman Legion, this is Climax. We shall commence in ten minutes. Out."

"Very well, gentlemen." Lorman grinned. "Let's try to keep up." We were there in case something went wrong. We had no idea how fast this new ship could move.

"Aye, aye, Captain. Helmsman, come around to zero-niner-zero."

"Zero-niner-zero, aye, sir."

Lieutenant Tower ordered our fastest speed. "Lee helm, ring up turns for flank speed."

"Turns for flank speed, aye, sir," the sailor replied. Then he muttered, "Snipes are gonna love this."

"The engineers are expecting it," Tower replied.

"Heading!" the helmsman called out. "Steady on course zero-niner-zero, sir!" The carrier was now directly astern of us. The OOD and JOOD went onto the open bridge to watch it. Captain Lorman put his binoculars down, closed his eyes and waited.

Combat Information Center reported, "*Enterprise* bearing two-seven-zero true, range eight thousand."

Four miles behind us, I thought. How are we on station?

The *Enterprise* began her run. The OOD watched it through binoculars. "Look at that rooster tail!"

"All eight reactors must be on line," the JOOD said.

"Mister Reynolds, I do believe you're right."

I couldn't see a thing. In a few minutes, I heard a very un-military report from CIC, "Holy shit! How fast is that thing moving?"

I grinned and asked, "CIC, Bridge, should I repeat that question to the OOD?"

"Hell, no! Hang on, Bridge. We're calculating the carrier's speed now." They soon reported, "Bridge, CIC. The *Enterprise* is doing forty-five knots! That's four five, forty-five! It's already passed up the first tin can!"

"Bridge, aye." I repeated the report. The two officers stared at each other, mouths hanging open.

Captain Lorman opened his eyes and laughed a little. "Gentlemen, why do you think I just sat and waited? Soon we'll all have a very clear view of her stern!"

The *Enterprise* pulled abeam of us. We were moving as fast as we could, and it was doing half again our speed. Then she kicked it up. Soon that ship, the size of the Empire State Building, left us "fast" destroyers far behind.

"Over fifty knots!" Reynolds exclaimed in wonder.

I compared the speeding carrier and our relatively low speed to my situation. My progress on the *Hestek* was agonizingly slow. But, like the destroyers, I was moving as fast as I could.

* * *

Skye got a report that another sailor died on a cruiser tied up at Mainside. It was another case of too much quinine in his heroin. He'd shot up in a workspace, in the middle of the night. He died with his needle next to him.

21. FIELD OPERATIONS

A lazy Monday morning. Skye got up after nine. She needed the sleep and had nothing else to do until later. She ate a leisurely brunch, then sat down to figure out a complex chess sequence.

About 1400 she called Jennie Powers. "Tell Gardner to be at the Tradewinds at 1600. I'll meet her for supper."

When Skye entered the club she found Gardner at the bar. "Hi, Ruth. What're you drinking?"

"Black Russian," she smiled. "Just one or two. With food."

"Oh, those are too heavy for me. I prefer a nice light Cuba libre. Let's get a table." They settled down to eat. "How's the boyfriend situation?"

"It's rocky. With me here, we're not together much. Friends back at Lakes tell me he's playing the field again." She emptied her glass shortly before the salad arrived. She looked at Rena. "Why did you call this meeting?"

Skye didn't answer because their supper arrived. They ate without speaking. The team leader paid for both meals. When they left the club it was already dark.

"Let's go for a ride," Skye said. "You can study while I drive around."

"I have an assignment?"

"Yes." Skye extracted a manila folder from under the driver's seat. Once off the base, she handed it to Ruth, along with a flashlight. "You need to know this by heart before we return to the base."

Gardner read for a while. "Who is this?"

"Shirley Card is a Wave. There's enough there for you to make up a story, if necessary, that you come from her part of the country. Look at the map. Your best bet might be that you're from Antrim, or Deering, or one of those small towns."

"Okay," Ruth answered. "Why?"

"You might have to become very good friends with her."

"Why? And how?"

"Or you might not. You have to find out who her boyfriend is."

"What's important about him?"

"She tipped us off that he might be on drugs. We have to identify him."

"Where is he?"

"Naval Air Station."

"She didn't give you his name?"

"No." Skye explained Card's call to Central. "Now we need to find out who he is, without alerting them."

"And after that?"

"We have others at NAS to watch him. We want to find his supplier. Meanwhile, memorize your information."

"You say I might not have to make contact with her?"

"It's best if you find out who he is without talking to them. Try to follow her. We don't want to tip our hand."

Gardner held up the papers. "So why do I have to learn all this stuff now?"

"Just in case. You might not be able to find out who the guy is. Then you'll have to make friends with Card. So you can get her to identify with you and get her talking about her man."

Gardner memorized the material within an hour.

Skye worried about how a meeting would go between the two, if it came to that.

22. PAYDAY

First of the month. The day the eagle shits. On paydays aboard the *Hestek* we filed down a companionway on the port side, passed the steam line, collected our cash from the disbursing officer on the mess decks, and exited through the scullery. When I stepped out onto the starboard side of the main deck, I saw Derella leaning on the bulwark, where he could easily see any approaching chief or officer. He held a small notebook in hand. Reston faced him, showing a mixture of anger and frustration.

"Come on! This is robbery!"

"Ya don't fuckin' like it? Pay up right away. Gimme my fuckin' money or I'll take it outa yer hide!"

"I don't have it! How can I give you what I don't have?"

I joined them. "What's the problem?"

"He owes me money, which is none of yer fuckin' business," Derella growled.

I ignored him and turned to Reston. "Hank?"

"I borrowed some money and I can't pay it back. I'm willing to pay his interest, but I owe twenty-eight bucks and he wants to add interest for the three dollars over the twenty five...."

"That's how I do business!" Derella snarled.

"Other slush funders add more interest only when it gets to the next five-dollar point!"

"Look, fuckhead, yer cut off. No more money 'til you pay every goddamn penny, accordin' to my calculations 'n' the way I figure the interest. Ya wanta play fuckin' games, yer out in the cold, asshole."

I glared at Derella. "Just shut up a minute." I turned back to Reston. "What's his interest?"

"Five for seven. Like most everybody, except he doesn't know when to...!"

I sensed that the loan shark was ready to jump in again, so I held my hand up to quiet him while I continued, "You said you owe him twenty-eight dollars?"

"Yeah, right now.... He says it'll be forty next payday."

I handed Derella three tens. "Give me my change and scratch his name off your list." The slusher did so. I thanked him and added, "Glad to do business with you. You know what you're doing is against the regs. And being such a hard-ass is a good way to get turned in."

"An' who the fuck do you think you are? Some kind of fuckin' cop, or somethin'?"

23. CHASKÉ

Did Derella really think I was a cop? Or was that just his mouth? I stood there staring at him for a moment. He pushed me away. "Get the fuck outa here! Quit bothering me!" Then he turned to Reston. "And you, shithead, don't ever come to me fer money anymore! Never!"

We walked aft.

"Eric, why'd you do that?" Reston asked.

"We're friends, aren't we?" I asked.

"Yeah, but what makes you think I can repay you when I can't pay him?"

"I hate people who take advantage of others. I paid for you to break the cycle. I won't charge you any interest. None. You can pay me a five spot each payday until you're clear."

I thought to myself, He's a good kid in a nasty trap. Maybe I can save him.

* * *

While we were at sea, Skye had some busy days. First, she did some research at the Norfolk Public Library while waiting to personally talk to Laura Jaf, another operative.

The research was the result of something I'd mentioned. Blink told me his bar was once a Quaker meetinghouse. Skye's instincts told her that was important. She didn't know why. She searched the library and gravitated to the local history section.

Old plantation houses. Titles jumped off the shelf. She pulled the volumes down and glanced through them. They were interesting but had nothing to do with any kind of churches.

She kept looking, but nothing clicked. She sat down a bit noisily, sighing, wondering where to look next.

"Problems?" a deep quiet voice asked.

She looked up. A big man, well over six feet tall, stood leaning against the nearest bookshelf, smiling. He held three books, two of them quite small. Skye recognized him from the photo she'd seen in her files.

"Hi, Rodney! Yeah, I'm having problems. I'm looking for something and don't know what."

He chuckled. "Hard way to do research!"

"Tell me about it!"

He sat down across from her. "By the way, my friends call me Chaské."

"Chuh-SKAY? What kind of name is that?" She looked him over. He had dark brown skin and a wide nose. His crew-cut hair was pitch-black. His eyes were dark brown, almost black.

His broad smile lit up the room. "It's a Sioux name for the first kid who's also a boy. We have special names for the first five kids, unique ones for boys and girls."

"I'm the oldest in my family. What would you call me?"

"Winona," he told her.

"Wih-NOO-nah. That's pretty." She pointed to the books he was holding. "What're you reading?"

"A book on the Civil War by Bruce Catton for me. And some books for my kid, quote end quote. Just in case we had to do our oral handshake."

"Now I'm curious. What kids' books could you use?"

"This one's called *Are You My Mom?* This little bird doesn't know where it comes from and asks all the animals if they're its mother."

Skye laughed out loud then put her hand over her mouth to muffle the sound. "And I guess I'd answer, Oh, yes, I know about some of the new kids books. Did you ever see *Green Eggs and Ham*? I used to read that to a friend's daughter. It's another funny book."

"Oh, please," he begged. "I ate at truck stops a lot while I was in college." He looked at the ceiling, thinking. "I've eaten green eggs, ...and green ham. Got sick afterwards, but...." Rena let out another burst of laughter. Chaské made a point of looking around them. "Shhh, you're goin' to get us kicked out of here."

She pointed to his books. "What's the other one?"

"It's called *Go, Dog, Go!* Different colored dogs, all sizes, movin' on everything from cars to skis. It's funny, but it tells about life, too."

Skye reached across the table. "Chaské Hunter, I love your sense of humor. I'm glad to finally meet you. You must know that I'm Rena Skye. How did you find me here?"

"Followed you. My people been pretty decent trackers for a long time. In your case, it wasn't too hard." He grinned. "They told me where you lived and worked, but I didn't think I'd be very welcome in that white bar. I went to your apartment. I got there just in time to see you get in your car. So I followed you."

"You might be all right at the bar. We have a few Negro patrons and they don't seem to have any trouble. Blink, the owner, was career Navy, since before World War Two, and he's seen all the races do their part."

He thought a moment. "I could be too sensitive. I am kind of dark and I wouldn't want to take the chance here in the South." He nodded towards her pile of books. "So what're you looking for that's so frustrating?"

She described Blinker's and the history about the Quaker meetinghouse that Blink had described.

"Eric's your boy friend?"

"Not really," she smiled. "He's one of us. I guess under different circumstances he could be a boyfriend."

"And the information about this place, what's botherin' you?"

She shrugged her shoulders. "I don't know. I have good instincts and my subconscious is screaming that there's something important there."

"Have you looked for books on Quaker meetinghouses?"

"Couldn't find anything."

"You know, I'm a trained researcher. My GI bill from Korea paid for college and I wanted to do somethin' interesting, so I majored in sociological research. Let me do some lookin'. I'll see what I can find."

"Thanks." Skye sat thinking for a while then shook her head. "I thought I had it. I'll have to let it bubble." She stood up. "Meanwhile, I was supposed to meet someone here today but she didn't show up. And I have to get some groceries or I'll be eating in restaurants."

"Well, have fun shoppin'," Chaské said. "See you later."

Laura Jaf got to the library late. She heard Skye and Hunter talking. She waited outside and followed Rena to the supermarket where she arranged an "accidental" meeting.

24. LIBERTY PORT

Ships move and visit different ports. Sailors see new and fascinating places. Navy recruiters don't hesitate to advertise this. Some guys sarcastically say they're swabbing their way around the world. But there's a certain degree of truth to the travel stuff. And sometimes the "exotic" ports are in the USA.

The *Hestek* pulled into New York City on a Friday afternoon. They set the special sea detail at Verrazano Narrows, where a huge new bridge is almost done being built. This made a long detail but let us see all the harbor attractions, the whole skyline and the busy merchant and ferry traffic. The Statue of Liberty welcomed us as she had many of our parents and grandparents. We wound our way up the East River to the Brooklyn Navy Yard, where we saw another huge new Navy carrier, the USS *Constellation*.

"You going ashore?" Shepherd asked.

"Thinking about it. How about you?" I countered.

"Yeah. I even have a new camera. I want to get as many pictures as I can."

"You turning into a tourist?"

"Hey, I've never been to 'The City.' You better believe I'm a tourist! Too many things to see. And I hear the women here are some of the prettiest in the world."

"What would your wife say to that?" I asked.

He rubbed his short-cropped hair as he thought a moment. "She'd slap me. Gently. And remind me that I can look all I want. Then she'd add that I better not touch or I'll get my fingers broken. Or some other body part!"

"Let's do it," I laughed. "But I have to get a camera, too. Lomax has some nice ones in the ship's store. And his prices are good. I'll check them out."

"Great. Tomorrow's Saturday. We can make a day of it."

The ship's store was a model of efficiency. It was maybe four feet square, including the shelves. Its Dutch door opened outward, the top latching to the bulkhead in the passageway so it didn't take away any usable area. Inside, Lomax got most items by twisting and reaching. He kept one of each large item for inspection, but stocked that stuff in secured storage compartments below. The store held candy bars, toothpaste, razor blades and packs of smokes, but if you wanted large amounts or expensive items, you had to wait until Lomax got them from storage.

I took my time checking out the three camera models. When he had time, Lomax demonstrated each one. I bought an automatic 35mm camera. Easy to use. Load the film, aim and shoot. I couldn't even make double-exposures—the camera locked the shutter until the film advanced. I could also use manual mode to adjust the aperture and focus. I paid thirty-five dollars, about half a month's take-home pay.

Saturday was cool and clear. The woolen blues felt good. The peacoats looked light, but were heavy enough to keep us warm.

Shep and I headed out. Our first adventure was finding the subway from Brooklyn to Manhattan. We returned to ground level in Times Square.

The frenetic activity all around astonished us. Hordes of people scurried in every direction under flashing neon signs that blazed advertisements and news. I'd been to Chicago many times, but never found it as frenetic as this.

"I've heard this place never sleeps. Never even slows down," Shep commented. "Wonder what it looks like at midnight. But I'll be too tired to stick around and find out."

The crowd almost carried us away. Shep pulled me up to a storefront. "Look! Hole-in-the-wall stores for any specialty you want!"

"The crowd's not as dense here either," I observed. "Let's walk and window shop." We strolled past numerous stores and stopped in front of an optics shop. "Look at that! One store, twenty-five feet wide, selling nothing but telescopes, binoculars, stuff like that."

"There's some really small pieces in there. I wonder how good they are," Shep mused.

"Let's go see," I suggested.

We were surprised. Some of the optics were amazingly good for their size. A telescope that could fit in my dress jumper's inside pocket intrigued me. "How much is this?"

"Twenty-five dollars," the shopkeeper said.

"You going to buy that?" Shepherd asked.

"Why not?"

"What're you going to do with it?"

"Well, it lets you see things at a distance...."

"God, what a wise ass!" Shep rolled his eyes. "What do you need it for?"

"Don't know. But I'm fascinated that this little thing does such a great job."

"You have the money for it?"

"Yeah. I don't go on liberty much and I don't drink a lot, so I've saved some. Gives me a chance to do something silly once in a while." I nodded to the storekeeper. "I'll take it."

We spent the day sightseeing. I used my new telescope instead of paying for one at the top of the Empire State Building. We roamed around the spacious UN building and Shepherd bought small flags of every country he'd visited. And we went to watch a show at Radio City Music Hall. We were both tired as hell when we got back to the ship.

The *Hestek* departed New York about noon the following day. On the way out, I used my new telescope to get close-up views of the *Constellation*, the skyline and the Statue of Liberty. I was especially pleased to pick out the windows near the top of the Empire State Building where we stood the day before.

Reston didn't go ashore at all in New York. This seemed strange to me. Everyone went ashore in a port like this, if only to grab a beer.

25. BOYFRIENDS

Gardner was assigned cleaning duty in her barracks on Mainside of the Norfolk Naval Station. She couldn't move around easily, but the Watch, Quarter and Station Bill was in the open. She noted Shirley Card's bunk, locker, and duty section.

Gardner followed Card when she went on liberty. The woman didn't leave the base. She walked north toward Willoughby Bay and along the waterfront, just west of the slip bordering the heliport. She joined a man at the water's edge.

Gardner continued walking along the road, mentally noting all the parked vehicles. If the man with Card owned one of them, she had his information.

Ruth returned to the curve in the road where the slip began at Willoughby Bay. She wrote a few lines on a piece of paper. Now she could say she was working on a poem. From her position, she could see the couple and all traffic.

After an hour, the pair returned to the street. They walked to an older car. He got in and started it. Card put her head through the open window and kissed him before he left. Ruth marked the vehicle on her piece of paper.

On her way back to the barracks, she stopped at a booth to phone Skye.

"Here."

"Gardner."

"Got something?"

"Yes. Ready to write?"

"Shoot."

Gardner recited make, model, year and license of the car driven by Card's boyfriend. "That's it."

"Okay. Thanks. Anything else?"

"Nope."

"Okay. You sure it's her boyfriend?"

"They met in an out of the way place for over an hour. He got into this car and started it up. And she poked her head through the open window to kiss him good-bye. Circumstantial, but...."

"Good enough. We'll go with it. Thanks."

"Anything else?"

"Not at the moment. Watch and listen. Remember, Waves are in danger, too."

"Yes, ma'am. Bye."

Skye called Charlie Knox at OCI Norfolk and repeated the information. "I need a full report on the owner. ASAP."

"It's base information. Easy fifteen minutes."

Fourteen minutes later Knox reported, "Here's your man. Divven, Randall. Called Randy. AQ3, Air Fire Control Technician third class. Stationed at NAS. His brother owns the car, but Divven registered it for base parking. Anything else?"

"Nope. Thanks." Skye called the men's barracks at NAS. She left a message for Tomas Morelos, her operative there.

Morelos didn't call back before she left for work.

Halfway through her shift, a man walked into Blinker's. He could've come from any Latin American country. He had well-trimmed black hair and smiling black eyes. He paused at the door, looked around, then took a seat where Skye could wait on him.

"Hi, Tom!" she greeted. "What can I get you?"

"Beer. Dos Equis, if you have it. Order of fries."

She soon returned with the beer. "He's making some fresh fries, so I waited."

"Thanks," he nodded. "So, what's up?"

"When I deliver your fries, I'll leave a name under your plate. Be sure he's a user."

"Then?" Morelos asked.

"Bring him in to the NAS Legal Office. We want to make a deal."

"Time frame?"

"ASAP."

"Got it."

* * *

Gardner cried herself to sleep that night, clutching a "Dear Jane" letter:

Ruth,
I could live with you running all over when you came home

regularly. But now I never get to see you. I love you, but I can't live this way when you're not here. Maybe it's time for us to split up. It was good while it lasted, babe. I'm sorry if this hurts you, but I don't know what to else do. I never wanted it to end like this. If you're coming back up here soon, let me know and maybe we can pick up again. I need you here.

   Bob

26. SLUSH NETWORK

The *Hestek* took on stores in Norfolk. All hands, third class and below, carried crates of food aboard all afternoon. It was exhausting work. Go to the pier. Pick up a box. Lug it aboard. Carry it down a couple decks, unable to see where to put your feet. Stand in line waiting for someone to rearrange stuff so you can put the box down. Return to the pier. Over and over again. The worst boxes were the wooden lettuce crates, so large that your knuckles smashed against the rims of the hatches as you went below. That was after you'd shoved a two-by-four sized splinter into your hand, which you couldn't take out because some senior petty officer would holler at you for stopping.

At least we weren't carrying ammunition. Anything was easier than carrying fifty-five pounds of explosives in a steel shell that was round with nothing to hold onto.

My muscles felt like we'd loaded ten tons of stores.

Now I sat on the 01 level, back against Mount 33's metal shield, relaxing as far from people and blowers as possible. I knew Rena wasn't working but had other chores. So I rested my sore body and gathered my thoughts.

After a while I heard Derella on the main deck talking in hushed tones. It seemed strange for him to speak so quietly. I moved to the edge of the superstructure, lying on the deck itself so I could look to the level below.

Derella about twenty feet forward, talking to someone on the USS *Joseph*, which was tied up alongside us. Friends on different ships often talked like this, so I sat back up. His friendships were his business.

I closed my eyes and relaxed. I could still make out a word now and then. Then I heard "interest" and a short time later, "slush." As a Navy cop I had a responsibility to get as much information as I could and pass it on, so I listened the best I could. I lay on the deck and looked over the edge again. I set my baseball cap to the back of my head so I could see better.

"I'll tell ya one las' time, Curtis," Derella said, "if ya don't like it, fuck off. Gimme my money back, 'n' go to hell."

"No, no, I like the arrangement," the other man laughed self-consciously. "But this is business and I was just trying to make a little more for myself."

"Seemed like you were tryin' ta screw over me. I staked ya a hundred bucks a few months ago with a fuckin' agreement. You loan out my money at five for seven. We split the take. That's a pretty fuckin' good deal. You don't even hafta use yer own dough."

Derella glanced around to be sure nobody overheard him. I ducked as low as I could, and wound up lying completely on the deck.

"I agree," Curtis nodded.

I lifted my head again, but I'd inhaled some dust. I rubbed my nose to stop a sneeze. Then a few drops of rain hit my neck. *Just my luck*, I thought. *The rain washes down the deck after I get a load of dust up my snot locker.*

"Same fuckin' agreement fer this hundred. Now you got two hundred of mine, an' you pay me forty fuckin' bucks every two weeks. You keep the other forty. Understood?"

"Yeah. I said I was okay with the deal. But what if I don't loan all of it out every payday? Do I still have to pay you forty bucks even if I don't pull in eighty?"

My nasal passages began to itch, way up inside. I pinched the bridge of my nose to stop the irritation.

"Hey! My goddamn money's still out on loan from me. I'm just givin' you a good rate of interest. Come on. It's startin' ta rain 'n' I'm not gonna stand out here arguin' with you. Take my fuckin' deal or leave it!"

My nasal irritation was getting worse. I thought about backing away from the edge but I was too interested in the conversation.

"I'll take it," Curtis said. "Something is better than nothing."

"All right."

I couldn't stop the sneeze. I tried to cover it up with my hand. The result was a muffled snort. I froze. For an instant.

27. INFORMATION AND THREATS

Skye picked up her ringing phone. "Here."

"Laura Jaf. I have a suspect report."

"Who is it?"

"Kent Eckersley, Seaman. Met him at the EM Club. From the cruiser *Orlando*."

"Symptoms?" Rena asked.

"Glassy eyes. Incoherent, dreamy speech. No sign of alcohol. His buddies helped him return to his ship."

"They didn't notice he hadn't been drinking?"

"I think they were too drunk."

"Could you determine what division he was in?"

"He wasn't wearing a striker's patch. His friends were technical, two electronic technicians and a sonarman."

"That's some help, though they're from different departments. Anything else?"

"He seemed friendlier with the ETs."

"Okay. Thanks." Skye hung up then dialed a number.

"OCI Norfolk," answered the voice on the other end.

"Skye here. Have Knox transfer Daniel Han from the USS *Plant* to the *Orlando*. As soon as he can."

"Reason?"

She explained Jaf's field report.

"Okay. We'll cut the orders right away."

* * *

Derella had heard my muffled sneeze. He whirled around, looking in my direction. "What the fuck was that?"

111

"Sounds like someone's up there." Curtis pointed.

"Well, let's just take a fuckin' look."

I pushed back. It was raining heavier now, and I slipped trying to get to my feet. I was almost up when Derella jumped, thrust up on the superstructure with one foot, grabbed the top of the bulkhead and pulled himself up over the edge. I jumped behind the metal shield. But not quite in time.

"Matthews! You sonofabitch! I'll take care of yer sorry ass! You been warned!"

I took Derella seriously. He'd never believe I hadn't deliberately eavesdropped on him. After my warning about slush funds on payday, he could easily convince himself that I was out to get him.

The *Hestek* left Norfolk mid-morning on Thursday. I hadn't seen Derella since Monday night. We worked in different areas and I steered clear of him at other times. It was tough, being sure we were never alone. But I couldn't avoid him forever.

One day, after using the head, I was returning to work on the main deck. As I passed the hatch to our living quarters, hands grabbed me and forced me to start down the companionway. Then I was shoved. I lost my balance and fell downward to the deck.

28. THE DEAL

Derella towered over me. He grabbed my shirt and pulled me to my feet. Considering his small size, he was pretty damn strong. Eyes blazing, he shook me and growled, "Why the fuck're you spyin' on me?"

"I'm not spying on you," I replied.

"You were on the 01 level, fuckin' watchin' us."

"I was not watching you!"

"You were up there, you cocksucker. I heard you fuckin' sneeze while we were talkin'. What'd you hear?"

"I didn't hear anything. I...."

He lifted me off the deck and slammed me into a bunk. I heard him through a fog of pain. "I don't wanna hear no fuckin' stories, boot. You're gonna tell me the truth!"

"I already am," I insisted. "I heard voices. I was curious. I looked over the edge to see who was talking. That's all." I relaxed, then tensed up, shot my hands up between his arms, and pushed outward. The move surprised him. I was free. "Why would I spy on you?"

He shook his finger in my face. "You ask too many fuckin' questions, you sonofabitch!"

I glared at him. "Is that a guilty conscience I hear? What else are you doing that's illegal, besides running a slush fund?"

"You stay outa my fuckin' business!" Derella shouted, sounding like he was trapped.

I wondered if he was a drug supplier. "Just what is your business? What are you really up to?" He tried to grab me again. I batted his hands away. "Keep your hands off me."

"And you, asshole, you steer clear o' me. I don't fuckin' want you anywhere near me. You see me, you go the other fuckin' direction. Next time you mess with me, you're gonna fuckin' get hurt, and hurt bad."

113

* * *

Skye told me about the deal the Naval Air Station Legal Office made after Morelos uncovered enough evidence to confront Shirley Card's boyfriend, Randall Divven.

Four people were at the meeting besides Morelos and Divven: Lieutenant Commander Brian Cecil, legal officer; his recording assistant, Yeoman third class Alan Noonan; Charles Knox, OCI's contract special agent; and a burly Master-At-Arms at the door.

They offered Divven immunity if he identified his supplier and went through treatment. If it meant busting open a whole drug ring, they would offer the pusher a chance to turn state's evidence. If he did, they'd also keep his record clean and provide him with a new identity, some schooling, and set him up with a new life.

Divven only knew his supplier's first name, Chuck. He couldn't describe his car or license plates. He'd never even seen a car. Chuck always stood in shadows. Divven described the pusher as big, a couple inches taller than himself, and heavier by twenty pounds.

Legal suggested he make a purchase while they watched. He agreed, but doubted it would work. Chuck was very devious.

Four agents watched Divven's every move. Three nights later, he made the purchase. Chuck kept in the shadows of a building on the Naval Air Station. This time he stayed in his car and drove away before the agents could grab him.

Knox, who'd set up the operation, didn't know why it went wrong. Morelos was furious. He asked where the agents in cars were and why didn't they have vehicles to block Chuck's escape?

Knox told Morelos to set up the next operation himself and walked away. But Morelos had watched the seller through binoculars. As it drove out of the shadows Morelos saw a 1961 Olds Eighty-Eight, Virginia plates, eight-seven-seven zero-two-six. He wrote down the information and passed it on to Skye so she could check it out.

The day after that, the Legal Office learned that Divven died in the cleaning closet of his barracks, where he'd shot up. His needle was on the floor next to his body, along with half a packet of unused heroin. It was pure and uncut. Another deliberate murder.

* * *

I had duty Friday so I could only watch Reston take off at liberty call. I went down to the living compartment to read the newspaper.

There was one really interesting article. It was about Neil Armstrong a well-decorated ex-Navy pilot who flew many missions in Korea. He was now flying experimental aircraft. Yesterday he set a world speed record in a Bell X-15 rocket plane. He flew the thing slightly over 4090 miles per hour. That was fast!

I was reading when Reston returned. He waved but didn't say anything. His eyes were unfocused and he was a bit unsteady. He hit the rack immediately.

I could call for a surprise locker inspection and get him for using drugs. But my job here was to track down his supplier. I had no choice but to take the time and follow him. I'd have to be ready every time without giving myself away.

Besides, I thought as I rubbed the scars on my right cheek, *I still want to save this kid if I can.*

* * *

I got off my 20-2400 watch and went up to the 01 level for a smoke before hitting the rack. As I leaned against the lifelines, the paint locker door opened and Monnyng came out. Nobody painted anything at midnight. Monnyng was wearing blues and nobody ever came near the paint locker in a good uniform. As he locked up the small compartment, he did so with one hand across his waist, like he was holding something in place under his jumper. His bulky peacoat reduced my certainty whether he was really hiding anything. He went aft, stepping as if he were adjusting something, and then he walked normally.

29. DEAD MEN AND QUITTERS

Liberty call on the *Hestek*. This time I didn't have duty and could follow Reston. I stayed close enough to see where he went, but far enough back for him to not see me.

It didn't work. I verified he ducked into that abandoned warehouse area. Once back there, where he went was anyone's guess. I stood alongside Hampton Boulevard, frustrated. But I couldn't stay there long. I didn't know when Reston would step out and see me. So I ran back to the bus stop near the D & S Piers gate. I went downtown Norfolk and did some book shopping.

I'd have to figure out some way to get into that warehouse area before Reston. But I really didn't want to go there every liberty day and wait.

Then, again, maybe I'd have to if I wanted to track down the scum that sold those drugs. It was my passion to clear them off the planet. I rubbed my cheek. I would do whatever I had to do to break this bunch of pushers.

* * *

The phone rang.

"Rena..." the voice on the other end said.

Skye recognized the voice but didn't like his tone. "Tom! What's wrong? Didn't you find him?"

"Yeah, we found him. His name was Charles Gaines. We...."

"Was?"

"We saw no trace of him for a whole day. The landlord opened his apartment for us. He was in there, dead."

"How?"

"Same way as Divven. He had multiple punctures on his arm. Blood dried around them. He'd struggled and was held down. There were bruises on his arms and legs."

"So, he was injected...."

"The packet was in the kitchen. Hundred percent pure."

Skye stared into empty space. This was totally unexpected. Morelos' voice brought her back. "And there were no fingerprints at all. They must have used surgical gloves." He took a deep breath. "What now? Start over?"

"What else? Watch the barracks, the clubs...."

"Will do. Later."

"Yeah." After hanging up she stood for long moments looking out the window at nothing. Thinking. She returned to the phone, picked up the receiver and dialed a number.

"OCI Norfolk."

"Skye here. I need to talk to Commander Blount. It's critical." The duty yeoman put her call through right away. "Sir, our deal backfired. Subject and suspect both killed."

"How?"

"Deliberate overdoses. Pure dope."

"More murders. What happened?"

"Don't know. NAS Legal made the deal. The only people who knew what was happening were the user, Morelos, the Legal Officer, his yeoman, Knox, and a Master-at-Arms. One of them was bought. I want all of them watched."

"Even ours?"

"Yes, sir. We can apologize later. I want that snitch."

"Okay, I'll have tails on them as soon as I can get operatives into place," the commander promised.

"Thank you, sir. And I don't want any more deals. We track down everyone. We grab everyone. We lock them all up. We make deals after we're done. We'll save lives that way."

"I agree, Captain Skye. I'll run interference for you if I need to."

* * *

I showed up at Blinker's for last call. Rena stopped me from helping her clean up. "Blink doesn't like it."

"Why not?"

She shrugged. "Something about working without pay. And really, it's not fair for me get out of here earlier than the others."

"All right. I'll sit and watch. How're things going?"

"Later."

I thought that was kind of strange. Rena had never acted that way before.

"Okay," I replied. I went to sit at the bar and wait.

117

"Hi, Eric!" Blink greeted, after he finished counting the bills in the register. "Want another drink?"

"Aren't you closed?" I asked.

He shrugged. "Nobody'd say anything if I gave you a free beer. And sodas are legal."

"I'll have a Coke, then." I turned to watch Rena.

"Here you are!" Blink said placing a drink in front of me. He put his cash in a bank deposit bag. He poured himself some coffee. "Well! I'm done," he said. "Let's go out there." We sat down in the middle of the restaurant. He pointed to Rena. "She is a pretty young thing, isn't she?" I took a sip from my drink, wondering where this was coming from. All I saw in his eyes was friendliness. I nodded in agreement. "You know, you two make a nice couple. Have you taken her out for a good dinner and dance or a movie?"

"Once in a while." I couldn't tell him she was really my boss, so I played along with the conversation. "But we can't do much on a seaman's pay. Dancing means buying drinks. That gets expensive."

The bartender nodded. "Yeah. But movies aren't too bad. And there are a couple good ones out now. Try 'Guns of Navarone.' That's my all time-favorite flick."

"She doesn't like war movies. And I see them on the ship."

"Okay how about a good Italian shitkickers."

I nodded. "Yeah, I like them, too. But she goes for the softer ones. She really likes Paul Newman."

Blink sipped his coffee. "There are some other good movies out there. Maybe they aren't Newman flicks, but she ought to enjoy them." We talked until Rena came over.

"Ready to go, Eric?"

"Hey!" Blink grinned. "I was saying that he should take you to see 'Breakfast at Tiffany's' or 'West Side Story.'" He put on a fatherly look. "And if you guys are strapped for dough, come in here, if you don't mind eating where you work. Just let me know. I'll save that corner booth for you. It's out of the way. You're a good enough worker, I'll give you a meal on the house."

"Thanks, Blink!" Rena said, smiling. She took my arm and tugged. "Let's go home, Eric. I'm tired."

"Go on! Get out of here!" Blink smiled, motioning toward the door.

Rena handed me the car keys. We got in and I started driving to her apartment.

"All right, what's so mysterious you can't tell me whether everything's okay or not?"

"Eric," she started. "We have a problem."

My heart skipped a beat. Was she talking about the two of us? The OCI team? I looked at her and saw the streetlights illuminating tears on her cheeks.

I started to pull over. "What's wrong, Rena?"

She swallowed hard. "Keep going." She took a deep breath. "We lost people."

I knew what that meant right away. "Who? How?"

"The pushers gave a user pure dope, and he OD'd."

"That's happened a couple times around here. Why are you so upset about this one?"

"We set him up to identify his supplier. We wanted the supplier to turn state's evidence. But they got into his apartment and forced an overdose on him, too."

"Their own street man?"

"Yeah."

"They must've been very afraid of him squealing."

"I guess so."

I reached over, put my arm around Rena and pulled her close. "This really shook you up, didn't it?"

"Yeah," she whispered. "I feel like we were the ones who killed him." She laid her head on my shoulder. I felt her sobbing. I held her firmly, comfortingly.

I pulled into her driveway. We sat for a while so she could compose herself. Finally, she dried her eyes with a handkerchief. Once inside, she was ready for business again. "How about you? Anything new?"

"Well, this isn't new...." I pulled her close and kissed her. "Mmmm, you feel good."

"You too," she murmured, resting her head on my chest. But then she tensed up and pushed herself away. "I'd love to continue. But I was asking about work."

"Why do you do that?" I asked.

"What?"

"Get real close, then go cold like that, all business and nothing else."

"Eric, I don't know how close I can get. Not yet."

"Why? Fraternization? You're the boss and I'm...?"

"No! Really, I could handle that."

"Then what is it?"

She swallowed hard. "I should have told you a long time ago." She paused. "Eric, I... I'm married."

I was stunned. I wanted to shout at her but nothing came out.

"I'm so sorry, Eric," she continued. "But it's not as big a thing as it sounds."

I finally found my voice. "Not such a big thing?"

"When I got assigned here, I was getting a divorce. As soon as I get back to California, I'll finish it." She reached up and placed a hand on my cheek. "If this wasn't in the way...." She took a deep breath. "Stick with me, please. Sooner or later...."

I didn't know what to do or say. I nodded, pulled her to me and kissed her forehead. "Okay. Now, about work...."

She took a deep breath. "Yeah."

"I've been trying to follow Reston on his liberty jaunts. I think he meets his supplier in an abandoned warehouse area. But I can't follow him too closely or he'd see me. I sure don't want to go there every day and wait. I can see myself sitting all alone, day after day."

"Poor dear." She tilted her head and smiled.

"Thanks. I could borrow your car...."

"We don't know what days you'd need it and I have to keep it handy for my work. Isn't there another way?"

"I don't know. When I see him leave, I need to reach the warehouses before he does so I can watch what happens. I'd have to move fast. I'll have to think of something."

We watched TV. I was getting ready to return to the ship when the phone rang. Rena answered it.

"Here.... Hi, Ruth...." I knew Rena well enough to hear the alarm in her voice. "Is everything all right?" She listened for a moment then motioned for me to listen. She held the phone so we could both hear.

"I want out." Gardner said in a very shaky voice.

"What do you mean?" Skye asked.

"I quit. I don't want to do this any more."

"Oh?" Rena had a hard time keeping calm. "Why not?"

"I just heard that Shirley Card's boyfriend was killed," Ruth sobbed. "And that his supplier was also killed by an overdose. And... it's... it's all my fault! I'm a corpsman! I'm supposed to save lives, not kill people! I want out!"

30. A RIDE IN THE NIGHT

"Snap out of it!" Skye ordered. "Right now! This shook me up, too. But either we do our jobs or let them get away with murder. And they'd kill a lot more people."

"I can't," Gardner whispered.

Rena thought for a moment. "Gardner?"

"Yeah?"

"I cannot accept your resignation over the phone. You'll have to go through the chain of command."

"What?"

"Find Jennie Powers. Tell your immediate superior that you want out. Got that?"

"Yes, ma'am."

Rena didn't wait for Ruth to hang up. She was grinning like the Cheshire cat from *Alice in Wonderland*.

"You're downright cold!" I said.

"What could I do from here? If she wants to quit, she can tell Powers herself." Rena smiled. "When Jennie hears this, she's going to chew Gardner up into little chunks and spit out the pieces!"

She stood staring at the phone for quite a while. She reached up and began twisting her hair around her finger.

"Rena is there something else wrong?"

"Eric, tell me the truth about something, will you?"

"Sure, if I can."

She looked me in the eye. "How did you really get those scars on your cheek?"

I tried to change the subject. "God, you're cute!"

"Eric, stop that! Tell me!"

"No." My heart was pounding. I was afraid if I told her the whole story

I would be accused of getting too emotional about my work—my overriding passion to track down and punish drug dealers. How I got my scars might psychologically disqualify me from this job. And I didn't want that at all. "No, I won't tell you. Not now."

"Eric, I'm your superior on this case. Tell me now!"

Why did every pretty woman think she could demand an answer for every question?

"Go to hell," I said and turned to leave.

Skye heaved a huge sigh. "Wait. I don't want to make an enemy out of you and it's a long walk or expensive cab trip. I'll drive you home."

"Thanks," I said. "And I hope it all works out with Gardner."

* * *

In the Wave barracks on Mainside, Powers spoke through clenched teeth. "You want to WHAT?" She jabbed a finger in Gardner's face. "You come with me."

They got into Powers' car, left the base and drove down Hampton Boulevard. Powers didn't say anything until they'd gone half a mile. "Okay, what's going on?"

"I want to quit."

"I heard that already, girl. Why?"

Gardner related her guilty feelings over the deaths.

Jennie responded: "Divven was an addict. He would've died anyway. But he tried to help us get that other guy, a belly-crawling, no-good, poisonous snake. Gaines deserved to die. An OD was too easy for him."

"But...."

"No buts! Look, lady, these guys did not die because of you. Divven died because he chose to help us. The other guy? No loss except we don't get to use him."

"Isn't that kind of harsh, Jennie?"

"Don't 'Jennie' me! I'm Powers, your senior. And you're right. That's harsh! What kind of joyride do you think we're on here? This isn't a pleasure cruise, girl."

"No shit. But I still want out."

Powers turned left onto Little Creek Road. "You can't get out. You're in the Navy. If we were at war, could you leave when it got uncomfortable?"

"No. But I'd be healing people. That's a hospital corpsman's job. I wouldn't be killing."

"Well, honey, you left that job to be part of OCI. Now we're at war. These drug-pushing low-lifes are killers. And we're on the side of the dead guys. That makes us at war." She drove on. "Besides, those deaths were not your fault."

"Yes they were!"

"Why not Divven's fault? He went along with the plan. Why not our other operatives? They persuaded him. Why not Rena Skye? She tried to get a pusher to turn state's evidence." Powers compressed her lips and shook her head. "No, you're a little sailor in a big war. And you've just been through your first battle, that's all."

They drove through the night. When Powers returned to the barracks, she turned off the engine and faced Gardner. She spoke calmly. "Now hear this! You cannot quit. Not until we're done. Go back to work. Do your job like a good sailor, no matter how easy or how hard. Now, get out of my car."

Gardner looked into Powers' glaring steely eyes. Powers' level voice, her cold tone, her complete lack of profanity, all telegraphed a single-minded seriousness.

Gardner was not going to get out of this.

"Yes, ma'am," she said groping for the door handle. She ran, crying, into the barracks.

Powers tried to calm her own shaky nerves. "God, that was hard!" she said in a trembling voice. "Almost like I was in a battle myself!"

31. ARRANGEMENTS

Skye ordered Gardner to meet her just west of Willoughby Bay, in the area where Ruth had first seen Shirley Card and Randall Divven. They would talk about wanting to quit. It was a setup. She sent Chaské Hunter to talk to Ruth. He was so smooth and "down home" that Skye believed he'd do Ruth more good than she could.

Hunter found Ruth standing on the grass near the water, staring at the ground. She subdued her sobs, but couldn't hide her tears. She didn't look up. After standing there for a few minutes, he asked softly, "Why so sad?"

Ruth shook her head.

His voice was low and comforting. "A woman back home cried for six months before she found out her dog wasn't dead. It ran away. Then she cried another six months 'cause the dog didn't like her any more. And she could've had a puppy from next door. But by then...."

"Oh, shut up," Gardner said. "I don't want to hear about anybody's stupid puppies."

"I guess not. Back home they tell me I'm a horseshit storyteller. I'll sit here and cry with you."

She halfway smiled.

"Well," Chaské said, "at least you're not a statue."

"What do you want?" she demanded.

"Nothin'. Just wondered why such a pretty woman was so sad. How can I help?"

Ruth lifted her head enough to see him. He had brown skin, a wide nose and jet-black crew-cut hair. "Where'd you come from?"

"I was just passin' by and saw you. I noticed your bright red hair first, before I saw the tears. And I'm a sucker for a weepin' woman."

"Sucker for a weeping woman, huh?"

"Sure! Why else would I be standin' here?"

Ruth shrugged. "Let me rephrase my question. Where's 'back home'?"

He looked around, scratched his head, and pointed to the west. "Somewhere that way. In South Dakota, Sioux country, my country. With us, if you like folks you tease 'em. And the more you like 'em, the more you tease." He paused. "Hmmm, I didn't know I liked you so much!"

Ruth laughed a little bit.

"That's better. Your green eyes look a lot nicer when you're smilin'. Want to go talk, have a cup of coffee? That's part of my culture, too."

"What is?"

"Offerin' a cup of coffee." He chuckled. "If you're at someone's home and they don't ask if you want some coffee, you better leave fast."

"But I don't even know you."

He looked around. "Well, all I can say is my mom would tell you that I wouldn't hurt a fly."

"Your mom, huh?" Ruth looked up in surprise. What would be the odds? She continued the sequence, "Uh... what would she say about living out in all that green prairie grass?"

"Maybe nothing. If you're there during the dry season, she'd take you out and show you the grass could be as brown as my dog's fur."

Ruth turned away from the water. "Let's go for coffee."

"By the way, my name's Chaské Hunter. Rena Skye asked me to check on you. Try to cheer you up."

"Why you?"

He shrugged. "Maybe she thinks I'm a good listener."

"Well, Chaské, I am looking forward to spending more time with you."

*　*　*

I watched the nightly movie, which was shown on the mess decks because we were at sea and waves were washing over the fantail. Then I sat there reading for a while. About an hour after taps I went back to the living quarters to hit the rack. Reston was standing still, leaning on his bunk. Just standing there. Staring into empty space.

I went over and whispered: "Hank, is something wrong?"

He didn't respond, except to turn his head. His eyes were glassy. He looked dazed. He mumbled something but was incoherent.

"Speak up!" I urged in a slightly louder voice. "What's the matter?"

"Shh. Quiet! Don' wake up...."

"What's the problem?"

"Tired. Need sleep. Help me... up."

What else could I do? I grabbed him under his armpits, lifted, and pushed him up into his rack. I was thankful that Reston slept in a middle bunk and not in a top one. Once in his rack, he laid there, eyes half open.

32. SECOND DATE

The *Hestek* came home for the Friday and Saturday of the Thanksgiving weekend. I wasn't getting very far with Rena, but I still liked spending time with her but I wouldn't be able to do that for another couple weeks. At least being with her was a good cover. Normality. Guy meets gal, and all that.

I had the duty Friday. I called Rena to tell her I'd be at Blinker's before closing on Saturday.

After work, we got into her Chevy, me driving. Rena asked, "So, how was your Thanksgiving?"

"It was great," I answered. She'd calmed down from the last time I saw her. "Big feed. Sure wish you could've been with me."

"Blink put out a banquet for us. Fed us all. The families, too. Must have cost a fortune, even if it was wholesale. They say he does this every year."

"Good. I'm glad you had a nice holiday."

"Yeah, it was great, except...."

"What?"

"You weren't there." She rested her arm on the back of the seat and put her hand on my shoulder.

Rena's mixed signals confused me. I drove without saying anything. She leaned back, eyes closed. "I really don't care," she said dreamily, "but where are we going?"

"Don't know. Let's go sit on the beach. I heard of a nice spot south of the city. Okay?"

"Sure, if it's not too cold."

Rena got a blanket from the trunk. We spread it out far enough from the surf to stay dry. I put my arm around her. She moved an inch or two closer and we watched the waves roll in. We were silent for a while. She looked over to me and said, "You're pretty quiet tonight. What's up?"

126

"Just thinking about something you said earlier."

"What?"

"You said Blink fed all of his employees and their families and he does it every year."

"That's what I heard."

"Every holiday, too? Christmas? New Year's? Easter?"

"All of them. Plus a huge picnic on July Fourth, with fireworks."

"The bar makes that much money?"

Rena laughed. "Everything works for him. He has customer loyalty. His eighty-cent lunches have two burgers so large you can't get your mouth around them, fries and two beers. In the evening he has a huge T-bone, baked potato, salad, all for a buck and a quarter.

"Everybody loves Blinker's. So they come in, eat and stay for the music. He hires good local bands for almost nothing. When the music starts, meals go up to four bucks and drinks to a buck fifty. That's for the simple mixed drinks. Liqueurs and special stuff run higher.

"Our wages are low, forty cents an hour. But the customers love us, so they tip a lot. You know, guys try to impress us. Or their lady friends. So we do all right even with lousy pay. Finally, Blink gets high school kids for the heavy cleanup and pays them better than the hamburger joints—and he feeds them, too. Even on dead nights, Nick Davenport banks nearly a grand. On Fridays and Saturdays he almost needs bodyguards. Yeah, he makes enough to pay for those feasts."

We sat for a while, before she continued. "I saw something odd the other day. I saw this local businessman on TV."

"He was odd?"

She slapped me on the arm. "Let me finish! His name's Frank Murphy. He owns Bogie's Club in Norfolk. Right after I got into town, he gave his church two hundred fifty thousand dollars for an orphanage."

"That's a lot of dough! So why did he make the news now?"

"Business was slow, so Blink put the news on. They showed the orphanage groundbreaking. I commented that Murphy must really be a wonderful man and that I'd heard folks called him 'The Saint'. Blink said 'Yeah, that's what they call him.' But I saw fear in his eyes."

"I wonder why?"

She shook her head without saying anything more. We watched the surf until she shivered. "It's getting chilly."

"Then, let's go."

We stood up. She reached up and gently touched the scars on my cheek. "You still won't tell me how that really happened?"

I shook my head and smiled. "Uh-uh. Family secret."

She pulled my face down and kissed me. "You are very considerate, Eric, but stubborn as hell. And I'd love to spend more time with you tonight. But I can't." She paused, looking down to her feet. She turned toward the car and said softly, "I'll drive you back."

I pulled her around to face me. "I was really hoping...."

She took my hands and held them. "I'm sorry. My divorce, remember? And I really do have some work to do."

I wondered just where I stood with this woman. "Oh, well," I said. "We're pulling out early. It's probably best if I get back now anyway."

"This job does keep the non-fraternization crap in place, doesn't it?" she said softly. She took my hand and turned to the car again. "Let's go before I forget about the regs. And the divorce."

I thought about that last comment for a week and finally concluded we might have something great as soon as she cleared up some stuff. That kept me going for a long time. What I didn't know was that Skye called for a copy of my medical records when she got home.

33. USER

We pulled out of Norfolk early Sunday morning. We were out of sight of land by noon. I loved to watch the ocean when we were at sea. That afternoon I sat on the fantail enjoying the sunshine. I'd meant to start Steinbeck's *East of Eden*, but laziness prevailed. Then running footsteps caught my attention. Davern, Messenger of the Watch, ran past me and dropped through a hatch into the compartment below.

I frowned. He was moving too fast to be just looking for someone. I followed him below, aft through the living quarters and into the steering gear room.

"Reston!" Davern was shouting. Hank sat in a corner of the after steering compartment. I recognized his stupor. I'd already seen him like this. "Hey Reston! Wake up!"

"Mmmmmmm?"

"What's the problem?" I asked.

"He's asleep. We couldn't reach him over the phones without alerting the OOD. So I came back here to wake him up. What the hell's the matter with him?"

"Nothin'... wrong... with me...."

"What did you tell the officers?" I asked, ignoring Reston for the moment. "You tell them where you were going so fast?"

"No. I said I needed a piss run and then I was gonna get coffee for the lookouts."

"Can you keep this quiet from them?"

"Only if we can get him to talk on the phones. He's gotta be ready to steer if necessary."

"I know." I thought for a moment. "How about if I take care of Reston. And the watch. Okay?"

Davern stared at me. "You sure? You qualified for this watch?"

"I'm sure I can take care of it. Go on."

"Well, I guess...."

"And, Davern...."

"Yeah?"

"Keep it quiet, even from the other guys up there, okay?"

"I hope you know what the hell you're doing."

"I do. Carry on."

Uh-oh. I screwed that up. Davern looked at me oddly. "That's a strange thing for a seaman to say. Sounds more like an officer."

I tried to laugh it off. "That did come out kind of weird, didn't it? Go ahead. I'll cover this."

He left, but hesitantly.

"What... you going to do..., Eric?" Reston mumbled.

I unsnapped the sound-powered phones' breastplate from his neck. I placed the headphones over my ears and snapped the straps on. "I'm taking your watch."

"Why?"

"Let's talk about that another time. Right now, I'm trying to save your sorry ass from a court martial."

"Thanks... for nothing...."

"Bridge, after steering," I spoke into the phones. "We're under control back here. No need to raise any flags."

There was no response. Finally the bridge talker replied, "Sorry for the delay. The OOD was looking right at me. I heard and understand. No flags."

"Thanks. I owe you guys one."

I sat there, watching Reston adrift in his private dream world. I liked him a lot. He had a sense of humor, a sense of loyalty all his own, and a sense of duty when he wasn't high. My own senses of duty and of helping others, namely this screwed-up kid, were in conflict. All I could do right now was cover for him. But I had work to do. Nice was not part of my job description. I had to prove he was an addict, find his supplier and then arrest him. There was no middle ground. It was my only reason for being on this ship. *Reston*, I thought. *What can I do with you? I really want to help you. But you're not making it very easy. Don't push this too far or I won't have a choice. If I'm in this kind of a bind too often, I'll have to take you in.*

34. HELPING OTHERS

The *Hestek* moved into position a thousand yards behind the *Valcour Bay*. A carrier always has a destroyer behind it when it launches or lands planes. Other ships are around it too, and the bird farm itself puts helos in the air. All in case a plane crashes. Splashed aircraft sink in minutes, usually taking their aircrews with them. These ships and helos improve their chances.

Some of us sat around "shooting the shit." Suddenly the *Hestek* sped up and heeled over like she was heading out for a rescue, but she quickly returned to position.

"Wonder what that was all about?"

"Be right back." Shepherd took off. He returned quickly. "After lookout said a helo crashed. One man was unhurt, one suffered face cuts, and one was killed."

"Where are they now?"

"They're in the drink with their life jackets. The two survivors are holding up the dead guy so they can send him home. Another helo is picking them up."

We tried to see whatever we could. I watched through my small "New York" telescope as the Air Ops Guard pulled the crashed helo crew out of the water.

After it ended, we settled down in the gun tubs again.

"Well," Shep began.

"That's a deep subject," Reston grumbled, taking a drag from his cigarette.

"What is?"

"Wells."

131

"What the hell are you talking about?"

"You said 'Well' and I said 'That's a deep subject.'" The seaman snapped. "Can't you understand a simple joke?"

Shep snorted. "Twenty thousand comedians out of work and you're telling stupid jokes like that."

"Get bent, man." Reston looked into the sky. He closed his eyes, took a deep breath, let it out slowly, and put his hands over his eyes. Moments later, he moved his hands down, trying to hide the tears that he was wiping away. Not knowing what his problem was, I wasn't about to ask in front of everyone. Shepherd continued.

"As I started to say, that's one of the main jobs of a destroyer."

"What is?" I asked.

"Saving lives."

"We didn't save any lives tonight," Reston growled.

Shepherd heaved a huge sigh. "But we were there to try. I can't help it if the Air Ops Guard beat us to the rescue. Anyway, I was reminded about that tin can in the Red Sea or Persian Gulf when we were in the Med."

"Gulf," Reston barked.

Shepherd looked at the seaman, frowned, and shrugged. "Anyway, they went into a port with a really narrow, winding channel. The safe speed was under five knots. The folks there were so glad to see the visitors that they had a big beach party for them. Then, just before liberty call, radio central received a mayday. A British merchantman was on fire and D-I-W."

"D-I-W?" I asked.

"Dead-in-the-water. That tin can put out to sea doing twenty knots through that channel. She passed three English destroyers on the way to the burning ship. But the fire was too hot to go alongside. So they pulled guys out of the shark-infested waters, gave them first aid and food and drink. After the heat died down a damage control party boarded the merchantman and put out the fire.

"Helping people. Saving lives. That's our job as much as fighting."

"Yeah," Reston mumbled. "Tell them the rest of it."

"The British ships arrived and took over 'cause it was one of their merchantmen. They took their people aboard and began to tow the burned out hulk. They secured the towline wrong and the merchant sank. It was all for nothing. Except the U.S. Navy had saved the English sailors."

* * *

Back in Norfolk, Skye met with Jennie Powers and Ruth Gardner over dinner.

"Ruth, can you handle talking about these men, now?"

Gardner nodded.

"The user is dead and so is the guy we were certain would turn state's witness."

"They must have been just as sure or they wouldn't have killed their own guy."

"So what do we do now?"

The discussion lasted considerably longer than dinner. They couldn't decide on anything, but Ruth promised to think of something.

*　*　*

That night I sat on the main deck watching the water slide past as I often did when thinking. The plankton in the wake sparkled, seemingly trying to outdo the stars in the sky above. On board a ship, the crew is your family. At least that's the way it's supposed to be. For me, the crew was made up of suspects. Even as close as Reston and I were, I knew that some day I'd have to arrest him. Even if I could get him off the junk and save him.

I was alone. Except for my feelings for the one person I felt close to in this OCI life, Rena Skye. I thought often about her and dreamed of being able to get closer to her. But when would she let me?

35. PORPOISES AND CHIMPANZEES

We returned to Norfolk long enough to resupply and refuel. We got some liberty for the married guys, but we were only in port for a week. Then we went back out to sea. A lot of ships left Norfolk together. We went way out into the Atlantic. The Plan of the Day said something about a Project Mercury space shot, but few of us knew any details.

The next day Reston grabbed me. "Look! Porpoises!"

Gray fins bobbed in and out of the water. I played ignorant. "Those aren't sharks?"

"Nah. These guys come above the surface then arc downward and dive. What they're doing is this." He moved his upright hand in an undulating motion. "Sharks cut straight through the water. Porpoises are mammals and they have to surface to breathe."

"They're keeping up with the ship! We're not going slow, either."

"That's nothing. Sometimes you can see them just in front of the bow. Like they're playing tag with us."

The swimming pattern changed. "What now? They disappeared!"

"Over to the other side!" He had me running back and forth across the ship in order to watch the porpoises play, diving under the ship and coming up on the opposite side, like we were their toy.

"I wonder how friendly they are," I said, still playing ignorant.

"Very. Sometimes they keep humans afloat so they can breathe. Even if the people are unconscious. They save lives, Eric. And they try to kill sharks. And when they're in danger they stick together and help each other." He put his hand on my arm. "Know what I mean?" Pain showed in his eyes when he mentioned saving lives and pleading showed when he spoke about helping each other. He was obviously begging me to help him. I wondered how I could save his life.

The Plan of the Day was right. We were in the mid-Atlantic for a

Mercury launch. Another historical date: 29 November 1961. NASA was sending Enos, a chimpanzee, into orbit to measure how space flight affected primates. This was the U.S.'s first orbital flight. A number of ships lined up along the trajectory of the space shot. On station, each ship hove to and waited.

There were some delays but they finally got the chimpanzee up. The bitch box announced: CAPE CANAVERAL REPORTS LIFT OFF! ENOS IS ON HIS WAY!

The crew waited. "Wouldn't it be great if we picked up that chimp?"

"Yeah. I hear we're close to the splash down spot."

"Hey! I thought this was gonna be a short trip. When the hell is that monkey gonna come down?"

"He's supposed to do three orbits around the earth. Hurry up and wait."

We waited. We watched, hoping to be the first to catch sight of the space capsule. It developed problems and they brought Enos down after only two orbits.

Finally the bitch box announced: SPLASH DOWN! THE MERCURY CAPSULE HAS LANDED JUST A FEW MILES AWAY ... FROM THE NEXT SHIP.

"Shit!"

"I didn't want to mess with no fuckin' chimpanzee, anyway."

"Well, I'm disappointed."

The chimp had flown for 181 minutes and it took almost another hour and a half to pull him out of the Atlantic.

Hearing the comments of my shipmates, I thought, Yeah. Sometimes your best-laid plans just don't work out. Hurry up and wait.

* * *

I dragged myself out of my rack to stand my 04-0800 watch. I was leaving when Le Blanc came down the ladder. I hadn't even noticed he wasn't in his rack.

"You have the mid?" I asked him.

"Yeah. I took starboard lookout for Burch."

"You're off watch already?"

"Got relieved early."

When I talked to Burch's relief, he told me he'd relieved Burch himself. On time. Le Blanc was nowhere around.

Why would Le Blanc lie? Maybe he wasn't sleeping twelve hours a night after all. I had to find out.

36. OTHER MYSTERIES

We pulled into Norfolk for a few days. Periodically I hit the beach with crewmembers. It would really seem strange if I never spent off-hours time with others on the ship. Also, I had to know these guys, evaluate them, understand their habits and their dreams.

Shepherd, Rob Roy Davern, Toby Burch and I returned from liberty. They hit the rack. I went to the port side of the ship to think. It was about 2330. As I stepped out onto the deck, I noticed the paint locker door closing. Other than Chief Gascomb, only Monnyng had a key to the place. My curiosity got the best of me. I invited myself in.

Monnyng was sitting on the floor. He slammed his metal box shut when I opened the door, but I saw some magazines and a couple decent sized bottles before the lid closed.

"Hi, Joe. What's going on?"

"None of your business."

"I saw you coming in. Thought I'd visit." I pointed to his metal box. "There's no taboo magazines among the crew. Why are you hiding those?"

"That's my business."

"It looked like dancers on the cover of the top one."

Monnyng chewed on his bottom lip a while before he flipped the top open again. "You've never given me any reason not to trust you, Matthews. Please don't now."

His treasures were a few ballet magazines and some high-priced classical phonographs from the Musical Heritage Society. The records were all ballets, including Swan Lake and The Nutcracker. "I like classical music," I said. "Even been to some ballets. I love Swan Lake. Why hide your music and magazines?"

"I got tired of being called names, queer and stuff, just because I like ballet."

"They taunted you so bad you had to hide your music?"

"They get on you for anything that's different."

"What got you interested in ballet?"

"I don't know. I was real young. I took lessons for ten years until I broke my ankle and it didn't heal well enough to continue."

"That's when you joined the Navy?"

"Soon after."

"Where'd you study?"

"In my home town, Philadelphia."

"How old were you when you started?"

"Six."

"Wow, that's young! As for your secrecy, I'd probably do the same thing. Who else knows about your love of ballet?"

"A couple guys. Shep and Zoss but they're cool. No problem. And Smith knows."

Ah! Our divisional asshole!

"You drink a lot?"

"Hardly touch the stuff."

I pointed at the two quart bottles that were also in the box. "Smith's?"

Monnyng nodded.

"What's in them?"

"Vodka. Big bang. No smell."

"He hasn't teased you publicly about your ballet? I find that hard to believe."

"One time, he pushed so far with the queer thing, I nearly broke down. I asked how I could get him to quit. He started to say 'No way.' Then he came up with this. I store his booze, fill his flasks and he has all he needs in port and at sea. I've done everything he wants and he's kept his mouth shut. So far."

"So Smith is as anti-homosexual as he sounds...."

"Worse. He's a dedicated queer basher. Least little hint and he's all over you, unless he can use you."

"Has he treated anyone else this way?"

"Reston had a friend, Cory Palm. They were real close, like brothers. Smith teased them mercilessly, calling them queer, homo, boyfriends."

"Were they?" I asked.

Monnyng shrugged. "I don't think so. They were really close. Went everywhere and did everything together. Then Palm got hurt and was highlined off the ship. Ever since, Reston doesn't go ashore for long. Never over night."

I stood thinking for a long time.

Monnyng motioned to the box. "You won't tell anyone, will you Eric?"

"No. And I despise guys like Smith. We should be able to get him off your ass. Let me think about it. Maybe I can come up with something. And, Joe, don't let his bullying get to you."

37. NEW PLANS

We pulled into Bermuda to refuel. This harbor looks open, but the channel winds through numerous reefs. It seemed like the ship had to circle the islands to reach the Navy base across the bay from Hamilton, the main town.

The crew got no liberty. Reston and I watched the Captain leave to pay his respects to the base commander. A driver stationed in Bermuda picked him up.

"Now, that's some sweet duty," Reston said. "Sit around and wait to drive some officer someplace."

"I agree. I hate all the watch standing. And I hate the standing more than the watches. We're always standing while at sea."

"Not me. I'm in after steering. I take a book, sit, read, and answer whoever calls me on the phones."

"Okay, wise-ass. Most of us stand on our watches," I grinned. "And we stand the whole time on Quarterdeck watches. My feet start hurting half-way through a watch."

"You have a driver's license?"

"Yeah?"

"Request duty as a driver."

"How?"

Reston shrugged. "Get a Navy driver's license. And you have to have a civilian driver's license to get one."

"So, I'm half way there."

Reston held out his left hand, palm up, and jabbed his right index finger on it, like he was going down a checklist. "Get the Navy driving test requirements from the ship's office. See what to do. Go take the damned test."

"That easy, huh?"

"That easy," he nodded.

We stayed in port for three hours. When we refueled and the Captain returned, we cast loose and left port.

I sat on the fantail, watching the water glide by, thinking. The last few days had triggered some conflicting thoughts. A Navy driver's license would help wrap up my end of this case. But the completion of those duties was incompatible with other things. "Helping others" and "doing my duty" chased each other around inside my head. I wasn't sure what to do. So I sat and flowed with the ship as it cut through the ocean.

* * *

Ruth Gardner walked along Willoughby Bay, where she'd watched Shirley Card meet Randy Divven. She was still looking for a way to make up for the deaths of Divven and Chuck Gaines.

She finally decided to do what had been going through her head for days.

38. SSN TRACKING

NOW, SET THE ASW ATTACK TEAM. SET THE ASW ATTACK TEAM.

We were running anti-submarine exercises. The sonarmen were excited. They'd soon be tracking one of the Navy's newest subs. I settled in to keep up the bridge's ASW Status Board.

"Matthews, you there?"

"Yeah. Who's this?"

"Zephyr, down in sonar."

"What's up?"

"That's some real hot sub out there. It's gonna be fun," he snickered. "Yep, just tracking a submerged sub. Watch the folks up there when you give your reports. Let me know what kind of reactions you see."

"Okay."

The first report came in. "Sir! Sonar reports contact zero-six-zero relative, seven thousand and closing."

"Very well."

We got another report in thirty seconds. "Bridge, Sonar. Contact zero-five-seven, range six-six-zero-zero."

"Have them check that," the OOD ordered. "It's too far from the previous position."

Captain Lorman looked up, but only smiled.

"Aye, aye, sir," I replied. "Sonar, Bridge. OOD says to check your information."

"Sonar, aye." Some seconds passed. Then they reported, "Bridge, Sonar. Contact bearing zero-five-four, range six-two-zero-zero."

There was dead silence on the bridge. The sub moved so fast that the JOOD grabbed a protractor and a pair of calipers on the quartermaster's table to lay out its track. He gasped. "It's doing fifty knots! Underwater!"

"That's correct, Mister Castle," The Captain said. "It's supposed to go exactly fifty knots."

"How can it go that fast, Captain?"

"It's our newest type of fast attack nuclear boat."

"That's almost twice as fast as our flank speed!"

The sub made six runs from six different angles, so sonarmen on all the ships could track it. I could now do my duties automatically, and I did a lot of thinking about my own situation. Like with the *Enterprise*, this submarine consistently outran us. My analogy still held true. My assignment was like our old destroyer. It moved agonizingly slow. All I'd discovered was that heroin was on this vessel. I knew of one user, but no supplier. And just like the *Hestek* tracking this sub, I could only go as fast as I was able. No faster. It was exasperating as hell.

The exercises took four hours. When we returned to our regular duties, my feet hurt. A lot.

"I don't know, Hank," I later said to Reston. "I'm really getting tired of all this standing."

"Well, when you get enough time as a seaman, you can always go up for third class. Or...."

"What?"

" Remember that driver in Bermuda? Get a Navy driver's license and get on the watch bill as a duty driver."

"I like that idea more every day. At least I won't have to be on my feet in port."

"Right on the mark, my man! Right on!"

39. SEAGULLS AND STUFF

The *Hestek* was south of the Vacapes operating area again. Raynes, Reston and I were watching the ocean go by. The ever-present seagulls soared through the air in their turning, diving search for food. The only time I didn't see these birds was during bad weather. I had no idea where they went then. I don't think anyone knew. Or cared. But the gulls always reappeared with decent weather.

Reston had been pensive all day. I felt that he had something to say but Raynes was with us. Then Derella came over.

"Watch this!" He looked up to the circling gulls. "Hey! You guys hungry?"

He held half a loaf of bread in one hand and threw small chunks into the air. A great cloud of gulls soon gathered. They gobbled up the bread that fell into the water. Soon they caught the pieces in mid air.

"Derella, you got those guys trained pretty well."

"Yeah. Now, watch this." He pulled a bottle of Tabasco from his pocket. He doused a piece of bread before he threw it up. One of the gulls made a perfect catch. Within seconds it screeched and dove directly into the water. Derella doubled up, laughing. "You ever see anything so funny? Watch, they never learn!"

He soaked another piece and fed a different gull, with the same results. Roaring with laughter, he continued his diversion.

"Come on, Derella, quit!" I demanded.

"Why? This is hilarious!"

"You're torturing them," Reston shouted. "It's downright mean. Stop it!"

"Who the fuck's gonna make me?"

"They're God's creatures," Raynes shouted. "You have no right to do this!"

Derella pushed him. "Get the fuck away from me, you religious nut! If your God doesn't want me doing this, He can stop me. Until then, get the fuck outa here!"

Raynes backed up, his eyes a kaleidoscope of emotions: fear, pain, irritation, anger, hatred. Preacher stood immobile for long moments before moving to the other side of the ship.

"Shit, let's get out of here," Reston suggested.

"Wait a minute." I walked over to Raynes. "Luke, are you all right?"

The man nodded, wiping at a water-filled eye.

"You sure?"

"Yes. Bless you for caring enough to ask. You're a good man, Eric. Why won't you let Jesus save you?"

"Like I said before, I follow my own path."

"Well, thanks for your concern. Go on with Reston."

"Okay, Luke, just don't let that guy get to you." Reston and I moved up to the 01 level near Mount 33. Cisco was up there reading, so we moved aft of Mount 34.

"Hank, what's with Cisco," I asked quietly. "Half the time, he's watching us. He's always reading. Big thick books. What's with him?"

Reston shrugged. "Dunno. He's always been that way. We've nicknamed him 'Professor' because of those books. He says he wants to leave the Navy one of these days and go to college."

"How long's he been in?"

"Sixteen years, maybe. He's always watching folks. And he does it in a way that makes you believe he's trying to figure it all out."

"Figure what all out?"

"Everything. People. Life. Nothing's ever come of it that I can think of. Maybe he's going to write a book."

We sat on the deck without talking for a full five minutes. "Eric," Reston started. A moment later he continued quietly. "Eric, why are you protecting me?"

I looked up, surprised. This was the first time he said anything related to his habit. "What do you mean?"

"You covered for me in after steering. You've seen me out of it and never reported me."

"I'm sure other guys have seen you out of it, too. And they never reported you."

"I don't think they've really seen me that often. Why didn't you report me?"

"Maybe I've been there."

He stared at me. "Bullshit. If you'd been through this, how'd you ever get in the Navy?"

"It was Sean, my brother. Not me. He was addicted to heroin. I stood

144

by him. I know what it's like to go through it. I've seen it with him."

"That what were you talking about up on the 03 level? When you said something about having such a rush?"

I stared straight ahead and replied almost inaudibly. "Sean persuaded me to try it. It was nice. But I liked it too much. I was so afraid I'd get hooked, I never used it again. And I don't drink much either. Same reason. I tried to take care of my brother, until he could take care of himself." I rubbed the scars on my right cheek. "But it never happened."

Reston nodded. The silence returned, but didn't hang over us quite so heavily.

40. INFORMANT AND UNANSWERED QUESTIONS

In the Wave barracks in Norfolk, Ruth Gardner's stomach churned with nervousness. She forced herself to approach the other Wave. She believed she'd caused the deaths of two people and needed to redeem herself. "Shirley Card?"

"Yeah?"

"I, uh, I heard about your boyfriend. Please accept my condolences."

Card looked at Gardner like she was crazy. "Who are you? How'd you know Randy died? Why should you offer me condolences?"

Gardner didn't want to talk there. The walls had ears. "Let's go to the gedunk, get a cherry coke or something."

"I want to know who you are before I go anywhere with you."

"My name is Ruth Gardner. Here's my Navy ID. Come with me and I'll tell you everything. I think we need each other."

"I'll get my coat. We get to the curb, you give me a better reason to go further."

When Shirley returned they stepped into the cool evening air. At the street, Card faced Gardner. "Well?"

Ruth swallowed hard. "This is against every regulation in the book. I can get into a shitload of trouble. But I want to make up for something I did." She stopped and took a deep breath. The other woman waited, looking at her uncertainly. "My name is Ruth Gardner. I'm a special agent working with OCI, the Office of...."

"Okay, I'll go with you." They walked away from the barracks. "Randy was being investigated, wasn't he?"

"Yes. Did you know he was using heroin?"

"I suspected. God, I loved that guy." She choked up for a moment, but quickly composed herself. "I called the Legal Office and talked to an officer there. I never mentioned Randy. I told Legal who I was and that I thought

146

my boy friend was using drugs. They asked what made me think that. I chickened out and hung up."

Gardner nodded. "That's how we got your name. I was sent to find out who your guy was."

"And you did...." She stopped under a streetlight and faced Ruth with tears in her eyes. "That's why he's dead."

"Lets go to the gedunk and talk."

"No! I don't want any drinks or ice cream or music or anything! I want to know what happened."

"I did identify him. He made a deal with Legal. He identified his supplier. We wanted that guy, the dealer, to be a witness for us."

"What went wrong?"

"We don't know. Somebody found out. It seems the drug lords deliberately gave your guy pure heroin so he'd overdose. They also killed his supplier so he wouldn't talk."

Shirley was silent for a moment, lip quivering. "Randy wanted to straighten out?"

Ruth nodded. "He must have loved you a lot, 'cause he was willing to make some real sacrifices."

"Thanks for telling me," Card whispered, wiping away tears.

"Now I hope you can help us get his killers."

She shrugged her shoulders. "How can I do that?"

"When Randy was using, was he ever with anyone else?"

Card thought for a moment, then nodded. "Sometimes."

"Who were they?"

"No! Don't kill any more of them!" She began to walk away.

"Shirley, wait! We've already changed our procedures. We have orders now not to make any more deals until...."

"Then they're all going to...?"

"Listen! Please! No more deals until we identify everyone and pull them all in. Only when we have the whole bunch, then we'll make deals to convict the top dogs. Until then, we'll only follow them to find out where they get their drugs." Gardner took a deep breath and looked up to the stars. "I want to get those guys, but I want to get them right, without anyone else dying."

Shirley slowly walked away. Ruth sensed she was trying to decide what to do. They walked silently for perhaps ten minutes. "You have something to write with?"

"Don't need it."

Card smiled. "That's good. No paper to be found."

"Right."

"Tom Dineen, AN, Roy Peale, AT3. Those were the friends he shared with. Both of them are at NAS."

"Thomas Dineen, Airman?" Gardner repeated. The informer nodded. "And Roy Peale, third class Aviation Electronics Technician." Card nodded again. "Thanks, Shirley."

The other woman looked at Gardner with pleading eyes. "Don't let them die. Deep down inside, they're good guys."

"I know. Most of them are. Good guys that made a wrong turn. That's what's been haunting me about Randy's death."

* * *

The *Hestek* came into Norfolk and tied up at the D & S Piers. But I had duty so I couldn't go ashore. I went to get some extra sleep before my 04-0800 watch. I noticed Le Blanc wasn't in his rack, which surprised me. Then I remembered he was on watch now.

Zoss was sitting on the locker tops reading his mail for the umpteenth time.

"Stephen, do you have family in Norfolk?"

He nodded. "Yeah, kind of. A fiancée. I'd like to share Christmas with her, but we'll be out. Not being with loved ones is the worst part of the Navy."

"I know what you mean." I paused. "Can I ask you a personal question?"

"Sure."

"Do you preach on the street corner, too? Like Raynes?"

"No. I feel there's something wrong with that. Seems like those folks are only trying to persuade themselves. That's no basis for faith. I often—shouldn't, but often do—question their sincerity. And I wonder what they're trying to cover up by insisting belief and faith absolve them of everything."

"So you believe more in deeds for salvation?"

"About fifty-fifty. I know all the stories. Jesus worked with both. But somehow I don't see Raynes in those stories. Not anywhere."

"Isn't it wrong, talking about him behind his back?"

Zoss smiled. "Yeah, I guess it is. Aren't we all sinners? That's why I need Jesus."

I hit the rack but woke up at 0215. Le Blanc still wasn't in his rack. I wondered where he was. I lay there trying to go to sleep again, but I couldn't.

So I thought about the case. Smith was a boozer. Monnyng had explained his locked steel box. The others, though? It was hard to say. Anyone could be doing illegal stuff. I had to find out. Even quiet, introspective Cisco could be hiding something. I didn't believe rebellious Toby Burch was disciplined enough to deal drugs and he never exhibited any symptoms of a user. I couldn't see lazy Brian Grengs doing anything illegal. He got too much attention being gross. Charlie Wu was almost too quiet and I watched him. Jax Jackson was quiet and hard working until someone used his given name, Clement. Then he drew a lot of attention to himself. To me, Raynes was a religious weirdo and I only wanted to stay away from him. Derella ran a slush fund network on a number of ships, but I believed he only dealt in money. I had no idea why Le Blanc slept so much. Reston definitely used but I hadn't found his supplier. Yet.

My mind wandered to Rena. This time it had nothing to do with romance. I wondered if she and others might be in danger after the botched Randy Divven affair. The drug bosses murdered him and Charles Gaines, but what of our agents? Who were the gang's leaders? What did they know? That really bothered me, now that I thought of it. How much did the criminals know about us?

41. WINDJAMMER

Two days later I applied for my Navy driver's license. It had become necessary for my work. I barely passed the Navy driver's test. It was tougher than the test for a civilian license. But I made it. I requested Duty Driver status instead of quarterdeck watchstander. The Navy, in all its wisdom, let me do both. If driving interfered with a Quarterdeck watch, a standby would be found for the watch.

The day after that was a lazy day. I finished my deck work early and showered up. I worked crossword puzzles for a while then watched Cary Grant and Tony Curtis in "Operation Petticoat." After the movie, I stepped out onto the main deck. When the cold hit me, I stopped to zip up my work jacket. Derella was nearby, talking to a guy on the *Kendrick*. He was counting money.

"Okay, Paulson, it's all here," He said.

Derella noticed me and stuffed the money into a pocket. I didn't look up as I passed him, but I didn't hurry either. He said nothing more until he thought I couldn't hear him.

"Like I said, it's all here. Thanks."

"Glad to do business with you."

I took a few more steps, turned, and leaned against the lifelines. I watched the two men out of the corner of my eye.

"Yeah, me too," Derella replied. He noticed me stop. "I'll catch ya next payday." He walked over to me. "Hey, shithead, I told ya to stop fuckin' with me."

"Can't I even stand here and enjoy the night air?"

"Not when I'm nearby. And you know what the fuck I'm talking about, asshole. When ya see me, start headin' the other fuckin' direction."

"Yeah, sure." I turned and slowly walked away.

On Saturday evening, Rena Skye went to the Windjammer, which was nicknamed the "Acey-Deucey Club" because it served only first and second class petty officers. She was going to meet Jennie Powers, who could be there because she was a second class Storekeeper. Undercover, but still.

Rena breathed a sigh of relief when nobody checked her ID. She wasn't supposed to get in without a senior petty officer accompanying her. She entered the main bar.

Two television sets, hanging from the ceiling at opposite ends of the room, competed for attention. One blared college football scores; the other blasted "Rawhide."

Skye looked around the room. Powers was in the most out-of-the-way booth. Rena sat down across from her. Jennie greeted quietly and lifted a glass. "Already have my drink."

"If they check, I'm your guest tonight. My ID says I'm an ensign." Rena motioned to the waitress.

Powers raised her eyebrows. "Isn't it against regs for an officer to even be in an enlisted club?"

Skye smiled. "They can remind me."

The server came over and asked Powers, "Another bourbon and water?"

"Not yet, thanks. What do you want, Rena?"

"Cuba libre, please."

The waitress nodded. "Coming right up!"

"So, what's new?" Powers asked.

"Wait until I get my drink. I don't want anything overheard."

Jennie nodded and sipped from her glass. When the new cocktail arrived, she opened with, "So what's up? New boyfriend?"

"How'd you find...?" Rena stopped in mid-sentence because of the amusement in her friend's eyes. "You're sneaky. What made you say that?"

"Remember how well I can read you, girl! You need a man, honey. It's been a long time, if I remember right."

"I'll ignore that part. I hope I'm not so transparent to the bad guys."

"They haven't been around you as long as I have. What's his name?"

"Archibald," Rena said.

"Come on, lady! You give yourself away. Who is it?" Jennie pressed. "You can tell your best friend!"

"Eric Matthews."

"Isn't he one of our operatives?" Skye nodded. "The tough lady officer is fraternizing?"

"We're the same rank. That's not fraternizing. Technically. Now end it! Please!"

"All right. For now. So what is the, uh, real problem?"

Skye shrugged her shoulders. "It doesn't seem like we're getting anywhere. And I don't know what to do now."

"Patience, girl. You knew this wouldn't be easy. We've been here about three months. For something this big, that's just enough time to get organized. Things will start hopping soon. Look at the bright side. Ruth did get the information on that guy at NAS. But the other one, Laura. She walks around like some kind of princess. Like everyone should wait on her. Uncommunicative. Watches everyone with an expression of disapproval. She gives me the heebie-jeebies"

"Who's she watching? You and Ruth?"

"It feels like she's looking down her nose at everyone. I don't know. I just get a weird feeling when she's around. She's a real arrogant one."

"Well, watch her. Watch Ruth, too, without getting in the way," Skye suggested. "She's young and inexperienced. You're her immediate supervisor. I gave her a big job to do and she did all right. But I'm not convinced she'll pull off every task as well."

"Why not get someone else?"

"Ruth's been on other investigations. She just hasn't been undercover before. It's time she got some experience with this kind of fieldwork. And she did get what we needed. Still, keep a close eye on her."

"How close? Am I her mother?"

"No. And you're not her baby sitter, either. But we can't jeopardize this investigation. Too many dead people. Remember the quinine, which gives users a greater-than-normal chance of dying. I really wanted to follow up on Card's lead. We need to find the dealers. We have to break them up and I want to nab the whole ring."

"Duly noted." Powers acknowledged. "Let me know when you make another assignment. I'll give her some extra attention."

They talked for another hour before going into the dining room, which would become the nightclub/dance hall when the band started. They sat to one side, out of the flow of traffic. A waiter appeared at their table. He was about five feet ten inches tall and had black hair, graying at the temples. He had a mixture of Negro and Latin American features: light brown skin, thin nose, full lips.

"Good evening ladies. My name is Tony Alvarez and I'll be your waiter tonight. Here's today's menu. Can I get you a drink?" They ordered what they'd had earlier. "Thank you. I'll be back shortly."

When he returned, they ordered dinner. They continued their conversation. Powers found it curious that Skye continued talking when the waiter made his periodic appearances.

"So, what's on the agenda for tonight?" Powers asked.

"As things stand, we go fishing. You know, a white girl and a colored girl out for a little fun. We can attract guys from either race. There are also other operatives in the crowd, here and at the Tradewinds."

"We have all angles covered, don't we?"

"I hope so."

"How about the O Club?"

Skye shook her head. "We don't know of any officer involvement. All the deaths were enlisteds. So I figured we'd go where the enlisteds go."

"Off-base clubs?"

"We can't cover them all. But I have six guys out there, four in white bars and two in Negro clubs."

By the time they finished eating, the room was filling up with people who came to dance. The women ended their shoptalk because they didn't want to raise their voices over the increased noise level.

The band set up. Their quality was evident as soon as they started playing. Their impressive repertoire ranged from popular to rock and roll to slow dance to jazz. As the women sat enjoying the music, two sailors asked them to dance.

After a few dances, the men joined them at their table. They talked, joked, and danced. Both women continued observing the crowd. Skye noticed a restless sailor nearby. He drummed on the table, the front of his chair, his knees, whatever he could reach, but he never kept time to the music. He reached into his inner jumper pocket and felt for something, reached down and checked around his ankles. He looked around the club like he was searching. He had trouble lighting a cigarette. He hugged himself with a look of pain on his face. He went through the same movements over and over.

"Another dance?" one of the sailors asked.

Skye sensed movement out of the corner of her eye. Glancing in that direction, she saw the door to the men's head closing. When she looked back, the restless sailor was up and moving toward the men's room.

"Let's skip this dance. I need a rest." Rena leaned back and stretched. She wiggled her fingers as if to work out some kinks in them. She caught the eye of a man in civilian clothes standing by the wall and nodded toward the men's room. He and another man in civvies entered the men's room. They loudly told cop stories while using the facilities.

Powers and Skye excused themselves and walked into the foyer. They stood so they could see the door to the men's head. Tony Alvarez, the waiter, sauntered to the front door. The restless sailor came out and returned to his table, more agitated than before. The plainclothesmen emerged in a few moments.

Another man in civvies soon exited. He immediately left the club. The women followed, but he'd parked close to the door and was already in his car. His tires screeched as he left the parking lot.

"Jennie, did you get the license plate number?"

"No. He was too fast. All I saw was a black '60 Ford Thunderbird with Virginia plates racing out of here."

Skye looked at Powers and shook her head. "So, all we have is circumstantial evidence."

42. COMBAT

"Nothing but circumstantial evidence," Jennie agreed. "So, what do we do now?"

Skye nodded to the entrance of the Acey-Deucey Club. "We go back. Keep our friends company a while longer. Maybe the guy at the other table will do something to give himself away."

They re-entered the building. Alvarez walked in behind them. He slipped a note into Skye's hand: "Va. 794-138." Skye smiled. Powers looked at the note in surprise, at the waiter's back and at her companion again.

Skye smiled. "Looks like we have some work for Central after all. We can identify him now."

When they returned to the table, one of the sailors asked, "Why'd you two go out there?"

"Girl stuff," Jennie answered, smiling sweetly. "But we came back, didn't we?"

"Yeah. Let's dance."

The song ended. When they returned to their table, the restless sailor was gone.

When Skye got home, she called Central to report the Thunderbird and its license number.

* * *

We'd been in port for a week and a half. The *Hestek* got underway on a Monday morning. My underway duties got changed. I was ecstatic. They put me in the Combat Information Center as a phone talker. I'd be able to sit down on watch.

Even so, the first time I showed up in CIC, I was apprehensive.

"Come in!" greeted a radarman striker. "You Matthews?" I nodded. I entered the dim room and looked around. Three radarmen were watching me, but one soon returned to his radar screen. An ensign, half asleep, sat at a far table.

"Shut the door. We need the darkness to see the stacks. Let me introduce us. My name's Grant Seales. This here's our glorious watch leader, Dan Hauser, RD2. Over there," he pointed to the man sitting in front of the upright box with a radar screen on top, "that's Buster Clark, RD3, on the stack." Clark looked up and waved.

"Okay, here's the deal," Hauser said. "We take turns on the stack and the phones, where Clark is now. We trade off every half hour, so nobody gets inattentive. At least they better not."

"But...."

"Uh-uh-uh, don't get your whatsis in an uproar. We'll teach you. Any questions whatever, ask. We got plenty of folks here who can answer." He looked at Seales and grinned. "Or some who can try. Sometimes even he has to ask. Oh, that's Mister Auburn. He's the ECM Officer, and the CIC Watch Officer in our duty section."

Auburn opened his eyes, gave half a wave and a warm smile, and closed his eyes again.

"What's ECM?" I asked.

"Ah, all the acronyms are new. ECM is electronic counter measures. That's the electronic garbage we throw at skunks and bogeys, if they don't talk nice to us. I do hope you know what skunks and bogeys are."

"Do I have to know about ECM to stand my watch?"

"Nope. But... come over here." Hauser pulled another tall stool up to the radar stack. "You will have to know what Buster's going to teach you now. Sit."

Clark looked up and grinned. "This is fun."

"What do you do?"

"First, learn how to sit on these stools. They tip over real easy. So, put your feet on the deck, or this railing around the bottom of the stack, and make a pyramid with your two legs and your ass on the stool.

"Okay. Look here." He pointed his grease pencil toward the radar screen. "This is the stack, also called a repeater 'cause we have a bunch of them repeating the radar display. The Old Haystack is always the middle of the screen, right where this sweep, this line of light here, is rotating from. When the radar 'sees' something out there, we get a blip on the screen."

"Yeah, I see our formation, kind of," I observed.

"'Kind of' is right. There's the carrier over there. But look carefully. How many destroyers do you see?"

"Five."

"And us in the middle makes six."

"I thought eight tin cans were around the bird farm."

"There are! See this white ring here, a little way out from the center?" I nodded. "That's sea return, a reflection off the ocean. The other two ships are in it, hidden. Here." He made a dot with his grease pencil on the glass screen. It showed up white. "And here. There's our formation."

I examined the screen, frowning.

"What's wrong?" Clark asked.

"Don't you have to watch really close? What if one of them gets out of position?"

"Give the man a see-gar!" Seales crowed. "He hit the bulls-eye on the first try!"

Hauser patted my back. "You'll do fine. That's the biggest danger in tight formations like this. Only plane guard is worse, when we're going maximum speed a thousand yards behind a carrier. That's very close when it comes to reaction times. And, if we have to pick up a downed flyer, we can get pretty close to other ships."

"All right," Clark continued. "One more thing. With any skunk or bogey, you have to let the bridge know its bearing and range. That's what these knobs are for." As he turned them, a thin non-rotating line moved around the screen from the center and a small bright dot ran in and out along that line. "See this blip here, the farthest tin can? I turn the bearing knob until that line runs right through the blip. The bearing shows up on these dials here. That one is relative and this one is true bearing. Report the true bearing. But if they ask you, you've got the relative. Okay, now...."

I pointed first to the range knob and then to the bearing line. "That bright dot gives you the range, doesn't it?"

"You done this before?"

"No, it just makes sense. When you moved the knobs around, I noticed the dot moving."

"Well, you've got it figured out. Here, tell me how far away that destroyer is," Clark invited.

I double-checked the bearing and moved the range marker out to the blip. "Four thousand yards."

"Right. We're all two thousand yards from the carrier, so the farthest can from us is the one straight on the other side of the *Valcour Bay*. Two thousand yards between each of us."

I settled quickly into the CIC routine. Everyone took turns watching the stack; nobody got so tired that they missed things.

Combat also had a number of speakers so we could hear voice communications from other ships. These were very busy during anti-submarine warfare exercises. A major job of destroyers is to sink submarines, so we constantly practiced our ASW techniques.

We often played games with subs. We made runs on them, coordinated by the sonarmen. Sometimes we'd fire a torpedo. Mostly we used hedgehogs, which fired a pattern of what amounted to super-sized underwater hand grenades. On the practices, of course, we used dummies, and a "hit" was scored if a unit hit the submarine with a dull thud.

One day another destroyer, recently modernized, used the fleet's newest ASW weapon. It was miles from the target when we heard the voice communication: "This is Turkey Trot. ASROC fired at the sub."

They scored a direct hit. A couple days later, that ship "sank" another sub from a greater distance.

"What the hell is ASROC?" Seales asked.

"Anti-Submarine Rocket," Hauser explained. "The rocket delivers a homing torpedo to the target area. It searches. Homes in on the sub. Boom! Gone!"

"I remember when we were tracking a nuclear boat going fifty or sixty knots, underwater," I said. "This ASROC can get one of those guys even if we can't make a run on it!"

"Oh, it gets better than that," Ensign Auburn woke up enough to point out. "ASROC can also carry a small nuclear depth charge. If that goes off within five miles of the sub, crunch! It's like crushing a milk carton."

I smiled inside myself. When we tried to keep up with the *Enterprise* during her sea trials and when we were tracking that SSN, I drew an analogy between the *Hestek's* slow pace and my personal lack of progress. The existence of ASROC, its ability to make up for the destroyer's slow speed in one gigantic leap of rocket energy, encouraged me. Something could happen at any time to speed up the pace of my investigation. *Hang in there*, I told myself. *Something will break this case open.*

* * *

I was learning a lot of new things on the CIC watches. It was a lot of fun. And I could sit down. One night, after standing a midwatch, I was tired but happy. I stood along the lifelines and watched the water. The ship was rolling a bit. One moment I was pretty high above the ocean. A few seconds later I could easily reach down and wash my hands. I was too tired to stay there long so I headed back to the living compartment. Suddenly someone blocked my way in the darkness. It was Derella.

"I told ya to stay the fuck out of my business."

"What are you talking about? I wasn't doing anything," I protested.

"I saw ya watching me again while I was talking to my friend on the *Kendrick.*"

"You're paranoid! What are you hiding, anyway?"

"None of yer fuckin' business," Derella growled. "What the hell are you tryin' ta do?"

"I'm not trying to do anything." I decided to go on a fishing expedition.

"But I am curious about something."

"What?"

"What you're doing besides running a slush fund."

"Nothing! An' why would you wanta know anything about me or my business?"

I tried to sound nonchalant. "Curiosity. It's a habit of mine. I'm curious about everything."

Derella glared. "Bad habit. You're a fuckin' cop, ain't ya?" His voice was steely cold. "Well, you ain't goin' ta watch me any more." With a quick movement that took me completely by surprise, he grabbed the front of my jacket, lifted me off the deck and threw me across the lifelines just as that side of the ship rolled toward the water. "Now you're gonna become shark food."

I twisted and draped myself over the lifeline on my stomach. My glasses fell in the drink. I was unbalanced and the water rose to meet me as the ship rolled. I wondered how to stay afloat long enough for the ship to turn around and rescue me—if they even noticed I was missing.

43. BLINKER'S AND LIFELINES

Skye's home phone rang shortly after 0430. She'd just had a conference with Commander Blount and Charles Knox after a busy day at Blinker's. She answered even though she didn't want to.

"Hi, boss!" a soft, laughing voice said. It was Hunter.

"Chaské? What have you been doing?"

"Beatin' my brains out lookin' for interesting things about Blinker's Bar and Grill. Someone went to lots of trouble to hide stuff."

"What do you mean?"

"It was tough finding anything. Any thing. And I still haven't found information about the Quaker Meeting House. There's just nothin' there."

"And you think someone's hiding it?"

"Well, consider this. Nicholas Davenport bought the building on 21 January 1952."

"Sounds right. He got it after retiring from the Navy. That date rings true."

"Oh, the date's not what's interesting. He paid cash."

"What?"

"Yeah. Hard cold cash."

"How much did he pay?"

"Twenty-five thousand dollars. And...."

"Chaské, how could he afford that? He would've had to save every penny he made in the Navy!"

"Unless he got money from somethin' crooked. Or got real lucky in Las Vegas. Maybe he sold his soul to the devil. I don't know how he did it."

"Was the place a bar then?" Skye asked.

"No. An architect's office. Davenport got remodeling permits within a week of the sale. I'd guess he started converting it immediately. He got his first liquor license four months after that."

"He had to have more money for remodeling."

"Here's the really strange thing. None of these documents were where they should have been. They were salted away in an obscure file where it made no sense."

"What do you mean?"

"They were with some procurement records. Of the Norfolk City Council."

"The *Norfolk* City Council?"

"You got it!" he chuckled. "The permits and liquor license were issued by Virginia Beach, where the building is located. But the papers were in Norfolk. No idea why." Skye sat thinking for so long that Hunter asked, "You still there?"

"Yeah. I'm trying to figure this out. What're you going to do next?"

"Find somethin' out about the Quaker Meeting House."

"All right. Let me know if you find anything."

"Oh, I'll find something," Hunter laughed. "I just don't know when or where. Talk to you later."

"Yeah." Skye hung up and sat mulling over this information in the dark. A half hour later she made a call.

"OCI Norfolk."

"Skye here. Let me speak to Charles Knox, please." He was on the line in minutes. "How long would it take to get someone's military records?"

"Depends when they served. For civilians it can take months."

"Can you expedite it?"

"They'd help us all they can."

"Good. I need the records for Nicholas Davenport, U. S. N. Career sailor, retired in '51, I think."

"Rate and service number?"

"Rating was signalman. Other information is unknown."

"That'll take longer."

"Can't be helped. I won't walk up and say, 'I'm investigating you. What's your service number.'"

The voice on the other end of the line laughed. "Of course not. I'll do what I can. Maybe the Commander can make the request. Or the Big Boss. That would help."

Skye smiled. "Do what you can. And, I need a few other things."

"Shoot."

"All of Davenport's bank accounts. They're probably in one or more of the cities around this area."

"Do you want me to limit the search to this area?"

Skye thought for a moment. "Check locally first. Then if you can, check up and down this coast. It seems that he's only served in the east."

"Okay. What else?"

"His police records. Local, county and state."

"Will do."

* * *

Thanks to Derella, I was draped over the lifeline, looking at the distinct possibility of swimming with fishes. I had no desire to do that. My glasses were in the drink, but I didn't need to see much right then. I shoved my left leg between the middle and top lifelines, bent my knee and stuck my foot back through the safety mesh between the middle and bottom lifelines. I locked my left foot behind my right leg and clenched my muscles. Derella grabbed my belt and tried to flip me into the water. I bounced around, but my locked legs kept me from going over.

I leaned as far forward as I could. The springiness of the lifeline helped me launch myself back and up. I swung my elbow around with all my might. It connected solidly with Derella's head. I felt him crumple.

I untangled myself, planted a knee on Derella's chest and had fun slapping him into consciousness. When I knew he could hear me, I seized his windpipe and squeezed enough to let him know he could die.

"You hear me?" Derella didn't have much freedom of movement, but he nodded. "Okay. Listen and remember. I'm not a cop. I'm not watching you. I do know how to protect myself. Don't mess with me. Understand?"

Derella nodded again. I stood up. "I'm not going to turn you in. I don't want to get even. But I'll tell you what you told me. Leave me alone and we'll be all right."

44. SHADOWS IN THE NIGHT

The task force often sailed in darken-ship condition, with all exterior lights off. Doors to the weather decks activated switches that turned off interior lights before they opened. Sailors used red-filtered flashlights to move around topside. The watches had a tough job at these times. Without running lights, it was hard to see the ships in the formation. We had to rely on radar and shadows to maintain the ship's position.

I took advantage of darken-ship to sit on the main deck amidships, low and close to the sea, and watch the small waves of the wake drift by. No lights interfered with nature. Plankton sparkled in the water, agitated by the vessel's movement. The gentle whitecaps shone brightly in the inky darkness. There are few places where the stars are so bright as at sea on a cloudless night. I'd never seen the Milky Way like this. The sky looked like randomly thrown diamonds on black velvet.

I shifted my gaze between the wake and the stars. I was swimming in a magical sphere, flashing and sparkling matter on all sides. I was a mite of dust in a room filled with points of light, floating in a world of peace and harmony.

My eyes became fine tuned to the darkness. In this scene painted in black and shadow, I marveled how well I could see along the deck and how the stars outlined the superstructure. I wanted Rena to see, hear, feel, float alongside me.

I turned my back to the sea and bent over to shield the fire of my Zippo as I lit a cigarette. I sheltered the burning end inside my cupped hand then returned to examining the scene around me again.

I noticed a movement on the fantail. Another guy was enjoying the night. Then he leaned on the lifelines, head bowed, hands raised to cover his face.

I frowned, wondering what his problem was.

He reached down and unbuckled his belt. He pulled something from it before buckling up again. He held a long, thin object in front of him. I was certain it was a seaman's knife and sheath. Suddenly he threw it into the water with a mighty heave.

Now he knelt on the deck, holding the lifelines with both hands and resting his head on his extended arms. I watched, shielding my cigarette rather than throwing it over the side and announcing my presence.

He knelt there for some time before he got up and entered the watertight door leading to the crew's quarters.

I felt my fingers burn. "Damn!" I said, throwing the scorching butt into the ocean. I licked my blistered fingers and blew on them to relieve the pain. "I've got to quit smoking!"

* * *

When the ship's store opened in the morning, I went to buy cigarettes. Reston was leaving. "What did you get, Hank?"

He held up a long, thin box. "Needed a new knife."

I frowned. "You had a knife. What happened to it?"

"Lost it over the side a few days ago when I was re-canvassing lifelines."

"What?"

"Yeah. I fitted some canvas over the cable and sewed it on. But it was about an inch too long. So," he reported sheepishly, "I used my knife to trim it and dropped the damn thing into the drink."

I grabbed his arm and pulled him off to one side. "Were you the guy I saw last night throwing a knife over the side?"

Reston looked trapped, but only for an instant. "What're you talking about, man? I wasn't out on deck last night. Must've been someone else."

He pulled away and stomped out onto the main deck. I was convinced he'd lied. I wondered what this was all about. "Something else," I muttered to myself, "to store away for the future."

45. CHRISTMAS

Captain Lorman worked hard to get the *Hestek* home for Christmas. The best he could do was get us in Christmas day morning. We had two days in port. I had duty, so I would feast aboard ship, the result of the best the cooks could do. I wouldn't be able to see Rena until tomorrow.

Liberty call went down after we tied up outboard the *Kendrick* and we secured the Sea Detail. Norfolk was cold with an inch of snow on the ground. Dejected, I watched the men cross the brow to the *Kendrick*. Most of them carried AWOL bags filled with a fresh change of skivvies and the Christmas gifts they'd kept on board. Wives and children met them on the pier. It was amazing how fast that wives' network relayed the news of a surprise return home.

Not everyone rushing to leave was married. Many guys had fiancées, girlfriends, and "shack ups" ashore. Some had parents here. And there were isolated individuals like Reston, in the middle of the crowd, hurrying off the ship.

With a sigh of resignation, I went below to change into dungarees so I could do some work before my afternoon quarterdeck messenger watch.

Reston returned shortly after noon.

"How come you're back so soon?" I asked.

"Just had to see someone. Now I can eat the feast they cooked up and settle in for some shut-eye."

"Yeah. We do lose a lot of sleep at sea."

"Agreed," he said over his shoulder as he headed for the mess decks. "See you later!"

Liberty call went early the following day to give the previous off-going duty section a full day with their loved ones. Zoss was grinning from ear to ear. He could be with his fiancée.

Rena waited at the gate. Now I was in the middle of the homeward dash. I carried my AWOL bag, hiding a wrapped gift. Even with my peacoat buttoned up to my throat, the walk from the ship was chilly. I jumped into the passenger seat as fast as I could.

"Hi! How're you?" I greeted, leaning over to kiss her.

"Better than an hour ago! I'm glad you phoned me when you tied up. This was a nice surprise."

"I'm sure that's what the Old Man meant it to be. I heard he called in some political favors from the high mucky-mucks to get us these two days." I opened my AWOL bag, extracted the gift and tossed the bag onto the back seat.

Rena glanced at the present. "What's that?"

"Something for a friend ashore." I held it on my lap.

"Who might that be?"

I shook my head, bit my lips and looked upwards. "Ah, you wouldn't know her."

"Eric!" She hit me on my arm. "God, what a tease!"

"Well, they say anticipation enhances a gift. And it's not much, so it needs all the enhancement it can get. Here, Merry Christmas!" Rena took the gift and placed it on the seat.

"Aren't you going to open it?" I asked.

"I'm driving, you dope! You want me to stop right here in traffic? What was that about anticipation? I'll open it at home."

I relaxed into the car seat.

"Have a rough time this trip?"

"It wasn't bad, but we're only in for two days." I paused. "Remember when I told you about Reston's liberty behavior? Taking off as fast as he can, getting a standby if necessary, but he's only gone a short time. And then I asked to borrow your car and we decided I had to think of another way. Well, I did. I got my Navy driver's license."

"Good."

"It's ironic. Reston and I talked a few times about me getting one to get off my feet on in-port watches. Now, I just might be able to be in a car when he leaves the ship."

"Aren't you supposed to drive officers around?" she asked.

"Yeah. I'll have to figure out a way around that."

"Right. Now, my news. Remember me telling you about Frank Murphy, the guy they call 'The Saint?' I met him."

"Where?"

"He stopped into Blinker's. Evidently he knows Nick Davenport. They talked a while and Murphy had a drink. Blink introduced us."

"What kind of guy is he? Does he live up to his nickname?"

Rena was silent for quite a while. "I don't think so."

"Why not?"

"Instinct. I got a strong feeling that he wasn't what his reputation suggested. And Blink was kind of nervous. At times he even looked fearful."

"Why would he be afraid?"

She shrugged her shoulders. "Don't know."

When we got home, she took my gift in one hand, my hand in the other and led me upstairs. "Okay, close your eyes." She unlocked the door then placed her palm over my eyes. She guided me into the room, shut the door and took her hand away. "Surprise!"

It certainly was! The table was set for a banquet. China instead of Melmac. Etched glassware. Candles and flowers. "Where did all this come from?"

She beamed. "Some weeks ago they told me that my transfer from San Diego was permanent. So I had everything shipped here. Sit down and relax. Luckily, I had a turkey in the freezer. It ought to be done in a little while."

"I thought you're going back to finish the divorce?"

"I'll take some leave. I'm here now. That'll be good for the two of us."

"If they let me stay around. Remember, I'm officially assigned to Great Lakes." I sat down on a kitchen chair. Rena sat on another and opened my gift. She extracted a key ring with a fob woven out of small twine.

"Like I said, it's not much." I shrugged my shoulders. "It is a hand-woven original by Matthews! And I was thinking of you the whole time I was making it."

"I love it, Eric! I love presents that people make rather than buy." She leaned over and kissed me. "I wish," she whispered, kissing me again with a touch of sadness in her eyes, "I wish I could give you the gift I really want to."

"What's that?"

She sighed. "Me. My love. Openly. But we have to wait until the divorce is final. I could lose everything I own if Gary found out and got mean. So, keep that anticipation of yours alive." She stood up. As she walked to the stove, she tossed her full head of auburn hair and teased, "Meanwhile, I can give you a great dinner by candlelight and my wonderful company!"

"I guess I'll take whatever I can get. And then hurry up and wait."

"Yeah. Besides, I am your supervisor and we should try to follow regulations." She stood facing the meal on the stove and breathed deeply. "But it's tearing me apart, Eric. Sometimes I want you so much I hurt. So I have to hurry up and wait, too. I'm sorry it has to be this way."

"Don't be. Deep down, I'm jumping for joy. At least there seems to be a future for us." I walked up behind her, put my arms around her and nibbled on the back of her neck.

"Stop it now!" Rena half sobbed, shaking me away. "Quit! I have to finish this dinner for you!"

"Okay," I whispered. "I'll stop." I let go of her and went to the television. "Wonder what's on the tube."

"Probably Christmas specials," she said, her voice carrying a touch of relief. "Or else the soap operas have holiday stuff. But the TV isn't working very well."

"What's wrong?"

"Reception's lousy. You have an electronics engineering degree. Why don't you fix it?"

"I'll try."

"I don't want to miss the Huntley-Brinkley report."

"Well, good-night, Chet...!"

"Should I reply 'Good night, David' back to you?"

"Nope." I paused. "You know, I come here for some hard-earned rest and recreation and you put me to work...."

"Oh, listen to that!" She rubbed her right forefinger across the thumb of the same hand. "You know what this is?"

I laughed. "Yeah! World's smallest violin playing 'My Heart Cries For You.' Etcetera! Etcetera! Etcetera!"

"Now you're the King of Siam?"

"No ma'am. Just the TV repairman. That's all I am, ma'am."

Rena came over and kissed me again. "You better be careful, mister, or you won't get any dinner tonight...."

She returned to the kitchen. I turned the TV set to look at the back of it. In a few minutes, I laughed. "Ha! All repairs should be this easy!"

"You found the problem?"

"Of course! I'm an engineer! What would you expect?"

"So what was it, genius?"

"The rabbit ears were loose. Really tough to fix!"

"Well, I don't know anything about that stuff."

"Maybe not. But, with a criminologist's trained eye, you could see a loose wire right out in the open!"

"Oh, you're asking for it." She turned in the kitchen and shook a fist at me. "If you're not careful, I'll give you a bust in the mouth."

"Really?" I grinned. "No I won't say it. I'll act my age and not be a crude wise ass. Even though I am a Navy enlisted man...."

"Only undercover. You're an officer and a gentleman." She paused for a moment. "By the way, I know your real age. What do you tell them on the ship about only being a newly advanced seaman?"

"We know I'm almost thirty. My service jacket says I'm twenty-three."

"I guess you could pass for twenty-three." She smirked, "If they don't look too closely."

"Thanks. I'll have to remember to return the compliment later."

"So how do you explain your age when you enlisted?"

"I received a draft notice, didn't open it for fear of going into the Army, and ran to join the Navy. Standard stuff. And believable."

I turned on the TV to check it out. "OK, what's on the tube?" The picture was perfect. I flipped some channels and turned off the set. "Nothing worth watching. You said I should remember that in real life I'm an officer?"

"And a gentleman!" she repeated.

"Yeah, by act of Congress! But what is real life in our undercover world? And what's unreal? If you ask me, most of it is unreal."

"Having trouble with reality? Shall I call in a shrink?"

"No need for that, boss," I quipped. "I was just commenting on the difficulty of playing the undercover game every minute of every day, seven days a week, trying to set up somebody I've come to like a lot. I've investigated people before, and I'm sure I'll be undercover again. But I never had to go after someone quite like this kid."

"Don't get too attached to him, Eric. Some day you'll have to arrest him."

I reached up and felt the scars on my cheek. "I can't help it."

46. MIDWATCH AND WATCHERS

We went back out to sea three days after Christmas. The seas were rough that night. And the *Hestek* was on a course that didn't let it go through its usual up-down-chatter-its-way-back-to-the-surface dance. Instead it bounced around a lot in an irregular and unpredictable manner.

Our berthing compartments had sets of three vertical bunks. Nobody ever wanted the bottom rack because of all the climbing in and out of bed to let people get into their lockers under the bunks. And the top rack was hard to get in and out of, besides being a bit crowded by all the cable runs and ventilation ducts. Because we had a few new people and I'd made seaman, I was able to claim a middle bunk. But it was still close to the companionway, so sometimes I woke up when people ran up and down the ladder.

At 2315, the Messenger of the Watch groped his way down into the compartment, trying to escape injury from the rolling and pitching. He slipped on the last step and his shoe slapped the deck. Pretty close to my head. I woke up, saw it was only the messenger and rolled over to go back to sleep.

Charlie Wu, the new arrival, went to Reston's bunk. He shook the mattress. "Reston! Wake up! Time to get up for your mid."

Reston normally woke up quickly. This time he didn't move. "Reston!" Wu called a bit louder. Hank twitched. "Come on, get up! What the hell's your problem?"

I propped myself up on my elbow to watch.

"Reston! I know you're alive! I can see you breathing."

It's an unwritten rule not to touch a sleeping man. There are still too many older veterans from World War Two and Korea who wake up swinging. Wu shook the mattress again and almost shouted, "Reston! Get your ass out of that rack! Come on, I've got other guys to wake up!"

Hank mumbled. He moved from lying on his side to leaning face down on his pillow.

I climbed out of my own rack. "Charlie! Go on to the others. I'll get him up."

"Thanks, Matthews. You know how midwatchstanders are if they miss their midrats."

"Yeah. Is he scheduled for after steering?"

Wu nodded.

The messenger returned up to the main deck. I grabbed Reston's arm and shook him so hard that the guy in the lower bunk complained, "What the fuck's goin' on? You're messin' with my sleep, man."

Reston woke up enough to look at me with glassy eyes. "Hank, get up! You got the mid!" He said something garbled. I kept shaking him. "Yeah... I'm getting...." He slowly draped his legs over the edge of his rack. "...up."

"Crap! Reston!" I hissed. "You can't stand a watch like this!" As I pulled him off his bunk, I saw a folded paper packet that he'd been lying on. I knew instantly what he'd done. I palmed the packet so it wouldn't be left lying around.

"I'm awright, Eric. I can stan' my watch. Done it before."

"Not tonight. You'd be asleep soon as you got down there," I whispered. "Why'd you do it so close to watch time?"

Reston shrugged. He let me steer him and lean him against my tier of bunks.

I tossed the paper packet onto my rack. I propped Reston against my bunk and went to search under his pillow. Nothing there. Searched between the mattress and the canvas of the bunk itself. Nothing again. Squatted on my heels and checked his locker. It was unlocked. I lifted the sheet metal locker top as far as I could without banging it into the rack above. Felt around inside. Found a small paper bag and took it over by my bunk.

The bag held folded paper squares like the one I'd found. Maybe eight of them. I dumped the bag onto my rack, the center one in the tier of three. I carefully opened one of the squares. Fine white powder. I stuck my finger into it and tasted it. Bitter. Heroin.

"Shit, Reston, you can't stand watch this way," I muttered. I scooped the packets back into the paper bag and returned them to Reston's locker, which I locked. I made my rack. While I was dressing myself, the messenger returned.

"Is he awake?" Wu almost whispered.

"Good enough to get to his watch. He must have been drinking."

"I didn't smell anything."

"They say vodka doesn't smell...."

The messenger noticed that I was getting dressed. "So what are you doing?"

"I'm going to stay with him so he doesn't fall asleep on watch."

Wu shrugged his shoulders. "Your loss of sleep."

"Yeah. If he looks like he'll stay awake, I'll come back."

The messenger nodded and left the compartment. I finished getting dressed, then helped Reston put on his dungarees. This could be a rough night and tomorrow I'd be very tired because I also had my own four-to-eight in CIC.

We made our way to after steering. The fresh air revived Reston enough so he could relieve the watch and report in on the sound-powered phones. He even sounded like a guy who got up to stand watch in the middle of the night. Luckily, the ship didn't have to be controlled from after steering and no tests were run. As the watch progressed, Reston dozed off. I sat beside him with the headphones on. My mind was going in circles trying to figure out how I could help this guy.

The station was called just once, about 0230. I responded, explaining that we'd been shooting the shit and Reston was making a trip to the head.

By the time the watch was almost over, Reston was in a state that could be taken for normal. I stuck around long enough to be sure he got back into his rack.

When waking up reliefs, the messenger evidently glanced at my rack, noticed it was already empty and didn't go near it. When reveille sounded, I was dozing in a chair in the corner of Combat.

* * *

Shortly after 1300 that afternoon, Chief Gascomb came up to me where I was working. "Matthews, come with me."

"Sure, Chief! What's up?" I thought maybe someone heard about me covering for Reston.

"We have to see the Exec."

"Should I change into uniform of the day?"

"Just come with me."

I frowned but didn't say anything else. I'd find out all I needed to know in due time. When we reached his cabin, Mister Monroe motioned to a chair. "Come in, Matthews. Sit down." He turned to Gascomb. "Chief, you can go. I'll handle this."

"Aye, aye, Commander," Gascomb said to a closing door.

The XO reached into his desk drawer, pulled out a packet of heroin and tossed it on the desk in front of me. "The reveille PO found this on your rack this morning. How do you explain it?"

47. NEW YEAR'S EVE

It seems that when I put away Reston's dope, I accidentally left one packet on my rack. Shepherd found it on my empty bunk when he held reveille. He turned it over to the Chief, who went straight to the Exec.

I was really pissed at myself for letting this happen. Still, it turned out all right. The XO and I talked things over. Twenty minutes later, I left his quarters. I kept a straight face. But I was smiling inside.

* * *

New Year's Eve was here! A Wave sat in the Tradewinds Enlisted Men's Club. She felt restless. Then she hurt. She twitched. She felt cold flashes and a slight case of goose bumps. But this was an evening for celebrating!

She went into the women's head. Sat in a commode stall. Put some heroin from a small package onto a mirror with a nail file then put away the file and packet. She rolled up a dollar bill, placed one end in a nostril, leaned over and sniffed. She knew it might take fifteen minutes to reach her peak. But this was safer than shooting up.

She felt the rush begin. She felt wonderfully warm. Her mouth turned dry. Her arms and legs become heavy. There was a welcome relief from her pain. Then she felt an awful nausea she'd never felt before. She vomited. She itched severely all over.

Her heartbeat slowed.

So did her breathing.

She went to sleep and slowly settled against the wall of the stall.

She never woke up.

* * *

It was almost midnight. The *Hestek* sliced through calm seas. Radarman Seales and I left CIC. We snuck down to the main deck, amidships, the in-port quarterdeck location. Reston met us there. I turned on the 1MC.

At exactly midnight, Seales rang the ship's bell—DING-DING, DING-DING—and all three of us shouted the announcement: NINETEEN-SIXTY-TWO ARRIVING!

Reston turned off the 1MC. We began to return to our watch stations, but we saw Le Blanc pass by on the main deck. I knew he'd borrowed ten bucks, at five for seven, from Derella.

"Why's he roaming around now?" I asked.

"He does that a lot," Reston replied. "Don't know why. This time of night, I'd rather be in bed."

"Where's he going?" I wondered. When I got to the open deck and looked out, Le Blanc was nowhere in sight.

"We better get back on watch," Seales said. We returned to Combat. Reston hit the rack.

Hauser was waiting. "Nice touch, guys! But be careful. The best laid plans, you know. Don't try that again."

"Yeah, not 'til next New Year," Seales quipped.

"Just a warning. You never know how things'll turn out. I suspect it won't cause any problems this time, 'cause this Old Man's pretty cool. But on another ship, who knows? And, like I said, sometimes things just go awry."

"You leading up to one of your sea stories?"

"For a change, no!" Hauser grinned. "Just being a good petty officer and trying to keep my guys out of trouble."

48. REFUELING DETAIL

The crew got everything ready for refueling then hurried up and waited.

NOW SET THE REFUELING AND HIGHLINING DETAILS. SET THE REFUELING AND HIGHLINING DETAILS.

We ran to our stations, put on the bulky kapok life jackets, and waited. I stood with Chief Gascomb. Other guys stood by the coupling where the refueling hose would connect with the pipe that went to the fuel tanks.

We pulled alongside an oiler instead of a carrier. The effect on the *Hestek* was the same. The water between the two ships was still choppy and dangerous.

I heard a familiar voice from the 01 level.

"You guys ready?" Shepherd shouted. I looked up. I saw him, Billy Bob Coe and Hank Reston.

"Ready," replied Coe.

"Okay, loop your safety belts around those lifelines," the petty officer ordered.

"All set," Reston pointed to his hook up.

"I'm all right, Shep," Coe shouted. "I've got my legs tucked around the lifeline. I'm secure."

"Coe!" Reston screamed.

"Coe, damn it! Get that fuckin' safety belt hooked up!" Shepherd ordered. "Or I'll hold up this refueling and put your sorry ass on report! I don't want another Cory Palm."

Grumbling, Coe looped his safety belt around the lifelines and clipped it at his waist. "I'm hooked up!"

"Keep it hooked!"

Coe nodded.

"Okay, heads up!" Chief Gascomb shouted.

We heard the line-throwing gun pop on the oiler. The plastic impact bulb arched toward us. The small nylon line snaked after it. The bulb hit the superstructure with a thump. The waves grabbed the nylon line and began to pull it into the water.

"Get that sonofabitch!"

One guy threw himself on top of the bulb. As he stood up, a breaking wave almost knocked him down again. He pulled the shot line over and grabbed the messenger, the first of a series of progressively larger ropes. He handed the messenger up to Shepherd, who routed it through a block and handed it back.

Gascomb had me string the messenger through blocks attached to padeyes on the deck and give it to the after crew to run it around. They pulled the span wire across until the end fitting was almost even with an already rigged pelican hook. Shepherd shouted to the men below, "Hold it! Pull in a little more. Hold it!" and to the topside crew, "Come on, pull it in! Grab that span wire and pull!"

The roiling water between the ships pushed the *Hestek* to starboard, away from the oiler. The retreating span wire yanked the line through our hands. I heard Reston shout, "Let it go!" After a muffled scream, Hank shouted again, "God! Pull him in!"

On the main deck, the line handlers had to let some of the line go. They would never be able to hold a destroyer upright anyway.

We rolled back to port. The span wire slackened. The line handlers pulled the end fitting in place again. The guys on the 01 level slipped the span wire end fitting over the movable piece of the pelican hook. Shepherd swung the pelican hook closed, secured it with its metal ring and inserted a cotter pin to lock everything in place. Now the machinery on the oiler would automatically adjust the span wire's tautness.

Finally, the crew pulled the fuel hose across. It rolled on trolleys hanging from the now taut span wire between the two ships. Finally, the hoses were connected to the special fittings leading to the fuel tanks.

I went up to visit Shepherd who was watching the span wire connection and the fuel hose coupling. Reston and Coe sat on the deck, propped against a couple of lifeline stanchions.

"Hi, guys! Was this a rough connection?"

Shepherd shook his head. "No. Pretty normal, in fact."

"Easier than some," Reston stared at the deck in front of him.

"Shep, how come you were so insistent on Coe hooking up his safety belt. And what's the story on Cory Palm?"

Reston heaved himself to his feet in one smooth motion. "Shit! A guy can't ever forget anything."

49. REVELATIONS

Reston moved off to watch Belisle, the Intercom Technician running the music system. I frowned. "What's his problem?"

"You couldn't see that Coe got pulled through the lifelines when we rolled away from the oiler," Shep explained. "That safety belt saved his ass," He lowered his voice and grinned. "I think it also changed his opinion about Negroes. Reston and I both offered to pull him back up. He chose my hand, saying, 'I guess Negroes ain't so bad after all, Shep!'

"Cory Palm was that seaman that we think you replaced. Coe is his replacement up here. We were refueling last July and the ship rolled like today when the span wire pulled away." Shepherd took a deep breath. "Palm hadn't hooked up his safety belt. Reston slipped and kicked Palm's feet out from under him. He lost his balance and fell to the main deck below. He hit flat on his side with a thud we could hear all the way up here. He actually bounced. Then he didn't move. Thankfully, he wasn't washed overboard. Doc Hamilton, the chief corpsman, suspected he had some serious internal injuries. We never saw him conscious again. They got him onto a Stokes stretcher...."

"What's that?"

"Those rigid metal tubing and wire stretchers hanging on the bulkheads. You can tie a guy in and he can't move. We highlined Palm to the carrier. Transferred him. We haven't seen him since. Some guys think he was killed."

I looked over the lifelines at the main deck below. "God! I can see where that could be nasty."

"Yeah. You showed up about a month and a half after that. Just long enough for NavPers to assign someone out of boot camp."

"So, why is Reston so sensitive about it? It was an accident, wasn't it?"

"Yeah, best we can figure. There were some questions about it, but I can't get into that. Confidential stuff. A lot of the fault was Palm's. He didn't hook up. Reston and Palm were real good friends, and Hank did slip and cause Cory to fall." Shepherd rubbed his chin. "I think Reston blames himself. But it's more my fault than his."

"Why?"

"I was the PO up here. I should have ordered Palm to hook up. Threaten to put him on report, like I did with Coe today." Shep stood there staring at the deck. "I don't feel so hot about the whole thing, either. But I can't seem to get through to Reston that it was mostly my fault."

"Want me to try?"

The boatswain shook his head. "No. Steer clear of it. Just let him be. Time heals, too."

* * *

Phil Le Blanc always hit the rack right after "knock off ship's work." I woke up after midnight a few times and saw that he wasn't there. He was usually gone when I got up for a midwatch and often hadn't returned when my watch was over at 0400. I had no idea where he went.

I decided to find out. I forced myself to stay awake one night, keeping my blanket up to my neck to hide the fact that I was still dressed.

I reviewed all possible drug users on the *Hestek*. I puzzled over who might be a supplier. There were no obvious choices for either. I still had my work cut out for me. When I began to doze off, I switched to thinking of Rena.

Le Blanc finally got up. When he reached the top of the companionway ladder, I got up and slipped into my shoes. It was cold outside, so I put on my foul-weather jacket. Le Blanc went forward along the starboard side of the ship. He slipped into one of the workspaces amidships. I stepped through the watertight door. A hatch went down to the forward fire room. A ladder went up to the 01 level and the hatch up there was open. I heard voices behind the wooden door to the ship's office.

"Okay, ready?"

"Yep. Just like always," Le Blanc said.

"Sit down, then."

"Deal, Max."

"All right, here we go. Five card stud, deuces wild."

I stayed long enough to be sure this was what these guys would be doing for a long time. They seemed to be pretty equally skilled, and the same amounts of money passed back and forth between them. I couldn't stay there long. What if someone had to go to the head?

I climbed up the ladder, went through the hatch to the deck above, and sat there, shivering. I waited. An hour later someone left the compartment below. He returned in a short time. Same thing happened forty-five minutes after that. I got up and went back to bed. This was frustrating as hell. For all my imagining some heavy drug acquisition and dealing, I wound up freezing my ass off monitoring a poker game. Le Blanc was an addict, all right—to gambling.

50. INFORMATION AND FIREWORKS

One evening, Skye found a note in her mailbox as she left for work.

> "Blue De Soto, Virginia 480-950. Noticed around Tradewinds selling something. When Shore Patrol approached, it raced away. Photos to follow. Glenn Oliver"

She went back upstairs and put the letter into her metal box with a combination lock on it.

After Skye got off work that night, she relaxed in the easy chair in her living room. It had been a busy night.

Her phone woke her from her nap. "Here."

"Skye?"

"Yes."

"Charles Knox, over at Central. There were a couple deaths two months ago, result of a deal with Randall Divven, AQ3."

"Yes?"

"We found who leaked the info about the deal to the drug peddlers."

"I knew of the leak. I called for agents to follow everyone at the meeting."

"That's interesting!" Knox chuckled. "My tail must have been good. I knew about the others. But I never suspected I was being followed, too."

"It's nice to know we can do something right."

"I agree. We can still stay on top of things."

"You found the leak?" Skye asked.

"Yes. Alan Noonan, the yeoman legal assistant."

"So what're you going to do?"

"The Old Man and Commander Blount just want to watch him. See what we can learn."

"I agree. Thanks, Knox. I appreciate the call," Skye said. "And I have something else for you to do."

"What's up?"

"We have a license plate to check." She gave him the description and license number of the De Soto that Glenn Oliver had reported.

*   *   *

I enjoyed being at sea. Even more than before. The sit-down CIC watches were fun. Even the difficult aspects of CIC became normal and more relaxed.

For most of this watch my mind drifted from duty to friends to Rena. One more night at sea and I be with her again. I got off duty at midnight, then stood on deck, watching the water go by, daydreaming.

I noticed a shadow an instant before I heard Derella say, "Now you're a dead man."

The right rear side of my head erupted in excruciating pain. There was an explosion of light, like fireworks, then darkness.

51. RECOVERY

I woke up in a strange bunk. When I moved a searing pain in my head brought me up short. I opened my eyes. I was facing a bulkhead. I heard a groan. It was me.

"Hold still," a calm voice said. "I'm fixing you up."

"Where am I?"

"Sickbay. You remember your name and ship?"

"Eric Matthews. USS *Hestek*."

"Good. This is Chief Hamilton. You have a nasty bump back here. Do you remember how you got it?"

I shook my head. "Ohhh, God that hurts! Guess I shouldn't do that, right, Doc?"

The chief replied softly, "I wouldn't if I were you. What happened?"

"Don't know. I was watching the water go by. Then I felt this intense pain. The lights went out. I woke up here. Do you know...?"

"Someone called the bridge, told them you were hurt and needed help. I found you on the deck, out cold. We got some help and carried you here."

"Who told the bridge?"

"Don't know. Hold still. I shaved the hair around your wound. Now I need to take some stitches. This could smart."

My breath hissed through clenched teeth each time the needle pierced my skin. In comparison, the slight tugs when the thread was pulled through were nothing. "How bad is it, Doc?"

"You might have a concussion but your skull's intact. I need x-rays to be sure it's not cracked."

"Can you guess how I got hurt?"

"I'd say someone tried to bust your skull open. Maybe with a dogging wrench. But you seem to have a hard head." The corpsman Chief tied another knot.

The pain stopped me from chuckling. "My Dad always said the same thing."

"One more stitch and we're done here. Then, it's up to your own healing powers. We can get x-rays tomorrow. Tell me, do you have any idea who did this?"

"No."

"The scuttlebutt is that you've had some pretty hot words with another guy on the deck force."

"That was only a slight disagreement. I don't think he'd try to kill me."

The Chief seemed to freeze. "Why would you say that? Nobody said anyone was trying to kill you."

I waited until Doc finished the final knot. "No need to. It's logical. I was hit on the head so hard it knocked me out cold. And the cut needed stitches. I'd say a desire to kill me might be a high probability."

"Well, your injury certainly didn't hurt your reasoning powers," Hamilton chuckled. "The stitches are tight and the cut is oozing very little blood, so I'll leave it unbandaged. If it starts to bleed, or if lots of fluid comes out, I'll cover it. Let's see if you can sit up."

I struggled to an upright position but it was painful to hold my head up. I noticed Contino, the other corpsman on the *Hestek*, standing behind the Chief. Reston stood in the doorway. I couldn't help laughing. "Hank, you look as bad as I feel!"

Reston smiled. "Still a wise ass. I guess he's going to be okay, huh, Doc?"

"You all right, there?" the Chief asked. "Not woozy or feeling like you're going to lose consciousness?"

"No, I'm all right that way. It just hurts like hell."

Hamilton nodded. "That's normal, considering. I'll get you some painkillers. They could make you lightheaded, so don't go out on deck. We'll get you clean clothes. You rest here tonight. Somebody will stay with you."

"Who whupped you upside the head?" Contino asked.

"I only have a suspicion but I'm not going to name anyone if I can't prove it."

The chief tilted his head as he regarded me. "Is that your final word on the subject?"

"Yep. Final word," I tried to nod. "For now."

* * *

After we tied up, the Captain visited sickbay. Hamilton looked up at his knock.

"Morning, Chief!"

"Capt'n!" Hamilton greeted, rising. "To what do we owe this honor?"

"Is your patient in good enough shape to talk?"

"Yes, sir." The corpsman waved his hand toward me. "Right there, sir." Both corpsmen left sickbay.

Lorman pulled a chair next to my bunk.

"Sorry I can't stand, Capt'n," I apologized.

"Stow the formalities for now, son. How are you?"

"Not bad, Capt'n, everything considered. What can I do for you?"

"Tell me what happened."

I repeated my story.

"You have no idea who attacked you?"

"No, sir. No idea."

"Well, I hear the scuttlebutt. So I believe you know, but I can't force you to tell."

"Yes, sir," I smiled. "I know you have a pretty good information network."

"Maybe a certain loan shark...." I looked up so sharply that I winced at the pain in my head. Lorman continued, "Maybe he thought you were some kind of police agent out to clean up slush funds."

I looked him in the eye and grinned. "Not me, Capt'n. I don't know anything about cleaning up slush funders."

"Just a seaman on the deck force?"

"Yes, sir, Capt'n."

Lorman examined my face for a long moment. "Well, if you ever need help of any sort, for any reason, don't hesitate to ask. If my crew's endangered, my ship is, too. Understand?"

"Aye, aye, Capt'n."

"Very well. Follow Doc Hamilton's orders and get better."

"Aye, aye, Capt'n."

Two hours later Contino and I were at the Naval Hospital in Portsmouth getting x-rays. They showed no skull fractures. We returned to the *Hestek* and the corpsmen made sure the pain medication was working without disabling me.

I could go ashore as long as I wasn't alone. I called Rena and had her pick me up.

"My God, Eric, what happened?"

"I guess someone tried to do me in," I quipped.

"Let me see." She gently pulled my head down to examine the wound. "Does it hurt a lot?"

"No. The pain killers are pretty good."

She shook her head. "This is kind of a shock."

"Yeah, it was for me, too."

"So what happened?"

184

"It was Derella." I told her of Derella's slush fund and his network on the *Joseph* and the *Kendrick*. "I guess he felt threatened enough to try to get rid of me."

A hard look came across her face. "He won't get another chance."

"What do you mean?"

"He'll be off the Hestek by this time tomorrow."

52. THEFT AND INFORMATION

Derella was indeed gone the following day. OCI agents simultaneously appeared onboard the *Hestek*, the *Joseph*, and the *Kendrick*. Also on the *Tatters* and the *Reilly*. They arrested Derella, Curtis, Paulson, and two others. I smiled. There had to be some happy men around who didn't have to repay what they'd borrowed.

Each day, I came in for morning quarters, though I could leave right away again on "recuperation leave." Then I'd go over to Rena's apartment where I got some extra sleep and played chess whenever she wasn't busy with work. She was a very good chess player; we must have played ten or twelve games and I didn't win a single one. At this time, for fun, she was working out defensive moves against the Ruy Lopez openings. Her thinking and her analysis of the game quickly lost me.

I was healing so fast that Doc Hamilton returned me to full duty status in just three days. The pain was gone, but my head was still tender to the touch and a lump remained.

It was warm for January, in the mid-forties. I sat outside, jacket zipped up, watching the liberty party. Rena was doing other things tonight so I stayed on the ship a while. All things in due time. I watched Reston leave as soon as he could.

I tried to follow him a couple times without being on duty and lost him. My duty driver plan had fizzled so far. I drove only when officers had to go somewhere. I never even got into a Navy car otherwise.

I found a comfortable spot on the 01 level. I should have changed into the uniform of the day, but I was still in dungarees, so I wasn't worried about getting dirty. I pulled out a paperback copy of *To Kill a Mockingbird* from my back pocket, leaned against a stanchion and began to read.

I looked up at each noise or movement. Even so, I read quite a bit. One of the movements I noticed was Reston's return. Again, he'd departed as soon as possible and came back earlier than anyone would expect.

Right after "knock off ship's work," I was in the washroom getting ready to go ashore. A few other guys were there, too, including Roma, the third class boatswain. When done and dried off, we each wrapped a towel around our waist. We returned to the berthing compartment. I saw Roma searching, frantically rifling through his locker. He stood up and opened his wallet a second time. "Damn!"

"What's wrong?"

"I put my wallet under my pillow before I went up to shit, shower and shave. Somebody found it and took fifty bucks. It was my money to go on leave with." He checked the compartment to see who else was around. "Raynes! You see anybody else down here?"

"No. Only me and Reston."

"You see anyone around my bunk?"

"Actually, I just got down here. Ask Reston."

"Hank, you see anyone else down here?"

Reston lifted his head. "No.... Di'n't see anyone...."

I noticed Hank's glassy eyes and wondered. I turned to Roma. "You ought to report it to the Quarterdeck Watch Officer."

"Yeah." The dejected boatswain's mate dressed, glancing at Reston every few seconds. Before leaving, he turned to me. "Watch the rest of my stuff?"

I nodded. I looked around the compartment. Reston seemed asleep. Raynes was the only other person there. I couldn't believe Raynes would, or even could, steal Roma's money? But Reston? I wondered.

Roma soon returned shaking his head. "Crap!"

"What did the Watch Officer say?"

"I didn't mark the money. There's no way to ID it, even if we found it. It's gone."

I squatted down and felt around my own locker. I pulled out some bills, counted out a few and put the rest back. "Roma!"

"What?"

I stood up. "Take this. Interest free. Have a good leave."

"How'd you get so much money?" He looked at me suspiciously.

"Saved it. I don't spend a lot," I explained. "And, hey! Don't look at me like that! I was with you the whole time you were in the washroom. And I returned with you."

"Yeah, I'm sorry. Kind of an automatic reaction. I didn't think any of us would steal from a shipmate."

"Me either. But I can help. Please let me. And if you lock it up tonight you'll still have it in the morning."

"Yeah, thanks. I sure appreciate this. I'll pay you back, I promise."

"You'd better!" I laughed.

I unfolded my dress blues. Looked them over. The bell-bottom pants were pressed inside out, as was the jumper. The white piping around the wrists and the large collar needed to be replaced. But a little chalk whitened them up and made them passable.

"You going ashore, Matthews?" Raynes asked. I nodded. He began one of his tirades. "You going off to fornicate? Don't you know that The Good Book says 'Thou shalt not commit adultery?' In plain English that means you shall not have sexual relations outside of marriage."

"Wrong," I replied. "Adultery is only if you're already married. But Jews believe—and it's their holy book—if both parties aren't married, it's not adultery. But having sex then actually marries them. Automatically."

"Good heavens! You don't look like a kike!"

"Well, Raynes, there's another reason not to like you. The proper term is 'Jew' or 'Jewish.' And I'm not."

"So how do you know so much about them?"

"Friends. And I'm not a blind ignoramus. I read and learn."

Dressed and ready to go, I studied Reston for a few moments. *Hank,* I thought. *You just might have crossed the line.* I really wanted to wrap this thing up now. But how? Others still had to fit their pieces of the puzzle together. And I still had to find Reston's supplier. Frustrated, I left.

My true love was waiting.

* * *

Rena and I watched television, snuggling, with drinks. We talked during the commercials.

"I'm glad Blinker's isn't open tonight." she said, moving even closer. "It's nice just sitting here with you."

"Yes it is. But aren't you awfully close to me, you being married and all that?"

She hit me gently. "Shut up. I'll be the judge of how far I can go."

"Yeah. And I'll sit here and hurt 'cause we don't go any farther." She hit me again. I changed the subject. "Speaking of Blinker's, what do you know of Blink's military service?"

"Why?" She sat straight up. "I just called for his service jacket a while back."

"I ran across two little bits of info. First, Blink and I were talking Saturday night while you finished up. By the way, does he sit in the middle of the room every night?"

"He started that some time ago. Why?"

"I don't remember seeing him do it before."

Rena shook her head. "I don't know why he does. Anyway, what's this information you discovered?"

"Remember the night Blink said he'd give us a free dinner?" Rena nodded. "Well, he said something about getting out as a Signalman Second."

"A second class? That's all? After twenty years?"

"It sounded strange to me, too," I said.

"Signalman isn't a frozen rating, is it?"

"Somewhat, maybe. But he should've at least made first in twenty years. Why'd you call for his service record?"

"On a hunch. Chaské Hunter found out that Blink paid cash for the bar and had enough left over to remodel it. That would have taken a lot of ready money." She told me everything Hunter reported.

"He paid cash? After getting out as a second class? What kind of savings account did he have? Or did he make some great investments?"

"Don't know yet. You mentioned there were a couple pieces of information. What else did you find?"

"I was talking to Dasso, an SM1 on the Haystack. He told about when he was a seaman apprentice aboard his first ship. He knew a signalman who was a lot like Derella. Always in trouble. The rumor mill had it that he even made first class a couple times and got busted. Said he was the fastest signal lamp operator he'd ever seen. But he ran a slush fund, which got him in lots of trouble."

"Did he mention this guy's name?"

I nodded, grinning. "Davenport. First name of Nick. He was so fast on the signal lamp they called him Blink."

"Small world, isn't it?" She laughed. "Thanks. I'll keep that in mind when I look over his service jacket. We may just have run across the reason why he never made a higher rate." Rena cuddled up again. "Okay! Now I don't want to think about this stuff any more tonight. I only want to think about you."

"Click. Just turned off the thinking machine. Let's get closer."

* * *

Three days later, Rena got a call from OCI Norfolk. "Skye? Knox here at Central. We got the bank and police records for Davenport. No police record at all."

"And his bank records?"

"Savings and checking accounts in Virginia Beach. In 1949, he put a fair sum of money into his savings and added to it. Twenty to fifty dollars every couple weeks. By the end of 1951, he'd saved about ten grand."

"I know he was a lifer. That's about when he left the Navy. So he didn't have lots of money then."

"In April of '52, he emptied his savings account and took possession of an old architect's office. The next tax cycle shows him as owner. But we couldn't find any bills of sale, mortgages, building permits, nothing like that. And his saving account stayed close to zero for years."

"Any idea how much he paid for the building?"

"Records indicate it had a tax value of $19,995. But that's always lower than market value. Evidently, the place was pretty run down. Its value dropped for a couple years before this. Maybe it wasn't being used."

"And he paid cash for it, right?"

"Where'd you hear that? We didn't find that."

"Hunter found it hidden in Norfolk's records. He also found a sale price of thirty-five grand. How did Davenport get that much cash when he only had ten thousand?"

"I wouldn't hazard a guess," Knox said.

"Then he remodeled the place, which takes more money. This could be pretty valuable information. But I'll have to let it simmer for a while. All right. Thanks a lot."

"No problem. Anything else?"

"Not right now. Call me if you find any more information. Thanks."

53. AWOL

My Navy driver's license wasn't doing much good. Once again I was on the quarterdeck watching the guys get ready to go ashore. At Liberty Call, Reston slapped me on the arm from behind as he passed me. "Take care of the Old Haystack!"

"Will do! See you later!"

He trotted down the brow. He was in a hurry, but not like on other days. I wondered how long it would take him to return.

He wasn't back by the end of my watch. I went below and changed into a grubby uniform, so I'd be comfortable watching the movie, Rita Hayworth, Robert Mitchum and Jack Lemon in "Fire Down Below."

In the morning, Reston's rack was empty. I frowned. It was rare for him to stay out all night.

At Morning Quarters for Muster, Chief Gascomb took roll call. Each man responded.

"Dean, I see you're here. Cisco. Monnyng. Hawksbill." He worked down the list of men in the division. "Lyell!"

"Here!"

"Reston!"

There was no answer. The Chief called out again. "Reston!"

Still no response.

"Has anyone seen Reston?"

"Here!" the seaman gasped, rushing up from the Quarterdeck. He was still in his liberty uniform.

"Where've you been? Watch out, you'll wind up on report."

"Already am, Chief. Mister Eglin didn't let me slide."

"When did you get aboard?"

"Five minutes ago. Mister Eglin got my name and service number, then told me to get up to quarters. He was filling out the report chit when I left."

"What happened?" Gascomb asked.

"My ride overslept. Guess he's on report, too, on his ship."

The Chief looked at Reston for a long time, shaking his head. "You know the Old Man could bust you for this?"

"Yes, Chief. I know that." He seemed quite contrite. "But my record's clean. Maybe I'll only get restriction."

"You better hope so."

After quarters the crew went about the daily grind. As afternoon ship's work began, the bitch box blared:

NOW THE FOLLOWING MEN LAY TO THE EXECUTIVE OFFICER'S CABIN: RESTON, SN - HILL, FN - SCHEFF, RM3. LAY TO THE EXECUTIVE OFFICER'S CABIN.

Reston told me what happened. The three men, ready for XO's Mast at 1300 hours, were in dress blues. Outside the Exec's cabin, Lieutenant Commander Monroe said, "A few words to all of you together. I don't have the authority to reduce you in rate. But the Captain does. I'll decide if you get Captain's Mast. All right, we'll start with highest rate first. Scheff, you may enter."

The man entered the cabin and the door closed. When the door opened, Scheff stepped out with a slight smile.

"Hill!"

"Aye, aye, sir!" The man stepped into the XO's cabin. Again the door closed. When it opened a moment later, Hill was not smiling.

"Reston!"

"Aye, aye, sir!" He took off his white hat as he stepped into the cabin. Monroe, sitting at his desk, motioned for him to close the door.

The Exec flipped through Reston's service jacket and looked over the report chit. "Absent Without Leave," he mused. "You almost got back on time. What happened?"

"I spent the night at a friend's. I made arrangements for a ride, but he showed up late, sir."

"The charge is not a deliberate breach of discipline," Monroe said. "And you have a clean record. I'll give you a choice, Reston. Captain's Mast or two weeks' voluntary restriction. The first goes on your record, the second doesn't."

"I'll take the voluntary restriction, sir."

The officer nodded. "I thought you would. You're on your honor. You won't have to muster with the restricted men. But the wardroom will know you're restricted and you won't be allowed off the ship."

"I'll stay aboard, Commander."

"Very well. But a warning. If you break your word, I will put you on report, a Captain's Mast will be automatic and we'll throw the book at you."

"I understand, sir."

"All right," the officer smiled. "Carry on."

"Aye, aye, sir. Thank you, sir."

Monroe shook his head. "Don't thank me. Just keep yourself squared away."

54. JUNK

Shep told me the truth when I first came aboard. Unusual sounds, even soft ones or missing ones, can wake you up. Maybe it was because there was no competition. No screw shaft noise. No waves slapping the ship. No other at-sea sounds to compete with a man's breath hissing through clenched teeth.

Reston was pacing, bending over, holding himself, pacing some more. His restriction was half over. He was antsier the last few days. His attention span was short. He was like a caged animal when not actually doing something.

I crawled out of my rack, dressed and led him up to the fantail where we could be alone. "Hank, what can I do for you?"

"Nothing!" he snapped.

"I've seen you a lot of ways, but never like this. How can I help?"

Reston looked at me through his pain. "I don't know. I hurt. My bones hurt, Eric. My muscles are jumping all over on me."

"Withdrawal," I stated.

"What the fuck do you know about it...? Oh, shit...." He held himself and groaned. "What was your brother on, Eric?"

"Heroin. But he only snorted."

"Yeah, that helps keep a habit secret. No tracks."

"Is that why you don't have any tracks?"

"Don't jump to any stupid conclusions." He stood there, shivering.

"Hank, tell me the truth. Maybe I can help. What are you on?"

"Who the fuck do you think you are? Joe Friday? The truth, sir, just the truth. Duuuum-da-dum-dum; Duuuum-da-dum-dum-duuuuum!" He half-laughed, then stared at the deck, arms wrapped around himself. He stood silent for a moment, then pleaded, "Eric, I gotta get offa this ship or I'm gonna go crazy!"

I grabbed his arms. "Don't go off the deep end. That'll get you in a brig somewhere doing cold turkey."

"What the hell do you think I'm doing now?"

"Hank, I have to know for sure. Are you on heroin?" He nodded without looking up. "Okay, don't do anything dumb. I'm going ashore to see what I can work out. I may get into a lot of trouble for this, but I'm going to try."

"What're you gonna do...?"

I didn't answer immediately. I was going to let friendship sideline duty. I checked my watch. "Just hang on. It's oh-one-hundred now. Go below and hit the rack. I'll be back as soon as I can."

* * *

Skye worked on Thursdays, but her cleaning took until 0230, sometimes after that. Since I didn't have the duty I went on liberty, to Blinker's.

A few customers were still there. Nancy, Sue Anne and Jeannie were working the floor. I looked all around. I didn't see Rena. "Blink, where's my girlfriend?"

"She took the night off." He grinned. "She didn't keep you updated, Eric?"

"Guess she forgot. Thanks."

Blink waved and went back to washing glasses.

Now I could only wait at the apartment. As I walked past the east side of Blinker's, I glanced down the private parking area. A couple older vehicles sat toward the front. Two very expensive cars were near the alley, beyond Blink's private entrance.

"Whew!" I whistled. "Look at those wheels!" I walked over to them. The new white Cadillac De Ville had all the plushest features. The dark blue Lincoln Continental had just as many expensive accessories. I admired the cars and noted their license plates. Habit, you know.

One of these vehicles could be Blink's—the bar made enough money. The other car could be a friend's. But nobody was at the bar with him. And nobody inside Blinker's looked like they could afford such cars. The patrons I'd seen were sailors. None of them would have that kind of money.

I waited on Rena's apartment stairs. She came home two hours later. "Eric, I thought you had to stay on the ship tonight!"

"Yeah. But something happened." I had to think how to say this. I decided not to go straight to my request. "You weren't at Blinker's tonight. Where you been?"

She frowned and opened the door. "It's your turn to watch me? I've been working. You do remember my real job?"

"Yeah," I admitted. "Sorry, but this is an emergency and I've been waiting for two hours."

She closed the door behind us. "What's wrong?"

"I need some stuff."

"What kind of stuff?"

"Stuff. Smack…. Junk…. H…. Blow…."

"Eric! Why?"

I tried to explain. "I want to keep him indebted to me. I want him to testify for us. He knows I know about his habit. If I can get him just a little junk to get him through this restriction, he'll never suspect I'm an agent. He'll be in the palm of my hand."

Rena shook her head. "I don't like it."

"Do any of us have a contact where I can get a five dollar bag?"

"What happens if Central finds out?"

"Guess my ass would be on the line."

"Not only yours." Her brown eyes blazed anger. "I'd be an accessory!"

"It's something I have to do," I insisted. "Either you help me or I start looking on the street."

"God, what a week. Last night Frank Murphy 'suggested' that I work at his club, Bogie's. It was all I could do to refuse. Long drive, my apartment was close to Blinker's, so on. Finally he backed off, but he wasn't happy. And now this." She plopped down in a kitchen chair and glared at me.

"Why does Murphy want you to work at his club so bad?"

"I don't know. Maybe he likes the way I look." She took a deep breath. "And now you want to buy a user some drugs. You know, Mr. Matthews, sometimes you can be a sonofabitch! Why the hell do you have to do this?"

At least she didn't refuse outright. I took a deep breath. "Reston's a bright guy. He's just hooked. He reminds me of someone else who never got the help he needed."

"Who?"

Well, here it goes, I thought. "My older brother, Sean. He was hooked when I was a teenager. Nobody helped him. Our parents swore it was his choice. If he were strong enough, he'd stop. They never believed heroin was so addictive. But he couldn't quit by himself. He died because they thought he didn't want to quit. And he did! He told me. But no one believed him. And they…." I swallowed hard and continued in a whisper. I touched my scars. "They never helped him. And I was too young to help."

"What really happened when you were twelve, Eric? I know you didn't get hit by a baseball."

"How're you so sure?"

"I checked your medical records," she said quietly. "You were in the hospital with a concussion for a week. And you weren't really healed for a month. What happened?"

I took my glasses off and wiped my eyes. "I stumbled on Sean buying some stuff. I attacked his supplier with a hefty chunk of tree branch I found on the ground. The next day the supplier and some of his friends found me and beat the shit out of me. That's how I got the scars. But they didn't hurt much because I was unconscious when they were treated and they'd begun to heal a bit when I woke up. I found out the hard way that I couldn't protect my brother.

"So I watched him drift away. And when he got some extra strong stuff and died...." I paused a moment. "I... lost my brother... because nobody would help him... and I couldn't.... Now I want to put all these sonsabitches behind bars. But I know I can help Reston. "

Rena sighed. "You've gotten way too close to him, Eric." She got up and walked around the room twirling her hair around a finger, thinking. She went to the phone and dialed. "Come on, Dave. Be there!"

Rena talked to Dave for a few minutes. After hanging up, she shook her head. "He's the only person I know who could help. But he can't get any without stealing from the police evidence room. I'm sorry, Eric. I can't do much more."

I couldn't talk for a long time. "Okay.... I better go back. Try to keep Reston from going off the deep end." I called a cab. "By the way, what kind of car does Blink drive?"

"An old Chevy."

"Nothing real fancy or expensive?"

"No," Skye frowned. "Why?"

I described the cars I saw. I gave her the license plate numbers. She shook her head. "I wonder what they were doing there? I've never seen anybody there that looked like they had that kind of money."

"Maybe they're selling stuff out of Blinker's."

"I never noticed a sale going down. And I keep a pretty sharp eye out."

"Okay. See you later." I leaned over to kiss her.

"I will check the license plate numbers, though, and get the numbers and car descriptions out to the other operatives."

"Got to go. Good night. I love you."

"Yeah, you're kind of special, too, even when you are a sonofabitch." Rena grinned and blew me a kiss. After I closed the door, she called Central about the fancy cars.

Suspicious by nature, Skye took a look for herself. She wore a dark coat and stayed as far from the street as possible and still look legal. She waited in the shadows of the yard next door to Blinker's. There were no lights inside the bar other than those for security. Blink's car was gone. The expensive ones were there. She checked her watch. It was almost 0400.

She started for home, then heard voices. She dropped to her knees behind the neighbor's hedge and looked over them. Two middle-aged men walked to the automobiles. They talked quietly enough that Skye couldn't understand what they said. She didn't recognize the voices and she couldn't see them well enough to describe them. Each climbed into a car and drove off through the alley. She stayed put. Both cars drove to the avenue on the other side of Blinker's. One turned toward Norfolk, the other toward downtown Virginia Beach, speeding by just yards from her. She waited another five minutes then walked home.

* * *

I returned to the ship and went directly to the berthing compartment. Reston was sleeping peacefully.

"Reston, did you get some stuff on your own?"

I doubt that he heard me but I swear I saw him smile, even as dark as it was.

I went up onto the fantail to think. There was only one answer to where he got drugs here. There had to be a dealer on board.

55. REPORTS AND NEW ASSIGNMENTS

Central reported on the expensive cars within two days. The Cadillac belonged to Frank Murphy, owner of Bogie's Club in Norfolk, which had a Humphrey Bogart "Casablanca" theme. The Continental was registered to a Eugene Rudolph, owner of Punk's Bar in Virginia Beach, not far from the waterfront.

Skye decided that we should watch Bogie's. Punk's didn't seem to warrant special attention. Still, her instincts screamed at her. These two men met for some reason at Blinker's. And even if it was a dead-end, she needed to clarify their relationship.

She phoned Everett Cobbe who was working with the Marine guard at Dam Neck. She heard the barracks office announce the call. Moments later he answered, "Corporal Cobbe here."

"Skye here. I have some extra work for you."

"Sure. What can I do?"

"There's a place in Virginia Beach called Punk's Bar. Ever been there?"

"No, but I've heard of it. It's supposed to be a pretty nice place."

"Good. I'd like you to begin hanging out there."

"Anything special you need?"

"The owner, Eugene Rudolph, met another club owner where I wouldn't expect him. I need to know more about him and his club."

"Who was the other owner?"

"Frank Murphy of Bogie's. They met at Blinker's, where I'm working."

Cobbe whistled softly. "There are stories about Bogie's. 'Bogie' is an unidentified aircraft. Guys joke about that bar having stuff to get as high as a plane."

"Hmmm. The owner could be a supplier. But we need proof."

"Yeah. That could be tough. That club is also supposed to be a classy place. And I hear the owner leads a charmed life. Friendly, magnanimous, never had a bad thing pinned on him. You going to send someone there, too?"

"Yes."

"Have him be real careful. I understand more than one nosey Norfolk cop either got transferred to a different precinct or demoted—or worse. Others who work around the area have no trouble. Who're you going to send?"

"I'll see if Morgan Delano will volunteer for some extra evening work. Del's good. He can handle two shifts for a while."

"From what I know of him, you're right. But warn him about the place."

"Will do. Thanks, Cobbe."

"At your command. Semper Fi. You know that."

Skye laughed. "Yes, I do. You be careful, too."

"You'll get no argument there. Talk to you later."

Skye laughed as she hung up. So, Frank Murphy led a charmed life in more ways than one. She first heard of him as a "saint," always helping the community and his church. But if nosey cops consistently got moved out of the way....

Skye called Morgan Delano, who was acting as a third class Electronics Technician at the Naval Operations Base. He was out on a repair call. The ET shop took a message. Just to be sure, she left another message at his barracks for him to contact her. He did so just as she was leaving for work. He agreed to his new assignment.

Shortly before midnight there was a lull in Blinker's business. Rena stepped outside through Blink's private door for a quick cigarette. Blink's old Chevy was the only car out there. She lit up. She was half done when someone rounded the corner at the back of the building. The overhanging roof blocked the light from the street lamp in the alley. The man stayed in shadow.

"Who's there?" Skye called, a bit louder than necessary.

"Glenn Oliver." His soft voice and Southern Negro accent confirmed his identity. Rena had worked with him in San Diego, so she recognized his voice immediately. They didn't need the oral handshaking. His semi-sweet chocolate-colored skin blended with the night. His heavy mustache was a shade darker than the rest of his face. "Here." He held out a small piece of paper. "Here's another car to watch. Saw him hangin' around the Tradewinds, acting suspicious. Y'all might have Central check him out. I wrote down on my note there what I could recognize, but the plates were in shadow so I don' know if I got the numbers right."

She took the paper and put it into her skirt pocket. She'd examine it when she got home. "Thanks, Glenn," she whispered. "Better go. Don't want anyone to see you here."

He flashed a big smile. "Yes, ma'am. I'm gone."

He disappeared around the corner. Skye ground her cigarette out with her shoe, opened the door and nearly walked into the bouncer.

"Who you talkin' to out there?" Bowser asked.

Skye looked up at Blink's bouncer. "What?"

"Who were you talkin' to out there?" he repeated.

"No one, why?"

He scowled. "I heard ya talkin' to someone."

56. STORIES AND A WATCHER

So Bowser heard Rena talking to Glenn. Did he also hear Oliver's voice? She didn't know but he gave no indication that he'd heard another voice. She thought fast. She shook her head and looked the big man in the eye and smiled. "I was going over my shopping list. Maybe you heard me talking out loud to myself."

Bowser nodded, grinning crookedly. "Yeah. That musta been it. I thought maybe somebody was botherin' ya. The safety of Blink's employees is part of my job, ya know."

"Thanks for being concerned." She patted his arm. "I appreciate it."

He nodded, beaming like a just-praised child.

*   *   *

We were at sea again. I really enjoyed CIC now. Even the more difficult aspects of those watches were becoming easier.

"Gather 'round, children, and I'll tell you a story," Hauser droned on a humdrum midwatch. "In the Med—that's Mediterranean for the uninitiated—every ship selects an orphanage or other institution for the crew to fix up, clean, scrape, paint, whatever.

"One ship, home ported right here in Norfolk, pulled into a small Italian town and started working their magic. It was October, but weather is milder there, so they could still paint outdoors. They kept warm by working hard. They discovered that the place's furnace was crapped out and the people who ran it didn't have enough money to buy another. It was nice having their woodwork painted, but it would be pretty cold in a couple months. Some Italian winters can be uncomfortable.

"Back on the ship, the guys spread the word. Within hours, the crew donated a hundred dollars out of their pockets, almost enough for a new furnace. By the time the ship pulled out, they'd collected another hundred. They had to go to sea to do their Navy stuff, so they left the money at the orphanage and departed.

"Their Old Man requested permission to return there for a few days instead of spending their whole next tender availability in Naples. The brass approved. Over half the men gave up liberty to repair and paint the whole orphanage, not just the outside. The snipes, who know a bit about boilers and such, installed the new furnace and checked it out. The crew also noticed the kids didn't have any playground equipment. So they grabbed what woodworking tools they could find, bought some lumber and built swings, seesaws and other toys for the girls and boys.

"This story made the newspapers all over Italy. Yeah, we're the ugly Americans, ain't we?"

"Great story, Hauser," Clark complimented. "I heard it from guys on that ship, so I know that ain't no shit!"

"And what's the moral of such stories?" Ensign Auburn answered himself. "Helping people. That's more important than anything. That makes friends and proves that we're the good guys. As far as I've heard, the Rooskies don't do things like that."

I swallowed hard. *And how does one help others, Mr. Auburn,* I thought, *when it conflicts with one's duty?* It felt strange to take lessons from a young ensign who was so new to life and friendship and duty.

* * *

After cleaning up, Skye headed home. The crowd tonight was insistent, so she was very tired. While walking through the winter cold, she scanned the area like she usually did. A green 1962 Pontiac Catalina was parked across the street from her apartment. She'd never seen it before and wondered if a neighbor just bought a new car.

Smiling at the idea of owning a brand new automobile, she unlocked her front door. As she turned to close it behind her, she noticed a slight movement inside the Pontiac. It looked like someone ducked when she turned around. Upstairs, she examined each room before going any farther. She pulled up a chair behind the front bedroom window so she could sit and watch.

Nothing changed. Enough time passed that she began to wonder if there really was anyone there. She went back into the living room and turned on the light. She ducked under the window to return to her chair. Within a minute, a shadow sat up in the front of the vehicle.

Her heartbeat thumped in her ears. Who was he? Was he watching her? She calmed herself. The man left after sitting there for ten more minutes.

Then she remembered the note Glenn Oliver gave her. She fished the paper out of her pocket, opened it and read: "1962 Pontiac Catalina – green – Virginia plates – ??4-218." Her heart beat wildly as she called Central. She was sure the car Oliver saw was the same one. When Central reported back in two days, the bad news was that they weren't able to match the license plate numbers.

57. THE TRAP

I watched the ocean go by while waiting in the paint locker line. When I got to the door, Monnyng and I talked a while. He seemed especially jumpy. I told him there was a way he could get Smith off his back, if he wanted to.

He didn't respond for a few seconds. Finally he asked: "How?"

"Set a trap," I said.

"What can we do?"

I liked that "we" part. He was ready to do something. "When you refill Smith's flasks, deliver them to him. Then drop the big bottles over the side and tell me. I'll set it up."

He hesitated. "I'll let you know...."

He was ready in a couple days. I paid a visit to the XO.

That afternoon two officers and the Chief held a surprise locker inspection. Smith's locker was the only one they inspected thoroughly. They found a full flask.

Smith had a shit fit. "Yeah, I got some booze here. But there's others who have a lot more."

"Who?" the Chief demanded.

"Monnyng's got more booze on board than I ever dreamed of having."

Everyone looked at the third class petty officer, standing near his locker. The Chief challenged Smith. "Can you prove it?"

"Sure. And besides, he's queer as a three-dollar bill," Smith ranted on.

"We need proof, Smith, not accusations."

"I'll show you! I know right where he hides it. Get him to open the paint locker."

"Monnyng, let's go."

"Sure, Chief! Glad to cooperate," he said. Gascomb followed him topside, holding the flask they'd found in Smith's locker. Monnyng unlocked his workspace.

"There!" Smith shouted. "In that metal box. His booze is in it."

Gascomb motioned. "Open it."

Monnyng did so. Everyone looked. There was no liquor. Monnyng had dropped the almost-full bottles over the side. All that the metal box held were a few classical music phonograph records, some ballet pieces among them, and the flowery stationery from his mother that the guys razzed him about. I had his other magazines for safekeeping.

Smith turned on the petty officer. "What did you do with it, you sonofabitch? I know it was there!"

Monnyng shrugged and smiled. "I don't know anything about booze around here."

"He hid it! He hid it somewhere in here!" Smith shouted. He grabbed the front of the bos'n's mate's shirt and waved his fist in his face. "Tell me where you put that vodka, you queer bastard, or I'll knock your block off."

The Chief and the two officers inspected the place from top to bottom. They searched behind the paint cans and shook most of them, listening for their normal gurgle and feeling for their proper weight. They even opened a few. They found nothing out of the ordinary.

Finally Chief Gascomb faced Smith. "How did you know it was vodka, Smith?"

"I... uh... just thought it was. I... uh...."

"Write him up, Chief," one of the officers ordered. "For alcohol aboard ship, disrespect to a petty officer, threatening a senior, defaming another sailor, conduct detrimental to good order and discipline, and anything else you can think of. Give him no chance to squirm out of the charges. We will not permit such behavior on this ship."

That evening I returned Monnyng's magazines. We talked for a long time. I told him I'd put an anonymous note under the Exec's door to trigger the inspection. I left him in the paint locker, feeling good. I returned to the living compartment thinking about something I'd observed during the locker inspection.

Raynes was the most nervous person in the compartment. I wondered why.

58. MORE REPORTS

Awake in my rack, trying not to let the gentle roll of the ship rock me to sleep, I reviewed everyone on the *Hestek* who might be a drug user. I puzzled over who provided Reston relief when he was on restriction. There was no obvious choice for that one. I still had work to do.

I lay there for some time then got up to go to the head. When I returned to the compartment, I heard someone talking very quietly. Of course, I had to investigate. Raynes was talking in his sleep, sometimes crying. "It's... my fault," he mumbled. "What... wrong? A .... divorce? ... Please don't...."

This piqued my curiosity. I wished there was a way for me to call Rena from the ship at sea.

* * *

Skye answered her phone. "Here."

"Tom Morelos. I witnessed a sale on the Naval Air Station."

"Who bought?"

"An AT3 named Roy Peale."

"Did you see the seller?"

"No. But it went down inside a black 1960 Thunderbird. Damned near new."

Hoping beyond hope, Skye asked, "License?"

"Virginia plates. Seven-niner-four one-three-eight."

"Photos?"

"Good ones, I think."

"Thanks, Tom. Great work. Get me more, if you can."

"I'll try. Adios."

Skye sat deep in thought for a long time. *So we've seen this guy before. He's an active one.* The phone jolted her out of her thoughts. "Here."

"Lunch, here. I have lots of info. I saw a sale and was able to follow the guy. It was easy. He's not too smart. He drives a bright red, brand new Corvette. Really spiffy. Not easy to miss."

"Their stupidity is our luck. You get the plates?"

"Virginia Alpha-one-three-nine, seven-eight-five. I followed him for miles. I watched him go to an out of the way spot, behind a Sears and Roebuck store."

"What was he doing?" Skye wondered.

"He met another guy in a Mercury and picked up some items. Not a lot, just a couple packages."

"You get any information on the other car?"

"Yes. He may be someone we haven't seen or heard of before," Lunch said. "This guy looks like an errand boy between the upper level supplier and the street people. He was driving a white '61 two-door hardtop Mercury 600."

"Did you get *his* plates?"

"Yes. When they split up, I followed the Merc long enough to get them. Virginia license one-eight-one, zero-five-zero."

"Great work, Brandon! Thanks! I'll get these checked right away."

"Sounds good. By the way, I got photographs all the way around, the sale and the meeting. See you later."

Skye hung up the phone and called OCI Norfolk to give them the information.

Central reported back that the driver of the Mercury was a man named Ronald Cronin, resident of Virginia Beach and employee of Punk's Bar. This connected a dealer with Punk's, though not necessarily with its owner, Gene Rudolph. What she found out about the red Corvette fit into an entirely different category. The agents had already identified two distributors: a groundskeeper at NAS named Dick Cunningham, who drove the Thunderbird, and an employee at the Mainside enlisted mess hall named Jerry Bando, who owned the De Soto. The Corvette belonged to Bennie Tappan, a crane operator at the Norfolk Naval Shipyard in Portsmouth. All these federal employees had Navy base passes. Once in, they could sell their dope.

"So," Skye mused, "we have insiders working the military bases...."

59. RECORDS AND NEW COLLISIONS

Skye received Nicholas Perry Davenport's service record. She read the file three times to understand him better. Then she let her subconscious work on the information.

She wanted to talk this over with me, but the *Hestek* was at sea. There was one other person on the team who was as close. She picked up the phone and dialed.

"Good afternoon. Wave Barracks. Darnell, SN, speaking."

"Jennifer Powers, SK2, please."

"I'll announce there's a call. Who's calling, please?"

"Rena, R-E-N-A."

A few minutes later, Powers was on the phone. "Rena?"

"Hi, Jennie."

"You sound like there's a problem."

"Yeah, I need to talk to someone about some info I got."

"And your boyfriend's not around, so I'm running second string."

"Oh, come on!" Rena almost shouted.

"Good Lord! I was just teasing you, girl!"

"I know. It's just that you hit the nail on the head. Eric's at sea. You know you're my best lady friend, but...."

"Uh-huh! But the man always takes precedence over the lady. Tut, tut! No snappy comebacks, now, are there? Don't answer. I've been there myself. So, what's bothering you?"

"It's too important to discuss like this. Find a secure phone and call me back."

"How about if I come over?"

"No! Don't do that!"

Powers was silent for a few seconds. Then she asked quietly, "Rena, what the hell is going on?"

"I'll explain when we're on a more secure connection."

"Ten minutes, honey. Bye."

Rena's phone rang in eight minutes and twenty-seven seconds. "Jennie here. Talk to me, girl."

"Where are you now?"

"Phone booth on a corner in North Chicago."

"Okay. First, I didn't want you here because I'm being watched. I don't want to give away any of the team." She described the green Pontiac Catalina and the man in it. "So I'm not meeting people unnecessarily."

"You tell Central about this?"

"Not yet."

"Why not?" Powers demanded.

"I want to be sure it's not a fluke."

"Let Central decide! Protect yourself, girl!"

"Okay, I'll call them. Now...." Skye reached for Davenport's service jacket. "A few weeks ago, Chaské Hunter found out that Blink paid cash for the bar. Also, some time back Eric was talking to Blink and found out that Davenport was a Signalman Second after twenty years in the Navy."

"Only a second class? That's hard to believe. Did he get busted?"

"That's the first thing that entered my mind, too. I got curious enough to call for his service record. I received it yesterday."

"Well, don't keep me guessing!"

"Okay. Listen," Skye began. "Born 20 March 1910, Jefferson City, Missouri. He joined the Navy at eighteen. Went directly to the fleet from boot camp. Spent a year on the deck force, before striking for signalman. Looks like he beat the Depression by re-enlisting for six years in '32. He got out in '38, with ten years of continuous service. But he went back in...."

"What rate was he when he got out?" Powers asked.

"Signalman Second."

"So he made rate fairly quickly. Why did he get out after ten years?"

"No clue."

"He didn't stay out?"

"No. He re-enlisted for four more years, two days after Pearl Harbor," Skye said. "He must have figured it was all downhill from there, so he signed up for his final six years in '45. Retired in '51 with twenty years—nineteen and six of actual time in service."

"Sure. Early re-enlistments cause time-in-service periods to overlap. So he was still a Signalman Second when he retired?"

Skye shuffled through the pages of the service jacket. "He made first class. Twice."

"What?"

"Each time he was busted. One Captain's Mast, one special court martial."

"What were the charges?" Jennie wondered.

"Usury. Both times. I quote 'Usury in that he did loan money and did charge exorbitant interest for said loans.' He ran slush funds and got caught."

"Twice."

"Right. The first time someone complained. A Captain's Mast busted him to second class. The second time, OCI swept through a whole destroyer squadron. This time he got a court martial."

"What did the court martial give him?" Powers asked.

"Reduction in rate by two pay grades, fine of half his pay for three months. Restriction to his ship for one month."

"They broke him down to third class?"

"Yep. He made it back to second, but didn't have time to make SM1 again before retirement. It ruined his pension. He didn't learn the first time, when he was fined as much as possible by his Captain's Mast. He seemed to learn from the court martial. There are no indications that he ever got into trouble again. Now," Skye said, "how was he able to pay cash for the bar when he got out?"

"Maybe he saved all the money he made with his slush funds," Powers suggested. "If they were good long runs, he could have put away a lot of dough."

"No, I have a report on his bank accounts. Central found that he only had ten grand when he got out."

"Where did they check? Just around the Norfolk area?"

"No, up and down the whole east coast."

"So how did he pay for Blinker's?"

"That's what I was asking!" Rena took a deep breath. "I don't know, Jennie. Not yet."

"Anything else interesting in that service jacket?"

"No. A few low quarterlies. AWOL a couple times, before the court martial. Looks like he might have done a lot of steaming."

"Running around doesn't build up a savings account. Looks like you have more questions than answers. I'm glad I don't have your job, girl. Field operations are just fine with me," Powers laughed.

"Guess I'll let you get back to your brand of fun. Thanks for talking this through with me. I'll have to think about what to do next."

"Any time, honey. Any time. Call me if you need my expertise and insights again. I'll check with you later."

"All right. Thanks."

* * *

The officers shuffled their watches so that when I was in CIC, the OOD

211

was Gunnery Officer Lt. Richard Ashe and the JOOD was Fox Division Officer Lt(jg) Eric Dapp. We never thought anything about the changes.

"Mister Dapp has the conn."

Every line officer must practice ship control. Nobody felt anything wrong. But Dapp evidently thought we were drifting too far to port. He commanded the helmsman to give the ship a little right rudder. Something else must've caught his attention because he gave no counter orders.

Any boredom on that watch ended with the message over the phones: "Bridge, Starboard Lookout! We're awful close to another can on the starboard bow!"

"All stations, Bridge. Captain has the conn! Emergency left rudder! Emergency full back!"

"Shit, we almost rammed it!" the lookout said.

Hauser was on the stack at the time. Mister Auburn looked at him. The radarman shook his head. "I didn't see a thing. Must have been hidden in the sea return."

Two days after that, Mr. Dapp did it again. Once more the Captain took the conn from him.

The bridge watchstanders told me after that, when Dapp had the conn, both the Captain and Mister Ashe watched him like hawks. They immediately corrected the junior officer's mistakes. A week passed without incident.

Then Mr. Dapp almost rammed another destroyer.

"Capt'n has the conn!" came the voice of the bridge phone talker. "Emergency left rudder! Emergency full back!"

Mister Auburn walked out of CIC's starboard door onto the 01 level. His face was ashen when he returned. He moved his mouth, but no sound came out. He swallowed and tried again, "I could have spit on the son of a bitch."

Twenty minutes later Dapp put on too much speed and we came much too close to the carrier.

"All stations, Bridge. The Capt'n has the conn!"

The following day Dapp was reassigned to be a CIC Watch Officer. He could no longer control the ship.

Dapp's career in the Navy was effectively over. He didn't have what it took. A line officer had to assume responsibility for his ship and the men on it. When he screwed up, he was done.

I wondered if I was on a similar track by not taking Reston in right now. Except my job was to find his supplier.

*   *   *

Around this time Ruth Gardner took a walk, staring out across the choppy waters of Willoughby Bay. She felt alone and lonely. She and Chaské had gone out a couple times. Then he disappeared. She didn't see him for weeks and she missed him. He'd filled a void, an empty place that was now almost bigger than she could handle. "Chaské, where are you? Why aren't you talking to me any more? I need you!"

60. OBSERVERS

Skye strolled home after work. Frank Murphy had visited again. He still wanted her to work for him at Bogie's. This time it wasn't a suggestion. Once again, she declined, repeating all her excuses. He was obviously irritated.

The green Pontiac was across the street, facing west. She went upstairs without looking at it. She entered her dark bedroom and stood to one side of the window thinking.

A while back Eric had asked why Murphy wanted her to work at Bogie's so badly. She had no idea at the time. Now, with the little thing she'd learned about Frank Murphy and with someone watching her, it seemed more urgent to get an answer to Matthews' question.

But no matter who or what Murphy was, this guy in the Pontiac was beginning to interfere with her work. There was no way any of her team could meet her here. She had to find out who this guy was. She was sure this was the same car Glenn Oliver reported. She decided to go out to get something. Anything. She forced herself not look at the other vehicle while she went to her car. She backed out of the driveway and drove east, opposite the direction the Pontiac faced. She drove normally, watching her mirrors.

The Pontiac's lights came on in seconds. The driver did a U-turn. When Skye was sure he was following her, she took a right and slowed down, hoping he'd come close enough to see his license plates. He didn't. She thought through her options. She decided to go to Cranston's, the all night café some blocks away. She drove so she could round the corner it was on and park right in front of the restaurant.

It worked. The Pontiac turned the corner as she got out of her car. The driver made eye contact, smiled admiringly, and continued down the block. Skye saw the plates: Virginia, 454-273. Glen Oliver reported the last three numbers as 218 and was missing the first two numbers. Now Central could get a good report.

She entered the restaurant and placed an order. She ate two doughnuts leisurely, sipping her coffee while she glanced over the day's newspaper. She forced herself to be calm, acting normal and unsuspicious in case the tail doubled back to check on her. When she got home she reported the information to OCI Norfolk.

She got an ID report a day later. The green Catalina belonged to a Robert Little, a welder at the Norfolk Naval Shipyard in Portsmouth, the same place that Bennie Tappan, the Corvette owner, worked.

* * *

The weather was as calm as it ever gets off Cape Hatteras. We were catching up on our work on the weather decks. It was tedious and boring—chipping old paint off the deck so it could be repainted. The mindlessness provided plenty of time to daydream. I dreamed of a slim, well-tanned, perky, dimpled, auburn-haired gal.

I stood up to stretch and do some head rolls to loosen my neck muscles. Cisco was on the 01 level, clutching his ever-present coffee cup. He motioned for me to come up. I pointed to myself, mouthing the word "Me?"

He nodded, pointed straight at me and motioned again.

I climbed up the nearest ladder. Cisco had moved. I found him sitting on Mount 34's platform.

"Sit down. I'd like to talk with you."

"Sure. What's up?"

He sat silently, looking straight ahead and sipping his coffee for almost a minute before he asked, "Where are you from?"

"You called me up here for that? I'm from Rockford, Illinois."

"That's not what I meant." He paused, looking down into his coffee cup. "I've been watching you. I watch everyone. I study people. I've wondered about you for a while. You're very good at what you do, Matthews. Took me a long time to realize you weren't just a boot on the deck force."

My heart was thumping so loud I thought Cisco could hear it.

"It took me a long time," he repeated. "By the way, I'm glad you were able to get rid of Monnyng's antagonist."

"How do you know it was me?"

"I watch. Put two and two together. I also know you're not what you're pretending to be."

215

61. SHADOWING

I tried to look at Cisco like he was crazy. I stood up to leave. "I don't know what you're talking about."

His hand motioned for me to sit back down. "Like I said, you're good. But there's a tiny crack in your armor every once in a while. It takes a very astute observer to see it. Took me a long time." He let that sink in. "And my suspicions were confirmed when I saw someone smack you upside the head with a dogging wrench, which he immediately deep sixed, by the way."

"You saw that?"

Cisco looked directly at me and smiled. "That got your attention, didn't it? I shouted at him. He ran away. Then I called the bridge to report that you were hurt."

"So I owe you. Thanks. Who was it that decked me?"

"Same person with whom you had an altercation in which you entwined yourself in the lifelines."

"You saw that, too?"

"You were in control, then. No need to interfere."

"Why didn't you report who hit me over the head?"

"I believe you're something other than what you seem. I thought you might have your own way to take care of him. Must have been correct, too. He's no longer with us."

"So, what do you want from me now?" I asked.

"Just listen to something I want to tell you."

"Okay."

"Remember the sea stories some months ago, the ones about our tour around Pompeii and Vesuvius and a cameo factory? The story about Derella and the admiral's barge?" I nodded. "Well, they left out some things.

"The excavators at Pompeii poured plaster of Paris into every hole they

216

found. We saw plaster casts of people covering their heads with their hands and chained dogs trying to get away. They all died, not from ash but from gas, kind of like stack gas, if you ever got a good whiff of that." He pointed over his shoulder to the exhaust coming out of the after stack.

"That house where Derella was so intrigued with the sex pictures, had a large courtyard in the middle with a beautiful garden. They made plaster casts to identify the plants. Then they replanted it precisely the same way with exactly the same plants. It was stunning.

"Our last stop that day was the cameo factory. The carvers, artists of some repute, claim each piece has a hidden figure inside it and that's what they carve.

"So here we have a whole city whose essence consists of many things of remarkable beauty hidden from casual observers and artists who see the essence hidden within each piece of their raw materials."

"That's almost mystical," I commented.

Cisco nodded. "Now I don't know why you're on the Old Haystack. I suspect you're checking someone out. I have an idea who that is. I ask you to remember that he's just like Pompeii, just like the seashells. He has great value hidden inside. You might even say something wonderful."

I was silent for long moments, wondering how Cisco read others so well. I debated how much to admit. He obviously could keep a secret. I took a deep breath. "We all have hidden wonders. I know he's a lot more special than the guy who attacked me. I'll hurt him as little as possible. I promise."

"Thank you. And good luck to both of you." I stood up to go. Cisco flicked a finger on the book in my back pocket. "What are you reading?" I pulled the book out and handed it to him. It was a copy of *Secret Agent* by Joseph Conrad. Cisco laughed. "Aren't you afraid this will give you away to others?"

I looked him in the eye. "I don't know what you're talking about. That's a novel about terrorists. It's kind of prophetic, considering what's going on in France now."

Cisco nodded. "Yes. Those Algerians are making life miserable, aren't they?"

"Yeah. I wanted to read something to help me understand what's going on." I nodded to the paperback in my shipmate's hand. "That book has nothing to do with me or who I am. May I have it back so I can return to work?"

Cisco handed me the book with a smile.

*   *   *

Coming home, Skye noticed Robert Little and his Catalina again. She'd lost track how many days he'd been there. She called Central.

"Skye here. Commander Robert Blount, please."

"He's out. Can I take a message?"

"Have him call me back. I'm at home."

"How important is this?"

"Priority."

"I'll let him know."

Rena's phone rang in twenty-three minutes. "Here."

"Commander Blount. You called?"

"Yes, sir. I need your help."

"What's going on?"

"Somewhere along the line I attracted attention. Now I have a tail who spends a lot of time watching my apartment. He often follows me. He's going to get in the way of future operations."

"I'm looking at your communications with Central now. Are you talking about Robert Little?"

"Yes, sir."

"What would you have us do?"

"That's the problem, sir. If we do nothing, he gets in the way. We have to have some kind of charges to arrest him and that could tip off the ring that we're on to them. Do you have any suggestions, sir?"

"Your assessment seems accurate. Maybe I can do something, but you're right, it's a tricky situation. Let me think this over. If you get any ideas, give me a call, high priority. That'll even get me out of a meeting."

"Yes, sir. Thank you."

"Okay, Skye. I'll get back to you as soon as I can."

The next day Blount let her know some agents would tail Robert Little to try to find something to charge him with. They'd also be there in case she needed help.

* * *

We pulled back into Norfolk late in the afternoon. Nobody did much the rest of the day. Except me.

I rushed to the car pool before the *Hestek* was tied up to the pier. This was my first time as duty driver without having to also stand watches. As I got back to the D & S Piers with the car that was reserved for me, the Captain's wife pulled up. The Quarterdeck Watch Officer was right—the Old Man was taking off as soon as he could. I'd only have to drive around a few isolated officers.

Liberty call went down. Reston was in the middle of the pack. I followed him. I slowly moved the car to where I could watch him. Daylight was growing longer and I followed him with relative ease.

Reston walked through the gate to Hampton Boulevard and turned right, as I'd seen before. He continued for a few blocks, passing some abandoned buildings. He melted into the shadows between two old warehouses.

I followed him in short increments, watching through the small telescope I bought in New York. It grew too dark to see much and I was wary of getting closer. But I identified the exact point where Reston disappeared. I drove beyond that point, made a U-turn and pulled over. I turned off the lights and the engine. I faced the direction Reston would take when he returned to the ship. I slouched down so I could barely see over the dashboard and wasn't too visible to someone outside. Reston stepped out of the shadows and hurried back to the D & S Piers. He never looked backwards.

I drove up a short distance. I left the car to examine the area behind the warehouses. Nobody was back there, but the space was large enough for trucks to turn and back up, room to load and unload cargo. Another row of warehouses lined the other side of the loading zone.

I looked for a way to drive into the area. There was a truck entry some distance farther on. Behind the second row of buildings was a smaller alley, just large enough for a car to turn around. I returned to the ship.

The messenger told me he'd just heard that the Old Man had awarded our boozing shipmate, Smith, a special court martial at Captain's Mast earlier that day.

I went to the public telephone on the pier to call Rena.

"Hi, Eric!" Skye answered. "Anything interesting happening?"

"Don't know yet," I said. "Check something out and we'll see."

"What do you have?" she asked.

"Remember the religious fanatic I told you about? Luke Raynes?"

"Yes."

"He was talking in his sleep. Crying about a divorce. If it's bothering him so much, maybe it's significant. Can you get information on him from before he joined the Navy?"

"I'll look around. Isn't Raynes the one who preaches on the street corners?"

"Affirmative."

"Maybe you should follow him on liberty, too. Watch him for a while."

"You suspect something?"

"No. But you know there's a supplier on the *Hestek*."

I laughed. "And you think it might be The Preacher?"

"Remember my instincts. Just watch him for a while. I'll get your info for you."

* * *

When Raynes and I both had liberty, I went into Norfolk to look for him. I took the bus after the one he took because it might look suspicious if I was on the same bus he was. I asked a few questions of some street people and was steered to where they knew a sailor preached a lot, on the corner of a very fundamentalist church.

Raynes was there. He preached non-stop for a long time. He also handed out pamphlets. He went on forever. I leaned against a doorway like I was waiting for someone and watched from half a block away. Periodically I used my telescope. I didn't notice anything obvious. But something felt odd. Raynes's movements didn't seem natural, but I couldn't put my finger on it.

* * *

Zoss sat down beside to me during supper.

"I have some interesting news," he said.

"What's up?"

"A friend at the base legal office told me about the court martial of someone who used to be in our division."

I looked at him and grinned. This could only be one of two people, and I was interested in both. "Go on, please."

"Our friend Smith got slapped down pretty hard. Three months brig time and an undesirable discharge. That might be chastisement enough for his un-Christian behavior." I laughed out loud. Zoss asked, "What's so funny?"

"Stephen, you're downright gleeful at someone's punishment and you even have a Christian reason for it."

His eyes twinkled. "Ah, yes" he said. "Doesn't the Lord work in mysterious ways? Perhaps I sin in being so pleased, but the man was ill mannered, uncouth and foul-mouthed. We're a better crew without him."

I nodded my agreement.

That night I followed Raynes again. He preached outside for a long time and handed out pamphlets. I observed him with my telescope. Then he went into the church. I waited outside but got tired and returned to the ship.

This whole thing still didn't feel right. I mulled over what I'd seen as I walked down the pier. A sound grabbed my attention, metal on metal, like a slide shoving a shell into the chamber of a .45. I jumped behind a nearby dumpster as a shot rang out.

A car screeched its tires as it headed for the parking area. I pulled out my telescope to see his license, but he'd already turned behind other cars.

Two watch standers ran from their ships onto the pier to investigate, but the shooter was gone.

"Was that a shot?"

"Sure sounded like it."

"Hey, you, did you hear a shot out here?"

"I heard it," I replied. "But I couldn't tell who shot it or at what."

When I got back onto my ship, I went to the mess decks for a cup of coffee. I sat and thought for a long time.

62. DANIEL HAN AND DEL

I thought a lot about the shooting incident. I didn't hear the bullet hit anything. I think the shooter fired above me. Maybe it was a warning. I must be getting close to something, but I didn't know what. Somebody knew who I was. That was certain. I'd attracted the wrong kind of attention somewhere along the way. But how? I didn't have any answers.

* * *

Blinker's wasn't very busy this early on Saturday evening. Skye noticed the man the instant he walked in. He was Chinese and not a lot of Asians came here. He chose a booth in the back corner. She took him a menu. He looked up at her with laughing eyes and a smile. "Hi, Mom!"

Skye chuckled. "Stuff it," she said quietly. "You're not supposed to know me."

"Okay. I'd like a beer, ma'am. Whatever's on tap."

"Show me your ID." He handed her his Navy ID card. "You're almost as young as you look, Daniel Han!"

He laughed. "Thanks."

"Anything else?"

"Let me look over the menu."

"Be right back with your beer," Skye said.

When she returned, Bowser was growling at Han. "What're you doing in here?"

"I stopped in for some supper. Why?"

"We don't want any Japs in here."

"That's all right with me," Han quipped. "I'm Chinese."

"All you slant-eye bastards are the same," Bowser said. "You fuckers killed my father. Get out of here!"

222

Rena put the beer on the table. "Here you are, Mr. Han!" She turned to Bowser. "Why should he get out?"

"I don't want any goddamn Japs in here."

"He's not Japanese. He's Chinese."

"You can tell by looking at him?" Bowser snarled. Han sipped his beer.

"I checked his ID. His name is not Japanese. He's Chinese," she repeated. "They were on our side during World War Two."

"Same difference to me. It was yellow, slant-eyed sonsabitches that killed my father on Tarawa. I get sick, just looking at him."

"Bowser, he wants to order food. His money is good old American green. Let him eat and then leave. Do that for me?"

"You're some kind of Jap lover and I'm supposed to...?"

"Should I ask Blink if we're chasing away paying customers? If looking at him makes you sick, go look somewhere else."

Lips pursed, Bowser growled, "You better watch your step. You don't want to cross me. And you're coming very close."

He strode away.

Skye looked at her customer. "Sorry about that. Some people get crazy when they lose a parent so young."

"That I understand. The bigotry takes me by surprise. I grew up in New York, but I haven't lived there for a while now. I never got this reaction back home. It's happened a lot since I left The City. Enough that I'm almost beginning to get used to it."

"Still, I'm sorry. Have you decided on some food yet?" She lowered her voice. "And do you have anything to give me?"

He pointed to the menu. "Yes. And the burger and fries look pretty good."

"They are. Burger and fries, coming up. You have my phone number?" she asked. He nodded. "Okay, call me. I'll be home about 0245."

"Will do." After finishing his meal, he dropped a five-dollar bill on the table along with the check and walked out.

Rena's phone rang soon after she got home. Daniel Han made his report. A couple days earlier, he had seen a large sailor, a seaman, Caucasian, built like a boxer, suspiciously hanging around the cruiser piers. The guy didn't seem to be doing much, just loitering. But Daniel thought he seemed suspicious. Han also gave Skye the information on a guy in a De Soto Fireflite who looked suspicious.

Skye was about to call Central when she got another call. "Here."

"Del here," Morgan Delano said. "I've been hangin' around Bogie's a lot lately, jus' like ya told me ta do, havin' fun, ya know, dinin', dancin', drinkin'—not too much, but enough ta hafta go out for the cool night air sometimes, ya know?"

"I gather you saw something, Del?"

"Yeah. And learned sumthin', too, ya know?"

Skye chuckled at the difference between the impression given by the man's speech patterns and his preciseness. "What did you learn?"

"I learned that a pimple-faced weasel-lookin' punk with a hot sports car can attract many more ladies than a handsome specimen like me, ya know?"

She laughed out loud. "Don't be too jealous, Del. When he's behind bars you can go pick up all his lonely ladies."

"Ya know, I never thought o' that!"

"Who is this weasel?"

"Guy named Ned Luce. He's kinda the right-hand man for the owner of Bogie's, a guy named Frankie Murphy, but lots a folks just call him Murph. This punk Luce runs all kinds of errands, ya know? Flowers for the wife. Messages ta friends. Good Kentucky bourbon for the mayor. You name it, he does it. An' he loves ta do these errands so he can drive his beautiful '61 Studebaker Hawk. White with black sculpted fins. Ohhh, bee-yoo-tee-full little thing, ya know?"

"Did you take your eyes off the wheels long enough to see the license plate?"

"Certainly. Virginia two-zero-six, six-four-two."

"Did he do anything illegal?"

"Haven't got in that good with him yet. But I'll keep trying. How ever, I did overhear him talkin' ta Murph one time. Now there's one slick mother-fu..., pardon my French, ya know? I don' think glue could stick ta this guy. Any ways, they were talkin' an' Luce made some comment about pickin' up a special package for the boss."

"What kind of special package?" Skye asked.

"Dunno. I'm not privy ta all their secrets. Not yet, ya know? They were talkin' in real soft voices. Then they moved further away an' I couldn't hear nothin' more. But I suspect you might want ta put a tail on this weasel ta follow him around town. Ya jus' might see somethin' interesting, ya know? But be careful. I hear he's got as nasty a personality as you'll ever find' in a human bein'."

"Thanks, Del. Keep watching for me, will you?"

"Will do."

"And, Del, if possible, try to get a key impression of Bogie's front door locks. We may need keys later."

"Okay, your wish is my command, ya know? Bye."

Rena hung up, and telephoned Central, "Skye here. Report from Daniel Han on the Orlando. He sighted some sales from a 1959 blue De Soto Fireflite, Virginia license four-eight-zero niner-five-zero. He'll mail photos directly to you. He also spotted a well-built Caucasian seaman on foot doing business. No other information. Also, I need some info about a Ned Luce who runs errands for Frank Murphy, owner of Bogie's. He drives a 1961

Studebaker Hawk with Virginia tags, number two-zero-six, six-four-two. See if you can find anything on him, all right?"

"We'll do what we can."

*　*　*

Next morning, I got up and noticed that, again, Reston hadn't slept in his bunk all night. This was quite unusual for him. So I went looking for him.

I missed quarters for muster and inspection because I found him. After searching almost every place I could think of, I was on the 01 level, heading back to the living compartment to get a pack of cigarettes.

As I passed Mount 33, I noticed some feet sticking out from the interior side of the gun mount's shield. I looked inside the gun tub. Reston was leaning against the shield. He looked dead. I checked for a pulse. I felt nothing.

63. TRAGEDY

I just stood and stared at Reston's body. A syringe was on the deck next to him. Alongside an empty heroin packet. He had a note in his hand:

> "Cory Palm was like a brother to me. But I killed him. I snorted up just before we had an unexpected refueling. I did the best I could, but the ship was rolling and I lost my balance. I pushed Cory off the 01 level and killed him. The more I thought about that, the more it ate away at me. I killed my best friend. Everything reminded me of it. We gave each other birthday presents. He gave me a knife. I used it every day and I saw his face every time I did. It all came crashing down on me. The missing people on the fishing boat. The death with the helicopter crash. Coe being forced to use his safety belt. All I saw was death. Everywhere. I threw the knife overboard. But I couldn't forget. So, I snorted more and more heroin, but that didn't work either. I couldn't forget. I could have gone through cold turkey, but that would have been a living hell. I've been living in hell ever since I killed Cory. So I'm ending it all with a nice overdose. I'll just go to sleep and it will be all over. All over."

I dreamt of helping Reston get the cure, freeing him from his enslavement. It would never happen now.

I sat down by the body. Thought of everything we'd done together. The help and support we gave each other. The jokes and tragedies we shared. I shed tears for this young man I'd wanted to help as badly as I wanted to help my own brother. Now it was too late.

I wiped my eyes. I felt like picking up the syringe Reston had used and throwing it over the side in pure frustration. But that would be interfering with the scene of the death. I saw Cisco farther along the 01 level.

"Cisco!" I choked up. Cleared my throat. Swallowed hard. Motioned for the second class bos'n to come over to me.

Cisco stopped at my side. He looked down at Reston. For the first time since I came aboard the *Hestek*, I saw him lose his composure. "Aw, fuck. What the hell happened?"

"He overdosed. On purpose. He never used a needle. Always snorted. But there's the syringe on the deck by him. And a note. He couldn't handle it any more." Cisco picked up the note, read it, crumpled it in his fist.

"So the essence of a good man got shot down by a needle on the Haystack."

"Yeah. Sometimes we win. Sometimes we lose. We lost this one."

"Go tell Chief Gascomb. I'll stand by here. Ask him to get the Doc up here. And to notify the XO."

The XO sent a messenger to clue the Captain in about what happened. Then he ordered Chief Hamilton and Contino, our two corpsman, to take Reston's body to sickbay and do what was necessary to send it home.

A few hours later the ambulance took Reston away. I sat and watched the dirty, oil-slicked water of the harbor. I realized I wouldn't be able to track down Reston's heroin source. I'd spent months on the Old Haystack for nothing.

I sat there feeling sorry for myself. But then it hit me. Someone had supplied Reston with drugs when he was on restriction, the night I tried to get Rena to find some dope for him.

I still had a job to do here—find that supplier.

I went out to the pay phone on the pier and called Rena to give her the bad news. I devised a plan on the way out to the phone. Skye agreed I should have another piece of equipment. She got Central to give me a telephoto lens for my 35mm camera.

On the way back I had another idea, one that energized me a bit. Maybe Hank Reston and my brother Sean were now friends wherever it is that people go after this life.

When I calculated that Reston would have gone looking for more stuff, I went over to the warehouses.

Evidently, I had some unsolicited help. Toby Burch, the Messenger of the Watch, told me that as I drove off, Lieutenant Semple, the Engineering Officer, railed at the Quarterdeck Watch Officer. "Where the hell's that duty driver going? He didn't have anybody in that car and he drove off! I have a dinner appointment at the O Club! Who is that driver?"

"Matthews," the watch officer answered.

"Give me a report chit. He's going to see the Captain."

"Lieutenant," another voice interrupted. "Please come here for a moment."

Semple turned to see the XO motioning to him. "Commander," the lieutenant said, "what's that driver doing?"

"Matthews is following my orders," the Exec lied. "I'm glad I overheard you. I never would have let your report chit get to the Captain anyway."

"How am I supposed to get to the O Club, sir?"

Monroe handed him a five-dollar bill and pointed to the phone on the quarterdeck desk. "Call a cab. I'll pay."

* * *

I maneuvered into the alley behind the second row of buildings in the warehouse area. I picked what I hoped was a good place for observation and turned the car around to make a quick exit if necessary. I threw my white hat on the car seat. It was too easy to see in the dark. I worked my way between two buildings.

Another car slowly entered the area with its lights off. I dropped onto my stomach. I put the telephoto lens on my camera, then placed the camera on the ground in front of me. I stuck my glasses into my jumper's inside pocket and watched through my little telescope. The car pulled up to the space between two warehouses nearer the city street. It was one building over, so I only had a little trouble seeing it. The black vehicle had a fin that looked like it went all the way to the front of the car, like a Thunderbird.

I took a couple photos. The car waited for just a few minutes before leaving.

It was getting dark. The car backed out slowly and turned to leave. I watched through the telescope. The driver turned the corner before putting his lights on. I never saw his license plates.

A half hour later, I was back on the *Hestek*. I entered a wake-up call for 0230 to phone Skye.

When the watch woke me up, I made my way to the quarterdeck. I pointed to the phone and asked the Watch Officer, "Mister O'Reilly, may I use that?"

"You got up at this hour to use the phone?" the officer asked.

"Yes, sir. She's been at work. And it's pretty important."

"Very well. But no longer than five minutes."

I took the phone as far into the thwartships passageway as I could and dialed Rena's number. "Be home, be home."

"Here."

"Eric, here. You just get home?" I spoke into the phone quietly, like this was a personal conversation.

"Hi, Eric. I've been home about twenty minutes. It was an easy cleanup tonight. What's up?"

"Rena, you sound strained or nervous. What's wrong?"

228

"Oh, nothing."

"Come on! I can hear it in your voice. Tell me what's wrong or I'm coming over there."

"It's nothing to worry about. I'm being tailed by one of the pushers or errand boys or someone. Central's on it."

"Then you shouldn't be as upset as you sound. What else is there?"

She heaved a huge sigh. "Tonight when I got home, there was a note slipped under my door."

"Up on the second floor?"

"Yes. It wasn't in the mail. No stamp, no return address."

"What was it?"

"It was short. A warning. It said: 'Be careful. They're watching you. Watch your back.' It's signed, 'A friend.' I have no idea who left it there."

64. WARNINGS AND CHALLENGES

So it seemed that more than one person was watching Rena.

"Want me to come over? Keep you company for a while?" I asked her.

She gave a nervous little laugh. "I'd love that. But what about tomorrow? Could you walk around work with me? I'll be all right. It was just a little unsettling." She took a deep breath. "Actually, I'm surprised none of us have been in danger before now. I was expecting worse."

"Yeah, but it's still a surprise." I decided not to tell her I'd been shot at. Not when others might overhear me. "Well, I went looking for our friends tonight, even though I no longer had my guide. I did see one of our friends but only from a distance and in the dark. But I saw his '61 black T-Bird."

"No photos?"

"I got some but it was really too dark to take pictures. He didn't use his lights where I could see them."

"Sixty-one T-bird? We may already have his license plate number," she said.

"Yeah! Too bad it couldn't work out."

"A guy with a new Thunderbird is definitely one of the dealers. Now we have to find his supplier."

"I'm also wondering," I said, "if you found out anything yet about our friend who's so religious?"

"No. Central hasn't reported back yet. Tracking all this back may take some time. Keep watching him."

"Will do. I can't wait for party time," I commented. "And you be careful. Call your friend the instant you need help."

"Okay. See you later." She blew a kiss into the phone. I returned it.

* * *

Skye dreamt of a ringing phone. She woke up to find the noise was real. Her clock said 0537. She shuffled into the living room to answer the phone.

"Here," she mumbled.

"Central here. Commander Blount wanted me to contact you the instant we got something on Robert Little."

Rena became fully awake. "What did you find?"

"We've shadowed him for a week. He's one of the street dealers. He picked up some drugs from a little guy in a Studebaker Hawk. Tonight he made two sales. We have both events on film. But Blount doesn't want to pull him in for this."

"Yeah, it would be a tip-off."

"That's his thinking. But we also saw Little stop a number of times at liquor stores and bars. It seems he drinks a bit. That might come in handy. The Commander wants you to hang in there until we can take him out of circulation."

"You're going to take him out?"

"That or pull him in. Commander wants you to call if it gets worse. Don't take more chances than necessary."

Skye chuckled. "Don't worry. I've never liked that idea. Thanks."

She hung up the phone, wondering what Central would dream up to pull Little in without tipping their hand.

* * *

During Quarters the next morning, Chief Gascomb mentioned that the compartment cleaner's assignment was ending. He asked for a volunteer to take the job. I thought about it for five seconds or so. Contrary to the military axiom to never volunteer, I said I'd do it. There were only positive aspects to this—a chance to watch the trash for interesting items like needles and packets, being right there when anyone came into the compartment, overhearing conversations and seeing strange behaviors. I start the first of the month.

* * *

The following Friday, I got a call from Rena. I knew Blinker's would be busy because it was the first night of a weekend. So I was surprised when she phoned me via the Quarterdeck phone at 1700. "This is unusual. What's up?"

"I got a report today you'll want to see. Meet me at the gate in half an hour."

"You're not working?"

"I told Blink I'd be late. See you soon."

She had me sit in the passenger seat. Handed me a report on the divorce of Luke Raynes' parents. They'd argued, viciously, often about him, so he felt the divorce was his fault. Actually, it was due to incompatibility, partly because his dad couldn't stand his wife's beliefs. He'd often called her a "religious nut."

After the divorce, the eight-year-old boy lived with his mom. She used her maiden name again and changed his legal name to hers, Raynes.

She committed suicide when he was fourteen. She shot herself in the head. He discovered the body. It was very messy. Luke, still a minor, had to live with his father, even though he hated the man. He joined the Navy right after turning seventeen, evidently just to get away. He kept his mother's maiden name instead of taking his father's.

I stared at the father's name. "No shit!"

"Mmm-hmm," Skye replied. "None other!" I placed the papers on the seat between us. She continued, "Watch Raynes like a hawk. If he's a supplier, he might get the drugs directly...."

"But why?" I interrupted. "Why, if he...? He does hate his father, doesn't he?"

"Maybe Dad is so overpowering that Raynes feels like he doesn't have a choice."

I definitely had to tail Raynes now.

Skye dropped me off at the gate. The *Hestek* was at the southernmost pier, so I cut through the enlisted parking lot to get to the ship. When I was fifty yards or so from the Haystack, a car pulled up at the head of pier, too quietly. I noticed it out of corner of my eye. It was moving slowly with no lights. I saw a glint of metal where the rider's window should be. I threw myself down just in time. The shots were muffled, like the gunman was using a silencer. This time the bullets thudded on the metal of the dumpster, just above me. These weren't warning shots.

65. A FLOOD OF INFORMATION

Skye accepted the long distance call, charges reversed, from R. H. in Richmond.

"Chaské! I haven't heard from you in ages!"

"Sorry. And I'm sorry about the collect call, but I'm at a pay phone. I found something about Blink's building. I had to get to some very old reports in some historical archives in Richmond. But, wow, what I found!"

"Don't keep me in suspense!"

"Okay. Before the Civil War, that old Quaker Meetinghouse was a station on the Underground Railroad."

"That means it would have hiding places," Skye mused. "That's what was bothering me! But Norfolk wasn't...."

"There were a number of different roads that runaways used. In the 1830s or so, some went to Cherokee, Creek, or Choctaw country to the southwest. Some routes went north up the Appalachian Mountains into Pennsylvania. Some went out by sea. Frederick Douglass escaped on a northbound ship from Baltimore."

"And the station at our Quaker Meetinghouse?" Skye asked.

"I guess they hid runaway Negroes until they could get them onto ships handled by the right people. Leaving Norfolk or Portsmouth, they'd take the runaways north from there."

"Does this building have a history of hiding places?"

"Yeah," Hunter said. "Places the authorities never found before the Civil War. And during the war, Northern spies were smuggled out when it got too dangerous. They mentioned the secret hideaways in their reports and memoires."

"I've never seen them. Blink's never said anything about them." She paused, frowning, thinking there was something new she was missing. Pushing aside her questions to herself, she continued. "Did the reports say

233

where the secret places were or how to get into them?"

"Sorry. Couldn't find anything more. I'll keep looking."

"When did you find this out?"

"This afternoon. Thought you'd want to know right away. But I figured you were at work, so I waited until now."

"Thanks. Bye."

She sat for a long time, thinking. She was still sitting there when the phone rang shortly after sunrise. "Here"

"Cobbe here. You have any info on a Ron Cronin?"

"Yeah. I have his car and tags. He works at Punk's."

"Well, he works directly for the owner."

"Gene Rudolph?"

"The same. Cronin is Rudolph's right hand man. His nickname is Shoop, whatever that means. I overheard him talking about him and another guy there, nicknamed Ruff, icing one of the pushers some time ago. Him and some other guys led by someone named Bowser."

Skye's heart skipped a beat. "Are you sure?"

"I overheard him talking. You sound surprised and upset at the same time."

Skye swallowed with difficulty. "I am. Both. Bowser's the bouncer at Blinker's. I suspect the pusher they were talking about was Charles Gaines. We already know about his murder."

"I'll try to get more details for you. We have to find enough information to put all of these guys behind bars for a long time."

"Be careful, Elliott. They're dangerous."

"Yeah. And I'm a Marine. Semper Fi, remember? You give the word, I do what I have to do to get the job done."

"I know. Just be careful."

"Yes, Mom," he replied with a chuckle. "Talk to you later."

* * *

Knowing who Raynes' father was gave me a compelling reason to follow him again. And Reston, my main lead, was dead. So I put the Preacher at the top of my priority list.

Raynes stood on a Norfolk street corner and sermonized. For a long time. He also handed out pamphlets. It felt like this went on forever. I leaned against a doorway like I was waiting for someone and watched from half a block away. As before, I used my telescope. I still didn't notice anything obvious. But, again, there was something strange about the way Luke Raynes moved as he handed out the pamphlets. The movements weren't natural. But only sometimes. I would have to do some research on this.

I was very watchful when I returned to my ship.

We went back out to sea the next day, so I didn't have the chance to watch him again for a while.

66. SOME ANSWERS, MORE QUESTIONS

Skye reached her phone on the third ring. "Here."

"God, you're hard to get! I've tried five times to reach you."

She recognized George Stolichek's voice. "Things are starting to move. What's happening?"

"You have any reports on a black Thunderbird?"

"Ye-es."

"How about a white Studebaker Hawk with black sculpted fins?"

"Yes!"

"Excited? Listen to this. I saw the drivers of those two cars making a deal. The guy from the T-Bird took a good size package from the other one."

"Great stuff. You get license plates?"

"You bet." He named two already-known license numbers. "And I got them on film."

"George, I love you. You just made one of the final connections we needed."

"Good. Let me know when we take them down."

* * *

Skye puzzled over how the drug ring worked. She called Lunch to meet her at the beach north of town. She waited for him, walking alone. The gentle breeze had a touch of spring. Some seagulls hung on mid-air currents. Others strutted across the sand, alternately calling each other and scolding the human for not feeding them. She walked a little farther and sat down on the sand. The small waves were hypnotic.

"Perhaps if I let myself go," she said to the breeze, "my subconscious can work it out." But she couldn't concentrate.

She looked out over the water. The soon-to-be-completed Chesapeake Bay Bridge-Tunnel was in the distance to her left. She wished the *Hestek* were making its way home instead of going out to sea again.

"Why?" she asked herself. "You won't let anything happen. What's the difference if he's in port or not?" A soft sob escaped her. "Stop this, damn it! You have work to do."

She turned toward a dog barking in the distance. She saw Lunch's Saint Bernard chasing gulls in zigzags. Tango almost reached a group of birds before they took flight. He watched as they settled back to the beach seventy-five feet away and galloped toward them again. Then he spied a different group to go after. He noticed Rena when she laughed. Evidently deciding he'd get more attention from her, he rushed over.

"Hello!" Lunch walked toward them. "I thought he might lead me to you!" He lowered himself onto the sand alongside to Skye. "So, what's going on?"

"I need someone to bounce ideas off of, Brandon, and everyone else is busy."

"Glad I can help. What's happening?"

She reviewed everything they'd discovered so far: user identities, the deal with Divven, the murders....

Lunch soaked up the information while he absent-mindedly threw a thick stick for the dog to fetch.

"Then there are the two boss's automobiles. Matthews saw them one night at Blinker's. We've identified them and three of their street dealers. We've photographed the street guys making sales."

"Are you certain that the nightclub owners are the drug bosses?"

"Gene Rudolph definitely is. I probably couldn't prove in court that Frank Murphy is. But there's a lot of circumstantial evidence against him."

"Were they selling at the bars? How about at Blinker's?" he asked.

"No."

"What makes you so sure?"

"None of us have noticed any suspicious activity in these three bars. None. I kept an eye out at Blinker's, just to protect myself. Also, here's another point: we only saw the bosses' cars there once. If they were using Blinker's for anything, I think they'd be there regularly."

"Maybe they were in a meeting the time you saw them...."

"I don't know." Skye took the stick from Tango, who wrestled with it for a moment. She threw it as far as she could.

"Here's something else. Blink told Matthews that the building was once an old Quaker meetinghouse. Another operative, Chaské Hunter, is doing some research for me. He discovered that Blink's place, the old Quaker meetinghouse, had been an Underground Railroad station."

"Really?" Lunch asked. "Oh, that's interesting."

"Yeah," Skye said. "Secret hiding places. The logical extension of that is...."

He smiled. "It hit me as soon as you said it. Dealers' cars at a building with a hiding place so secret it took months to discover, even when we're looking for it."

"So if Blinker's is really where they're hiding their stuff, I've been standing right above it for months! But how do they get it in and out?"

Lunch chuckled. "My supposedly stodgy New England ancestors were conductors on the Underground Railroad going to Canada. They had a secret room. And they always made sure they had a second way out in case the main door was discovered. I'll bet Blinker's has an entrance from inside and another somewhere outside."

"I have to set a watch over Blinker's itself. We better find those entrances before we raid the place. And we have to follow the dealers to a pickup."

Lunch stood and helped Rena up. "Just in case the ring uses some other vehicles?"

"That, but mostly to see how, who, when they're moving stuff around," she said. "We'll need more people than we have. I'll get in touch with OCI Norfolk and have them ask for more operatives from the FBI, Treasury, wherever."

"What shall I concentrate on now?" Lunch asked.

"We need good people on the three night clubs. So, I'm going to pull Everett Cobbe out of Dam Neck. He's already my full-time customer at Punk's. You can stay there at night with him. Also watch Punk's after hours. You can sleep from sunrise until the afternoon."

"Fine. Have him get in touch with me. And the other places?"

Skye closed her eyes and moved her hands, like she was moving pieces on a chessboard. "I'll put Len Ford watching Blinker's with Hillory Tuttle. Morgan Delano is already working Bogie's. Robert Alban can help him watch there after hours. That takes care of our three suspect clubs.

"Tony Alvarez stays at the Windjammer and Glenn Oliver at the Tradewinds. They and the Waves can cover Norfolk Naval Station. Tom Morelos stays at NAS. George Stolichek keeps Little Creek. Charlie Williams moves from the Negro clubs in Norfolk to a grounds crew job at Oceana Naval Air Station. Rupert Vincent leaves the clubs and goes to Dam Neck. He served in the Marines and can take Cobbe's place in the guard job. Chaské stays at Portsmouth shipyard."

"Chaské?"

"Rod Hunter. Chaské is his Indian name. Okay. These teams watch all of these bars and bases. And... and...."

"What?" Lunch asked.

"Central can ask the Coast Guard to watch the waterways. Albemarle

238

and Currituck Sounds in North Carolina and southern Virginia Beach are part of the Intracoastal Waterway. Let's catch some smugglers, too."

"How soon do you think we can end this?"

"Let's get all our ducks in a row first. I want the whole network. We know most of the distribution and sales. We need to nail down supply. And I don't want to move until all the ships with our guys are in port. So, get together with Cobbe and watch for those cars. Track their every move. I'll let you know when to take them down."

"We'll be watching. See you later." He turned to the dog. "Tango! Let's go home!"

That night, Skye ordered full stakeouts during and after hours at Blinker's, Punk's and Bogie's.

* * *

Rena dozed in the easy chair in her living room. She bolted awake when the phone rang. It was 0402. "Here."

"Skye?"

"Yes."

"Dave Walden, Norfolk P. D. I haven't heard from you for a while, so I didn't know if your project was still going on."

"Sure is. But it's big. Our net's getting bigger and bigger, like a slow motion movie of ripples when you throw a stone into a calm lake. It takes time to set up, then find all the information we need."

"Understood. There's some buzz on the street that someone's watching a very politically popular nightclub owner in Norfolk. He's so powerful that Norfolk's finest can never prove anything he's involved in."

"Damn! I was hoping nothing would get out."

"Nothing leaked," he reassured her. "One night I met a guy named Del."

"Yeah?"

"Don't worry, he didn't compromise himself. He was a bit tipsy and sitting on the curb. We talked. He said he'd been hanging out around this club a lot 'cause his lady left him, but he wasn't used to drinking much yet. Sounded like a guy getting acclimated to undercover. I knew your operation was on so I thought I'd double-check. Is Del one of yours?"

"Affirmative. Just how widespread is the word on the street?"

"Don't worry. Just among some of the undercover boys. Sometimes we can spot an active operation a mile away."

"But there's no need to tell anyone else," Skye cautioned.

"I won't even clue in the Jakes. And, like I said before, we'll help if we can. This citizen is slippery. If you can get something to stick, there'll some very relieved people around here. I believe he's playing with Harry, you know, the Big H. Coke and Mary Jane as well. But we can't nail a thing on him."

"I think I know why not."

"He's an angel. He helped build his church—from scratch. He gives thousands to the Boy Scouts and Girl Scouts. Tens of thousands to the United Fund. Everyone in city hall believes he's a saint. Going to heaven the instant he croaks. I know better.

"Every time we have something on him, he's got a witness to testify he was somewhere else. Often more than one. Nothing sticks. He either buys himself out of trouble or buys the best legal beagles around. We even had a case where his favorite hit man was practically being driven to the slammer. Most of our proof was circumstantial but logically watertight. And up came two witnesses swearing that Grizz was in Baltimore when the victim was done in."

"Grizz?"

"Yeah, short for Grizzly. The headman's number one boy, Ned Luce. Little piss-ant thinks he's the hottest thing going, him and his pretty little Hawk."

"He's been up for murder already?"

"Oh, he's a mean little shit. He's a little squirt, but his confrontational personality has led his coworkers to give him his nickname. Other names would fit him better. He's scrappy as a badger and mean as a copperhead. He'll take anybody on. And he's ruthless. He's so smooth with the ladies they think he's God's gift, but he is one nasty little bastard. And his helper is a guy nicknamed Burp. I even don't know his real name.

"Anyway, I liked Del, so tell him to be extra careful around these guys. They're dangerous. Truly dangerous. Killers."

67. THE SHED

Central "transferred" the OCI operatives for Skye. The orders looked official, but the agents knew to check in with her for their new assignments. Robert Alban, BT3, received orders to the naval base in Naples, Italy. He went to watch Bogie's with Morgan Delano. Corporal Everett Cobbe got orders to Sasebo, Japan. Skye had him and Brandon Lunch watch Punk's, especially after it closed. Hillory Tuttle's orders transferred him to Port Hueneme, California, to a ship nobody ever heard of. Skye sent him to help Len Ford stakeout Blinker's. They parked on the neighborhood street so they could view the customer parking lot west of the building. The place was closed now and there should be no activity at all. There were no cars on either side of the building.

Another car, holding FBI agents, was on the street one block to the east. They watched the private parking lot where I'd seen the Cadillac and the Lincoln.

Ford and Tuttle took turns napping. Ford ate to stay awake—candy, sandwiches, potato chips, you name it. He became famous for his eating on stakeout.

When he couldn't keep awake he called to Tuttle, who instantly woke up. He said he'd always done that. And he could sleep in short segments all day long. Evidently President Kennedy could do the same thing.

Tuttle was a quiet, patient man. He surveyed the scene then double-checked the settings on his camera so he could take good night shots.

He was also a musician who composed his own songs. He was rewriting some melodies in his head when a De Soto entered Blinker's parking lot. At first he didn't pay much attention because another car had turned around and left right away. This one stopped near the rear of the club.

They'd seen two other cars pull in this week, the Studebaker Hawk and the Mercury 600. Those drivers walked around the building and entered

241

Blink's private entrance. Now the De Soto appeared. All came well after the owner left for the night. Minutes later the Mercury showed up again. It pulled alongside the first car. Tuttle took lots of pictures.

The drivers left their engines running. They talked for a short time before the Mercury driver entered a shed at the rear of the property.

Ford ate a sandwich and a small bag of cookies. Tuttle took more photos. He also pulled out a microphone to a police-band radio in the glove compartment. He asked Central to notify Skye about the meeting going on.

They watched.

Ford ate.

Skye came on the police radio. "Foxtrot, this is Lady. What's happening? Over."

"Lady, this is Foxtrot," Tuttle replied. "Not much. The Mercury and De Soto drivers talked for a while, then Mercury man disappeared into a small shed back by the alley. De Soto man's standing guard. No idea what they're doing. Over."

"OK. I'll stay here. Keep me updated. Out."

The Mercury driver reappeared. He gestured as he talked, first holding up four fingers then pointing to the south. He seemed to ask a question, because the De Soto driver nodded in agreement. They talked a while longer then drove away.

Ford got ready to start the car as Tuttle reported, "Lady, they're leaving and going in two different directions. Which one should we follow? Over."

"Foxtrot. Did you get photos? Over."

"Lady, I got a shot every fifteen, twenty seconds when they were both there, every thirty seconds or so when De Soto man was alone. A few rolls of film altogether. Over."

"Foxtrot, wait a while. Check out that shed. Then come home and develop that film. Out."

They waited twenty minutes. The shed was empty. There was no indication of any means to leave it other than the door they'd been watching.

68. ATTACK

I was now the compartment cleaner for our living spaces on the *Hestek*. The compartment had been well cared for, so the work wasn't difficult. Mostly simple cleaning and running the laundry bags back and forth to get clothes washed.

So far I'd seen nothing out of the ordinary. But I didn't expect to make any major breakthroughs in three days.

One day Commander Monroe came down. He pretended he'd gotten a report that the cable runs across our overhead were decaying. We talked in spurts, between people coming down to the living quarters or going to and from the engineering shops located just forward of the compartment.

He'd heard that I volunteered for compartment cleaning duty, which most guys hate. To him it looked like I was restricting my freedom of motion. I explained that I knew we had a drug supplier on board and thought it might be someone in our division. He understood that being here every day positioned me very well.

After he left, I went back to work while thinking a lot about Raynes and his preaching. Preacher's motions on the street corner still felt wrong. His moves weren't natural for giving leaflets to others. Something about them reminded me of... what?

I took out a deck of cards. Went through the motions of handing out pamphlets. Held the cards different ways until my movements imitated Raynes'. By the time I was done, I knew what Raynes was doing.

* * *

Blink's waitresses cleaned up. It had been busy for a Wednesday, so it took longer than usual. Skye left Blink sitting at a table in the middle of the restaurant area. She walked home leisurely, wondering when they could break this case open. The Pontiac Catalina was not across the street.

Her internal clock normally didn't let her sleep until dawn, so she settled down to read.

If the drug ring operated out of Blinker's, they wouldn't move anything until they were sure everyone was gone, including the drunks passed out in their cars. She hoped they had no idea that OCI was watching from across the street.

The telephone rang. "Here."

"Morelos. The De Soto's at the mess hall on Mainside and...."

"At this hour?"

"They're doing some painting and stuff."

"What were you doing over on Mainside?"

"Some of the base security people know the vehicles we're watching. They let me know he was here."

"So what's going on?"

"I can see through the windows. Some people are working and some are cleaning up, so they may be leaving soon. Do you want me to follow this guy?"

"Yes. I'll get my radio ready right now. Try to determine what gate he's heading for."

"Will do. Want me to follow him out?"

"Don't know yet. Something's bubbling in my head. I'll let you know."

She went to her bedroom, switched on the table light just inside the door and turned on the police-band radio in her closet. The room was cool. She went to get a sweater from the dresser. She passed in front of the window, illuminated from below and behind by her bedside lamp. A shot rang out. The glass shattered and the thin curtain billowed inward.

69. CONTRABAND

The bullet zipped inches above and in front of Skye's face. She never remembered hitting the deck. She raised herself up to look out the window, barely lifting the curtain. She saw the rear of a green automobile seconds before it disappeared. How had the shooter missed her? She analyzed the scene. The table lamp had cast her shadow high and from an angle. When he shot, he must have miscalculated her location from her silhouette.

She immediately called Central. "That S.O.B. in the Catalina just shot at me. Busted my apartment's front window."

"You all right?"

"Yeah. A bit shook up. Can you do something about him? Or should I get ready to shoot back?"

"We'll take care of it, Skye. Hang in there."

"Hanging kills people!" There was silence on the line. She took a deep breath. "Okay, I'll wait."

After Skye hung up she draped a blanket over the curtain rod to keep out the cool air. She grabbed her area map and returned to the police-band set. She took a deep breath and keyed the microphone. "Everyone, Lady is on line."

Everyone on-station reported in. Skye used this listening time to think of a strategy.

"Foxtrot, this is Lady. Go to Naval Air Station's Gate 22."

"Lady, we're on the way. What's up?" Ford asked.

"We may have a fish in a net. More info as we go on. Lady out." She paused for a moment. "Central, are you there?"

"Lady, that's affirmative," Charles Knox answered.

"Will you get some teams out to watch the other gates?"

"Will do!"

"ASAP, please. Here's the data on the De Soto...."

"Already have it. I'll pass it on."

"Okay. Thanks. Out."

Some time passed before Morelos got on the line again. "Lady, this is Mike. Over."

"Go ahead Mike. Over."

"Lady, our guy is leaving. I'll tell you where he's headed soon as I can determine it. Out." Morelos was back in ten minutes. "Lady, this is Mike. He's going to Gate 22. Over."

"Mike, this is Lady. We have it covered. Stand by. I may need you again. Thanks."

"Will do, Lady. Out."

* * *

Len Ford left Blinker's upon getting the order. When he got to Gate 22, he backed into a dark spot facing it. Ford's new partner was Evan Nye, an FBI agent. Skye had Tuttle swap with him so there was an OCI agent in each car. The operatives settled in to wait.

Ford continued eating: sandwiches, cookies, candy bars, who knows what else. When Nye commented that he should weigh three hundred pounds, Ford replied that he got lots of exercise when not on assignment. He hiked the White Mountains back home in New Hampshire.

Fifteen minutes later the De Soto left the base.

Nye reported in. "Lady, this is Foxtrot. He's coming out of Gate 22. How do these guys get base passes? Over."

"Foxtrot, this is Lady. Follow him. They get passes because they work on various bases. Where's our De Soto going? Over."

"South on Granby. Over."

"Keep me updated. Lady out." Skye settled down for a long night. "Central, this is Lady. Over."

"Central here. Over."

"Central, call out my whole team. Get them in their cars. Over."

"Lady, you really want a full call out to tail one car? Over."

"Affirmative, Central. Playing a hunch. I did a lot of this as an operative in Dago. If I'm wrong, I'll buy breakfast for the whole team. Over."

"Lady, this is Central. We'll make the calls. Out."

* * *

The De Soto went to Blinker's. Two men in dark clothing got out. One entered the shed and re-emerged in ten minutes. Nye took pictures. The agents followed the car into Norfolk, where it pulled into an all-night restaurant.

They watched through the diner's windows for half an hour. Other agents came on line. Skye placed them in a large circle around the De Soto and Foxtrot.

"All stations, Lady. These positions let you close in if Foxtrot loses them. This is the latest we've seen them out. We have to find out what they're up to. Out."

Foxtrot followed the De Soto south. Nye watched through binoculars. Ford used all the tricks he knew to prevent detection. He fell back in thin traffic. He turned the car lights off, then on again shortly afterwards to make it seem that a car had left and another entered the road. He slowed down before turning the lights back on. When traffic picked up, Ford let other cars between them and the De Soto: he could easily follow the vehicle's triple vertical taillights. Once, he exited with another car then made a U-turn and returned to the road. He varied his speed to make himself look like different drivers.

As they went farther south, Skye had a flash of insight. She may even have quit twisting her hair. On her maps, she noticed that North Landing Road had a fishing turn-off where it crossed the North Branch River.

"All stations, this is Lady. Let's start moving into a tighter circle." She gave the directions.

The De Soto turned down Indian River Road, northwest of North Landing Road. Ford and Nye followed carefully with their lights off. They crawled along until their eyes adjusted to the darkness of the new-moon night. After a mile and a half, the car ahead stopped. Ford pulled over, hoping the shoulder would support his vehicle. To their right a swampy creek flowed into North Landing River.

They sat, waited, watched. There was very little moonlight. An umbrella of trees blocked the starlight. They opened the car windows hoping to hear something.

The muffled sounds of oars soon slid through the darkness. A light flashed once from the creek. The De Soto answered with a single flash of its lights. A shadow turned toward the riverbank. The De Soto's trunk light came on. There was a flurry of activity, shadows moving between car and boat. The trunk lid was closed. The rowboat backed away, turned, and retreated downstream.

Nye used fast film and long exposure times in his camera.

Ford reported, "Everyone, this is Foxtrot. They're leaving. They made a pickup where Indian River Road crosses a small, swampy creek. Lady, you might tell the Coast Guard that the small boat is now heading south. It has to go into North Landing River to get out of here. We heard no motors. I think they were rowing. Out."

"Central, this is Lady. Are you still there? Over."

"Lady, that's affirmative. We're notifying the Coast Guard now. Over."

The operatives followed the De Soto. They expected it to return to Blinker's but it remained on North Landing Road. It eventually headed into downtown Virginia Beach. The smugglers turned into an alley and stopped in the shadow of a building.

Nye called in: "Lady, they pulled up behind Punk's Bar. What now?"

"Foxtrot, sit tight. See what happens. Lima, you've been following Foxtrot, go around the corner. Park about a block farther on and watch the front. Out."

The agents saw little activity in the shadows. Then three men carried items from the De Soto into a shed behind Punk's Bar. They let Skye know.

"Foxtrot, Lady. Punk's has a shed, too?"

"Lady, Foxtrot. That's affirmative."

"Foxtrot, Lady. When they leave, take a look inside that shed. Be careful. We know they'll kill. Everyone else, go home and get some sleep. Out."

Ford took the microphone from his partner. "Lady, we'll take a look. But I doubt if we'll find anything. I remember another out building like this, an empty one, at the rear of another bar. Over"

"Yeah, Foxtrot. I hear you. Out."

When the drug runners left, Nye and Ford waited fifteen minutes before they checked the shed. It was empty.

70. THINKING

The operatives ashore had a breakfast meeting at Brandon Lunch's apartment. Almost everyone was confused.

Skye voiced their perplexity. "Blinker's has secret hiding places from its Underground Railroad days. Matthews saw the drug lords' cars there. Ford and Tuttle saw a man enter an empty shed and not come out for a long time. So why didn't they take the smuggled stuff there to hide?"

She looked around. Lunch was smiling. He motioned for her to remain silent. He nodded to the others.

"There must be an explanation," Everett Cobbe laughed.

"But what?" Ford asked. "Let's review what we know."

"Aw, come on, Len," Stolichek groaned. "We've done that already."

"Hunter, where's your two cents' worth?" Cobbe asked.

Chaské held out his cup. "I need more coffee."

Lunch refilled his cup from the pot on the table. "Any ideas? Rena and I thought we'd figured it out the other day."

Hunter sipped his coffee. He nodded to himself. He grinned. "Copy cats."

"What?" Cobbe asked, puzzled.

"Think it through," Hunter suggested. "Lot's of people know about secret places at Underground Railroad stations. If you suspect someplace was part of it, you look for the secret hiding places. Right?"

Everyone nodded.

"If I were a drug lord and owned an old Railroad station, I'd be afraid of that 'cause, bang! That's the first place they'd search."

He sipped his coffee. "But it's a damned good hiding place. So, what could I do?"

"Build a another like it where there never was one!" Stolichek blurted out. "Why didn't we see it before?"

"Too obvious?"

Chaské nodded. "It's a good idea. Copy cat."

"Hold on!" Ford protested. "They carried the stuff into the shed at Punk's. That's not a secret hiding place. Yet we didn't find what we saw them take inside. It went somewhere. From inside the shed...."

"Brandon?" Skye said.

"Coming from an old New England family who participated in Underground Railroad activities...."

"In New England?" Stolichek asked.

Lunch nodded. "Indeed. During one period the Federal Government returned every runaway they caught. Many families built secret rooms to hide refugees."

"What's this leading to?"

"Every hiding place had a second exit," Lunch explained. "In case the authorities raided them. Now, I'll just bet...!"

Ford slapped the table. "The shed's the back door!"

"Yep," Chaské agreed. "I'll bet it has a spring release to lift a trap door, with a tunnel under."

"Okay, we've got this about locked up. When do we take these guys down?" Stolichek asked.

"Patience! Patience!" Rena demanded. "All the ships with operatives are in port except the *Hestek*. Let's party the night after *Hestek* pulls in. Take them all at once, pushers and users. You guys working Punk's, get impressions of the locks so we have keys if we need them." Cobbe and Lunch nodded. Skye took a deep breath. "That said, I may have to call for the raids sooner. Bowser, the bouncer and head of security at Blinker's, is watching me. A while back, I was being followed, and I was shot at from the street when I was in my apartment."

Comments of surprise and reaction filled the air.

"What?"

"When?"

"Who was he?"

Skye raised her arms for silence. "Central said they'd take care of it. But I'm sure Bowser's in on this whole thing. Last night I went to work and mentioned that someone shot out my window. Must be some kids, I said, with pretty powerful pellet guns. I tried to hang in there, cussing out those kids. Trying to take the suspicion away from me. But if it gets too hot, I'll call for the party to begin immediately."

"Are you protecting yourself now, Rena?"

She patted her purse. "I carry a friend with me." She looked out the apartment window. "Looks like we have a bit of a storm out there. Best hurry up and get home. Tomorrow is Ash Wednesday. Hope all of you have a nice Easter. We're close enough to wrapping this up; work this weekend only if you have to."

*   *   *

The *Hestek* was just south of Cape Hatteras. The seas were beginning to get a bit rough, but, even so, I was able to get some painting done. I was back in a corner of our living spaces. Raynes came below decks. He didn't see or hear me. I peeked under the bunks to watch him. He opened his locker. I was off to one side and could see under some of his raised locker top. Just enough. With one hand he lifted something up and all of the clothing in the front of his locker came up, too. He had something large under his stuff. Or a false bottom in his locker.

He stood up, looked around, evidently to be sure no one was watching. He stuck something in his dungaree pocket. He locked up, looked around again and went topside.

*   *   *

The storm's intensity had increased by the time Skye walked to work. The winds were high, driving the rain almost parallel to the ground. She got quite wet on her short walk, even though she had a good raincoat. Her umbrella offered her no protection at all.

After work, Blink approached Skye with a strange look on his face. "Rena...."

"Yeah, Blink. What's up?"

"I, uh, was told, uh, asked to give you a message. Frank Murphy really wants you to go work at Bogie's."

She shook her head. "I already told him that I couldn't. Too far for me to travel to work. I like my apartment. I like this job. I like the people here. I've turned him down a couple times. Doesn't he understand 'No'?"

Blink shrugged his shoulders. A sad look hung over him. "We're not close enough for me to know what he does and doesn't understand."

Skye fought the storm all the way home. It was worse than during the afternoon. Her raincoat offered no protection and she got home soaking wet all over. She undressed, dried herself off, and got into some dry clothes.

She sat at a window, nursing a cup of coffee and watching the weather. The rain came down in sheets. It pounded on the window so violently that she backed away, frowning. I sure hope this isn't an omen of how violently our project here is going to wind up.

She thought about Matthews' question a while back. Why did Murphy want her to work at his club so badly? She was quite certain by now that he was one of the drug bosses. Did he suspect her? Think she was a cop? Did he want to keep a closer watch on her?

251

She watched the storm through the night in wonder and awe. Its violence was increasing by the hour. By the next day, Ash Wednesday, the storm was almost a hurricane. She wondered how high the waves were over at the beach. But it certainly was too nasty out there to go and look. She remained inside, reading and playing through some historical chess matches.

71. MORE MURDER

Noting happened for a few days because the *Hestek* still wasn't in port yet. Skye got up before noon on the following Sunday morning and made coffee. She went down for her newspaper. She looked across the street. The Catalina wasn't there. Little wasn't showing up this early. Yet.

The landlord stepped out onto the porch. "Hello Rena! Happy Easter! How are you today?"

"Just fine, thanks, Mr. Scott."

"Have you recovered from that gunshot yet?"

"Yes. But I'm still wary of walking in front of the window. I'm glad the living room isn't in front."

"I don't know what this world is coming to. I can't imagine going around shooting at shadows in a stranger's window."

"Neither can I. It doesn't make sense," she agreed. "Thanks for fixing it so quickly."

"Oh, I had to! I couldn't let you get chilled. If I can do anything else, Rena, let me know. I'll take care of it immediately!"

She went to her door and opened it. "Thank you, Mr. Scott. I appreciate that."

Skye went back upstairs. The chill outside had awakened her but she still fixed her cup of coffee. She opened the paper on the table. The front page continued the coverage of the storm that had raged through the area from Tuesday through Thursday. Hundreds of homes and resorts along the Atlantic coast had been totally destroyed. Virginia Beach's concrete sea wall and boardwalk were gone. The Chesapeake Bay Bridge-Tunnel suffered a major setback and some specially built construction equipment had been destroyed. Farther north, in Maryland, there had been sixty mile-an-hour winds and twenty-five foot waves. A beach in Delaware had suffered forty-foot high waves. Forty-five thousand homes were destroyed in New Jersey alone. Forty people had been killed and over a thousand were injured. Some people were already calling this storm the worst Atlantic storm ever. The Weather Bureau didn't go quite that far, but was calling it the "Great Atlantic" storm.

"I have a very bad feeling about this," Skye mumbled. "My intuition is screaming at me. Something about our case here is not going to go very well...."

She finally broke away from the headlines and turned to the local section. An article there caught her eye immediately: "Drunk man drives off bridge."

"What's this?" she asked. "Robert Little, 32, of Virginia Beach... speeding on the Hampton Roads Bridge-Tunnel... lost control... crashed through the railing... dropped into the water... drowned before help arrived... determined that he was drunk... already calls for stronger railings. Well! That takes care of him!"

She could imagine OCI operatives in a few cars boxing Little in. Making him stop. Forcing whiskey down him, to get the alcohol into his blood stream. Taking him to the Bridge Tunnel very early in the morning. Forcing him through the guardrail into Chesapeake Bay. "Too bad he had to die, but he was willing to kill. Let's hope the drug bosses don't get suspicious. Still, I'd better be extra careful at work."

* * *

When Skye got to work that evening, Blink was there with a broken arm and a bandaged head.

"What happened to you?"

"I tripped and fell down some stairs," he replied without looking at her.

"What?"

"That's what I said," he snapped. "Don't you believe me?"

"Yeah, Blink. Sure."

Frank Murphy didn't show up. So after closing, Rena approached her boss. "Do me a favor?"

"If I can."

"When you see Frank Murphy, tell him I'll work for him. But not until March fifteenth. Makes it easier for accounting purposes. Do that for me?"

He looked at her and nodded without saying anything. But his eyes held thanks and concern and regret.

* * *

This is another event we pieced together from the stories of witnesses after they were arrested and started making excuses for themselves.

254

Early one morning Brandon Lunch parked in a spot just around the corner from Punk's Bar in Virginia Beach. He glanced at his watch—it was 0330. The place should be deserted. He wanted to examine the shed. He checked his back pocket to reassure himself that he had his flashlight. He walked down the alley behind the bar.

He wished Tango was with him. The dog could be a great lookout. But then, he could also be too playful when absolute silence was necessary.

When Lunch got to the shed behind Punk's, he leaned against it, listening for sounds of activity. There was no noise from anywhere inside or outside the rough-hewn shack. He stepped around the structure, silently opened the door and slipped into the shed. He closed the door tightly so nobody outside could see his flashlight. He began his inspection.

He planted his feet firmly and tried to minimize the steps he took. Under the floor, there was almost certainly a stairway or ladder and tunnel, an empty space that could reverberate like a drum. He didn't want these guys to catch him alone. He regretted not telling the others what he was doing. But it was too late for that now.

He took his time, carefully examining the shack. He looked for a doubled stud, a seemingly loose board, anything that might be a trigger to open a trap door. He identified a few possibilities, then began to carefully push, pull and twist those pieces of the little building. Nothing moved. Nothing happened.

Frowning, he stood and thought for a moment. Perhaps he was standing on the section that opened. He quietly stepped outside. Holding the door open with his body, he reached into the shed and went through all the pushing, pulling, and twisting again. When he pulled on a particular section of a wall stud, it moved a fraction of an inch. One side of the floor popped up. He lifted it all the way up. He saw a stairway going down to some kind of underground space.

A man grabbed him from behind. He twisted Lunch's arm up behind his back and growled: "Get your ass down there."

The man pushed Lunch until he stood in a fairly large room. A number of others faced them.

"See, Bowser, I told you somebody was up there."

"Yeah, Ruff. You told me. Tie him up," Bowser ordered.

Two other men lifted Lunch up, dropped him onto a chair, tied his hands behind him and his feet to the chair legs.

"All right, Tick," Bowser directed. "Search 'im."

A diminutive, squinty-eyed man ran his hands over the agent. He held up two items. "Flashlight, wallet."

"What's in the wallet?" Bowser demanded.

"Not much. Couple o' dollars, Connetticut drivers license...."

The leader heaved a sigh of exasperation. "Tick, what's his name?"

"Uh, Brand, no Brandon, Lunch."

"Lunch? How'd ya like ta have that name?" one of the burly men snorted. "I can hear his lady now." He screwed up his face and spoke in a falsetto: "I wouldn't want to lose my Lunch!"

Everyone burst out laughing. The agent looked around, tried to figure out his situation. He saw five men near him, three very big guys, the pipsqueak, and another diminutive man with a mean look in his eyes.

"Good one Ruff. Now shut up." Bowser stood in front of the prisoner. "Mister Lunch, my name is Bowser, 'cause I'd just as soon bite as make a friend. This here's Ruff, 'cause he's just plain tough. Shoop is that guy over there, and the really mean sonofabitch there is Grizzly. Maybe he don't look like much, but you know about grizzly bears out west? Nastiest, meanest disposition of any animal there is. That's him. Now, what're you doin' snoopin' around here?"

The agent calculated that he wasn't going to survive the night, not with characters like these. But he'd try. "I'm a student of architecture. I was curious why such a small shed would be behind a major nightclub. It didn't make sense to me."

"That's a pretty lame story," Bowser said. "Now how about telling me the truth?"

Lunch shrugged. "That is the truth. What more can I say?"

"All right. Have it your way." He turned to the small man with evil in his eyes. "Grizzly, do your stuff. No bruises. Yet."

The man responded with a short, painful jab into the solar plexus. Lunch found it difficult to breathe for almost a minute.

"So, now you appreciate the pain our Grizzly here can inflict. You want more?"

"No," Lunch gasped. "Not really."

Bowser nodded. "Okay. One more chance. What're you doin' around here?"

"I already told you. I'm a student of architecture and...."

Bowser nodded. Grizzly hit the agent a few times, spaced so that he was only able to take a single breath between punches. "You ready to talk yet?"

"I already told you," the prisoner repeated, staring at the floor. The leader of the tough guys heaved a huge sigh.

"Mister Lunch, I don't think you quite appreciate the situation you're in. You answer our questions or you're goin' to die. It's that simple. And it's your choice."

Lunch looked around. He recognized chopped up marijuana. And there were piles of a couple different kinds of powder sitting in front of small paper packets, some filled and some empty. He took a deep breath. "I don't believe you're going to let me go, no matter what I say."

Bowser pursed his lips and nodded. "You're right, Mister Lunch." He turned to the tough guy. "Grizzly, go ahead and play with him for a while. You other guys, go get the stuff we'll need."

The men scurried to obey. Bowser spoke again: "Okay, Grizz, hold up. Mister Lunch, we're going to put you to sleep. We can make this shorter or longer. It's up to you. Answer my questions, you go to sleep quick and easy. Or Grizzly can have his fun for quite a long time."

The agent refused to say anything.

"Grizz, make him hurt. A lot. Then we'll take care of him like we did our friend Chuckie."

The other men returned with the items Bowser had ordered. He prepared the heroin right in front of Lunch, making sure he took his time, performing each step of the process between painful punches. Finally the agent was almost unconscious.

Bowser checked his watch. "Sunrise. Let's get this done. You guys have to check in with Gene and Murph. And I want to go home and get some sleep."

"Ya want me to bare his arm and hold it?" Ruff asked.

The leader shook his head. "No. Hold his head. I'll shoot it right into his jugular so it can go all the way through him before it hits his brain. Let him think about dying as the stuff makes its way through his whole body. He'll go quickly enough."

Bowser prepared the syringe. He jabbed Lunch in the neck with the needle and pushed the plunger. "Throw him under the table. Shoop, call Burp. He's at Blinker's. Have him get over here and dispose of the body."

72. PARTY TIME

The *Hestek* pulled into port the same day, after spending two weeks off Cape Hatteras. Some officers were having a party at the Breezy Point Officers' Club, which they often did on returning to port. As duty driver I had to take them there.

While on a run, Skye phoned. When I returned the Petty Officer of the Watch told me she'd called.

"Sir, can I use the phone?" I asked the Quarterdeck Watch Officer.

He nodded. "Keep it short."

"Aye, aye, sir." I dialed Rena's number. "Hi! Eric here."

"Hi! It's party time! We'll hit twenty locations at 0230. Got that?"

"I got it. See you later."

"Bye." She blew a kiss into the phone. I responded the same way. Hanging up the phone, I grinned at the quarterdeck watch and purred, "She loves me toooo much!"

"You have more officers to take to the club."

I nodded and sauntered back to the car. So, this was it. I reviewed the places: Blinker's, Bogie's, Punk's, the homes of Davenport, Murphy, Bando, Rudolph, and twelve known street dealers. Also, all the operatives on ships and in barracks would arrest known users.

I signed the wake-up list for a call at 0230. Luke Raynes had the midwatch as Messenger. That should make my job easier.

* * *

Skye was frantic. She'd tried to reach Brandon Lunch for hours to give him his assignment in the coming raids. She couldn't find him anywhere. No agents had seen him. What could have happened? He was one of the most reliable people on the team.

The last person she telephoned was Cobbe. "Everett, have you seen Brandon or heard from him today?"

"He hasn't returned?" he replied. His tone sent shivers up her spine.

"Returned? From where?"

"Shit! I never should have let him go alone. But he demanded. He...."

"Cobbe!" Skye screamed. "What the fuck are you talking about?"

"Oh, God. He... was going to go...."

"Everett, what happened?" Skye interrupted, her tone icy.

Cobbe spoke in a low, dull voice. "He went to the shed at Punk's."

"What?" She turned cold inside.

"He wanted to look for trap doors, like he'd seen in New England. He said he'd just inspect the shed and leave."

"Why?"

"He wanted to get in the back as easily as the front on the upcoming raid. I would've expected him to report in to you."

"He didn't and I can't reach him," Skye managed to get out. "Pray, Everett. Pray that he's still alive. We're going in at 0230. I want you at Punk's."

She sat periodically dialing the phone. She tried for over an hour to contact Dave Walden, the Norfolk Police Department street man. Finally, he answered. "Yeah?"

"Skye here. I have a heads up."

"Going down tonight?" Dave asked.

"Yes. Thought I'd clue you in."

"Thanks. Anything specific we should know?"

"Only that the supply will plummet soon. You locals will see some real crazies and some very sick people. Thought I'd give you some advance warning."

"Yeah, there'll be a pretty big ripple effect. Pushers and suppliers gone. Users who support their habit by selling won't be able to get their stuff to sell. Users going cold turkey. Like you said, there'll be some crazies. I'll pass the word around the department. Tomorrow. After you're done. Wouldn't want to compromise anything." He chuckled. "The boys in blue will get to play social worker, push a few folks into rehab. It's going to be rough for a while, but we'll be glad to see those assholes behind bars."

"Me, too. It's been a long time coming."

"Listen, if you ever work these streets again, let me know. I'll help whenever and wherever I can. Thanks for the heads-up. Don't get hurt."

She choked up for a second, then regained control. "We'll try not to, Dave. Bye."

"Bye."

Skye put the phone back on the cradle. "Yeah, we'll try not to let anyone else get hurt."

73. THE BUST

At 0230, Morgan Delano, Robert Alban, Chaské Hunter along with FBI and Treasury agents raided Bogie's Club in Norfolk. There were no problems thanks to the homemade keys. Frank Murphy, owner of the club and of the white Cadillac, had already left. The FBI put out an APB for him.

They searched the place from top to bottom. Ned Luce and his helper, "Burp," tried to run with six kilos of uncut heroin, three of cocaine, and many bags of chopped-up marijuana. They didn't make it. The drugs on their person will serve as indisputable evidence at their trials.

Other federal agents helped Len Ford and Everett Cobbe take down Punk's Bar. Ford and Evan Nye waited at the shed with drawn pistols and a walkie-talkie. Cobbe pounded on the front door of the club and shouted, "Open up! Law enforcement officers!"

Gene Rudolph was leaving to drop off the day's take at the bank. The agents met him at the door.

"Who are you guys?" He demanded.

"Naval Office of Criminal Investigation. You're under arrest, Mr. Rudolph."

"Don't know what you'd charge me with. I haven't done anything wrong. Besides, I'm a civilian. You can't touch me." Three other men pulled out FBI, Treasury and county sheriff IDs. He protested again when an agent put handcuffs on him. He screamed for his lawyer.

Cobbe whacked him in the ribs with his pistol. "Shut up, slime bag! You'll have plenty of time for your lawyer."

They looked for the secret room. They searched the basement for ten minutes, but found nothing except storage spaces and refrigerators. Using his walkie-talkie, Cobbe told Ford to go through the shed.

Ford and Nye searched thoroughly, pushing and pulling on studs. Ford felt a slight movement, but nothing happened. They moved outside and pulled the stud. The trap door popped up an inch. Ford opened it, jumped down the stairway, rushed through a short tunnel and burst into the secret room. Two men were at a table, making little paper packets of heroin.

One man pulled out his piece. The shot was deafening in the confined space. The concussion on the left side of his chest slammed Ford back. Nye opened fire. The man with the gun dropped. Another man pulled a lever to escape into the club's basement. Four lawmen were waiting for him.

Cobbe entered the secret room. It was full of heroin, cocaine, and marijuana. He dropped to one knee, examined Ford, then had another man call for an ambulance.

He looked across Ford, to the area under a table. Ford, surprised at the sudden paleness of his fellow operative, turned to look. Lunch's body lay there, hands tied behind his back, a large bruise on his neck where he'd been injected.

A third party assembled outside Blinker's Bar and Grill. Jerry Bando's 1959 De Soto Fireflite was in the private area. Skye positioned Glenn Oliver, Tom Morelos and her other men to cover the doors on either side and to watch the rear. "Keep a close watch on that shed."

When they pounded on the front door they heard Blink's voice. Sue Anne opened the door. Skye entered, shouting, "Federal agents! This is a raid!"

Nick Davenport sat at a table in the middle of the establishment, drinking coffee. Jerry Bando and some of the street people stood in the middle of the large room. Most of them raised their hands. Blink stayed seated, smiling.

Bowser drew a pistol from under his sports jacket. One shot rang out from a T-man's piece. The big bouncer went down. Skye kept her pistol aimed at Blink as she approached him. She flashed her badge. "Office of Criminal Investigation. You're under arrest, Davenport."

"So it's you!" Blink said. He kept his hands above the table. "You'll get no trouble from me, Rena. I called you guys in the first place."

"What?" she asked.

He said in a low voice. "When you get them out of here, we can talk."

Skye motioned for the other agents to continue their work. "Cuff these guys and get them into the cars. Then search the place."

She pointed to the groaning bouncer on the floor. "You know, Bowser sure makes you all look guilty."

"I won't dispute anything you find here. As for that son of a bitch, he was here to watch me. But I'm sure he also coordinated a lot of the activities."

Skye motioned for a local officer to come over. "Watch him. I'll be back soon."

The Treasury men placed all the dealers in handcuffs while Skye opened the trap door to the basement. The FBI agents inspected the place. They uncovered very little.

"Gentlemen, there's a secret room and a second way out. Look for hidden door releases," Skye said. They found nothing. After fifteen minutes of fruitless search, Rena returned to Nick Davenport's table. "How do we get into the secret room, Blink?"

"I honestly don't know. I didn't even know it existed until last year. I'd help you if I could, but they never told me how to get into it."

Glenn Oliver sauntered up to Skye and held out a note. "It's from Cobbe."

She read the note. She closed her eyes and heaved a deep sigh. She asked, "Did you read this?"

Oliver nodded an affirmative. "Okay, hold up a minute." She turned to Blink. "You said 'they' never told you how to get into the secret room. Who is 'they'?"

"Frank Murphy's the big boss. Gene Rudolph is his partner. Bowser, Luce and Cronin run the ring for them and buffer them from the operation so they stay clean. Murphy uses his money and influence to get the guys off if anything ever gets public."

Skye motioned for him to stay where he was. She turned to the other agents, motioning to certain people. "You two, stay here and keep Mr. Davenport company. You guys go below and stay in the basement. Be ready for a door to open up anywhere along the eastern or southern walls. The rest of you, come with Oliver and me. Cobbe has told us how they opened Punk's trap door. Let's see if it works here."

They found the latch. They followed the stairs into the secret rooms. They found many kilos of drugs, as well as all the damning evidence they'd ever need: almost a quarter million dollars in cash, as well as a ham radio set with call letters for Bogie's, Punk's, the street dealers, and a schooner out of Miami. Finally there were books for the whole operation. Skye returned to Davenport's table.

"There's enough here to prove almost any charge we'd want to make."

"I'm glad I could help. Did you also get Murphy and Rudolph and their henchmen?" he asked.

"If it went well we got everyone from the street people to the smugglers. And we'll have enough to put Murphy away, too. Some of them will go up for murder first. They killed one of my officers at Punk's."

"I'm so sorry, Rena. I wish you could have gotten them before that happened."

"Thanks. They left a few other dead people lying around, too, murdered with pure heroin overdoses. Did you know they were selling heroin and cocaine?"

Davenport nodded. He looked down and spoke in a low voice. "Like I said, I found out last summer. That's when I called OCI in August. When I hired you, I also hired another waitress and a bartender. I suspected one of you was an agent, but I didn't know which. I tried to warn you by putting a note under your doors."

Skye thought back to the warning she received in late February. She nodded. "I wondered where that came from. I walked a little more carefully after that. And it may have worked. They tried to shoot me from the street."

"I'm glad they missed. You can't believe how much I worried about whoever was investigating these guys, knowing what they were like."

*   *   *

Raynes had the midwatch, from 2345 to 0345. Over these months on the *Hestek* I'd developed the ability to set an internal alarm clock. I was awake when the messenger came to get me up at 0230. I got dressed and went topside for a smoke. At 0245 I got the Exec. He and I went to the compartment to break into Raynes' locker.

"Can you figure out the combination?" he whispered.

I nodded. I got the lock open quickly. We held a private surprise inspection. The XO held the flashlight while I went through the Preacher's possessions. I found the false bottom. It was only an inch above the deck, but it was big enough to hold packets of heroin and cocaine. The only indication we had that he was dealing was my use of the deck of cards to analyze how he handed out his pamphlets. He was passing drug packets under them.

We had no proof he was a user, but possession was a crime.

We'd return when he got off watch.

*   *   *

The raids were uneventful everywhere else. Frank Murphy wasn't home when the agents took over his house. The lawmen occupied Rudolph's, Bando's, and Davenport's houses without consequence. No drugs were found in any of them.

The sheriff's department tracked down the street people. They captured Dick Cunningham quietly. They chased Bennie Tappan down from multiple directions. He jumped from his red Corvette, gun blazing. The deputies killed him. All who were captured alive were charged with murder as well as drug related allegations.

*   *   *

Rena sat across from Davenport. "Tell me, Blink, how'd you get mixed up with this bunch? I never got the feeling you were that kind of person. My intuitions are usually pretty accurate."

"I've made some big mistakes and this was one of them. After I retired from the Navy, I was looking for something to do. I really wanted to own a bar or restaurant. I made some friends. One guy, Terry Blanco, was a nephew of Frank Murphy, a Norfolk bigwig I didn't know anything about. One night we were talking about my dream of running a bar. Terry said 'I'll see if my uncle can help you. He's loaded.'

"Murphy had eyed this building for some time and he showed it to me. Somehow he'd discovered the secret room, but I didn't know about it for years. All I knew was this was some old architect's office up for sale. It was open, with small offices along the sides. Murphy and I struck a deal. I put in five grand and he loaned me thirty grand more to buy the place. He set it up like a mortgage. Ten percent interest for a period of fifteen years. With a penalty clause: if I missed or was late with any payment, he'd raise the interest half a percentage point on the life of the loan. It really wasn't a penalty payment but a recalculation. Every time I screwed up."

"Why did you fall for it, Blink? With your experience as a slush funder, you should've seen what that was."

"You know, hindsight's as clear as hell. I was a total novice at business. But I did wonder about that contract. My friend Terry Blanco set me up with a lawyer friend who looked it over and declared that it was 'pretty standard' and 'nothing to worry about.' So it seemed okay. It never dawned on me he was on Murph's payroll.

"I knew I could manage a bar, do well by the people. I never suspected I'd ever have any trouble with those payments. So I signed the contract, in front of three witnesses. The payments started immediately, even before I was ready to open. That was the first real problem.

"It took me three months and the rest of my own money to put in booths, build the bar with a kitchen behind it, build the wood dance floor and the raised bandstand. Friends at the Portsmouth shipyard got me some Navy surplus for the signalman decorations. I bought a stock of liquor, beer, and food. By the time I was ready to open, I had nothing to live on.

"So I missed some payments. 'Well,' Murphy said like a father, 'you know, it takes time to get something going.' I didn't realize how bad it was. The interest went higher. To live, I paid late a couple more times. The interest went up some more. By the time I was able to make a living from the place, the interest was up to thirteen percent.

"Then came the first property tax bill. Murphy rolled it into the mortgage. That raised the payments. I missed a couple more times. Murphy's goons beat me once for non-payment. They told me the boss was thinking of foreclosing. Murphy sent Bowser over to be my 'head of security.' The interest rate was now fifteen percent. And I was making huge monthly payments. But I had my own business and I was very proud of that.

"I began living low and paying on time, through 1960. Things improved. These guys became friendlier. I'd talk with some of them when Bowser wasn't around; I never trusted him very much. Over time, I got hints that other stuff was going on right under my nose. I heard about a year long, slow, careful excavation project over at Punk's Bar, owned by Gene Rudolph. The excavation was of a secret, hidden room 'just like here.' 'Just like here?' I wondered. 'What the hell are they talking about?' But I didn't ask 'cause the guy who made that comment came in a few days later with lots of bruises and a busted arm. I realize now that the secret room was very useful and they duplicated it at Punk's. I still don't know why a secret room was here in the first place."

"You know this was an old Quaker meeting house," Skye said.

"Yeah, I've known that for quite a while. A sailor with an architecture degree mentioned that it looked like a Quaker church. I was able to find public records that confirmed that."

"Many Quaker places were part of the Underground Railroad. They built secret rooms and multiple exits in case they were raided. This was one of them. We think they kept escaping slaves here until they could arrange passage on merchant ships."

"That explains a lot. Then I heard references that didn't make sense. Things like 'after-hours business,' 'big deals,' and 'why do you think nothing's ever put in the shed?' I'd never been around the drug scene and I didn't understand a lot of the terms I overheard.

"But at least I owned my own business. I started making a decent living from it, if I lived carefully. It got easier as the place became better known and made more profit. I always treated my employees well. I knew from the Navy that a guy who treats his people well gets a lot more out of them. I figured it was the same for civilians. So, as soon as I could, I provided Thanksgiving and Christmas meals and Fourth of July picnics. In time, I provided more. Bonuses at Christmas, stuff like that.

"One day last year, I forgot my jacket at the bar and went back for it on a chilly Sunday evening. I saw Murph's Cadillac and a Lincoln Continental parked behind the building. I came inside to get my jacket. Nobody was here. When I went out, the big cars were still there. I waited around a while, but nothing happened. Finally I got tired and left. On a whim, I circled the block and returned through the alley. Murphy and Rudolph were just getting into their cars.

"I asked what was going on, where had they been? Rudolph quipped, 'Ask no questions, we'll tell you no lies.' Murphy added, 'You'll also stay healthy.' This ate away at me. A month after that my bouncer quit. Murphy told me Bowser could take his place. After that, there were a few times, not many, but a few, when some pretty unsavory characters met with Bowser.

"There was a guy in the crowd named Wiley Steckel. We nicknamed him 'Coyote' of course." Blink laughed. "Yeah, Wiley Coyote. He was one of Murph's pushers. It got where he had too much. His nerves were shot. He pulled out, went straight. I always got along with him, and he told me to be very careful because Murphy, Grizz, and Bowser would kill me if I let on that I knew what was going on. My curiosity was peaked. I asked, "What the hell *is* going on?" Steckel couldn't believe I didn't know. He told me about the whole operation, drugs smuggled through various waterways, the use of the secret rooms, selling drugs to civilians and sailors and Marines all over the area. He told me that if these guys ever got brought to trial, he'd testify, but all of them had to be locked up before he'd return. Then he took off for someplace in the Rockies. He moves a lot. He gave me the name of another guy who always knows where he is, so I can get in touch with him to get him back for a trial.

"One day I asked the cops to watch my place during the off hours, especially Sundays and Mondays. After a month they reported they'd seen nothing unusual. Now I was obsessed, afraid I could lose everything. So I made it a habit to drive by the place, many times at three or four in the morning. I'd go from west to east so I could see the back of the building. Sometimes I'd see other cars, Bando's Fireflite, Luce's Hawk, Bobby Little's Catalina.... What ever happened to Little? You know?"

"Some of it. He was the one who shot at me. OCI Central took care of him."

"Yeah, didn't they? We knew he drank a lot and no one thought anything strange happened. He got too drunk and drove off the Bridge Tunnel. Anyway, I'd see these cars parked here in the middle of the night.

"The cops never saw anything. Rumor said that Murphy bought off the Norfolk police. Maybe he bought off the Virginia Beach cops, too. So who could I call? Then I remembered the OCI. They caught me slush-funding the second time. I was impressed with them. They seemed fair. Some guys they caught were sent to the Portsmouth Brig and got a bad discharge. Some of us, who didn't have huge slush lists, were left to the mercy of our commanding officers or lower courts martial. I was one of them.

"I thought if Murphy and his guys were pushing drugs to sailors and Marines, the Navy should know. So I memorized OCI's phone number. I began going out to establish a 'normal pattern.' Then, one evening, on the way home I called OCI...."

"Nick..., Blink...," Skye stammered. "I don't know what to say."

Davenport shook his head. "Don't say anything. Take me in. Just keep me out of their reach. Please. I'll turn state's evidence. I know it'll be difficult to convict Murphy and Rudolph. They keep pretty clean. Between my testimony and that of Wiley Coyote Steckel, we might provide enough to convict them. Along with what OCI has gotten. Take me in and let me redeem myself. Maybe they'll let me come back and run my business in peace. Or let me go somewhere else and start over."

"We'll take you in and protect you. And I'll put in a good word for you. But OCI doesn't control the courts. Technically, you were part of this ring."

"I know." Blink stood up. "Let's get out of here."

* * *

Mister Monroe and I sat on the mess decks talking and drinking coffee. He told me about Cory Palm's accident and the suspicions about Reston's drug use.

The *Hestek* had been refueling. Shepherd, Reston and Palm were at their stations. According to Shep, Reston seemed out of it and Palm wasn't wearing his safety belt. The ship was taking heavy rolls. Palm stepped outside the lifelines to get a better angle while connecting the refueling hose. Reston's feet slipped on the wet deck and he kicked Palm's legs out from under him. Palm fell off the 01 level and hit the main deck flat. Witnesses said he actually bounced.

The XO checked his watch. It was 0335. The midwatch would be over in ten minutes. We knew Raynes would go to the living compartment as soon as he could to get a few more hours sleep. He wouldn't get them tonight. We made our way down to the compartment. All was quiet. The new watchstanders were gone to relieve the mid. Everyone else was asleep.

We waited.

Raynes came below. We had him open his locker. I went directly to his stash.

"How'd you know...?" Raynes cried. He inched toward his work uniform hanging from his bunk chains.

"You showed me, when you went there one day," I replied. "All your clothes in the front of the locker got lifted up at the same time. Gave you away."

"Well, you're not taking me in!" he shouted, pulling a knife from its sheath on his dungaree belt. He waved it at us. "I'm leaving. Don't try to stop me." He spoke hysterically. "I'll use this! I really will!"

A couple guys woke up. Stephen Zoss frowned. The Exec and I didn't move.

"Let me out of here! I mean it!" Raynes shouted.

Zoss quietly slid from his rack. He came up behind Raynes and gently but firmly grasped the wrist of the hand holding the knife. "Let's pray, Luke. Think about what you're doing. Pray for wisdom. Pray for God to help you decide what's right."

Raynes lowered his arm. Started to sob. Zoss took the knife and handed it to me.

"Zoss, please go get Chief Hamilton," the XO commanded. "Have him meet us in sickbay. We'll be coming up soon." Stephen nodded, quickly slipped into his work clothes. He buttoned his shirt as he went topside.

I took the drugs out of Raynes' locker and handed them and the knife to Commander Monroe. He put everything in a bag. I took Raynes' arm. "Come on, Luke. We have to go."

When we got to sickbay, I told Hamilton: "Chief, I'm actually a Lieutenant, senior grade, with the Office of Criminal Investigation. Raynes is my prisoner."

"I suspected you were more than a deck hand when you got bashed on the head."

"Thanks for not pushing it," I grinned. "Please inspect every part of Raynes's body for track marks. Check unusual places, between the fingers, between the toes, in the gums, groin, everywhere."

The Chief nodded, took Raynes in and closed the door. Commander Monroe went to have the messenger of the watch get a master-at-arms to guard the prisoner.

Rolles, a gunner's mate, arrived with a .45 strapped to his waist shortly before reveille. When Hamilton came out, he said: "You had a good hunch, Mister Matthews. He has track marks between his toes."

"Thanks, Chief. And thanks for fixing me up. Can we keep Raynes here for a while? Rolles will guard him."

"Certainly. What are you planning?"

"I want to get the three of us some breakfast. Then we have to check out with the Captain."

Commander Monroe held out his hand. "Good to work with you, Lieutenant Matthews. It was quite an experience."

We shook hands. "It turned out to be a good thing when I accidentally left that packet of heroin on my bunk. Thank you for keeping my secret."

"All part of ship's operations. I did let the Captain know, by the way."

I grinned. "I expected that, sir."

An hour later we were at the Captain's in-port cabin. I held up my OCI identification and told the Old Man who I was. "Captain, I'm leaving your ship this morning and I'm taking Raynes with me."

He registered little surprise. "So it's happening. But Raynes?"

"Yes, sir. I volunteered to be compartment cleaner because I knew there was a supplier on board. That's also why I didn't leave when Reston died."

"The supplier was Raynes?"

"One of them, yes, sir."

"Rolles, please stand guard outside the door. You two, come in," Lorman invited. "Raynes, sit over there." He pointed to a chair as he turned to me. "I already knew who you were, Lieutenant. I've been expecting your visit for a while, now." Lorman chuckled. "When you were hit on the head, I figured you were someone special. After your XO's Mast, Mister Monroe told me about you. So I already knew about the drugs, too. I suspect you were the response to my call to OCI."

"I believe I was, Captain."

"After Seaman Palm's accident, we felt something was very wrong. That night, Chief Gascomb, Cisco, Shepherd and I discussed what went wrong. The Chief suspected Reston was using drugs. So I called OCI."

"You weren't the only one who called us. Admiral Terry lost a few people on Mainside to overdoses. We had over twenty agents on this case and I expect that tonight there were OCI, FBI, Treasury, and a few local jurisdictions involved. We weren't only after Reston, but his suppliers. I believe we'll get everyone. The whole ring."

"So if we have more addicts aboard, we're likely to see some severe withdrawals?"

"I kept my eyes open, sir. I don't think you're going to have any more trouble."

Lorman glanced at Raynes. "What's the story with him, Lieutenant?"

"He was also using drugs, sir. Heroin. And he had a large stash under a false bottom in his locker. I believe he was also selling. At least he shared some dope with Reston at one time."

"How will you charge him?"

"That's up to legal. But I think they hope to make a deal with him, Captain." I turned to my prisoner. "Luke, the OCI is a police force and doesn't do the legal stuff. But here's the plan, as I know it. You help us, we help you."

"Yeah, I'm sure you can protect me too."

I knew what he meant, but I had to ask. "Would you explain yourself?"

"My father is very dangerous. I'm not saying a thing."

"Who is your father, Raynes?" Captain Lorman asked.

The prisoner hesitated, so I answered. "His dad is Frank Murphy, owner of Bogie's Club in Norfolk."

Lorman looked like he was actually taken by surprise.

I turned back to Raynes. "Your father will at least be in prison for the rest of his life. He may be executed for murder."

Raynes snorted. "You have enough to get him this time?"

"Absolutely. He'll get life or the death penalty."

"Guaranteed?"

"Guaranteed."

Raynes thought for a moment. "What's the deal?"

"I'll highly recommend you get a general discharge, or at worst an undesirable, instead of a dishonorable. If you testify for us and complete a rehabilitation program, I will recommend that you get no brig time. Don't know if I can swing all that, but I'll try. Your assistance and rehab will help."

"No harangues? No making me feel guiltier than I already feel? No berating me or belittling me?"

"Why would we do that?"

"That's what I've gotten my whole life. My parents blamed me for their arguments. Mom was very religious and Dad always harassed her about it. It was really bad living with him after mom died. He teased me mercilessly for being a Christian. He blamed me for the divorce and constantly warned me not to become an overzealous religious nut like her. He blamed me for the way she died." He choked up at that. I let him take time to compose himself.

"When did you become so religious?"

"My mother set the stage. But I really got serious while I was at Great Lakes. I tried to regain my balance. After boot camp, I was homesick—I do love this area—so I requested any ship in Norfolk. That's when I made the biggest mistake of my life, contacting my father. He took to calling me a religious nut case and treating me like he did my mom. I went downhill and eventually got where even religion didn't help. I became convinced I'd never been any good. Started using drugs." He shook his head. "A friend had some stuff and I actually felt good again. I started using more and more."

"Where did you buy your stuff?"

"That friend gave me a connection with a dealer. I didn't know the dealer worked for my dad. When my father found out, he had me sell and I got my drugs for free." Raynes swallowed hard. "But I never sold to shipmates. It's too dangerous if someone's under the influence on duty. I only sold once to a shipmate. Reston got some when he was restricted."

"But you didn't care about other ships or guys on the base?"

"I never thought about them very much."

"Did you sell to folks on the street? I watched you hand out pamphlets and it looked like you were hiding packets inside them."

"I sold packets that way to selected customers."

"Did you see me tailing you?"

"No. My dad insisted I have a bodyguard. He was really there to keep me in line. He noticed you."

"Did you have him shoot at me?" Raynes kept silent. "You did, didn't you?"

"It was my father. The bodyguard was supposed to scare you." He paused and took a deep breath. "I'll testify. With that sonofa... gun out of my life. Maybe I can do something good for myself. Come on. Get me out of here."

270

I turned to Captain Lorman, who had been listening without comment. "Sir, we do have to leave soon. Would you please have the personnelmen cut orders for both of us this morning and send them to OCI on Mainside?"

"I can have them do it now," the Captain offered, picking up his phone.

"Thank you, sir."

"No problem, Lieutenant. I'll also call for the quarterdeck to get a duty driver ready for you."

NOW ALL HANDS TO QUARTERS FOR MUSTER AND INSPECTION. COLOR GUARD LAY TO THE ARMORY. ALL HANDS TO QUARTERS.

We waited for colors to be over. During the lull in the conversation, I became aware of the sound of the ship's blowers, the slight motion of the deck beneath my feet. I heaved a sigh.

"Impatient to get moving?" the CO asked.

"No, sir," I chuckled. "I was just thinking that I'm going to miss the feel of a ship, now that I'm used to it again."

Lorman smiled. "Yes. Once in the blood...."

The phone rang. Lorman picked it up and listened for a few seconds. "Your orders and a driver are ready, Lieutenant. Any time you are."

Rolles, Raynes and I went to the quarterdeck. The duty driver was waiting for us. Cisco, the Petty Officer of the Watch, made the log entries for our transfers. I saw a question in Cisco's piercing blue eyes and asked, "What?"

"Can I ask you a question alone?"

I nodded. We stepped inside the superstructure. The boatswain's mate looked around then whispered? "What's with Raynes?"

"User and supplier. By the way," I smiled, "thanks for all you did. Not just for scaring a guy away from me. You told some pretty good sea stories, too."

Cisco smiled. He offered his hand, which I willingly shook.

Rolles, Raynes, the driver and I stepped off the brow and headed for the Navy car. A young seaman passed us on the pier. A middle-aged man stepped out of a Cadillac De Ville. He held a pistol. "I've been waiting for you, Luke!"

"No, Dad! Don't!" Raynes shouted.

Rolles saw the man aim at the prisoner. He launched himself at the Preacher, taking his feet out from under him. Murphy's bullet grazed his son's arm as he crumpled.

Raynes fell over Rolles, pinning him down. The duty driver dove behind his Navy car. The young seaman we'd just passed jumped behind a dumpster and called out to the quarterdeck watch. "Cisco! They need help!"

I could see Murphy was aiming for another shot at his son. Without thinking, I hit the deck in front of Raynes.

Cisco drew his .45 and clip of ammunition. Slammed the clip home. Pulled and released the slide. As he rammed a round into the chamber, he shouted to the Quarterdeck Watch Officer: "Permission to shoot, sir!"

He held his piece steady with both hands.

"Granted," the officer replied instantly.

Cisco pulled the trigger. His shot and Murphy's second one were almost simultaneous. The criminal's bullet hit the pier under me. Concrete chips ground into my side. The ricocheting bullet hit Raynes in the leg.

Cisco hit Murphy in the chest with a bullet designed to rip apart drugged-up Moro warriors in the Philippines. The drug lord died before he hit the ground. Rolles drew his .45. He and I went over to be sure Murphy was no longer a menace.

The seaman scampered from behind the dumpster and ran aboard the *Hestek*. I heard Cisco's greeting loud and clear, "Cory, you got fixed up!" I spun around to look. The petty officer motioned to me. "Matthews, uh... Mister Matthews, you won't believe this!"

The Officer of the Deck was calling base security. He motioned for the seaman to wait off the quarterdeck.

Cisco released the clip from his pistol. He pulled the slide back to eject the bullet now in the chamber. Put the shell back in the clip, which he returned to his pistol belt. He put the piece back into the holster.

Rolles and I inspected the Preacher's wounds. Neither was serious, but the second bullet had gone through a fair amount of flesh. Rolles pointed to the quarterdeck. "Go ahead. I'll stay with Raynes."

When I got back on the Old Haystack, Chief Hamilton had already arrived. He taped a patch on my wound, which looked a lot worse than it was. Then he went to attend to the prisoner.

Cisco took me over to the seaman and introduced us.

"Cory Palm?" I asked. He nodded. "Everyone thought you were dead."

"Nah. The hospital fixed me up great. But it took too long to get me back to the Haystack. I was sent to a ship out of Newport, Rhode Island. We just got back from the Med. This is the first chance I've had to come and visit."

"Reston was sure he killed you, knocking you off your refueling station the way he did."

"Oh, hell no. If I'd listened and belted up.... Where is Hank?"

"He was so sure he killed you, he took a deliberate overdose of heroin last month."

"He killed himself?"

I nodded.

"Oh, crap." Tears filled Palm's eyes. "We were like brothers. Now I'll never be able to share my news with him. I met a nurse in the hospital.

We're getting married when I get out of the Navy in a year."

A short time later, base security took away Murphy's body and his Cadillac, which had a base pass. We never found out how he got it. They took Raynes to the base infirmary for further medical attention, and then put him in the brig on Mainside.

74. FUNERAL

The OCI operatives gathered at Arlington National Cemetery. Fifteen men, four women, and a large Saint Bernard. We stood in the rain. The chaplain prayed. The flag-draped casket rested above an open grave.

Skye had gone to Brandon Lunch's apartment to get Tango. The big dog remembered her. She fed him, walked him, brought him to her apartment. Now he lay on the ground, head on his paws, mournful eyes staring at his master's coffin.

The chaplain finished. The honor guard folded up the flag and gave it to Lunch's next of kin. The pallbearers lowered the casket into the ground. Each person dropped a handful of dirt into the grave.

"You guys can go," Skye said. "We'll stay a while longer. See you back in Norfolk."

Tango gazed into the hole in the ground, whining. Rena knelt on the wet grass and put her arm around him. I stood behind her, my hands on her shoulders.

"Good bye, Brandon," she whispered. She rubbed the big dog behind his ears. "I'll take care of Tango for you. Thanks for everything. Rest in peace. You deserve it."

I helped her stand up. "Come on, Tango. Let's go home." The dog didn't move. Rena leaned over to whisper in his ear. "Tango, he's at peace now. Let's go."

The dog looked up at her, wagged his tail and plopped his head back down onto his front paws, whimpering. "All right." Rena said, dropping back onto the wet ground. "You're too big to pick up and carry, so I guess we'll wait for you."

We stood in the drizzle. Looking down on Tango, Rena couldn't hold back. Tears ran down her face. When a sob escaped her, the Saint Bernard lifted his head to look at her. Almost like he was convinced that his old friend was gone and a new friend needed him, the big dog stood up and nuzzled Rena's face. She scratched him behind the ears again. "Ready to go now?"

Tango wagged his tail as Rena stood up. The three of us walked quietly away from the grave.

Rena finally spoke: "You get your new orders yet?"

I nodded. "They're going to use my electronics expertise. I'm going to Great Lakes, to Fire Control Technician school."

"I already knew. Are you going to be an FTG or an FTM?"

"Guns." We walked a few steps in silence. I swallowed hard. "I'm going to miss you."

Rena looked at the ground as we walked. "I got some news yesterday, Eric," she said quietly. "OCI got my divorce done for me. Gary was very amenable. He gets our property out west. He gave my half of its value to OCI, which passed it on to me. So that's over with."

My heart skipped a beat.

She looked up at me and took my hand. "I think we both have a lot of anticipation to take care of. If you know what I mean."

"Yeah, I think so...."

She let go of my hand and hit me in the arm. The big Saint Bernard looked up at me and growled. "Don't worry about him, Tango," Rena said. "I'll square him away."

Then she took my hand again. We walked out of the cemetery side by side, the dog between us.

I was all smiles.

GLOSSARY

This glossary is for landlubbers; sailors will know these terms, no matter how long ago they served. I use naval terminology throughout the book because that makes the story real. I have read numerous comments by Navy veterans about a book they read and they say something like this: "It was obvious from page two that the author was never even on a ship." I include this glossary because I hope a lot of people who never served in the Navy will also read this book, and it is here to help them.

NOTE: Naval terms in the body of an entry may also have their own entries, so you can look for more detail there. This is a general glossary and some entries may not have been used in this novel. Hopefully there will be sequels.

01 (oh-one) level. The deck immediately above the main deck of a ship.

1JV phone circuit. Primary maneuvering circuit of the ship. Carries speed, direction and movement commands and reports. Typical stations on this circuit are bridge, engine room, forecastle, fantail, after steering, and the stations taking care of mooring the ship.

1MC (one-em-see). The "PA System" aboard ship, with control boxes ("broadcasting" stations) on the bridge and amidships, near the quarterdeck areas. There are speakers in all compartments, so persons everywhere on the ship can hear all announcements. The system is nicknamed the "bitch box."

after steering. An emergency station to allow a ship to be steered if the bridge is damaged during battle. Steering orders would be provided over the sound-powered phones.

Air Ops Guard. Air Operations Guard. The helicopters sent up by a carrier during launch and recovery operations, to try to save the crews of aircraft who crash.

all hands. Everyone aboard ship, officers and men.

AN. Airman, an enlisted level E-3, in the Naval Air group. See rate.

AQ. Aviation Fire Control Technician, the rating that maintains the equipment used to control airborne guns and missiles.

ASAP (AY-sapp). Abbreviation for "as soon as possible." Pronounced as a word, never spelled out.

ASROC (AZZ-rock). Anti-Submarine ROCket.

ASW. Anti-Submarine Warfare.

AWOL (AY-wall). Abbreviation for Absent With Out Leave, a court martial offense.

barbette. A large hollow metal tube going down into the ship beneath a gun mount (5-inch guns or larger) or a large gun director. It serves a number of purposes: as a base for the mount to rotate on, as a location to store heavy duty motors that turn the mount or director, and as a place to store immediately available ammunition very close to the guns.

bird farm. An aircraft carrier. Carrier personnel generally consider this to be a belittling name, but it is commonly used by personnel not associated with the Naval Air forces.

bird farmer. A person in the Naval Air branch. Considered by some sailors to not be a real sailor, because carriers are too large to have very much roll and pitch.

bitch box. The 1MC system, the ship's PA system.

Aye, aye. A naval affirmation meaning three simultaneous things: I heard, I understand, I will obey.

baseball cap. Navy personnel are required to have their head covered at all times when they are not in a building or the interior of a ship. The most common head cover is the white hat. Generally, however, when wearing the dungaree work uniform, the head cover is a blue baseball cap. When going indoors, sailors uncover. They usually fold the bill of the baseball hat in fourths and stuff the folded bill in a back pocket. Petty officers (first class, second class, and third class) generally wear a golden metal crow, about one inch high and one-half inch wide, on the front of the baseball cap. Compare to white hat.

bight. A spliced loop at the end of a heavy line, especially a mooring line.

bitt. A pair of metal horns welded to the deck of a ship. Bitts are used to secure mooring lines going to a pier or to another ship.

block. A pulley.

block and tackle (TAY-k'l). A set of two blocks (pulleys) and a good length of line used to lift or pull up a heavy load.

bluejacket. There are two definitions for this term: 1. A light cotton working jacket. 2. A Navy enlisted man. (capitalized)

blues. The winter uniform of enlisted men. Compare with whites. It consists of two options:

Service Dress Blues: black shoes, black socks, blue standard- or 13-button trousers (pressed inside out with the crease on the side), long-sleeve blue dress jumper (pressed the same way as the trousers), neckerchief, white tee shirt, and white hat. Stripes or crows and hashmarks are worn on the left sleeve and ships patch at the upper right seam. The dress jumper has white piping on buttoned cuffs and on the large collar.

Undress Blues: No neckerchief. Undress jumper (blue wool, no piping, cuffs not able to be buttoned). Stripes or crows and hashmarks are worn on the left sleeve and ships name patch at the upper right seam.

boat. There are two definitions for this term: 1. A small vessel that can be, and normally is, carried on a ship. 2. A submarine.

Boats. Name often used to address a boatswain's mate.

boatswain's (boh-suhn's or boh-zuhn's) mate. The rating that performs deck duties on a ship. Responsible for the upkeep of all rigging, ground tackle, and canvas. Operate and maintain the ship's boat(s) and refueling and cargo handling equipment. Often serve on damage control parties and gun crews.

bogey (BOH-ghee). An unidentified aircraft.

bollard (BAH-l'rd). A cylinder on a pier, which has small horizontal sections, which keep lines from coming off unless deliberately taken off. Bollards are used to secure mooring lines.

bridge. The command center of a ship, where the captain remains while the ship is underway. Stations on the bridge include the Officer of the Deck, Junior Officer of the Deck, helmsman, lee helmsman, bos'n mate of the watch, quartermaster of the watch, and various sound-powered pone talkers.

brow. The walkway between a ship and the pier or adjacent ship. Often misnamed "gangway."

bulkhead. A wall.

caliber. The size of a gun. The USS *Hestek* had 5"/38 caliber guns for her main battery. This means that each barrel was five inches wide in the inside (i.e., it fired a five-inch diameter shell), and 5x38 (190) inches long. Newer destroyers of this period had 5"/54 caliber guns.

can. Possibly short for "tin can" q.v. However, some believe this term comes from the "can do" attitude typical of the crews on these ships, but that sounds too "Navy," as if an officer were explaining it to civilians or new recruits. Destroyermen were very proud of being on their small ships and being the closest possible to sailors of old, in the days of "ships wood and men of iron," compared to the modern navy which was often described as being made up of "ships of iron and men of wood."

Captain's Mast. What is classified as non-judicial punishment. A ship's captain has the privilege of meting out a certain amount of lesser disciplinary actions. When a man is placed on report and the Executive Officer clears him for mast, the commanding officer (Lieutenant Commander or higher) can provide any of the following punishments (disciplines): up to 30 days restriction to the ship, up to 45 days of extra duties (no more than 2 hours per day) to be performed on personal time including holidays, reduction in rate by as much as two pay grades, brig time up to 30 days or three days in the brig on bread and water, a fine equal to no more than half of pay for two months, a detention of pay equal to no more than half for three months, or a court martial. There may also be issued a combination of some lesser disciplines, such as restriction and extra duty. A Captain's Mast may also be held to praise or commend a person or make an award (such as a medal for bravery).

carrier, aircraft carrier. In the 1960s, carriers were generally named after famous battles (*Lexington, Saratoga, Coral Sea*) or older famous ships (*Wasp, Enterprise, Constellation, Constitution*).

cast loose. To untie from a pier or from another ship in a nest in order to get underway.

chambray (sham-BRAY) shirt. A light blue (in weight and color) work shirt worn as part of the dungaree work uniform. The shirt can be long sleeved for colder or milder climates or short sleeved for warmer climates. The shirt may be dispensed with entirely in tropical climates (see dungarees).

chipping. Hitting a metal surface with one of a number of different tools to chip away paint on that metal. The idea is to take the metal down to a clean surface and be sure there is no rust, as preparation for repainting. Those doing the chipping often consider this to be nothing but busy work.

CIC (see-eye-see). See Combat Information Center.

chock. A set heavy metal horns curving in toward each other, standing about a foot off the deck. These are designed to provide a path for mooring or towing lines be brought onto a ship without rubbing and fraying. Such open chocks are typically located on the bow and on the fantail. Similar devices, often solid at the top, are placed along the sides of a ship, and are also used to route mooring lines.

cleat. Generally a pair of metal "horns" sticking 180-degrees from each other and laying parallel to the deck. The cleat is welded to the deck and used to tie things down.

CO (see-oh). Commanding Officer.

colors. The American flag or ensign. Also the act of raising of the ensign at 0800 and the lowering of it at sunset.

color guard. Five or six men assigned to raise the ensign at 0800 and lower it at sunset. Two men handle the flag and the others are armed with rifles, with which they salute while the ensign is being raised or lowered.

Combat Information Center. The combat nerve center of a ship. Its personnel also perform many crucial duties when the ship is underway. This is where the major surface and air search radars are carefully watched. Ships and aircraft in the area are closely watched, sometimes tracked on large status boards. IFF is used here and watched for correct responses from unknown units. In conversation, often abbreviated to "combat."

commode (kuh-MODE). A toilet.

companionway. A stairway between decks, generally with a hatch above it.

conn. Having control of a ship when it is underway. The officer who issues the commands on the bridge is said to "have the conn."

compartment. A room.

court martial. The Navy equivalent of a court trial, except there is a court of some number of officers instead of a jury. The three levels of courts martial are: Summary - a trial by one officer; Special - a trial by three or more officers; and General - a trial involving a law officer and at least five other officers. If requested by an enlisted person, other enlisted persons may be named to a Special or a General. Only a General may impose the death penalty, dishonorable discharge, imprisonment of over six months or hard labor for more than three months, loss of over 2/3 or for more than six months.

crow. Insignia for upper enlisted rates. The name derives from the eagle that forms the top portion of the insignia. Chevrons (pointing down) indicate the rate for the middle levels: one chevron for third class petty officers (PO3, E-4), two chevrons for second class petty officers (PO2, E-5), three chevron for first class petty officers (PO1, E-6). Chief petty officers (CPO, E-7) add an upward curving semi-circle between the chevrons and the eagle (a "perch" for the crow). Senior Chiefs (SCPO, E-8) add a single star above the eagle and Master Chiefs (MCPO, E-9) add two horizontal stars above the eagle. The rating insignia is located between the chevrons and eagle or between the chevrons and the perch. The crows for a white uniform are Navy blue. The crows for a blue uniform are red (normal) or gold (12 years of service that are qualified for a Good Conduct Medal).

D & S Piers. During the 1960s, this was an area of piers, separate from Mainside (q.v.) where all the destroyers and submarines tied up.

deck. The floor.

deck ape. Most specifically, workers on the deck force, i.e., boatswain's mates and the seamen working with them. By extension, any sailor who worked topside, outside of the engineering spaces, and not part of the supply or operations divisions. Not considered a complimentary name by deck force people. Compare with snipe.

deep six. Throw over the side of a ship. Toss into the ocean.

destroyer. A small ship of the line generally having two or more gun mounts and a number of anti-submarine weapons. In the 1960s, destroyers displaced 2250 tons (old Fletcher class) or more. The primary jobs of destroyers are anti-submarine warfare, anti-aircraft warfare, shore bombardment, gunfire support (of troops already ashore), guarding aircraft carriers and other larger warships and transport vessels in a convoy, and plane guard detail (to try to rescue the crews of crashed aircraft). Destroyers were consistently named after naval and Marine heroes.

director, gun director. A box-like unit, in which two to six men are stationed during battle. The director holds telescopes, radar equipment, and often a rangefinder. These are all pieces of equipment used to find, lock on and track targets. Thus, the director sends signals to direct the rest of the fire control equipment to calculate where the guns should be pointed to shoot down an enemy target.

DIW (dee-eye-double-you). Abbreviation for "dead in the water." Designates a ship that has lost power and cannot make headway.

dog watch. A watch that is only two hours long instead of the normal four. This usually happens as the result of splitting the 16-2000 watch in two, the break being at suppertime. Dog watches provide a rotation so watchstanders do not get the undesirable watches all the time.

dogging wrench. A piece of pipe, roughly a foot long. Older watertight doors had progressively raised areas over which a heavy rotating latch, called a "dog," rotated. As the dog moved, it compressed a seal around the door to make it watertight. The dogging wrench provided extra leverage for a person to manually secure the dogs on these older doors. Newer watertight doors used a linking mechanism and a long central lever to dog the door down, tightening all the dogs at the same time.

douche (doosh) kit. A shaving kit, roughly eight inches long, six inches high and three inches thick. Used to hold one's razor, shaving cream, comb and brush, soap inside a plastic soap holder, and other appropriate items.

dungarees (DUNG-guh-REEZ). From a Hindi word for blue denim cloth. Dungarees are the working uniform of Navy enlisted men below chief petty officer. The uniform consists of denim trousers, chambray (a lighter weight blue material) shirt, and blue baseball cap. The shirt may be long or short sleeved. In tropical climates, the work uniform may dispense with the shirt altogether, permitting sailors to work in their white tee-shirts. Civilians generally call dungarees "jeans" or "bluejeans."

ensign (ehn-s'n). There are two definitions for this term: 1. The American flag. 2. The lowest rank of naval officer.

ET. Electronics Technicians, responsible for maintaining the ships radio and search radar equipment. Fire control technicians and sonar technicians maintain their own electronics equipment.

evolution. An operation or procedure, generally a large scale one. This includes highlining, refueling, and stores replenishment.

fart sack. A mattress cover. It replaces sheets on a bunk aboard ship.

flag bag. A container to store signal flags. Each side of the signal bridge has one, one on the port side and one on the starboard side. Each flag bag is approximately four or five feet wide and about three feet deep. The flags are stored in them in a logical and consistent manner so that a signalman can automatically reach for the correct flag when making up a signal that needs to be raised quickly. Other flags are stored furled (rolled up and tied) so they can be raised in a manner that no one can determine what they are; then on command, the halyard can be yanked to unfurl the flags so other ships can execute the signaled command.

flank speed. Maximum speed a ship can make.

flat hat. Also called a "Donald Duck" hat. A flat blue Navy hat with a ribbon around the bottom section. It was worn as part of the dress blues uniform. It was officially discontinued in 1963.

flying bridge. Sections of the deck above the bridge that protruded from the remainder of the deck. They give the Captain, a pilot, or the officer with the conn the ability to walk out so far he could be even with the side of the ship. This provided greater maneuvering control when going into and out of port.

FN. Fireman, an enlisted level E-3 in the Engineering group. See rate.

forecastle (foke-s'l). The forward part of the main deck, in front of the forward gun mount.

foul weather gear. Special heavy, waterproof clothing worn to protect personnel from cold and drenching water (rain, sleet, or waves). Most personnel receive a foul weather jacket for work assignments. Outdoors watchstanders may also receive foul weather pants. Newer and more expensive foul weather gear is often serialized and may be received only with a signature recognizing receipt.

FT. Fire Control Technician, the rating that maintains the equipment used to control the shooting of shipboard guns and missiles. FTs are further designated as FTG for gunfire control or FTM for missile fire control.

fuck, fucking. The universal expletive and adjective/adverb. Some sailors use this expression so much that it becomes meaningless, and simply turns into a means to intensify an expression, statement or story. Other raunchy expressions and expletives are also used, but this is by far the most common.

FUBAR. Stands for "fucked up beyond all recovery." Polite people say it stands for "fouled up beyond..." Used to describe a situation that the speaker believes to be hopeless.

gedunk (GHEE-dunk). Most commonly, sweets or candy, and by extension, junk food in general. Also the place to buy these items. Also see pogey bait. Most strictly speaking, ice cream or ice cream products.

grab assing. Skylarking. Frolicking. Wrestling. Physically working off steam.

gun director. See director.

hashmarks. Diagonal service stripes worn on the lower sleeve of a long-sleeve uniform. Each stripe stands for four years of service. The hashmarks for a white uniform are Navy blue. The hashmarks for a blue uniform are red (normal) or gold (12 or more years of service that are qualified for a Good Conduct Medal).

hatch. An opening in a deck with a ladder or a companionway to allow movement between decks.

head. The compartment in which one finds urinals and commodes (toilets).

heaving line. A lengthy piece of light line (about the thickness of clothesline), with a weighted end (see monkeyfist). Half of the line would be coiled and held in the throwing hand. It and the weighted end could be heaved or thrown with a long sideways motion, while the remainder of the line was held fast and connected to a heavier line (often a mooring line) to be pulled across the open space. A good heave could throw the weighted end forty or fifty feet. Any requirement to throw across a longer distance requires a shotline.

helmsman. The sailor on the bridge (or in after steering) who steers the ship in accordance with the commands of the bridge officer who has the "conn."

helo. A helicopter. The term "chopper" was generally not used in the Navy. That was more of an Army term.

highline. A means of transferring relatively light loads on a trolley riding a heavy line held taut between two ships. This is the normal way to transfer movies and mail when at sea. One person at a time can also be highlined.

holiday routine. Routine where the only ship's work done is sweepers and those standing watches. Reveille is not announced, and the mess decks serves brunch instead of separate breakfast and dinner. Normal routine on Sundays and holidays.

IFF (eye-eff-eff). Information Friend or Foe. In critical circumstances, ships' radars can electronically challenge detected units. If the unit is friendly, it responds with a specific coded response, which shipboard equipment can detect. If the other unit does not make the proper response, it is considered a non-friendly unit.

JA phone circuit. A sound-powered phone circuit that serves as the commanding officer's primary battle circuit. Stations with phone talkers on this circuit include the bridge, after control, and CIC.

jack. In the 1960s, a small flag consisting of the blue field and stars from the American flag. Flown in port on the bow of the ship.

jackstaff. Flagstaff on the bow of the ship on which the jack is raised in port. The staff is lowered and/or disassembled and stowed when the ship is underway.

leave. A period of time that can be considered the Navy's version of "vacation." The government gives active military people 30 days of leave each year, which can be carried over from year to year. Compare to liberty.

lee helmsman. The sailor on the bridge who sends ships speed, via a special telegraph device to the fire rooms and engine rooms, in accordance with the commands of the officer who has the "conn."

liberty. A short period of time off ashore, specifically when not having the duty and not being required to perform ship's work. Compare to leave.

lifeline. A series of cables or chains, connected to stanchions all around a ship's decks, to keep personnel from falling overboard in case of a sudden roll or pitch. Lifelines are generally three high and often have a woven mesh between the deck and the lowest lifeline. They do not always work. A man is sometimes swept overboard by a wave. Sometimes a hated or despised man is lost in the middle of the night when nobody can call for a search.

line. There are three definitions for this term: 1. A fiber rope. (A metal cable, however is called rope.) 2. A piece of cord. 3. The group of officers who are able to take command of a ship. These officers are called "officers of the line." This does not include such specialist officers as supply officers.

Mainside. In the 1960s, Norfolk Naval Base had two major pier areas, The D & S Piers (q.v.) was a smaller area a short distance and separate from the remainder of the base, which was called "Mainside." This was the location of the cruiser, carrier and supply ship piers, recreational clubs, administrative buildings, supply centers, etc.

MAA (em-ay-ay). See Master at Arms.

main battery. The largest guns on the ship. Destroyers primarily had five-inch main batteries (different calibers, depending on the class of the ship), light cruisers had six-inchers, heavy cruisers eight, and battleships anywhere from twelve to sixteen, depending on when they were built.

marlinspike seamanship. The art and craft of taking care of, handing, and working with all types of line and wire rope. The name comes from a metal spike tool used separate strands of line in order to splice lines together.

mast. See Captain's Mast.

Master at Arms. A duty watch for a senior petty officer. Kind of a duty barracks policeman.

mayday. A call for emergency help. Supposedly from the French "M'aidez" which means "Help me."

Med. Common abbreviation for Mediterranean.

messenger. There are two definitions for this term: 1. A watchstander who carries messages, wakes up watch reliefs, and runs general errands such as getting coffee for other watchstanders. 2. A light line used to pull a heavier line over a distance, as between ships.

midrats. Short for midnight rations. A special snack for sailors standing midwatches and the people from the eight-to-twelve that they relieve. The food is generally chicken soup (broth and noodles) and crackers, but a cook who is feeling especially good (kind of rare at this hour) may cook up something extra.

midships, amidships. The area roughly halfway between the bow and the stern of a ship.

military time. See time.

monkeyfist. A complicated knot tied to completely encompass the weight at the end of a heaving line.

mooring line. A heavy line with a large spliced bight, used to tie a ship up to a pier or to another ship.

muster. A head count, to determine who is present and who is absent (unauthorized or accounted for).

NAS. Naval Air Station.

NavPers (navv-perz). The Bureau of Naval Personnel, which makes sure that ships are manned at their proper level, among other duties.

Navy Exchange. The Navy's equivalent of the Army PX (Post Exchange). Basically a small department store, where sailors could buy all-important items and many luxuries.

neckerchief. A square of silk or synthetic fiber, folded in half (to make a triangle) and rolled (starting with the points across from the folded side) to about a one-inch diameter. Often tied with black thread so it does not come unrolled. Passed under the large collar of dress blues and dress whites, and tied in a square knot at the jumper's "V." The knot is to be tied so that it presents a flat front. This makes it look like the neckerchief comes from under the collar, through a holder at the "V" of the jumper, and hangs down from there.

nest. A grouping of ships tied alongside each other, in order to better utilize available pier space. The inboard ship is tied up to the pier and outboard ships to other ships. Thus a crewmember of an outboard ship must cross some number of other ships to get to his own.

non-skid. A series of paths on weather decks laid down to provide better footing. Whereas the decks are normally painted a dark gray, the non-skid consists of black paint combined with a sandy compound.

Norva. Norfolk, Virginia.

NS. Naval Station.

O-Club. Officers' Club.

officers' call. The morning muster of ship's officers to receive special orders and assignments to pass on to their divisions.

overhead. The ceiling.

padeye. A round tie-down ring welded to a deck or a bulkhead.

passageway. A hallway.

pelican hook. An emergency breakaway connection on spanlines that go between ships. It has a hinged section that is held in place by a ring that is held in place with a cotter pin. In an emergency, a heavy hammer can break the ring loose, causing the hook to open up and release the spanline.

Plan of the Day (POD: pee-oh-dee). Usually a single sheet (possibly two sided) mimeographed listing of the date, tides, sunrise and sunset, duty officers, a listing of watchstanders, special orders, and other items of special interest or emphasis.

PO (pee-oh). Abbreviation for "petty officer."

pogey (POH-ghee) bait. Candy. The name derives from an old, old time enticement for homosexual favors by a "pogue," or (cabin) boy. It seems that officers and crew (well, at least the crew) overlooked such ventures at that time.

pelorus (peh-LOR-russ). A compass with sighting equipment on a ring around it, so that it can be turned in any direction to sight a bearing to other objects.

piping. Thin white decorative stripes on the cuffs and collar of the dress blue jumper. There are three stripes at each location. They can be scrubbed with a toothbrush to clean them. White foreign substances (toothpaste, chalk) have been known to be put on dirty piping to try to fool the JOOD and get going on liberty.

port. There are two definitions for this term: 1. The left side of a ship or boat. 2. A harbor or a city on the ocean where ships may visit.

quarterdeck. That part of a ship onto which an arriving person steps from the brow. There is a quarterdeck area on the starboard and another on the port side, generally amidships, though sometimes aft. On larger ships, with a Command Duty Officer (CDO), the quarterdeck watch includes the Officer of the Deck (OOD), the Petty Officer of the Watch (POOW), and the Messenger. On small ships, the OOD may take the place of the CDO, in which case the quarterdeck officer is the Junior Officer of the Deck (JOOD).

quartermaster. The rating that works with ship control, navigation and bridge functions. Responsible for the upkeep of the ship's charts and navigation aids. Keeps logs of every action, course/speed change, and command of the CO/OOD while at sea. Serves as helmsman and lookout supervisor.

quarters. This term has two meanings: 1. The living spaces for the crew. 2. A gathering of all hands in their divisions for muster and for dissipation of plan of the day and special orders or assignments.

rack. A bunk.

rank. The levels of commissioned officers. "Commissioned" means that they get their position and authority from Congress. Note, there have been changes in the name and possibly the duties of "Commodore" in the late 1900s. From lowest to highest, the naval officer ranks are:

Ensign (Ens), pay grade O-1. Wears one one-inch stripe on the sleeve, single gold bar on the collar.

Lieutenant junior grade (Ltjg), pay grade O-2. Wears one one-inch stripe below a half-inch stripe on the sleeve, gold double bar on the collar. In conversation, this rank is often shortened to "j-g."

Lieutenant senior grade (Lt), pay grade O-3. Wears two one-inch stripes on the sleeve, silver double bar on the collar.

Lieutenant Commander (LtCdr), pay grade O-4. Wears two one-inch stripes on the sleeve with a half-inch stripe between them, gold oak leaf on the collar. This is the normal rank of a destroyer's Executive Officer, or a larger ship's department head.

Commander (Cdr), pay grade O-5. Wears three one-inch stripes on the sleeve, silver oak leaf on the collar. This is the normal rank of a destroyer's Commanding Officer (Captain) or of a larger ship's Executive Officer.

Captain (Capt), pay grade O-6. Wears four one-inch stripes on the sleeve, silver eagle on the collar. This is the normal rank of a larger ship's Commanding Officer (Captain). The Commanding Officer of any ship carries the title and honors of Captain.

Commodore (Comm), pay grade O-7. Wears one two inch stripe on the sleeve, one star on the collar. Wartime rank only. In peace time, senior Captains are named to the positions (and the honors of) Commodore when in charge of smaller collections of ships (divisions and squadrons). Now known as Rear Admiral (lower half).

Rear Admiral (RAdm), pay grade O-8. Wears one two-inch stripe below a single one-inch stripe on the sleeve, two stars on the collar side by side. Now known as Rear Admiral (upper half),

Vice Admiral (VAdm), pay grade O-9. Wears one two-inch stripe below two one-inch stripes on the sleeve, three stars on the collar in a straight line.

Admiral (Adm), pay grade O-10. Wears one two-inch stripe below three one-inch stripes on the sleeve, four stars on the collar in a straight line.

Fleet Admiral (FltAdm), pay grade O-11. Wears one two inch stripe below four one-inch stripes on the sleeve, five stars on the collar in an octagon. Extremely rare. Like a Five-Star General. Nimitz held this rank during World War II, and was equal to Eisenhower and MacArthur.

rat guard. A set of two slightly conical segments, attached to each other on one side, and having perpendicular sections that are tied around mooring lines after they are in place. The outer edge of the cone faces the pier. This prohibits rats and other such pests from climbing up the mooring lines and getting aboard a ship.

rate. The "ranks" of enlisted men. From lowest to highest, the enlisted rates are:

Seaman/Fireman/Airman Recruit (SR, FR, AR), pay grade E-1.

Seaman/Fireman/Airman Apprentice (SA, FA, AA), pay grade E-2.

Seaman/Fireman/Airman (SN, FN, AN), pay grade E-3.

Petty Officer third class (PO3), lowest of the non-commissioned officers, pay grade E-4.

Petty Officer second class (PO2), pay grade E-5.

Petty Officer first class (PO1), pay grade E-6.

Chief Petty Officer (CPO, XXC), pay grade E-7.

Senior Chief Petty Officer (SCPO, XXCS), pay grade E-8; created in 1958.

Master Chief Petty Officer (MCPO, XXCM); created in 1958.

When rate abbreviations are placed after a person's name, the "PO" or "XX" mentioned earlier are replaced with the abbreviation for the rating.

rating. The occupational specialty of an enlisted person. Each rating has a two-letter abbreviation, and sometimes a third letter for a subspecialty. Thus a fire control technician is an FT. If in a rate lower than the chiefs, FTs have a subspecialty of "G" for gunnery or "M" for missiles. Thus a second class gunnery Fire Control Technician would be abbreviated FTG2. Some other common abbreviations are: bos'n's mate (BM), gunner's mate (GM), hospital corpsman (HM), signalman (SM), sonarman (ST, for sonar technician), radarman (RD), and electronics technician (ET).

red lead. A paint primer for steel and such metals. Not used on aluminum.

recovery, recovery operations. Landing operations. The procedures carried on by a carrier to recover its "birds," i.e., land its aircraft.

regs. Short for "regulations."

report, on or to be (placed) on. To be officially written up for an offense of some sort, such as AWOL, dereliction of duty, disrespect to a senior, sleeping on duty, etc. The report is processed through whatever legal channels are in place. Many are simply taken care of by a Chief Petty Officer: do this and such, and I won't turn this in. The Executive Officer has the power to make an arrangement with the person on report: restrict yourself for two weeks and this goes no further. These kinds of deals can be made if the infraction is relatively minor. The person on report would generally agree to such deals because the punishment is usually less than that likely from a Captain's Mast and because the disciplinary action is kept off the record. Serious offenses, such as those named above, almost always result in a mast, and often a court martial.

roach coach. A mobile food vendor, generally a snack truck whose sides could be lifted to display assorted junk food and gedunks, q.v.

roostertail. The plume that rises from the surface of the water behind a ship going very fast. It is caused by the actions of the ship's screws (propellers) in the water.

SA. Seaman Apprentice, an enlisted level E-2 in the Deck group. See rate.

salt, old salt. An experienced sailor.

scrambled eggs. The decorative gold braid on the bill of a senior officer's hat.

screw. A propeller of a ship or boat.

scuttlebutt. 1. a drinking fountain. 2. rumor, the rumor mill

seabag. A canvas bag large enough to hold all of a sailor's standard issue clothing. The open end folds so that some grommets slip over an elongated heavy wire link. A heavy strap sewn in the middle of the bag has a hook that clips onto the link. A combination padlock is then placed through the link to keep the contents secure and to keep the seabag from opening.

sea bat. The sailors' version of a snipe hunt. See the chapter with this name.

sea cabin. A special stateroom, complete with commode and shower facilities, for a ship's commanding officer, located just aft of the bridge. When underway, the captain of a ship is in one of two places: the bridge itself or his sea cabin.

section, watch section, duty section. That part of the crew, which stands watches at the same time. At sea, there are generally three watch sections, each standing watch for (usually) four hours, and then having eight hours off. These watches are dogged daily or weekly so that one section does not get the most undesirable watches all the time. In port, the crew may be in three or four duty sections, standing the in-port watches every three days, except the same section would have duty on both Saturday and Sunday (weekend duty), thus providing a rotation, which permits another section to have a 72-hour weekend liberty (Friday, Saturday, and Sunday off), the third section to have a 48-hour liberty (Duty on Friday, with Saturday and Sunday off).

service jacket. The complete records for an officer or enlisted man. It includes records of ships or stations served on, advancements, quarterlies (semi-annual evaluations), and disciplinary actions. All this is kept in a single file folder with fold-over clips to hold all the papers in place.

ship. An ocean going vessel too large to be placed on another ship, except for a submarine, which is called a boat.

ship's office. The office where the yeomen (YN) and personnelmen (PN) work, where the ships written communication is taken care of, where transfer orders are cut, and where the service jackets of the officers and men are kept and updated as events occur.

ship's patch. A small patch with the name of the ship (or other duty station) in white letters on a blue background. Worn at the top of the right sleeve.

ship's store. The small store aboard a ship where crewmembers can buy cigarettes, razor blades, candy, soap, deodorant, and a few specialties such as knives, cameras, etc. The larger the ship, the larger the ship's store.

shootin' the shit. Participating in general conversation, joking around, and telling sea stories.

shotline. A light line connected to a rod with an impact bulb. The rod is placed in a special gun and shot across a relatively long distance, acting as a heaving line.

sideboys. Sailors in full dress uniform who stand in pairs facing each other. They provide an honor for very senior officers who walk between the saluting sideboys as they come aboard the ship. The higher the officer's rank, the higher the number of sideboy pairs. There can be from two to eight sideboys. A boatswain's mate usually accompanies the honors with a specific series of whistles on the boatswain's pipe.

signal bridge. A section of the superstructure behind the bridge and main battery gun director. It is the primary workspace for the ship's signalmen and the location of the flag bags, one on the port side and another on the starboard side.

Signalman (SM). The rating responsible for sending and receiving messages, especially those utilizing flags or flashing lights. Also adept at using semaphore flags. They also handle the ensign and personal flag (commodore's or admiral's flags) at sea for honoring passing ships.

skosh. Pronounced with a long "O". A little bit. From the Japanese word "sukoshi," which literally means "small" or "little." Sometimes "skoshi," especially when doubled for emphasis: "skoshi skoshi."

skunk. An unidentified surface target.

SN. Seaman, an enlisted level E-3 in the Deck group. See rate.

sound-powered phones. Telephone sets powered by the spoken word generating electrical signals as the sailor speaks. Thus, communication can be maintained even when the ship loses electrical power. A set consists of a pair of headphones and a microphone section attached to a chest plate that is strapped around the neck.

snipe. Member of the Engineering ratings, many of whom worked in the bowels of the ship (boiler rooms and engine rooms). Others supported the efforts or were related to the work of these engineers (electricians, inter-com technicians, enginemen, damage controlmen, etc.). This is an uncomplimentary name often used by the "above-decks" ratings. Compare with deck ape.

span wire. The cable supplied by a tanker, carrier or supply ship that is held taut between that vessel and a replenishing ship. A trolley rides this heavy-duty cable and carries the refueling hoses or hooks and nets carrying supplies.

special sea detail. Special assignment for all hands to take the ship out of port or bring it into port.

stanchion (STAN-sh'n). A metal post or pole.

starboard (STAR-brd or STAR-b'd). The right-hand side.

Stokes stretcher. A stretcher made out of metal tubing, with heavy wire mesh shaped to be form fitting for the human body. It was designed to move strapped-in wounded people up and down ladders and companionways without exacerbating their injuries.

striker. A seaman recruit, seaman apprentice or seaman who has completed school for a rating and is thus qualified to wear that rate's insignia. Also a seaman who has taken the exam for third-class petty officer but did not pass it.

stripes. Rate insignia for the lower enlisted rates: seaman recruit (one diagonal stripe), seaman apprentice (two diagonal stripes) or seaman (three diagonal stripes). Seaman stripes are white (on blues) or blue (on whites). Fireman stripes are red. Airman stripes are green. Construction rates are light blue.

superstructure. Everything on a ship above the main deck.

tender. A large ship with many specialty shops and trained crew whose purpose is to make repairs to destroyers (if an AD, or destroyer tender), submarines (if an AS, or submarine tender), or seaplanes (if an AV, or seaplane tender). Many repairs can be made by the tender, so that shipyard time can be reserved for truly serious repairs and upgrades.

tender availability. A period of time when a ship is scheduled to tie up next to a tender and get some repair time.

thirty-day wonder. Generally, a college graduate who became an officer by going through Officers Candidate School (OCS), a considerably shorter training period than that provided by ROTC (Reserve Officers Training Corps) in colleges, and immeasurably shorter than that provided by the Naval Academy at Annapolis. The end result was all too often (but not always) an officer of somewhat poorer quality and knowledge.

time, telling military time. Each hour has its number, and is put in terms of hundreds. The hours in the second half of the day use the numbers thirteen through twenty-four. Thus, 7:00am is 0700, pronounced "oh-seven-hundred." A half hour later is 0730, "oh-seven-thirty." Noon is 1200, "twelve hundred." In the evening, 8:00pm is 2000, "twenty hundred." When designating watches, the time is often abbreviated: the afternoon watch can be called the 12-1600 or "twelve-to-sixteen hundred." Midnight can be either 0000 (not spoken often) or 2400 ("twenty-four hundred").

tin can. Nickname for a destroyer. This term comes from the fact that they bob around in the water like a floating empty tin can, or like a cork. But also see "can."

topside. The level of the ship above and outside of where one is.

uncover(ed). In the Navy, all personnel must wear a head cover outdoors: a white hat or baseball cap for enlisted, or the officer's style hat for chief petty officers and commissioned officers. When going indoors (entering a building or the superstructure of a ship), personnel should "uncover," i.e., take their hats off. Personnel salute superior officers only when covered.

Watch, Quarter and Station Bill. A chart of all hands and their living and duty stations under all conditions.

weather deck. Any deck outside open to the weather.

white hat. Navy personnel are required to have their head covered at all times when they are not in a building or interior of a ship. The most common head cover is the white hat. When going indoors, sailors uncover, either carrying the white hat or folding the firm rim of the hat into the cloth cap portion and stuff one of the resultant ends into a back pocket. Compare to baseball cap.

whites. The summer uniform of enlisted men. Compare with blues. It consists of four options:

Service Dress Whites. Same as undress whites with an added neckerchief to the jumper, rolled about one inch in diameter, and tied in a square not at the jumper's "V." Stripes or crows and hashmarks are worn on the left sleeve and ships name patch at the upper right seam. See neckerchief.

Undress Whites. Black shoes, black socks, white standard button trousers (pressed inside out with the crease on the side), long-sleeve white jumper (pressed the same way as the trousers), white tee shirt, and white hat. Stripes or crows and hashmarks are worn on the left sleeve and ships patch at the upper right seam.

Tropical White Long. A white short-sleeve button-down shirt replaces the jumper and neckerchief. Stripes or crows are worn on the left sleeve and ships name patch at the upper right seam.

Undress Tropical Whites. No shirt or jumper is worn, just a clean white tee shirt. No stripes, crows, hashmarks or ships patches are worn.

Vacapes (vay-capes). Virginia Capes Operating Area.

XO (eks-oh). Executive Officer, the second in command and the administrative head of a ship.

A NOTE ON OCI PERSONNEL

The Office of Criminal Investigation (OCI) is my invention. It is very loosely based on the Office of Naval Intelligence, Criminal Investigation Division. I don't know if ONI CID used the racial and gender diversity that I use in this book. I only saw ONI and CID operatives work from the outside.

I decided to use the wide variety of people I did for two reasons. First, it simply makes sense (to me) for this kind of operation. It would help placing agents in better locations and make collecting the necessary data/evidence easier. Second, other agencies, such as the various spy networks, certainly did use more than white males as operatives. Therefore, I integrated the Office of Criminal Investigation and added women appropriately.

Richard Bergeron

ABOUT THE AUTHOR
(Photo © 2012, Barry Kleider)

Richard Bergeron grew up all over the U.S.A., but primarily in Rock Island, Illinois. In 1960, he joined the Navy at age 19 and stayed in for ten years. After boot camp at Great Lakes, he trained to become a Fire Control Technician (FT), and then had five and a half years of sea duty, mostly on destroyers. His final assignment was as an electronics repair and maintenance instructor in Newport, Rhode Island.

Bergeron moved to Minnesota in late 1969, where he worked at Control Data Corporation (CDC), the Red School House in Saint Paul, Minnesota Educational Computing Corporation (MECC, the "Oregon Trail" people) and August Technology Corporation. Finally he served two years in AmeriCorps and a year as VISTA Leader with the Minneapolis Public School system.

Bergeron used his G.I. Bill to obtain a Bachelor of Elected Studies degree, summa cum laude, with an American History major and an American Indian Studies minor, which led to an involvement with the Native American people in Minnesota. He became a traditional dancer and was adopted by a Dakota Family. He and his wife worked with the Minneapolis Juneteenth Committee for eleven years. Now retired, Bergeron is finally able to do two things he has always wanted to do: teach American Indian Studies, which he does as part of the Minneapolis Schools' Community Education Program, and write books.

Bergeron wrote extensively at every civilian job. He wrote a number of articles in CDC corporate publications. Some of his college papers were published in general systems and futures studies peer-reviewed journals. He has a (not self-) published book of poetry called *Where Did the Sunrise Go?* and a number of poems published in Guild Press anthologies. His "Three Acadian Generations" concerning his French Acadian ancestors, was initially published by Yvon Cyr on his Acadian Genealogy website. This novel, *Needle on the Haystack*, is his first published fiction.

He married his wife Barbara in 1968. They have three sons.

His website is richard-bergeron.weebly.com. Among other things there, you can find a diagram of the USS Hestek and a map of the Norfolk-Virginia Beach area.

www.ingramcontent.com/pod-product-compliance
Lightning Source LLC
Chambersburg PA
CBHW071254170626
46809CB00001B/214